# TUMBLE

# FALL

# TUMBLE

# FALL

## ALEXANDRA COUTTS

Farrar Straus Giroux • New York

## Acknowledgments

With many thanks to Wesley Adams and the team at FSG, and to Joelle Hobeika, Sara Shandler, Josh Bank, and the rest of the hardworking crew at Alloy Entertainment.

A big thank-you to Faye Bender, for the sound advice on everything from contracts to sleep training.

With love and gratitude to my family, my husband, Eliot, and most especially Evangelia, whose gentle spirit—and epic newborn sleep—allowed me to finish this book.

Farrar Straus Giroux Books for Young Readers
175 Fifth Avenue, New York 10010

Printed in the United States of America
Designed by Elizabeth H. Clark
First edition, 2013
1   3   5   7   9   10   8   6   4   2

macteenbooks.com

Library of Congress Cataloging-in-Publication Data

Coutts, Alexandra.
    Tumble & fall / Alexandra Coutts.
        pages cm
    Summary: With an asteroid set to strike Earth in just one week, three teens
on an island off the Atlantic Coast wrestle with love, friendship, family, and
regret as they decide how to live their final days.
    ISBN 978-0-374-37861-5 (hardback)
    ISBN 978-0-374-37862-2 (ebook)
    [1. End of the world—Fiction.   2. Interpersonal relations—Fiction.
3. Conduct of life—Fiction.   4. Family life—Fiction.   5. Islands of the
Atlantic—Fiction.   6. Science fiction.]   I. Title.   II. Title: Tumble and fall.

PZ7.C8329Tum 2013
[Fic]—dc23

2013012969

Farrar Straus Giroux Books for Young Readers may be purchased for business or
promotional use. For information on bulk purchases please contact Macmillan Corporate
and Premium Sales Department at (800) 221-7945 x5442 or by email at specialmarkets@
macmillan.com.

**Stand By Me**
Words and Music by Jerry Leiber, Mike Stoller and Ben E. King
Copyright © 1961 Sony/ATV Music Publishing LLC
Copyright Renewed
All Rights Administered by Sony/ATV Music Publishing LLC,
8 Music Square West, Nashville, TN 37203
International Copyright Secured  ·  All Rights Reserved
*Reprinted by Permission of Hal Leonard Corporation*

*For Evie, Princess of Naps*

*If the sky that we look upon*
*Should tumble and fall*
*And the mountains should crumble to the sea*
*I won't cry, I won't cry, no I won't shed a tear*
*Just as long as you stand, stand by me*

# DAY ONE

# SIENNA

THE DAY SHE GETS OUT, IT FEELS LIKE THE END.
It's funny to think about endings now. Now that all there is to do is wait. Now that the real end is coming, all of the other endings feel like something else completely. All of the goodbyes, and leaving the people she loved. The people she loved leaving her. They felt like endings at the time. But the next day, she had gotten out of bed, and maybe there was a hollow pit where her stomach used to be, maybe she didn't feel like eating or talking or seeing people for a while, but mostly, things stayed the same.

Sienna's last day at the House is like that. From the second Valerie knocks on the door, business as usual and passing out morning meds, Sienna is already feeling dramatic. The two plastic cups Val holds out like presents, one half-full of lukewarm water and the other rattling with tiny pink pills—*these are the last plastic cups.* The congealed, microwave-flavored scrambled eggs Sienna shovels down with a plastic spork, alone in the empty House kitchen—*these are the last scrambled eggs.*

And when Val walks her out to the porch, and they sit with the sides of their knees pressed together on the slats of the rickety swing, listening to the kind of quiet Val taught her to notice, the kind of quiet that feels full and on purpose and like everything's going to be okay—

*This is the very last quiet.*

She knows that there might be other endings, bigger endings, soon. The end of everything. The end of time. But it doesn't matter. All that matters now is that things are changing again, just when she'd started to hope that they wouldn't.


"You look fantastic."

Sienna's dad is a first-class professional liar.

*Lawyer.* Not liar. She always does that.

There's a reason he's the best at what he does, a reason his office is wallpapered in plaques and awards and framed photographs of thick-haired famous friends. He's the best because he only lies when he wants something badly enough; and usually, what he wants is to be telling the truth.

The morning he arrives at Sutton House, he's on debate-club fire. Proposition Number One involves convincing them both that, despite all evidence to the contrary, Sienna does not have "nursing-home hair." Nursing-home hair: an institution-related phenomenon occurring when a person, usually a patient of some kind, spends much of the day sitting in the same corner of the same couch and/or can't be bothered to shower. The resulting self-adhesive updo can be described in many ways. *Fantastic* is not one of them.

"They have mirrors here, Dad," she reminds him, pulling open the heavy door of his old BMW—"old" in that it's older than the new one he bought right after she was sent away.

"Unless *fantastic* is legalese for *homeless and lacking shampoo*, I'd say you're trying to make me feel better."

Dad rushes around from the driver's side to pry the beat-up duffel from her fingers. He tosses it with a flourish onto the backseat, as if ushering her luggage those last few airborne moments deserves applause or a cookie. He settles for a hug. "Thanks for coming to get me," she says, breathing into the warm, reddish stubble at his neck. She says it like he had a choice.

Val waves from the porch. Dad looks offended that she doesn't see them off, but Sienna knows how it is. Inside the House, Val's on her team. She's everything Sienna needs, whenever she needs it. Outside, it's different. Parents aren't really Val's thing.

And besides, Val and Sienna have had plenty of time for goodbyes. For the past week it's been just the two of them, roaming the halls of the converted mansion on the corner of Wilson and Rye. Even though the news reports had started out vague, it wasn't long before parents started showing up. Val said it wasn't supposed to happen so fast, they were supposed to have time to finish out their programs, however long they had left, but after the "precautions," people were starting to panic. Sienna's roommate, Mary Beth, was one of the first to go. She hadn't even stopped bleeding through the bandages on her forearms when her parents came to take her home. The rest of them weren't too far behind.

Dad had been away on a tax case in San Francisco. He made it back just before all flights were grounded, landing at the airport the very night it closed. He says it was eerie-calm, untouched, as if crowds of people had been abducted all at once. Newsstands with colorful displays, the food court neon and blinking. He says it was like sneaking into an amusement park after hours, or getting locked inside a museum.

The official release called the suspension of air travel "temporary," just until the FAA could be sure that satellites and navigation systems wouldn't be disturbed. But to most people, to Sienna, it felt like the world was shutting down for good. Sienna didn't mind being stuck in the House while it happened. She was used to the routine, the PG movies, the mindless crafts. And there wasn't exactly a whole lot to look forward to about going home. If Dad and her little brother, Ryan, could have moved into the House with her and Val, she probably would've voted for that option instead.

The car purrs and Dad clicks through the radio stations. Sarah Vaughan is slinking through a version of "Lullaby of Birdland." Dad raps his fingers against the steering wheel. "Really missed you, Goose."

He looks over his shoulder, into the road. There are no cars, but he doesn't pull out, just stays twisted like that, his thick blond eyebrows low and serious, watching the stoplight as it changes. Red to green to yellow. Red again.

She knows there are things he wants to say but can't, at least not without his face crumpling like tissue paper, the way it did when he dropped her off. He probably thinks she didn't see, that she was too far gone back then to notice.

There are things she wants to say to him, too. Things she's said before and will say again, things like *It's not your fault. You did the best you could. You gave me more than I was worth.* Val says it's good she can talk to him like this. That she's one of the lucky ones, lucky enough to realize how lucky she is.

But there is one thing. One thing she can't say, one thing she'll never be able to hear echoing back at her in the thick silence after she's said it.

*I was trying to leave you. I was trying to leave you behind.*

They're heading south on 95. She doesn't notice that they've been driving too long until the sky gets big and the car smells like ocean.

"Nice nap?" Dad asks, turning off the AC and rolling down the windows.

Sienna stretches her arms and presses the tips of her fingers against the windshield. There was a lot of day-dozing at the House and she's starting to feel like it might be a tough habit to kick. "Where are we going?"

She should be seeing pine trees and winding suburban roads lined with manicured hedges and boxy McMansions. Instead, as they pull off the highway and onto a narrow street, she recognizes the shingled shacks and souvenir shops near the harbor.

"Thought it might be good for us to be by the water." Dad winks as they pull down a long, paved road. He stops at the ticket booth, and the boat attendant, a college kid with a farmer's tan and a spray of freckles on the tops of his hands, checks their name off a list.

"Good for us?" Sienna scoffs. Even Sienna can imagine that being surrounded by water might not be the safest choice.

"You know what I mean." Dad sighs, and she does. He means in the bonding sense. The nostalgic sense. The senses that might be important if this really is the end.

It isn't lost on her now, the irony of it all. She had wanted nothing more than to die, to disappear, and now it looks like there's a good chance that she will. They all will. There were days in the House when somebody would sneak a few minutes of CNN, or hear some new projected date on the radio, days that she'd feel strangely at ease. As if, after months, years, of feeling at odds with the universe, things were finally working out in a way she could understand.

Her hand is on the door before they've come to a full stop. She weaves between rows of cars in the standby line, overflowing with mainland supplies. There's the usual summertime staples, paper bags of groceries, spare pillows, dog beds, mixed in with some more serious-looking emergency gear. A truck packed with gas-powered generators. An entire backseat stocked with plastic jugs of filtered water. Sienna eyes the drivers, most of them riding solo, anxiously waiting to board the ferry. The line of cars is much shorter than usual.

But the harbor itself looks exactly the same. She had no idea how much she'd missed it, all of it: the creaking of the docks, the bustle of steamship employees as they ready the passenger ramps. Val liked to say that depression has blinders, a physical barricade between a person and the things that once made her the most herself.

She half skips out to the end of the dock and shields her eyes from the sun. The ferry is just making the turn, gliding to shore as the big door to the lower deck pulls open. She doesn't hear Dad until his heavy palm falls on her shoulder.

"Just in time, Goose," he says, squeezing her into his side. She smiles and leans against him, remembering for the first time in a long time the leg-flailing tantrums she used to throw if they didn't get to watch the boat pull in. When she was little enough she'd sit on Dad's shoulders, and Mom would tug at her ankles, pointing at the horizon and racing to catch the first glimpse.

"So."

Dad's back in the boat's lounge from the snack bar, a Coke for Sienna and a plastic cup of foamy Sam Adams for him. He stretches his arms out wide behind him, his long, skinny fingers rolling over the edge of the booth. As much as a sixteen-year-old girl and her father can inhabit the same physical frame, Sienna and her father do. Same light, straight hair and low, furrowed brow, same long, sloping neck and thin, ropy arms. Same wide, knotted knuckles on bony, witchlike hands. Mom used to say if she hadn't pushed through twenty-three hours of agonizing labor, she would have believed that Sienna had sprung directly from one of Dad's shoulder blades, like some winged mythological creature.

It's one of the new boats they're on, imposing and spotless, with elevated loading decks and shiny new fiberglass tables. High above Dad's sand-colored cowlick, a Red Sox rerun plays on the flat-screen TV. He swivels around to catch the third and final pitch of an inning, guffaws like it matters, and turns back to steady his elbows on the table.

"So," he says again. Sienna looks out at the water. It's choppier than she would have imagined, sharp little whitecaps rolling over the glassy blue-gray.

"I have some news." His voice cracks, but she's still staring at the ocean, waiting to see the first shadows of land. This was the other game they played. Dad would claim to see the contours of the island first, long before the route they were traveling made such spotting humanly possible.

"It's pretty exciting, and I've been really looking forward to telling you, but I wanted to do it in person, so . . ." Dad shifts closer to the window so that she has no choice but to look him in the eyes.

"What's up?" Sienna asks. He turns back to the water, and behind the sharp profile of his nose, her nose on his face, she sees it: the snaking line of the harbor town, the scattered rooftops, the bridge, and the boats. "There it is!" she calls out, even though it's clear she's the only one playing.

"Sienna," Dad says quietly. Her stomach flips and wrenches. She can count on one hand the number of times he's called her by her real name.

*Sienna, your mom's going back into the hospital.*

*She's gone, Sienna, I'm sorry.*

She half expects to see tears when she looks back at his face, the tears that, when she was younger, seemed to be constantly pooling at the corners of his light blue eyes, rarely spilling over but always there, a watery threat. But all she sees is the same shaky smile.

"I'm getting married." His eyes are staring into her face like she's one of those 3-D pictures, like he's waiting for the real Sienna to pop off the page. The TV blurs behind him, everything blurs, until his face looms, distorted and unsteady, like a giant parade float. "Nobody you know, I don't think. Her name is Denise. I was doing some work pro bono for the Boys and Girls

Club. She's on the board of directors. It hasn't been long, but . . . well, with all that's going on . . ."

He lowers his voice and gestures outside, which is, she's noticed, what people do when they talk about what's happening. As if Persephone—the mile-wide asteroid poised to collide with some unlucky part of the planet, strong enough perhaps to knock them all off of rotation and into some eternal darkness they can't begin to understand—is nothing but an oblivious child, just out of earshot.

"We're going to do a ceremony, and a big party afterward. Next week at the house. Denny's never been to the island before—"

"Denny?" Sienna spits before she can help it. Her voice trembles from the racing of her pulse and she watches her fingers shake. She tries to freeze them with a sharp, steady gaze.

Dad coughs, a stalling clear of his throat. "I thought it would be nice for us all to spend some time together," he says. He reaches across the table and covers her trembling wrists with his hands. She tries to swallow but her throat is scratchy and dry. She wants to rip her hands away. Instead, she tenses the muscles of her forearms, pressing her fingers deeper into the table.

She feels tricked. He knows she won't put up a fight. She's done her fighting. Sienna was the one who had always fought to keep them together. And when it wasn't enough, when nothing got better, when things inside of her only got darker, she fought against the darkness. She fought until it was too much, and then she gave up.

And now she's back, with new meds, new "coping strategies." Just in time to wait for an asteroid, and a wedding. She isn't sure which is worse.

Sienna carefully frees one hand and takes a long sip of soda, realizing after she's swallowed, after the cool, bitter foam has coated her tongue, that she's grabbed his beer instead. Dad raises one eyebrow high above the other. "Something you picked up in rehab?"

She draws the back of one hand slowly across her mouth, refusing to let him see her smile. The boat shudders and shakes, the doors folding open as they pull into the dock. A hurried voice on the PA directs all passengers back to their cars. Sienna stands first and Dad touches her shoulder, pulling her in for an awkward sideways hug. "It's a good thing," he whispers into her hair. "I promise."

She follows him down to the car, where they sit and they wait in a new kind of quiet.

# ZAN

"I KNOW, I KNOW, I'M SUPER LATE. I'M SORRY."

Zan pauses at the bottom of the rocky ledge, stepping out of her flip-flops and looping them around one finger. She is racing the sun—if she gets to their spot before sunset, they'll have plenty of time to talk before dark, before the mosquitoes swarm her ankles and her mother starts to wonder where she's been.

"I've been trying to get out of there since three o'clock. I swear Miranda thinks she's running some sort of factory in our house. I thought when she closed the gallery she'd chill out or something, just work in the garden and read and listen to music—you know, the stuff she said she wanted to do when she retires. I mean, if ever there was a reason to force retirement I'd say the end of the world is it, right?"

Zan catches her breath at the top. She drops her shoes and heavy canvas bag into the sandy patch between two rocks and scales the tallest boulder up to the point, where she has the clearest view. The ocean stretches out for miles, the red clay rocks of the beach below changing colors as the waves roll in and retreat, leaving behind a labyrinth of shallow, misshapen puddles. Just beyond the next cliff, sprawling summer estates jut out toward the horizon. Leo likes to laugh about how expensive it must be, pretending to own this view, when they've always been able to get it for free.

"Which isn't to say that she's not doing those things," Zan goes on, her voice a sharp trill. "She's doing the shit out of them, like some kind of neo-hippie drill sergeant. She has a calendar on the dry-erase board in the kitchen now. There are allotted times for everything. Feeding the animals, harvesting—fine, I get it, but 'Free Read'? 'Correspondence'? It's like a boarding school in nineteenth-century England. I can't stand it."

Zan stretches her legs out from one rock to the other, tensing and releasing the short, sturdy muscles in her thighs. She wishes for the gazillionth time that she had legs like Miranda, her mother, who used to be a dancer, as she allows exactly nobody to forget. Long, graceful legs with narrow, lovely knees, instead of her own stubby calves and wide, boxy ankles. Leo says he loves her just the way she is, his little spark plug, hard to spot in a crowd but near impossible to push over.

From the bag, she pulls out a bottle of champagne—the good stuff, stolen from a crate in the basement, left over from a gallery opening where, as usual, the guests were outnumbered by hopeful bottles of booze. She bites into the foil and spits it out, uncoiling the wire and tugging at the chubby cork.

"I have no idea what I'm doing." She laughs, embarrassed, as always, not to be an expert at something the first time around. Eventually, the cork pops free, not arcing out into the distance as she'd hoped, but sticking in the cup of her palm. She tosses it into the sand.

A soft, steamy fizz puffs into the air and she lifts the bottle to

Leo's rock, her toes still grasping to hang on to the bumpy surface. "Bet you thought I forgot. What with all of the commotion. Did I tell you my dad is building some kind of art machine? It's an installation piece. He's working on it day and night. I have no clue what it does, something about guilt and forgiveness, something totally weird, I'm sure."

Zan rests the bottle on her lower lip and breathes in the sharp scent of the champagne. She takes a careful sip, a few sticky drops landing on the top of her thigh. She wipes them up with the hem of her denim miniskirt, Leo's favorite.

"Two years," she says. "Two years ago, I sat right here and waited for the sun to set, thinking that you'd have to come in eventually. I had no idea how long you'd stay out there; that just because all of the other surfers were trudging out of the water didn't mean you were close to done. I must have sat here for an hour, getting eaten alive, with my dumb little notebook, scribbling stuff down for that lame article I was writing. I can't believe I talked Miss Kahn into running it. 'Born to Surf.' And I can't believe you agreed to answer my questions. Even if you did make me promise not to write about your secret spots. I kept my promise, didn't I? And it was a pretty good profile, if I say so myself. I still read it sometimes. I practically have it memorized."

Zan takes another sip, a bigger one, and closes her eyes as the bubbles pop all the way down, warming her insides and bouncing around in her stomach.

"He did, too, you know."

The voice floats up from a lower ledge. Zan shifts to her knees, peering out over the edge of the cliff as Amelia hoists herself up.

Zan feels her face getting hot. She's already brimming with excuses, but nothing makes sense. She's sitting barefoot at the top of a cliff, chugging champagne from a bottle and talking to herself. It seems a lot to explain to anyone, let alone to Leo's little sister.

"Don't worry." Amelia sighs, out of breath from the climb. She wipes her hands on her long cutoff shorts. Zan can't help but think that the very same shorts would be closer to capri pants on her. Amelia is a head taller than Zan and then some, which might not be especially noteworthy—everyone is taller than Zan—except that Amelia has just finished the seventh grade. "I used to talk to him all the time."

Amelia sits on Leo's rock with her back to the water. She tilts her chin up at the underbelly of the cliff, where shrubby branches stretch up and over their heads. Zan fights the urge to ask her to move. Or to leave.

"Not anymore, really, but for a while it was, like, every night. It's weird, right? Just because he's gone it doesn't mean you don't still have stuff to tell him."

"It's our anniversary," Zan hears herself saying, as if it makes a difference. "I mean, it would have been." Usually she's good about catching her tenses in public. Her mom has corrected her a few times, and Zan has laughed it off as best she could. Inside, though, she felt like she'd been cut open with a knife, her secrets slithering into the sun like restless snakes.

Amelia cocks her head to one side like she's adding up a long list of numbers in her head. She reaches into her faux-leather backpack. Zan recognizes it as a birthday present from Leo, probably the last gift he ever gave. He'd ordered it from an eco-friendly Web site after Amelia became a vegetarian and vowed to wear only hemp shoes.

Zan tucks the bottle of champagne behind her rock and digs it into the sand. When she looks up, Amelia is passing her a square of something loosely wrapped in a brown paper bag.

"I thought maybe you'd be here," Amelia says. She doesn't look away until Zan has taken the package and opened it. "It's something you should have."

Zan reaches into the folds of the thick paper and pulls out a tattered paperback book. *The Rum Diary* by Hunter S. Thompson, a book Zan already owns. Leo bought her a copy the second month they were dating. It wasn't really her thing, too gruff and drug-addled and mean, but she loved that Leo loved it. That he wanted her to love it, too.

"Thanks," Zan says, laying a palm over the water-stained cover. "I'm just about done with the rest."

After the memorial service, a perfectly Leo-esque hodgepodge of surfers, greasy-haired kids from the skatepark, jocks, part-time librarians, and heartbroken teachers, Leo's mom had presented Zan with five enormous boxes of books. Leo had an obsession with used bookstores, and once he'd exhausted his favorite sections of the two small shops on the island, he'd drag whoever was willing along on mainland excursions. To Boston, Providence, the Cape. He'd hit as many as he could in a day, and spend hours flipping pages on the invariably gray and threadbare carpets. Zan could close her eyes and see the way he looked, hunched over a rare edition of essays or poems (the Beats, Bukowski, Brautigan) or an illustrated copy of some dense classic he'd read a thousand times.

The boxes sat in Zan's closet for a few months, until she decided to push her way through them, one book at a time. That's why she started coming back to their spot, the very place she used to sit in awe as he ranted or raved about whatever he was reading. The very spot his ashes were scattered. Now it was her turn. She'd show up, hoping to impress him (she knew it was crazy) with her scathing feminist criticism of D. H. Lawrence. When she started to run out of books, she got nervous and slowed down. What else would she say to a rock?

But Amelia was right. The fact that he wasn't there in body hardly mattered. There were still things to talk about. There would always be things to say.

"This is really nice of you," Zan says again, turning the book over and glancing up at Amelia. Zan wishes she'd called her, at least once, since the accident. Leo would have liked that.

Amelia nibbles at the inside of her cheek and presses her long fingers into the crevices of the rock. She'd played center on the basketball team this year, Zan remembers, noticing the broad expanse of her palms.

"Mom kept it on purpose," Amelia says, almost apologetically. "I guess she thought it would tell her something. But so far, it hasn't had much to say. And besides, it would probably be talking to *you*, you know, if it did."

Zan flips superficially through the book's thick pages, cool and stiff at the binding. She tries to imagine Leo's mom, a sunny dental technician unabashedly obsessed with pop stars and boy bands, poring over half-fictionalized accounts of a drunken journalist wasting time in the tropics.

"It's the last one," Amelia says quietly. "I mean, it was Leo's last one. It was in the truck, that night . . ."

Zan freezes, her fingers stuck between two pages, her pulse pushing in like the tide in her ears.

"That's why I thought you should have it." Amelia stands, her tall, distorted shadow falling across the pebbled sand. "Mom doesn't know I'm here. She's, you know, busy, these days, so I didn't think she'd notice. But I had this feeling, like I had to give it to you . . . like Leo was telling me it was the right thing to do. Do you ever feel like he's telling you things?"

Zan looks down, hoping to hide the hot tears that have sprung out of nowhere, blurring the black-and-white image on the book's ratty cover. She's imagining how the book sat, probably wedged against the console of Leo's truck, the way it must have gotten tossed around when he spun out in the rain. Did it come loose when the cab struck the telephone tower, the one so poorly and strangely disguised as a tree? Did it fly over the guardrail with Leo? How long before somebody picked it up?

"Anyway. I'm late for dinner." Amelia turns and shimmies down the path, lowering first one foot and then the other. "Maybe I'll see you around?"

Zan looks up just in time to see the end of Amelia's long braid disappearing down into the grassy trail. "Thanks," she tries to call after her, but the words are stuck in her throat. "Thank you," she whispers again. She wipes at her eyes with the heels of her hands and looks out at the water. The clouds are on fire, broken threads of orange, pink, and yellow. The sun has already set.

* * *

Miranda is outside when Zan gets home, lowering boxes full of produce into the backseat of Zan's car. "You forgot again, didn't you?" she says flatly as Zan crunches up the gravel walk. "It's your night for deliveries. We're late for a committee meeting at the Center, or I would have already done them myself."

Zan stares longingly past her mother's clenched fists, back at the farmer's porch and open screen door. She was hoping to curl up with the book in bed. Maybe she'd read it again. Maybe she'd just keep staring at the cover, holding on to the last book Leo held ten months earlier, on the night that he left her for good.

"People are depending on us, Suzanne. You know the rations are all processed junk, and there are some people who can't get downtown to wait in line, even if they wanted to." Miranda slams the back door and folds her arms around her still-slim waist. She's wearing the floor-length jumper, a black-and-white striped and shapeless thing with big silver buckles that Zan has seen in pictures from her mother's New York City days. It's the kind of outfit Miranda used to wear with chunky combat boots or dangerous stilettos, but now pairs with a sweater and sensible flats.

"I know," Zan says quietly. She slides into the driver's seat and fishes for her keys in the cupholder. "I'm sorry. It won't happen again."

The car smells of dirt and cilantro, and as Zan pulls out of the driveway she wonders again if anybody is actually eating this stuff. She thinks of the people she sees through windows on her route, the housebound elderly couples anxiously watching the news, the young single moms who seem to be constantly chasing their wired toddlers around the kitchen, or bribing them into the bath. She can't imagine what these people do with the bags of fresh greens she leaves at their doors. She wouldn't blame them for tossing it all in the trash.

Zan starts down the hill at the top of Amity Circle, where the dirt road bends and meanders in both directions, all the way down to the beach. There are seven stops she has to make before turning around at the bottom, where the chalky dirt turns to smooth black pavement, and five more houses to hit on her way back up.

She has it down to a science: make as little noise as possible pulling in the driveway, leave the car running, knock twice on the door if it's closed (or not at all if it's open), and hurry on her way. The only exception is Ramona.

The house at the bottom of the circle is hidden and set back from the road, though Miranda likes to say it's not hidden enough. It's an old, falling-down ranch with missing shingles and a colorful collection of trash cans, usually overturned by greedy raccoons in the night. It's by far the most ramshackle house on the road, but Zan likes to think that with a fresh coat of paint, a quick clean, and some basic landscaping, it could almost be considered cute.

Zan turns off the car and grabs the biggest box from the back. The sliding door is open, as usual, and she pulls at the screen with a satisfying swoosh.

"Ramona?" Zan calls into the quiet of the kitchen. The sink is stacked full of dishes, crusted with bits of pasta sauce and stray noodles, and there's a forgotten mug of coffee, now cold, on the counter. Zan remembers the nights when she'd come looking for her half sister, Joni, and find her and Ramona in a halo of smoke on the back porch, whispering. The place was never exactly tidy, but it couldn't have been as bad as this. "Hello?"

Zan opens the fridge and begins unpacking the lettuces, spinach, and kale, shoving aside six-packs of cheap beer and bottles of empty condiments that leave filmy rings on the shelves. When the bag is empty, she peers around the corner, into the darkened living room. The TV is on, a talk show rerun reflected in flickering blue in the big picture window. Ramona is sprawled out on the couch, her head lolling on a cushion with her mouth puffed open, like a fish. Her knee twitches and she stretches in her sleep, turning her face to the wall.

Zan stands in the doorway, looking at the pile of Ramona's wild red curls. Joni used to say that Ramona had to be the world's most stunningly beautiful alcoholic. Zan is inclined to agree.

The toilet flushes at the other end of the hall and a door creaks open. Zan takes a step back into the kitchen and holds the bag closer to her chest. Caden doesn't look up.

"Sorry, I didn't realize she was sleeping," Zan says, gesturing at the couch.

"She's not sleeping, she's passed out," Caden corrects as he walks into the living room. He kneels on the carpet to tug at the slippery sleeve of a windbreaker, stuck beneath one leg of the couch. "There's a difference."

Zan forces a smile. Caden looks thin, almost unrecognizable as the little boy she used to follow home from the bus stop after school. The only things that haven't changed are his wavy mop of dark red hair and the tear-shaped birthmark near the top of his left cheek. His green eyes used to catch the light when he was up to something, but lately they've looked empty and flat.

"I left some stuff in the fridge," Zan says as Caden rifles through Ramona's purse, left open on the table. He pulls out a wad of singles and keeps looking. "I'm pretty much done, I could stay and cook something if you want . . ."

"No thanks," Caden grumbles, shoving the bills into the pocket of his loose-fitting jeans. "Carly will be home soon. She'll figure something out for Sleeping Beauty, if she ever wakes up."

Caden pauses on the other side of the sliding glass door, and it takes a moment for Zan to realize that he's waiting for her to leave. She hurries out to the porch and he slams the door shut behind her. He jogs to the road and waves an arm high over his shoulder, all before she has a chance to offer him a ride. He always says no, but it makes her feel better to ask.

Zan stares at the book on her bed, warily, like it might actually start talking.

Her parents are still out. She'd felt relieved to see the empty garage and hurried upstairs to her loft, skipping the leftovers she knew her mother had stored in the fridge and taking the crooked steps three at a time.

The loft has low, pitched walls and no real windows. When Zan was little, this was Joni's room. She remembers sitting on the beanbag chair in the corner while her half sister stood on the bed, waving illicit smoke from her American Spirits up through the dusty skylight. She'd stare at the clouds and talk about all of the places she was going to visit when she finally got off this "Godforsaken rock." She promised that Zan could come visit.

After Joni ran away, Zan tried to find a picture of the two of them. In the only one her mother hadn't stashed away in the basement, they're at the fair, Zan hugging the neck of the stuffed giraffe Joni won on the rope-ladder race. Zan is blinking and Joni is staring off into space, but Zan framed it anyway and set it out in plain view, at the center of her bedside table.

Next to the photo is another in a frame: Zan's favorite shot of Leo. He made the frame himself, from scraps in his dad's wood-shop last Christmas. They're at the beach. She's leaning on his legs, his head tucked in the crook of her neck. A tangled strand of her wet, dark hair runs like a scar across his forehead. They look happy, full, attached.

Zan looks from Leo to the book on her bed and flips open the cover. In the top corner of the title page, there's a pencil scrawl: "$3. Used." Zan turns another page and a flimsy piece of paper flutters to the ground.

She bends to the floor to pick it up, recognizing the faint printed numbers on one side. A receipt. She squints to get a better look, but the letters and numbers have faded. Ink bleeds through from the other side and she turns the paper over in her palm. Written in dark black pen is a series of numbers, separated by dashes. A phone number. Beneath them, one word: "Vanessa."

Zan holds the paper out, as if it might make more sense seen from a different angle. Vanessa? She doesn't know any Vanessas.

Leo didn't know any Vanessas, at least not that he ever talked about. Why would he know a Vanessa and not tell her?

Zan shrugs. There's a new tightness in her stomach, but she breathes it away. The receipt must have been left in the book by a previous owner. A previous owner who met a Vanessa and asked for her phone number. A previous owner who probably never called.

She folds the paper back inside the book, closes it, and holds it in her lap. She takes a few breaths and tries to talk herself into doing something else. Taking a shower. Reading a book.

A different book.

Quickly, she pulls out the receipt and flicks on the lamp at her feet, holding the paper under the light and looking closer at the faded blue ink. She can just barely make out the word at the top. "Grumpy's." A chill spikes the hairs on the back of her neck. It's their favorite hangout, a coffee shop in town. Her chest tightens and she thinks of their table, the one on the porch, the mismatched chairs and the porcelain creamer in the shape of a cow.

She is ready to tuck the receipt back between the pages when she notices the printed date. The numbers are light and sketchy, but under the lamp she begins to make them out. This time, she gasps.

It's a date she knows too well. The date Leo was supposed to take her to the last movie at a film festival in town, a documentary about the importance of keeping bees. The date his best friend Nick asked him to do an emergency favor, something having to do with a part for Nick's boat in New Bedford. The date Leo said yes, because it sounded like an adventure and Leo always said yes to adventures, and what's the big deal? They'd catch the movie on DVD, and since when did she care so much about bees?

The date he left in the rain, and never came home.

Zan slams the book shut. Before she knows why, she flicks it like a Frisbee across the room, where it skids along the floor and stops at the wall with a dull, lifeless thud.

# CADEN

CADEN CALLED IT.

Not that anybody will believe him, and not that he cares if they do or they don't. He knows what he knows, and he knows that he knew. He knew the world was ending.

It all started back in the seventh grade. He managed to convince Dr. Stratton, the craggy-faced earth science teacher with bushy gray eyebrows that moved like baby squirrels when he talked, to let him write his final report on black holes. This was before the big growth spurt, before his skin cleared, before he gave up video games and comics and calling the hallway closet his "lab." This was before he started hanging with the Roadies, the kids who live all the way across town, in the island's only public housing development. The kids whose parents don't care how late they stay out, or what they smell like when they get home.

Caden doesn't have parents. He has Ramona. Yes, she gave birth to him. Yes, she gives him the money he needs, when he needs it (meaning he takes what he needs from her pockets and purse). But parental, she is not.

He has a dad, too, or used to. A guy who always wore a wool hat—the newsboy kind with a short, stiff brim—in pictures, and, for a time, sent him useless crap like personalized key chains and packs of candy cigars on his birthday. Caden doesn't blame Ramona for trying so hard to forget him, though it'd be nice if she did it someplace else. There are days when she transitions from deathly hungover to semi-sober to blackout drunk without ever leaving the sofa. There are nights like this one, when Caden walks three miles by himself without a flashlight, just to get out of the house.

He crosses the street at the end of Amity Circle and cuts through the path to the beach.

Black holes. It wasn't the black holes he cared about. It's what he learned when his research went off track. He was Googling for hours in the back of the library, waiting for Ramona to remember to pick him up. It was all over the Web back then. NASA and the budget cuts. People screaming online that asteroid research would be the first to go. With slashed funding, would there be enough attention paid to predictions, to tracking the routes and habits of all of those massive chunks of space-waste, some the size of small planets, hurtling around in no particular orbit?

Caden wasn't the only one who had a feeling that Persephone was going to be a problem. He read about scientists in the 1800s tracking her orbit and making predictions about a potentially destructive return. A century later, when she did come back, she was even closer. Scientists adjusted their calculations, and the overwhelming consensus was that her next visit would be the last. At the very least, she would do severe localized damage, interrupting satellites, making mass communication and air travel next to impossible, and putting on one hell of a show.

At the very worst, it could be the end. The end of everything. But that was all they knew, back then.

Caden went home that night and booted up the old desktop computer he'd salvaged from the freebie pile at the dump. He'd logged in to his online journal and typed quickly: "We're all going out with a bang."

Walking along the beach after dark, it's hard for him to imagine that all of this could be gone. Gone *how*, nobody will say. But Caden has looked into this, too. First: water. Massive tsunamis if an ocean took a direct hit, washing away entire coastlines. Then: fire. The displaced embers of Earth's very core, falling chunks of flaming hail. And last but not least: ice. A frozen planet, shrouded in clouds of debris, hidden from the life-giving forces of the sun.

Not that any of them would necessarily be around to witness it. They could all be gone, the way of the dinosaurs. But still, it seems impossible as he walks under the quiet glow of the moon, beside the soft, steady roll of the waves. It seems impossible that even this beach, this beach that he knows like his own back-yard, could be the first to turn against him.

He's never been afraid of the beach at night. As soon as it's warm enough, he likes to walk down to Split Rock, the big-ass boulder at the end of the point that looks like somebody sawed it in half. He rolls a joint from the baggie full of shake, stolen from Ramona's not-so-secret bathroom stash. He takes a few thoughtful hits, and falls asleep in the dunes. Nobody bugs him. Sometimes he wakes up to the early morning joggers, or a dopey retriever licking the salt from his face.

Tonight, he passes Split Rock and keeps walking. The way to the docks is longer by the water, but he prefers it to taking the streets. He tries to guess who will be out at the landing tonight. There's always the core group of Roadies: Justin, Kiefer, Lou, and Deck. Then there are the hangers-on, the kids like him who live in other parts of town and join the ongoing party whenever they can sneak away. Some of them have parents who try to track them down. They pull up in their SUVs at the end of the dock, headlights streaking across the parking lot. They call out into the darkness.

Some kids try to run, some sulk to their cars, stoned and reeking of cigarettes. They don't care about getting in trouble; nobody does anymore. It's just that some of them feel guilty. They shuffle their feet and climb inside, carted off to the warm light of living rooms and last-minute bonding.

Caden never feels guilty. Sometimes he wishes his sister wouldn't try so damn hard. He knows she's doing her thing, that she goes to Al-Anon meetings at the Center because it makes her feel better. But Caden wishes she wouldn't waste her time. Carly thinks this could finally be a way to get through, a way for Ramona to find something to hold on to. To live whatever time she has left with them, for them, clearheaded. But Caden knows better. Ramona was always going to die a drunk. Why would she change her mind now?

In the distance, Caden sees the deep orange light of a fire. There's over a mile still to go. It must be one hell of a bonfire if he can see it from here. He picks up his pace, shortening his steps until he's in a full sprint. Lately, he's realized how much time he spends getting places.

* * *

"You wanna go for a walk?"

Caden's feet are half-buried and there's a girl in a light blue sundress, kicking the sides of his toes. He doesn't know how long he's been lying here, his legs heavy in the sand where it starts to get damp and slopes down toward the water.

"Who is that?" he asks, struggling to lift his head. It feels like he's stacked full of bricks, like that game he used to play with Carly. She would pretend to cut an incision in his forehead, tap her fingertips like she was pouring cement, and fill him up. First to the knees, then to the waist, then all the way up to his collarbone until he was totally frozen, a concrete statue of a boy in the grass.

"Eliza," the girl says, plopping to her knees and tracing big circles in the sand with her fingernail. "We had after-school together once. I gave you money for the vending machine."

"You did?" Caden props up on his elbows, his brick-head throbbing. He wishes he'd brought along a bottle of water, wishes there was something to drink at the party besides cheap vodka and warm, flat beer.

Eliza nods. "Yup." She scoops a pile of sand and lets it sift through her fingers, pouring a steady, tickling stream onto the tops of his shins. "You got pretzels. And you didn't even share."

Caden is confused. He hates pretzels. And the sand on his legs feels warm and cold at the same time. He shifts back and bends his knees. Now his head feels light, like a balloon, like there's nothing keeping it from floating away. "What time is it?" he asks, looking around. The fire is dying but a small group of kids is still gathered around the glowing scraps, bottles and cans piled like pieces of abstract art at their feet. "I think I need to go home."

"Come on," Eliza says, leaning toward him. The light from the fire dances in the shallow creases of her slim, tanned shoulders. He gets a clear look at her face and places her at last. One of Deck's old girls. He's heard stories but he can't remember details, and he doesn't want to try. "Don't you want to go for a walk with me?" She rests her hands on the points of his knees and tilts her forehead toward his.

Months, even weeks earlier, there were few things Caden wouldn't have done to be asked to go for a walk by a girl like Eliza. The amount of time he'd spent conjuring up scenarios much like this one, scenarios in which a decent-looking female was not only interested in but maybe even enthusiastic about getting him alone, added up to a significant percentage of his waking (not to mention dreaming) teenage life.

But now that it's happening, now that Eliza—and it isn't just Eliza, it's been almost a full month of Elizas—is exactly where he never thought she'd be, saying the things he never allowed himself to dream she'd someday say, all he wants to do is disappear. Sink into the sand and let the waves pull him out to sea.

"Or we could just stay here," she's whispering now, inching her face closer to his. "You do look pretty cozy." With a jolt like a spasm, her hands are on the sides of his face, and she's pressing her lips onto his. Her tongue is cool and tastes like fruit punch and tobacco. Caden lets the weight of her fall into him, his mouth hung open and slack. He tries not to move. He tries to keep up. Of course he'll keep up. Who wouldn't?

He's on his feet before Eliza can catch herself, toppling

face-first into the leftover imprint of his body in the sand. She doesn't move, and for a minute he's worried she's not breathing. But then she starts to laugh, a quiet cackle that crescendos into a maniacal guffaw, somehow getting louder the farther he gets down the beach.

He's walking fast, trying to erase the memory of each individual moment with his steps. If he keeps walking by the water he'll have to pass whoever's left, he'll have to explain why he's leaving. Instead, he cuts through the parking lot.

He doesn't notice the town car until it switches on its lights. He can't tell if it's just pulled in or has been sitting there, hidden in darkness. At first, he assumes it's another anxious mom or dad, red-faced and feigning anger, but actually just relieved to have a chore, somewhere to be, a simple task with a beginning and an end.

The car creeps along the asphalt and Caden looks at it again over his shoulder. He shortens his steps and heads for a trail in the bushes. He hears the car accelerate, pulling up and matching his pace. The front window slides down and he can see two men, one driving, one inching an elbow out of the passenger seat.

"Excuse me," the passenger says. He's bald, with a long, oval head and a shiny black goatee. "I'm looking for Caden Crawford."

Caden stops. He feels his heart freeze and jump-start. He wonders if he's dreaming. He's back on the beach, with Eliza. He stayed, her body pressed warm and hard against his. Afterward, they fell asleep.

The thick-necked driver says something under his breath. The passenger nods twice, two quick, precise bobs of his egg-shaped head.

Caden is running before he knows why. There's a sharp squeal of tires as the car cuts him off, blocking his path to the trees. Both doors open and the smaller man is on him first, holding his wrists and twisting his arms in awkward angles behind his back. The driver lunges forward. There's something in his hand that feels warm on Caden's face, covering his mouth and nose. It's damp and smells medicinal.

Caden struggles, trying to free his hands, trying to look somewhere, anywhere else. He can't open his eyes, the weight of the cloth keeps them shut, and in the cloudy dark he thinks he sees a face. A girl. Not Eliza. His sister, Carly. They're little again and he wants to ask what she's doing, how she found him here of all places, but she's already tapping sand into his forehead, filling his arms and legs, until even his eyelids are heavy. He takes a breath and heaves forward, sticky leather slapping the fronts of his legs. The car jerks into the night.

# SIENNA

DENISE LOOKS LIKE SHE PLAYS A LOT OF TENNIS.

This is what Sienna thinks as she sets the table. The bags of groceries Dad brought from off-island have been unpacked and put away, and he's already stationed himself at the grill, wearing an old apron of Mom's that says "Kiss the Chef" over a cartoony pair of pursed, painted lips. Denise—Sienna so far has refused to call her "Denny" despite many cheerful prompts—walks back and forth from the kitchen to the dining room, asking where to find things like napkins and serving spoons and offering Sienna lemonade every fifteen seconds.

She hasn't stopped moving since they arrived. Which is odd since, when they pulled in the driveway, she seemed relaxed and content, flipping through a travel magazine and having a colorful drink on the upstairs deck. Sienna had to avert her eyes as she waved hello, so as not to see directly up Denise's short, pleated skirt. Her legs were bronzed and shining, like they'd been oiled to star in a commercial for disposable lady razors, and her thick blond hair was pulled back in one of those fake-messy buns, exposing a patch of darker roots at her temples.

Ryan says she wears makeup to the beach. He was waiting outside when they showed up, concentrating hard on a sign made from the taped-together insides of broken-down cereal boxes. "Sienna Welcome Ho" it said in meticulous green crayon. Sienna scooped him up, mid-scribble, swinging his scrawny legs back and forth like floppy, defective windshield wipers. His hair smelled different; less sweet and more sweat. He felt different, too, more hard preteen angles, less soft little boy.

At first, it looked like he was going to cry, and not because he was happy to see them. Dad had told him they wouldn't be getting in until later. They'd messed up his plan, and Ryan hates surprises. He was only two when Mom died, but Sienna thinks he tries so hard to be perfect so nothing bad will ever happen again. She tries not to wonder how much he knows about her, what she did, and where she's been.

"I won't look," Sienna promised, shielding her eyes from the unfinished sign and lugging the rest of the bags up the steps.

Dad kicks open the door to the back porch, carrying a tray of charred burgers and deformed-looking hot dogs. "Who's hungry?" he asks in his very best TV sitcom voice. It's not clear right away if the poor showing is a result of meat that has been stockpiled in the freezer for months, or Dad's overall culinary deficiencies. Either way, Sienna finds herself surprisingly homesick for the Tater Tots and frozen pizzas they served most nights at the House.

"It's nice to find a man so useful in the kitchen," Denise whispers to Sienna like they're suddenly girlfriends, quiet collaborators. To Dad, she makes an overly enthusiastic *mmm*-ing sound, which leads Sienna to suspect that Dad has met his match in the false-truth department. Either that, or she never actually eats anything he cooks. Maybe that's how she stays so thin.

"Wanna put the paper away, Bud?" Dad forks the burgers onto the open buns and passes them around the table. Ryan ignores him and stares with fierce concentration at the newspaper in his lap, tracing words with his finger across the front page.

"It's all right, Mark." Denise touches Dad's forearm as she reaches for the ketchup. "Let him read. I don't mind."

Dad shrugs and gives the table one last glance before settling into his seat at the head.

"I'd like to make a toast," Denise says. Sienna raises her full glass and tries not to look bored already. Denise's nails are filed into perfect squares with shiny white tips, and they clickety-clack on the table as she clears her throat. "I'd like to make a toast to—"

"Nuclear bombs!" Ryan blurts, lifting his glass high above the rest. The semicircle dimples cut on each of his freckled cheeks get deeper as he smiles.

"Ryan," Dad snaps. Denise lowers her glass and tucks a strand of her fried blond hair obsessively behind one ear. "That's not funny."

"I didn't say it was funny." Ryan shrugs. "I think we should toast them. They're probably going to save our lives."

Ryan unfolds the paper on the table, pointing at a headline on the front page. "What are you talking about, Ry?" Sienna asks patiently. Denise is smiling, but Sienna can tell it's forced.

Dad lifts up the paper and scans the front page. "Where did you get this?" he asks, distracted. "Is this today's . . ."

"It was in the neighbor's trash," Ryan says calmly, pushing at the forlorn-looking pieces of lettuce on his plate. "It's not stealing if they threw it away."

"What does it say?" Sienna asks, shoving her plate to one side and leaning across the table.

Dad clears his throat. "It's the new Space Alliance. NASA with Russia and China. They're sending a nuclear-tipped rocket directly into Persephone's core," he tells them. "It looks like they're trying to blow the asteroid up."

"I thought they decided it was too risky," Denise says quietly. Something about her has changed, Sienna notices. She looks smaller, like she's shrinking into the furniture.

"It is risky," Ryan explains. "But it's the only option left. Right, Dad?"

Dad scans the rest of the article. "I'm not sure yet, Buddy." He flips through the pages of the section, hurrying to find a continuation. He spreads his arms wide, accidentally knocking Denise's glass onto her plate, her burger bun quickly drenched in lemonade.

"Denny, I'm so sorry." Dad grabs his napkin and sops up the leaking puddles of juice from the table.

Denise doesn't move and the spill begins to drip onto the tanned tops of her knees. Her glossy lower lip does an abrupt little quivering thing, and her eyes look like they are straining to stay focused on her plate. There's a pause that feels too long, and then the squeal of her chair as it slides back across the polished floor.

Dad stands and tries to stop her but she shakes her head and gestures for him to sit before rushing out of the room. The bottom step creaks loudly as she hurries upstairs.

"What was that?" Sienna half mouths, half whispers across the table. Dad glances at the ceiling, following Denise's footsteps as she shuffles down the hall, toward the master bedroom. The door clicks shut, and Dad exhales. He stares at the food on his plate. He looks suddenly tired and old.

"This has all been hard on Denise," he says quietly. "She's . . . I don't know. She's scared." Dad looks at the top of Ryan's head, buried once again in the newspaper, and back at Sienna. "We're all scared. But we're all here together. And I'm just . . . I'm trying to make this a comfortable place for her. For all of us."

He doesn't ask them to give her a break. He doesn't have to. They finish what they can of the burgers in silence.


Sienna offers to do the dishes. The floorboards shift and groan and she can hear the gentle murmur of voices, Dad and Denise smoothing things over. First, there are flashes of shame, hot waves rushing to the back of her neck. She's done enough damage already. The least she can do is let him be happy now. What if this—this time together in the place they've always loved—what if it's all that any of them have left?

But then, as she dips her hands in the warm, soapy water, something shifts. The dull, familiar ache in the pit of her belly, the steady burn of all the things she can't have back. It's not fair. It hasn't ever been fair. And if this is really it, why should they have to share him? If everything's so scary, why should any of them have to tiptoe around a stranger?

Sienna hauls her bags up to the guest room at the top of the stairs. It's her de facto bedroom, where she's allowed to sleep when there aren't any guests. (She tries not to think about what kind of "guest" that makes Denise.) Otherwise, she shares the middle room with Ryan, which isn't so bad. There are two single beds built into the wall, meeting to form a giant L in the corner. He doesn't snore or mess up her things. Mostly, she's the one who has to worry about breathing the wrong way or accidentally messing up his.

The guest room smells musty and damp. She pushes open the door to the upstairs deck, which wraps around the house and ends at a pair of sliding glass doors leading to Dad's room, on the other side of the hall.

Outside, she can hear the rhythm of the waves, the low howl of wind in the trees. The night feels cool and moist, like the inside of a cloud. She tries to remember the last time they were all here together. After Mom died, they stopped coming every summer. Dad said the old renters called, that they made him an offer he couldn't refuse. Sienna was grateful for the story, but they all knew the truth. This was Mom's place. It didn't make any sense to be here without her.

There's a window open somewhere down the hall and Sienna hears a soft, conciliatory laugh. Before she can stop herself she's imagining them brushing their teeth side by side, changing unabashedly in front of each other, climbing into bed. She feels suddenly seasick, not just nauseous or dizzy but like the house is actually floating, stubbornly bucking against stormy seas.

She pads softly down the stairs and sneaks through the open front door. She's not wearing shoes and the gravel pricks the soft bottoms of her feet. She crosses to the grass and walks along the road, letting her eyes adjust to the dark.

She doesn't know where she's going, only that it's time to leave. This happens a lot. Sometimes it feels like there are answers inside of her, answers to questions she doesn't remember asking. The answer tonight is *Walk*. The answer six months ago was *Wait until Ryan's in bed. Dad's sleeping pills are in a blue bottle, hidden behind a stack of self-help books on his bedside table. Swallow them with a big glass of orange juice. See what happens.*

She spent six months in the House trying to figure out the question she was answering that night. She's still not sure what it was, but she has an idea. Something about how to make it stop. How to stop trying to fill up all of the spaces her mother left behind, without getting sick like her, too. It was impossible, so she decided to disappear instead. She'd be nothing, feel nothing. Nothing was better than not enough.

As Sienna walks around Amity Circle, she considers the latest news. Another nuclear rocket. Another chance for people to get their hopes up. To pray. Sienna used to pray. After Mom's last episode, after she flooded the kitchen, painted numbers on the walls, and locked them all out of the house, Sienna looked up to the sky. She prayed that things would change. That someday, they'd go back to the way they'd been before. She prayed for her mother back. There were even some days, when the meds kicked in, when her mom got dressed and knew who they were, that she thought somebody might be listening. Turns out, she was wrong. Now, especially now, she knows better than to ask favors from the sky.

At the end of the road, she sees the covered shed. Sometimes there are bikes wedged up against the outside, but tonight it's deserted. Dad says it's a bus stop, but she's never seen a bus, or a single person waiting for one to arrive.

41

She pushes through the tall grass up the hill. There's a crushed soda can in the dirt, a few cigarette butts, and a Kit Kat wrapper stuck in the slats of the old wooden bench. Behind the bench is a bulletin board. Lonely, leftover thumbtacks polka-dot the empty cork, a multicolored constellation.

She sits on the bench and stares across the street, where the paved road starts and, on the other side, a covered path winds out toward the water. There's a rustle in the trees at the bottom of the hill, and in the full-moon haze Sienna can barely make out the shape of a person at the end of a driveway. A light breeze moves the branches and a new pattern of dappled moonlight falls on the road. She realizes that she's been holding her breath, like she's caught in a game of hide-and-seek.

"Somebody there?" a voice calls out. It's a male voice, deep and low.

Sienna stands up fast, like she's in trouble. "Sorry," she says. "I mean, yeah. I am. I was just . . ."

The boy walks deliberately up the hill. Sienna sits back on the bench—he's walking fast and it feels like the right thing to do. He's tall and lean and he moves like he hasn't stopped growing yet, like he hasn't quite gotten used to the proportions of his limbs. "I thought so," he says when he reaches the shed. Sienna still can't see much of his face but it sounds like he's smiling. "I saw your feet. What happened to your shoes?"

He points at Sienna's bare feet and she shrugs. "I forgot them," she says. "My house is just down the hill."

The boy takes a step back and a patch of moonlight falls across his face. His hair is dark brown, thick and to his shoulders, but not scraggly or unkempt. His skin is creamy and his eyes are a warm chocolate brown, with a few oversize freckles on the bridge of his long, narrow nose. She looks away, hoping she hasn't been staring, and knowing that she has.

"Owen," he says. "I live a few streets over." He holds out a hand in the darkness, and slowly she reaches out her own, gripping his fingers to shake. She cringes when instead of an empty palm, her hand grasps a thin piece of paper. "It's a flyer for this show we're doing tomorrow night," he says. "I'm supposed to be hanging them up."

Sienna looks at the flyer, feeling all of the blood rush to the tops of her cheeks. She wonders if he knew she was trying to shake his hand.

"It's at the Community Center in town. Kind of a Battle of the Bands type thing, except, you know, everybody wins."

Sienna holds the flyer into the light. It's photocopied and black-and-white and there are a lot of hyphens and crazy-looking type. "Oh," she says dumbly. "Thanks."

"No problem." Owen shuffles his feet and Sienna thinks he's walking away, but when she looks up he's still standing there, his arms crossed over the front of his navy-blue T-shirt. There's a white emblem that looks like a wave peeking out over the tops of his tanned forearms, and beneath it the shirt says BALI. Owen cocks his head to one side and squints his eyes. "Sienna?"

Sienna is so surprised to hear her name that it takes her a moment to recognize it. "Yeah," she says at last. "How did— Do I know you?"

"This is so weird," Owen says, almost under his breath. "I

was just thinking about you. I mean"—he clears his throat and shuffles his feet again—"not like, *thinking about you*, but I don't know, something about being on this street . . ."

His hands move quickly to his forehead, where he runs his fingers in long strokes through the roots of his hair. "Owen," he says again, slowly, this time pointing to himself, to the empty blue space between the bubble letters on his shirt. "You don't remember me at all?"

Sienna shifts on the bench so that her back hits the wooden panels of the shed's far wall. She's trying to see him better in the light. "I don't think so," she says, hearing the familiar apology creeping into her voice. Val says not to worry, that it happens all the time. She says depression is a mental bully, co-opting more than its fair share of brain-space in order to make room for all of the compulsive negative thinking about things that will probably never happen, which makes it hard to remember some of the things that actually did. "Sorry," she mutters softly. "I don't."

"We were really little." He sits beside her on the bench. The soft cuff of his T-shirt brushes the outside of her shoulder. "And I think my hair used to be blonder. At least it is in pictures. Sometimes I don't really believe it was me."

He stretches his long legs out in the grass and crosses one flip-flop, tan leather with two red stripes, easily over the other. "We used to play together at the beach, every summer," he says. "I probably had seaweed on my head most of the time."

Sienna smiles. "Seaweed?"

"It was a phase." Owen shrugs. He tilts his head to the side. "You don't remember? You, me, and Carly?"

"Carly," Sienna repeats. The name feels comfortable and

strange at the same time, like one of those words you read a lot but never say out loud.

"Yeah," he says, nodding at the hidden driveway across the street. "She lives right there. We were just rehearsing for tomorrow—she's got this, like, unbelievable Janis Joplin–y voice, like sandpaper." He shakes his head and she feels him turn to study her profile. "You know, I think we even used to have dinner at your house some nights. Your mom used to make those, like, popover things. She's a really good cook, right?"

He intertwines his long fingers together, cracking his knuckles all at once, a loud, resounding pop. There's something about the noise that feels like she already knew it was going to happen, and something inside of her snaps. She remembers. There aren't any flashes, no pictures or memories or scenes she can see, but she knows that she knows him. That she knew him, when she was young and Mom was a good cook and everything else was so far away.

"Yeah," she says vaguely. She feels lighter, almost relieved, before she remembers the question she was supposed to have answered. "I mean, yeah, she was."

"Was?"

"She died," Sienna says quickly, in the way she always says it, the steady voice that is meant to convey a range of non-emotions: stability, acceptance, perfectly *all right*. "A while ago. I was eight."

Sienna holds her breath, waiting for the wave of consolation she'll have to nod through, preparing her subtly grateful half smile and the litany of follow-up assurances that everything is fine.

"Man." Owen knocks his head gently against the side of the shed. "That sucks."

He doesn't look at her. She waits for him to go on; she waits to feel offended when he doesn't. But he doesn't, and she doesn't mind.

"So what are you guys doing back here now?" Owen asks. "I mean, most people are trying to *leave* the island these days. At least the people with other places to go."

Sienna shrugs. "I really have no idea," she says. "I guess my dad's an optimist."

Owen slaps absently at a bug on the back of his neck. He checks his hand for evidence. "Not that it matters much anyway," he says. "I mean, if this thing hits . . . I've got a bunch of buddies building some type of amphibious boat. If you ask me, they're the only ones who stand a chance."

The word *amphibious* scrolls through Sienna's head and she smiles, imagining a bunch of Owen-clones riding the back of a mechanical frog. She thinks about the rocket in the paper and wonders if she should bring it up, but just the idea of the asteroid makes her veins twitch, her pulse race uncontrollably. Casual conversation about a nuclear space explosion isn't really an option, just yet.

"I should get going," Owen says. "My parents are all worked up about family nights these days; they made me promise I'd come straight home. We've been playing the same game of Monopoly for, like, weeks."

Sienna has a weird panicky feeling in her stomach, like she wants him to stay and go at the same time. For months, she only spoke to people who were paid to listen, or to the other kids in Group—kids who refused to talk at all, or were awkwardly learning the language of recovery. How to assess their symptoms, manage impulses, regulate nonproductive thoughts. Small talk wasn't exactly on the agenda.

"Try to make it tomorrow night," Owen calls as he shuffles down the hill, careful not to trip on any of the gnarly hidden roots. "It was really nice seeing you again."

Sienna thinks about calling out a goodbye, but quickly decides against it. She waits until she can't see him anymore and then takes off toward her house. The walk home feels shorter and she's halfway to the door before she realizes she's still smiling.

# DAY TWO

# CADEN

THERE'S AN ELECTRIC THROBBING THAT WAKES
him, an obnoxious grinding noise that might be inside his head.
He opens one eye and waits for the room to make sense.

It's oddly shaped, with dormer windows and steep, sloping
walls. The sheets on the bed are clean, white, with lace at the
edges. Caden's faded black Vans hang limply from his feet. He's
wearing most of his clothes.

The mechanical whirring stops. A vacuum, or a blender
maybe. Downstairs? Which would mean that he is upstairs. He
doesn't remember stairs of any kind.

He remembers running. The car. The men. And then, quiet.
Darkness.

Caden sits up too fast. The pounding in his head feels familiar: the thickness of a hangover, but worse. Way worse.

He walks to the window and pulls back the sheer ivory curtain. The house is on a bluff, jutting out over the ocean. If he
presses his face against the screen he can follow the curves of a
paved, narrow road. At the end of the road is a stoplight.

There are no stoplights on the island.

The light in the room is soft and there's something strangely familiar about the color of the walls, a green so pale it's almost white, and the dense, floral pattern on the bedspread. It's like he's dreamed of waking up in this room before.

Or maybe he's dreaming now.

On the back of a chair by the door is his sweatshirt. He swipes it free and digs into the pocket for his phone. But all that's left is a handful of sand.

Caden swallows hard and looks back outside. He's three stories up. There are a few sturdy-looking branches that might hold his weight. He tries to guess how quickly he could make it to the end of the road, the stoplight. The ground below is rocky and uneven. If he's really dreaming, he'll be fine. If not . . .

The blender starts up again. There has to be an easier way out.

He opens the door and peers down a long, quiet hall. He scans the walls for photographs or other clues, but there's nothing but kitschy watercolors of boats, and hand-painted signs with feel-good quotes like "You and Me, By the Sea" and "It's Never Too Late to Live Happily Ever After."

His head is still foggy and his feet feel stuck. He finds a bathroom and shuts himself inside. There are peach-colored soaps in the shape of scallop shells, and matching towels neatly stacked on a shelf. He looks at his face in the mirror, the dark circles under his eyes, the greasy red mop of his hair. His own reflection is by far the scariest thing in the room.

He follows the grinding noise down a wide, marble staircase, around a corner, and into a kitchen, all shiny black countertops and sleek, modern appliances. There's a small, plump woman in an apron, tilting a heavy blender over a row of glasses. Her bare arms are caramel-colored and her silky black hair is knotted in a bun.

As if she's been expecting him, the woman turns. Caden ducks quickly back into the hallway. He's suddenly afraid. Is this a dream? How can he wake himself up? And if it's not a dream, where is he, and how can he get the hell out?

There's a swishing sound behind him. The long panels of a floor-length curtain sway in the breeze, revealing a pair of white French doors, propped open just a crack. A misty light filters through. This is how it must be in dreams, he thinks. You ask for a door, and you get one.

The doors open onto a smooth, stone patio, lined with sturdy wooden lounge chairs. The chairs are arranged at precise intervals, surrounding a bean-shaped infinity pool. The water is perfectly still and artificially turquoise, a shimmering frame that mirrors the garden behind it.

Caden blinks purple sunspots from his eyes.

"You're up."

He jumps at the voice, knocking against the ceramic lip of a massive potted fern. The wind rustles and through the leafy fronds he glimpses a pair of long, tanned legs, outstretched and bent at an easy angle. Two narrow feet wiggle back and forth, light purple polish glinting in the sun.

Caden slowly sidesteps the plant.

"Hey," say the legs.

For the first time all morning, Caden hopes that he's really awake. He knows that he's staring, but there doesn't seem to be anywhere else to look. "Hi," he squeaks. He clears his throat and tries again. "Hi," he says, this time too loud and drawn out across many ridiculous syllables.

The woman—girl? Dark, oversize glasses shield her eyes and

make it hard to guess her age—pushes herself up to her elbows and smiles.

"Caden, right?" She pushes her glasses up into her hair. Her eyes are brown, but not a boring brown. A light, full brown that looks like melted pennies, flecked with orange and green. She's definitely older than he is. Not by much. Twenty-four, he guesses, though he has no idea why.

"Hi," he says, for the third time. "I mean," he stumbles. "Yeah."

"I'm Sophie," she says, holding out her hand. Caden shakes it, grateful for another opportunity to look at her face. Her hair is honey-colored and pulled back in a low, loose ponytail. It drapes over one shoulder and curls up like an inverted question mark, circling the dip in her neck. "It's nice to finally meet you."

Sophie lets her hand fall onto her bare stomach, tanned and toned and still wet from a swim. Caden averts his eyes to the top of his shoes and wishes they were cooler, or at least less grimy and gross. "Finally?" he manages. "Who . . . I mean . . . where am I? What is this place?"

Sophie chuckles. "I ask myself that every day." She fumbles with something on the ground and Caden hears the snap of a bottle of sunscreen. He keeps his gaze trained on the grassy cracks between the stones as she rubs lotion onto the bronzed top of her shoulders.

If this isn't a dream, he thinks, it must be some kind of a prank. Somebody has kidnapped him primarily in order to mess with him. His eyes dart around the pool, to the corners of the arbor overhead. Surely there are cameras, somewhere. Somebody's twisted idea of end-of-the-world reality TV.

Instead of cameras, he sees a shadow, stretched long from behind another wall of potted shrubbery.

"We're over here," Sophie calls, without looking up.

A man turns the corner. If it weren't for the hat, Caden might not have recognized him right away. He's slender, and much taller than Caden remembers, with smooth, expensive-looking skin and sharp green eyes. The hat is wool with a short leather brim, and not at all weather-appropriate. It's the same hat he wears in the pictures, the pictures Caden used to say good night to. The pictures he used to stupidly ask for help, before he grew up and realized that nobody was listening.

Caden hears his pulse, his blood a rushing river, flooding in his ears. The woman on the chair is moving. She kisses the side of the man's neck on her way back inside.

"Looks like you guys have some catching up to do." She smiles at Caden before disappearing into the kitchen.

Caden feels suddenly hot. There's something fierce and glowing inside of him, like a light or a magnet.

"What am I doing here?" he hears himself asking. His hand flutters at his side, like a foreign object he can't control.

Caden's father crosses his arms and leans back against the planter. He narrows his eyes into discerning hyphens. "You're smaller than I was, at your age," he says, angling his head to one side. His shoulders are too broad for his frame, and his forearms are covered in thick, dark hair. "Shorter, I mean."

Caden feels his spine straightening. His breath catches in his throat and the glowing thing inside of him changes, like a flickering flame, though he can't tell if it's getting bigger or going out. It's like a thirst and he almost thinks to ask for water, until he swallows. Tears, he thinks. He feels like crying.

"Caden, I know this wasn't the only way to do this—"

"Do what?" Caden coughs, which is better than crying, though he doesn't like the girlish squeal in his voice. He takes another breath. "What do you want from me? Why am I here?"

His father doesn't move or speak. He stands and stares, just like he does in the photographs, two-dimensional and somewhere else.

Caden feels his hands moving again, and he stuffs them into his pockets. He's surprised to feel the jangle of his house keys inside. His house. Where he should be. This is all really happening. He's been kidnapped by his father. Literally: *kid*napped.

It's absurd. Caden almost laughs. He takes a steadying breath and eyes the French doors behind his father. "I always knew you were an asshole," he says evenly, a new strength finding him. "But I didn't realize you were completely insane."

Caden shakes his head and pushes past his father, toward the open living room. It's not a dream, or a movie. It's real life, and he can leave whenever he wants to.

Just as he reaches the door, a second man appears from nowhere. Caden sees the watch first, then the man's giant, solid torso blocking his path.

"Easy, now, pal," the man says, holding up a fleshy hand and pressing it firmly into Caden's shoulder. Caden squirms out of the man's heavy grasp and turns away from the house, running past the pool, toward a low, stone wall.

But the man follows, shoving himself between Caden and the wall. He holds his arms wide, like he's attempting to corral a wayward bull. Caden bolts through a gap in the shrubs. He can outrun this guy, no problem. But his shirt snags on a spindly branch, and there's a hand on his back, a thick, sweaty arm scooping him at the waist and leveling him, horizontal.

"Where do you want him?" the man asks. His breathing is jagged, his shoulders shudder as he pants. Caden tries to wriggle free, but it's no use. He starts to feel dizzy, blood rushing to his head. He stares at the shiny tops of his father's shoes as the man carries him, like a piece of living luggage, back inside the house.

# ZAN

TWO THINGS PEOPLE MAKE TIME FOR AT THE end of the world: free food and a party.

Miranda has been on the Community Center board since Zan was in preschool, organizing fund-raisers, art shows, and live music. This is the first time more than a small, devoted group of gallery coworkers and local divorcees, lonely and bored on a Saturday night, have shown up. Zan can tell that her mother is pleased, though she hasn't stopped moving around long enough to really show it.

The second band of the night is playing on the makeshift Center stage, a group of stoner guys Zan knows from school. One of them sporadically strums a heavily stickered mandolin, another sits behind half a set of drums, and a third is doing some kind of unidentifiable yell-rapping. It's like an afterlife drum circle with Jerry Garcia and that guy from Sublime. On weed.

"What is this?" Daniel, Zan's father, asks, rearranging the tray of organic cupcakes that Miranda and Zan spent all morning baking. He points at the stage with frosting on his finger. "Not bad."

Zan smiles. Her father tries very hard to be hip, open-minded, slow to judge. He considers himself one of the "cool" teachers at school, the kind that kids actually want to hang out with. His shaggy gray hair is always tousled in a sort of old-man mullet, and he wears the same leather jacket every day, even in the middle of summer. Zan pretends he annoys her, but they both know they're a team.

"It's not *bad*," Zan allows, filling paper cups with glugs of homemade hibiscus iced tea. "It's a disgrace. My eardrums are crying."

Daniel taps his foot defiantly, his hard, weathered face a scrambled mix of phony enjoyment and fear. Out of nowhere, Miranda pops between them, her sunken cheeks flushed from walking in tight circles around the room. "How's it going here?" she asks, quickly surveying the spread. "Do you need more napkins? There's another box in the kitchen. Are people reusing their cups?"

Miranda reaches forward to rearrange the trays and Zan stares at the swinging tail of her mother's long, graying braid. "What does it matter if people recycle anymore?" she grumbles. She doesn't mean to say it out loud. Her father's foot stops tapping and Miranda's shoulders tense. Zan wishes immediately she could take it back.

She steels herself for a lecture. A reminder that *"Everything matters."* That *"Nothing is certain. We're here until we're not."* That *"Living clean is living well. And we're all still living, aren't we?"* Lectures that started long before the announcements, the panic, the endless waiting.

But Miranda's shoulders relax. She passes the clipboard to Zan's father. "Daniel, I've been working on getting sign-ups for help with your installation. Why don't you see who you can nail down outside?"

Daniel wipes a few telltale cupcake crumbs from the corner of his mouth and takes the clipboard. He gives Zan a warning glance as he passes, and Zan feels herself shrinking even smaller.

Miranda arranges the remaining brownies and cookies in precise little rows before clapping her hands together and glancing warily at the stage. "This is awful," she sighs. "I'm going to ask somebody to turn down the amps."

Zan watches her mother stalk across the crowded room. She wonders if she's ever felt as strongly about anything as the way Miranda feels about, well, everything. Maybe Leo, but that's it.

Leo's face flashes in her mind and she feels her heart swell, then stick. *Vanessa.* She has the Grumpy's receipt in her pocket, hasn't been able to stop thinking about it and what it could mean. Her mind loops in vicious circles. It's nothing. He ran into somebody he knew before he left. A friend of Amelia's, maybe, or his mom. Somebody who worked at a bookstore off-island, someone with access to a rare, out-of-print collector's item. He said he'd call to pick it up.

Nothing.

Or maybe it was something. Something more. Something she can't even imagine, something that rips the air from her lungs when she even begins to see it.

No. It was nothing. Zan pours more iced tea. A never-ending drum solo rattles her bones and she looks for her mother. As soon as Miranda comes back, Zan will sneak outside for a break, where she can take a full breath and maybe even hear herself think.

"What are you doing out here?"

Zan jumps to her feet, wiping the dirt from the back of her white mini-shorts. A dark silhouette shuffles toward her, across the spotlit green of the tennis courts. She doesn't recognize Nick until he's only a few feet from where she stands, frozen at the end of the net.

"I thought you were on refreshment duty," Nick says with a toothy smile, leaning into the sturdy post with one hand. His short blond hair looks wet and sticks to his forehead in choppy triangles.

"Hey," Zan says, looking down at the tops of her worn suede sandals. "I didn't see you inside."

Nick shrugs. "I got antsy, went to the beach." He tosses his head back in the direction of the path to the ocean. Zan remembers their Community Center Camp days, when Nick and Leo would talk her into skipping out on whatever bizarre homemade craft project Daniel had prepared. They would start running on the other side of the courts, snaking through the tall grass, across the dirt road, and all the way to the beach. They wouldn't stop until they were underwater.

"How are you doing?" Nick asks. He's using *the voice*, the "I really sincerely mean it" voice. But from Nick, it's okay. Usually she wants to shrivel up and vanish when people look at her that way, like she'd ever in a million years say anything other than "Fine" or "Hanging in there," her two automatic replies.

But Nick deserves to ask, mostly because he already knows. He knows she's just as lost as she was ten months before, when they sat together on Leo's mom's couch. Besides, with Nick, it isn't a *voice*. Nick really sincerely means everything that he says, which is one of the reasons Zan has always had a hard time understanding how he and Leo could be so close.

"I'm okay." Zan shrugs. "Basically just trying to ignore all of the obnoxious comments Leo would be making if he were here."

Nick smiles, pulls in some air between his teeth. "Yeah, he wasn't really into the jam-band thing, huh?"

"No." Zan laughs. "He wasn't."

There was a period of about a month after the funeral when Zan and Nick hung out all the time. It was the height of hurricane season, and without ever saying anything about why, they started meeting up at the beach, watching the diehards get tossed around the angry surf; not talking, not crying, not pretending to be anything but the empty human shells they'd suddenly become.

And then, as abruptly as the quiet comfort of their routine began, it ended. School started. Zan spent all of her free time reading Leo's books, and Nick went back to work, fishing with his dad. They'd barely run into each other since.

"I've been thinking about you," Nick says now, his big blue eyes looking into hers. Leo used to say that as far as Nick was concerned, you could never have too much eye contact. At first, Zan thought it was creepy. Even now that she knows it's just the way he is, ever-present and alert, it makes her borderline uncomfortable, like it's a test that she's destined to fail.

"Yeah," Zan says, scuffing her sandal against the asphalt. "It's weird, all this . . ."

She trails off, not exactly sure what she's saying. All this what? The fact that even though people are freaking out, stockpiling like they're headed into a war, nobody has any idea what's going on? Or the fact that whatever happens, Leo is still dead, and always will be? The fact that maybe the rest of them will soon be, too?

"Totally," Nick agrees. "My dad is still committed to the full-time denial route. We're out on the boat every morning at four-fifteen, like nothing's changed."

"Maybe he has the right idea," Zan says. "I mean, if the rocket thing works . . ."

"That's exactly what he says." Nick smiles and picks at a flaky piece of skin peeling from the bridge of his nose. His cheeks are freckled and pink. "He's actually looking forward to the day when everyone else realizes how much time they've wasted sitting around doing nothing."

Nick tries hard to sound teasing, like he sees his dad as a simpler version of himself, but Zan can hear the respect in his voice. Nick is looking forward to that day, too.

Zan leans against the net. It's been years since she held a tennis racket, but her skin still bristles at all of the things they are doing wrong. Wrong shoes on the court; carelessly stretching out the net. She wishes she didn't keep so many rules alive inside of her. Leo used to say she and Miranda were more alike than she thought. Nothing made her more furious.

Nick tucks his hands into his pockets and looks over his

shoulder at the glowing windows of the Center's main building. A new band has started, a bunch of old guys with fiddles and guitars. "Guess I should head back," Nick says with a smile. "Good to see you, Zan."

He leans in to give her a quick hug, crooking his elbow around her neck and awkwardly pulling her in. Zan flops an arm half-heartedly around his waist—she's never figured out how to hug boys she's not in love with—and pulls back to watch him go. There's something about seeing him walk away that makes her start to panic, like she's already lost her chance. Like the question she wants to ask and also doesn't want to ask will never be answered.

"Nick," she calls out. "Wait."

Nick turns and walks back, his eyes already searching hers with alarm. "What's up?"

Zan reaches slowly into her pocket. For a moment she allows herself to hope the receipt won't be there, that she's left it at home, in the book, or maybe it fell out somewhere on the way. But the flimsy paper sticks to the top of her damp fingers and her heart sinks as she pulls it out. She stares at it for a quiet moment before passing it to Nick.

"I found this in one of Leo's books," she explains, watching Nick's face pucker as he tries to read the numbers and scrawled ink. "It's dated the day that he died."

Nick swallows, the lump of his Adam's apple suddenly clear and pronounced. He flips the page over to the side with the hand-written note. Zan immediately wishes she could rip the paper out of his fingers.

"I don't know," she says, backtracking. "I'm sure it's nothing,

I just thought, you know, since you were the reason he went out that night . . ."

Nick doesn't move. His eyes stay trained on the smudged black print, but the air around him feels different. Charged.

"I'm sorry," she says. "I didn't mean, I didn't mean that it was . . ."

Nick puts a hand on the side of her arm and she stops talking. Right after it happened, she was careful with her words, sensitive not to say anything that might betray the way she sometimes felt. *If only you hadn't cared so much about your stupid boat. If only you hadn't asked for his help. If only you'd waited the night.*

"Nick," she starts again. "I'm so sorry."

Nick shakes his head, his hand still on her shoulder. "No," he says quietly. "I'm sorry. I should have told you before . . ." He passes her the paper. His voice sounds cool, far away and different.

"What do you mean?" Zan asks. She crumples the receipt and watches as Nick's hands return to his pockets. He's staring at the clean white lines of the court. Zan's stomach twists and coils. "Told me what?"

"I lied," he says, so quietly it's almost lost in the amplified chords of the music behind them. "I promised him I'd never say anything, before he left, and when he didn't come back, I didn't know what to do."

The outlines of Nick's hands turn to tight fists in the wet pockets of his cargo shorts. She can see his skin changing color in the dark, from pale pink to red, like a brutal, sudden sunburn.

"What?" Zan says. She takes a step back. "What are you talking about? What did he tell you? Look at me!"

Nick finally lifts his eyes, and this time, Zan knows she will win. She will keep his eyes on hers as long as she possibly can, until they've told her everything. "Nothing," he says, pleading. "I swear, he told me nothing. But he made me promise I'd go along with his story. He made it up. I didn't need anything for the boat that day. He needed an excuse, said he needed to take care of something. That's all I know, I promise."

Zan feels her heart pounding in every square inch of her body. She takes another shaky step back and is quickly on the ground, the cool grass tickling the outsides of her knees.

"Zan." Nick crouches beside her. "I'm sure it's nothing. I'm sure he was just on one of his adventures. He was probably trying to surprise you. That's why I never said anything. He made me promise, and it's not like I had any idea what he was up to. You know the way he was."

Zan feels Nick's arm around her back. She tries to focus on the in and out of her breathing. The wet of the grass. The white of the painted lines on the court.

"I have to find her," she says quietly.

"Find who?"

"Vanessa."

Nick laughs, but Zan can hear he doesn't mean it. "The girl on the receipt?" he asks. "Zan . . ."

"What?" she hisses. "I'm the one still here. If there was something going on, you don't think I deserve to know about it?"

Nick peels his arm away from her shoulder and rests it on his lap. "No. I mean, I don't know," he stutters. "I don't know what I think. I just don't . . . I don't see how it will help."

"Help what?" Zan cries. She's practically yelling now; she can feel the force of her words as they hurtle through her and out into the night. "He's already dead, Nick. Don't you think I should at least know the truth about what happened?"

Nick picks at the grass between them. "I know he's dead," he whispers. "I meant that I don't know how it will help you."

Inside, a song ends and the crowd erupts into boisterous applause. She feels Nick turn to look at the side of her face, feels him watching the single tear that's sinking toward her chin.

"Zan, you have to let him go."

A quick, shifting breeze flips a lock of her dark curls across her nose. She tucks it back, wiping the wet marks on her cheek and pushing up to her feet. She brushes her hands on her shorts, feeling the grass marks indented into the skin of her palms.

"No," she says firmly. "I don't. Not yet."

# SIENNA

"DON'T PLAY WITH YOUR FOOD," RYAN COMMANDS, with all of the authority of a sixty-five-year-old governess. Sienna pushes a snakelike pile of cold sesame noodles around on her plate. The two of them are settled at the empty end of a long table, tucked in the back of the Martha's Vineyard Community Center. Many of the hundred or so people crowding the old converted barn are already up and dancing, or at least that's what Sienna guesses they think they're doing. Dad and Denise included.

"Fine." Sienna shrugs. "I'll play with yours." She reaches across to Ryan's plate, piercing a piece of pasta salad with her recycled bamboo fork.

"Cut it out!" Ryan whines, boxing her out with his elbow. She rolls her eyes and turns back to the stage. A group of older men with long gray beards are playing old-timey bluegrass music on instruments that appear to predate the Civil War.

If it hadn't been for Ryan nosily spotting the flyer on the floor of her room, they would never have come to the Community Center concert. But he was drawn to the cartoon lettering, and soon the four of them were piling in the car, stopping at the only bakery still open to purchase a last-minute pie, and swinging into the overflowing parking lot.

On stage, the music stops abruptly and the old-timers are taking curt little bows. The next group files quietly in behind them, and it isn't until the bearded banjos are cleared from the stage that Sienna spots Owen. His long dark hair is tucked behind his ears and he's wedged impressively behind a portable keyboard, with two separate levels of keys and a series of pedals at his feet.

There's a drummer, a girl with short blond dreadlocks, and a skinny Asian kid playing guitar. The three of them immediately dig into their instruments, and a heavy wall of sound fills the room. From behind a curtain pulled to the side, a girl walks slowly and deliberately to the microphone.

Sienna doesn't recognize her right away. Her small, curvy body is tucked into a floral-print dress with a narrow leather belt cinching her tiny waist, and on her feet, brown suede ankle boots with tassels on the sides. Her shoulder-length fire-red hair is teased so that it looks like it's been through a tornado.

But there's something about the way she walks—slow, almost dreamlike steps—that feels familiar. In a flash, they're on the beach. Sienna is running, being chased by a boy with seaweed in his hair. Behind them, a little girl drags her feet lazily through the waves, a rainbow on the belly of her faded one-piece suit.

Sienna looks up at the stage. Owen plays with his eyes closed and his body hunched and tight, his long fingers frantically stretching across the keys. He's good, but he was right; Carly steals the show. Even before she's opened her mouth to sing, Sienna can't stop staring. Neither, it seems, can anyone else in the crowd; at the sight of her, they immediately start cheering and hollering like crazed college football fans.

And then there's her voice. Owen was right about that, too; it is like sandpaper. Gravelly and gruff, but tinged with little girly riffs and a strong, belting vibrato. Instead of the indie hipster music Sienna expected, the band plays a full set of standards, up-beat love songs and bluesy ballads.

"Wow." Sienna turns, after what feels like ten seconds but must have been at least four songs, to see that Ryan is gone. Dad is squeezed into the flimsy folding chair beside her, his blue eyes glassy and focused on Carly. Sienna knows what he's thinking before he says it. "Your mother would have loved this."

Sienna's stomach twists into a knot. They used to be able to talk about her, not all the time, but after a while they'd each found their own way to say her name out loud. But now it feels different. It feels wrong and cheap and forced, as if Dad's making a special point to remind her that just because he's seeing somebody new, she's not forgotten.

"Where's Ryan?" Sienna asks flatly, pushing back from the table and scanning the length of the room.

"He went with Denny to get more food." Dad gestures to the buffet behind them. "Said something about you contaminating his plate?"

Sienna rolls her eyes and fakes a smile. On stage, Owen is in the middle of a solo. His hands are flying over the keys, alternating quick, short runs with full, complex chords. Carly sways beside him, and every so often he looks up from the keys to catch her eye. It's as if he needs to know she's watching, like he's playing just for her. Sienna feels something hard in her chest, followed by a sinking numbness.

She doesn't realize that the music has stopped until the applause is almost over. She joins in late, clapping as Carly and Owen hug on stage. Owen hops to the floor and Sienna watches as he's swallowed by a crowd of his friends.

She gets up to refill her plate. The Center is packed with bodies and all of them seem to be funneling her into the buffet line. There are rows and rows of dishes and plates, half-ravaged pans of lasagna, big chopped salads, and cooling ears of corn on the cob. Sienna lifts a plate from the top of a short pile and is hovering over the selection of salads when she hears a familiar voice behind her.

"You showed up," Owen says, nudging her with his elbow and plunging a spoon into a sheet pan of lukewarm mac and cheese. He steps back and Sienna sees that Carly is hovering behind him. "See?" Owen gloats to Carly. "I told you she was real."

"Oh my God," Carly says quietly. Her speaking voice is a full octave higher than when she sings, and Sienna has a hard time believing that this is the same girl she just saw swaying seductively up on stage. "You look exactly the same. The hair, the freckles, the perfect teeth."

Sienna lets her tongue run along the inside row of her bottom teeth. She's never thought of them as perfect. She's never thought of them as anything, except teeth.

"So." Owen reaches around her to grab silverware. "What'd you think?"

"Ugh." Carly groans. "Don't interrogate her. If she wants us to know, she'll tell us."

Sienna smiles. "You guys were awesome," she says. "Seriously."

"Didn't I tell you this girl can sing?" Owen wraps an arm around Carly's waist and hugs her to his side. Sienna's stomach does another surprising flip-flop and she can feel her heart clanging against her ribs. Across the room, another band is setting up, and Owen surveys the crowd. "Come on." He gestures with a toss of his head. "These guys are great."

Carly finishes piling her plate with hearty scoops from the various trays and follows him away from the buffet. Sienna stands as if glued to the floor, her empty paper plate still flapping in one hand. Owen turns around. "Coming?" he calls back.

Sienna shakes her head. "My brother's over there somewhere," she says, gesturing to the tables. "I should go find him."

Owen smiles and waves, placing a protective hand on the small of Carly's back and leading her through the groups of jostling fans. Sienna tosses her plate in the trash and looks around for the door.

What she really wants is a cigarette.

She found Dad and told him she wanted to leave, that she didn't mind walking. It wasn't far. But he insisted he was ready, too. Denise wanted dessert but then they could all head home. That was twenty minutes ago.

Sienna finds an old rope swing with a paddle seat, hung low from the branches of a towering oak. She gives the rope a good tug and sits down, pushing off with her heels.

She didn't smoke until she got to the House, and even then it was only once in a while. The House was a mix of teenagers and college-age kids, and the over-eighteens were allowed to smoke in the courtyard with permission. Sienna would occasionally bum from one of them and sneak out late at night, when whatever staff was on duty had less of a chance of telling the difference.

She hated it at first, hated the taste and the chemical smell it left on her hands, but she liked the excuse it gave her to get outside. It was the one time of the day when she felt free.

From the dark shadows of the trees, Sienna sees Dad and Denise before they see her. Denise is carrying a plate full of leftovers, Dad's walking close beside her. From here, they look like strangers, a happy couple she doesn't know.

Sienna drags the tops of her feet and hops off the swing to the gravel. Dad turns at the sound. "There you are," he calls. "Ryan's washing his hands. Meet us at the car?"

Sienna nods and sticks her hands in the pockets of her shorts, watching as Dad and Denise shuffle slowly toward the back parking lot. She sits on the bottom step of the Community Center entrance, next to a sandwich-board sign that reads "All Are Welcome!"

Sienna takes her phone out of her pocket and checks the time. She's starting to wonder why she doesn't just wear a watch; she never uses the phone for anything else.

"You'd get better service out by the water."

She turns over her shoulder to see Owen. He sits on the other side of the steps and passes her a paper plate. "Doughnut?"

Sienna tucks her phone back into her shorts. "No thanks," she says, hugging her knees between the insides of her bony elbows.

"Come on," Owen pleads. "They're not popovers, but they're still pretty good."

Sienna smiles and relents, carefully picking up the sticky treat. It's honey-glazed with rainbow sprinkles. She wonders if there has ever been a more disastrous food to eat in public.

"So, I had this idea." Owen leans back against the concrete and stretches his long arms. He turns his head away, like he's looking for someone. Sienna is grateful for the opportunity to take an unobserved bite.

"It might sound totally insane, or, like, random, or whatever . . . and, I mean, I haven't really thought it through but I figured that's probably okay. Do I really need to think everything through all the way? I mean, does that even make sense?"

Sienna stops chewing, a few sprinkles stuck to the outside of her lips. "What are you talking about?" she mumbles through a mouthful.

Owen turns to face her and she can tell that he's trying not to laugh. "Well, first of all, you have frosting all over your face," he says drily. Sienna swallows and shields the bottom half of her face with her hands.

"Second of all," he says, cracking his knuckles one at a time, "I was thinking maybe we should go out sometime."

Sienna licks the tips of her fingers and runs them along the corners of her mouth. "Go out?" she repeats.

"Yes," Owen says softly. "Like. A date. Is that crazy?"

Sienna stops with one finger frozen near her lips. "A date?" she repeats. "Um, yes. That's crazy."

Owen looks away and his nose twitches, the few dark freckles stretching out across his skin. "Yeah," he says. "You're probably, like, really busy with family stuff, right? It's not, like, the best time to just . . . hang out, I guess."

Sienna stares at him. *Family stuff?* "I mean, it's crazy because of Carly," she says. She drops the doughnut on the plate and balances it on the step.

"Carly?" Owen asks. "What about Carly?"

"Aren't you guys, like . . ." Sienna is whispering. She doesn't know why.

Owen stares over her shoulder, the corner of his mouth pulling in. "Sienna," he says softly. "There's something I guess you don't know about Carly."

"Oh, yeah?" Sienna asks. "What's that?"

"Let's just say I've never really been her type."

Sienna feels a hard laugh escaping and rolls her eyes. She knows these excuses. There were days when she used to feel like she *invented* these excuses. "Why?" she scoffs. "You guys are just better as friends? Or, let me guess: she never dates guys in the band."

Owen hurries to his feet and stands in front of Sienna, so that she couldn't move if she tried. "Yeah." He nods. "All that. And she's gay."

"Who's gay?"

Sienna turns and sees Ryan standing in the door. The light of the entryway behind him sticks to the top of his parted hair and casts the rest of his face in dark shadow. His arms are crossed and he's glaring at them like they've done something wrong.

"Nobody," Sienna says. "We were just . . . never mind." She pushes herself up and holds out her hand. "Let's go, Ry."

Sienna reaches for Ryan's shoulder, catching Owen's eye over the top of her brother's head. She smiles sheepishly, wishing she had more to say.

"Wait!" Ryan squeals, wriggling from Sienna's grasp. "What about the president?"

"The president's not gay," Sienna assures him, steering him down the steps.

"I know that," he insists. "But he's about to make a speech."

Ryan stops in his tracks and points through the window. Owen runs up the steps and peers inside. "It does look like people are waiting for something to happen."

Sienna and Ryan follow him inside and they wait by the door. There's a buzz in the crowd, a confused murmur as people stand in clusters facing the stage. They hear a high-pitched squealing noise, feedback from the speakers, and then a woman's voice.

"Ladies and gentlemen, if I could have your attention for just a minute." The woman is tall and thin. She clutches a clipboard to her chest and huddles at one corner of the stage. "My name is Miranda Lowe, I'm on the board of directors here at the Community Center, and . . ." She takes a deep breath and fiddles around with the microphone, sending more piercing feedback into the crowd. "I'm sorry about that, I'm just, I wanted to use this time to thank you for coming, but I've been told that the, uh, the president, is holding an emergency press conference. I figured it's something you'd all want to hear, so . . . Daniel, if you would . . ."

Miranda nods offstage to a gray-haired man in a leather jacket, busy rigging up another microphone and holding it out to an old-fashioned boom box.

"What's going on?" Sienna asks. Owen shakes his head and Sienna feels Ryan's small hand slipping inside her own. A crackle fills the air, followed by loud, offensive static. The man plays with a knob until a clear, familiar voice comes through.

"Good evening." The president's voice is fierce and sudden, and a thick, reverent silence settles into every corner of the room. "As of six o'clock this evening, we have new information about the asteroid Persephone and her course. As many of you may be aware, under my authorization the Department of Defense has approved a new mission, in conjunction with NASA officials and the International Space Alliance: an attempt to deflect the asteroid away from a potential collision with our planet."

There is a pause, a somewhere shuffling of papers. People turn their heads at similar angles, glancing around as if the president could very well be among them. On the radio, he clears his throat. "According to plans I have reviewed with my advisers and other world leaders, the B-eighty-three one-point-two-megaton nuclear-tipped rocket will be launched from a classified location shortly, and will indeed make contact with Persephone, exactly three days from today."

There is a ripple through the crowd, people turning to their neighbors with questions in their eyes. Sienna feels a tightness closing in around her heart. Owen's shoulder is pressed against hers, and she feels herself leaning into him just slightly. Up near the stage, there's a celebratory shout, and a group of guys are slapping each other on the backs. They're starting to get rowdy when somebody else across the room yells, "Quiet!"

The static is back and the president's voice returns. This time, he sounds less certain and rehearsed, like he's suddenly gone off script. "As you . . . as you know, there's no way we can effectively predict what will happen from here. We can't guarantee that even the most successful impact will destroy the asteroid completely. And there are, of course, risks involved. But we are . . . very . . . hopeful that this course of action is the single best chance we've been given to steer Persephone in a different direction."

The high-pitched buzzing is back and all around the room people are cheering. On the stage the woman taps repeatedly into the microphone, and the man with the gray hair is waving his hands over his head. The president is still talking, but nobody cares. Sienna strains to listen.

"I must caution you all that there may be changes in the coming days. Persephone's course has been tracked and studied for many, many years, and we now know, with what I'm afraid is great certainty, that if left unchecked, she will strike our planet in less than one week."

Sienna feels Ryan's fingers untangle from her wrist and she looks to see that Dad is there, too, lifting Ryan to his hip and whispering steadily into his hair. Sienna stands frozen and wonders what to do now with her hands. They're shaking at her sides as she looks around the room. She remembers Owen and feels him shift beside her. She's worried he might leave, worried she might fall if he moves, but he takes her hand and folds it inside his long fingers. She feels a heartbeat in her palm and doesn't know if it's his or her own.

"We have been given the gift of one more chance," the president continues, his voice soft and still shaky. Sienna feels Owen squeeze her hand and she feels warm and, strangely, happy. Happy, for once, to be a part of something. To feel the things that other people are feeling. Happy to not be alone.

"I ask only that, whatever happens, you remain calm. How each of us handles the next few days, who we become and what we do, will be critically important as we are forced, as a nation, to face an uncertain tomorrow. God bless you all, and may God bless America."

# DAY THREE

# ZAN

ZAN TAKES THE TURN AT THE BOTTOM OF THE hill, her feet settling into a steady rhythm as she starts up the narrow footpath. She untangles the delicate wires of her headphones from around her elbow, careful not to dislodge the tiny white earbuds as she keeps her comfortable pace.

The streets are empty and the air is morning-cool. There are few cars on the road, not another person on the path. Normally, this section of the road is congested with a mix of recreational bikers and people on their way to the pharmacy or grocery store. But as soon as she stepped outside, she could tell that something was different. She knows it's because of the announcement. People aren't sure whether to be quietly relieved, or riotously excited, or if they should simply just hunker down and wait. She wasn't sure either, when she woke up. It's why she decided to run.

That, and the fact that there was no way she could handle being around her parents, each lost in uniquely dysfunctional methods of denying that anything at all was amiss. Daniel locked himself in his studio as soon as they'd gotten home last night, working furiously on his latest project. "The Forgiving Wheel," he's calling it. For her part, Miranda will be spending the next few days much the way she spends every day. At least, every day since Joni left. Making lists. Making plans. In times of uncertainty, she wants to feel useful and needed.

Usually, Zan listens to music while she runs. Something upbeat, something she can get lost in, something to make her forget how far she's gone or how long it will take her to get back home. She needs the music, because running isn't enough. She doesn't do it for the escape, the way some people say they do—in fact, she's found it almost impossible to be so alone with her thoughts since Leo died. But the movement is what her body craves, like stretching after a long car ride, or being underwater and coming up for air. If she goes more than a few days without lacing up her sneakers and at least jogging down to the beach, her legs tingle and her skin feels too tight.

She'd had another restless night of half-dreaming, strange involuntary visions that sometimes haunt the foggy space between awake and asleep. Every time she closed her eyes she'd see Leo in the distance. As she walked toward him—she was always walking toward him, he was always standing still—she'd realize that something was off. He was wearing an unfamiliar piece of clothing, like a cup-brimmed baseball hat he'd never be caught dead in, or a stiff, three-piece suit. One time, when she got close enough to see his face, he looked back at her with different-colored eyes, one his own, bright blue, and the other pale and milky, the soggy white of a half-cooked egg.

She takes a few thirsty breaths of summer air. With every heavy step, she feels sturdier, less off-balance. Past the post office, she cuts into one of the Land Bank trails, the one that winds through a dense patch of forest and opens at the entrance to the Arboretum.

The Arboretum was one of Leo's favorite spots. He knew everything about every tree. He'd memorized all of the engraved bronze plaques, the long Latin names for scraggly shrubs that Zan would never have looked at twice. Leo's memory was nearly photographic, a fact that Zan admired but also secretly found a little annoying, especially since he was constantly on academic probation at school. It was as if he stuffed himself so full of fictional characters and random statistics and the names of small villages in countries most people couldn't point to on a map that he didn't have room for things like the periodic table or vocab lists. She was mostly jealous, she knew, but sometimes she wished he'd just get it together long enough to pass the tenth grade.

She was jealous because he didn't need her for anything. He was always the one taking her places she'd never been, dropping names of people she pretended to know. She never questioned that he loved her—he told her constantly, in quirky and meaningful ways. But sometimes she found herself wondering why.

And ever since she'd found the receipt, that half-forgotten wistful wonder had turned to nagging curiosity, and maybe even doubt.

She ducks through the tangled vines of wisteria that cling to the wooden Arboretum welcome arch, pounding into the mossy earth with a new, raw energy. She refuses to let herself think this way. For ten months, Leo has been gone, and for ten months the certainty of their love for each other has been all that's kept her going. Now, now that nothing is certain, anywhere, for anyone, now she is going to start asking questions?

Of course he loved her. Wasn't he always underlining passages in books that made him think of the two of them together? Didn't he surprise her dozens of times after school, with a single wildflower under her windshield wiper, or steal her away on a Sunday afternoon for a just-because picnic at their spot on the cliffs? He loved her. There was a lot she didn't know, a lot she needed him to explain, but this much she knew for certain.

So why was she being so insane? Why was she torturing herself over something that clearly, like everything else she'd ever wondered about Leo, had an explanation, an explanation that would probably just make her love him even more?

Ahead, Zan spots their tree, hidden by the more popular magnolias and purple-blossomed rhododendrons. *Enkianthus,* "the Showy Lantern." She can hear the jump in Leo's voice as he talks about the different phases: the bell-shaped flowers that fall near the end of spring, replaced first by miniature brown berries and later by ragged leaves, like golden paper flames.

She settles into a dip in the trunk, just enough room for two people if they sit close together. She waits a moment for her breath to even out, her pulse to fade from her ears. She unplugs the headphones and pulls the Grumpy's receipt from the pocket of her hooded sweatshirt.

She exhales and feels a new calm in her blood, her bones. Leo is still Leo. They will always be the way they were, tucked against this tree, everywhere attached and breathing the same, newborn air.

She navigates the boxy screen of her phone, dialing the number with careful taps. The phone crackles and rings. She'd forgotten that cell service on this part of the island can be spotty, but each ring sounds more confident than the last. Zan drums her fingers against the curve of her kneecap.

After the sixth ring, there's a mechanical click, a stuffy pause. A man's voice answers, rehearsed, as if reading from a script:

*"Thank you for calling Lulu's Lounge. We are located on the corner of Tremont and Dartmouth in Boston's South End. For reservations, please press one. For hours of operation, please press—"*

Zan cancels the call and stares at the phone in her hand. Lulu's? The South End? There's a flutter in her throat. She isn't sure if it's a laugh or a cry. It's a bar. In Boston. What could a bar in Boston have anything to do with Leo on the day that he died?

Whatever it is, whatever it means, it's not Vanessa. There is no Vanessa, today. Today, there's only Zan. And Leo. Still together, still sitting in a tree.


"Zan!"

A dusty blue truck slows beside her. The front wheel tucks into the bike path, leaving her no choice but to jog in place. She tears the headphones from her ears and props a hand on her hip as she catches her breath.

"Hey, Nick," she pants. Ordinarily, she might feel embarrassed to stop and chat, with the collar of her sweatshirt damp and sticking to the bottom of her throat, her hair caught in frizzy loops like spiral antennae attached to her head. But for some reason, it's different with Nick. Maybe it's because she knows he looks at everyone the same way, his eyes so direct and unwavering. It's easy to wonder how much of anyone he actually sees.

"Hey." He shoves the gearshift into park and leans across the passenger seat. The door swings open. "I was just on my way to your house."

"You were?" Zan squints. The sun is higher now, and breaking through the early fog. She checks the time on her phone. Just after nine. "Why?"

Nick pats the cracked vinyl of the bench seat beside him. "Hop in," he offers.

Zan wipes a layer of sweat from her forehead. "Oh," she manages, gazing at the bike path stretching out beyond the nose of the beat-up truck. "Um. That's okay. I'm not far and I took a long break. I should keep going."

Nick grips the steering wheel with both hands and stares ahead through the glass. She's never noticed how steep the slope of his nose is from the side, how perfectly arched like a ski jump.

"I've been thinking about what you said," he says. He keeps his eyes trained ahead and the fact that he isn't looking at her, that he *won't* look at her, makes her stomach twist. Everything in her wants to run, and keep running. She wishes she'd never said anything about the receipt. Not to Nick. Not to anyone. "I have an idea. At least hear me out?"

Zan clenches her teeth and forces a deep breath. "All right," she agrees reluctantly, hoisting herself into the cab. She lugs the door shut and Nick turns the heavy wheel, pulling the truck back onto the empty road.

"What's going on?" she asks, trying to steady the tremble in her throat. She looks down at her feet. The truck is surprisingly tidy. Leo's truck was constantly littered with trash. In order to sit down she'd have to wipe aside sticky candy wrappers, half-empty bottles of soda, surf keys, mysterious tool parts, and handfuls of loose change, all caked in crusty layers of sand.

In Nick's truck, a full bottle of Gatorade sits patiently in the center console, and something that looks like a catalogue for specialty boat parts flaps around on top of the dash. Otherwise, it's spotless.

Nick rests one freckled arm on the open window, his fingers drumming against the outside of the door. "Nothing, really. I was just . . . I was thinking about what you said. About . . . Leo. And what happened that night."

Zan feels her hands starting to shake and squeezes them under the sides of her spandex shorts. "You were?" she asks, turning to stare out the window. They pass Dana Duffy's flower shop, boarded up with a "Closed" sign hung out front. Dana had been one of the first to leave the island, wanting to get as far away from the water as possible. Zan had overheard her in line at the library. Back then, everyone thought she was being hysterical. Now Zan wonders if maybe Dana had the right idea.

"Yeah." Nick nods, reaching for the bottle of Gatorade and twisting the cap with one hand. "And I just wanted to say, you know. I can help. I mean, I know you're not going to leave this alone. And I guess I feel kind of, I don't know, responsible . . ."

"You're not," Zan interrupts. "I shouldn't have said anything. It has nothing to do with you, Nick." Her words are sharper than she means for them to be. She tries to smile, but knows she's not doing a very good job.

"Well, but it does, kind of," Nick insists. He takes a sip, glancing at her sideways. Zan shifts uncomfortably. "If I hadn't lied for him, or if I had at least told you sooner that I did, you wouldn't be . . ."

"I can handle it." Zan tugs the sleeves of her sweatshirt down over her thumbs. Her mouth is dry and sticky. "Really, I can. But thanks."

Nick slows at the corner, behind a catering van. A big piece of cardboard has been taped to the back window, with the words "Jesus Loves You" scrawled across it in red block letters. There's something about the chaotic slant of the handwriting, or maybe the dramatic hue, that leaves Zan not entirely convinced.

"Well." Nick clears his throat. "I think we should call that number, at least. I'm sure it's nothing, but won't it feel better to—"

"I called it," Zan blurts. She feels her heart pounding in her ears and sits forward in the front seat, as if they might reach her house faster that way.

"You did?"

Zan swallows. "It's nothing." She shrugs. "Just some bar in Boston. And you're right. I do feel better."

She puts on her best, most reassuring smile, and hopes it doesn't look half as forced or foreign as it feels. Nick tries to hold her gaze but this time she looks away.

"Really?" Nick asks. "A bar?"

"Lulu's," Zan says, with another, bigger shrug. "In the South End."

"We should go!"

Zan sinks deeper into the seat, the muscles in her legs suddenly limp and exhausted. She can't tell if it's from the run or

90

from trying so hard to look normal. "Yeah, right." She smirks. "I'm sure that's exactly what you want to be doing with your last week on earth."

"Don't say that," Nick says. He digs into the brakes as they reach her road, taking the corner slow and wide. There's something new and severe in the blue of his stare.

Zan looks at him. His mouth is set and serious. "You're not kidding."

"No," Nick says. "Somebody at the bar has to know this Vanessa person. Maybe she worked there."

Zan stares at the skin around her nails, dry and cracked. No matter how many times she tells herself it's nothing, hearing the name *Vanessa* still nags at her heart.

"We have to find out," Nick continues. They bump up the dirt road to her driveway and the truck lurches as he rolls to a stop. There's power in his voice. He sounds almost mad. "I mean, Leo lied to me, too. In a way. He could have easily told me what he was doing that night. But he didn't. He made me promise to cover for him, and I did it, no questions. That's the way it always was with us. He was my best friend. I told him everything. But I always got the feeling he didn't want it to go the other way. Like he was keeping some part of himself separate from everything else."

Zan stares at her front porch, her eyes soft and out of focus. She'd never thought about Nick. She knew he felt bad for not telling her the truth about what happened that night. But she'd never thought about what all this might mean for him. That he might be trying to find something, too.

"How would we get there?" she asks. The boats would stop running, if they hadn't already. The better question was how would they get back.

Nick fans out his hands across the steering wheel, stretching the tight skin over his palms until it looks like it hurts. "My dad finally called it quits," he says. "Says there's no use going out fishing when nobody is buying anything he hauls in. I think my mom made him feel guilty for spending so much time away from home."

Zan pulls at her hair, twirling a few dark ringlets down around her chin. She can hear the loss in his voice, the empty hopelessness. She thinks of her mom, the way staying busy keeps her from feeling left behind. Maybe Nick needs to be needed, too.

"We could take our boat," Nick explains. "And we still have the car parked off-island. It barely runs but it should get us to the city and back."

Zan stares at the dashboard, the print on the trade magazine blurring as her mind wanders. For some reason, she thinks of the last time she saw Leo. They were on the path to the beach. He had just gotten out of the water and was wrapped in a threadbare towel printed with pictures of red and gold parrots. He shook water out of his ear and nuzzled his salty hair against her cheeks. He said he'd pick her up for the movie at six-thirty. He'd pack the snacks; the popcorn they sold at the theater was always stale and cold.

When he walked away he tripped over an exposed root and jogged it off a few steps, like he did it on purpose. He turned back and gave her a goofy wave. There was a ribbon of muddy sand wrapped around the back of his ankle.

She always thought he was waving goodbye. But maybe she was wrong. Maybe he was asking her to follow him.

She remembers what Amelia said on the cliffs. *"Do you ever feel like he's telling you things?"*

Maybe the receipt was a message. Maybe he'd wanted her to find it all along.

"I was thinking about what you said." Nick leans over the console, so close she can smell the salt on his skin, sweet citrus on his breath. "And you're right. We're the ones left. And we deserve to know the truth."

There's a ball of tightness in Zan's stomach, like a fist. She wishes, not for the first time, that she could go back. Back to before Amelia gave her the book, before she found the receipt, before she started asking questions. Back when Leo's memory was simple and true.

But she can't. She's opened something, a door that leads to another door, a trail that twists her farther away from what, and who, she thought she knew. Or maybe the trail is a loop, and she'll end up believing for certain what she's known all along.

He loved her. He did.

"So," Nick says, one hand frozen on his key, turned in the ignition. "What do you say? Are you in?"

# CADEN

SO FAR, BEING KIDNAPPED HAS ITS PERKS.

After a convincing sit-down with George, his father's thick-necked bodyguard, Caden resigned himself to an afternoon of soaking in the outdoor hot tub, drinking smoothies made-to-order, and watching pay-per-view movies on the forty-inch flatscreen tucked into an antique armoire in his room. If he was going to spend his last days on earth as a prisoner, he might as well try to enjoy it.

The TV was set up with seven hundred channels and the Internet. Not that there had been anything on worth watching since the announcement. Late last night, George had escorted him to the living room, where they'd all gathered to watch the president on TV. While George shook his massive head, swearing lightly under his breath, and Luisa, the Brazilian housekeeper, repeated a prayer in Portuguese, Caden tried not to notice Sophie, or the way that Arthur was stroking her hair, tender and protective.

The announcement itself Caden hadn't found all that impressive. They were going to send yet another nuclear device into space, hoping that *this* time, it might make a difference. What else could they do? The president had to give them something. He couldn't just twiddle his thumbs and say: *Well, we've done what we can. Let's just wait and see how this thing shakes out . . .*

Which is what Caden would have said, if he had been president. Persephone was either going to hit them, or she wasn't. This was real life, after all, not some big-budget Hollywood movie. There was no last-minute Bruce Willis space-cowboy, riding a rocket to save them. If there were any way to weaken the asteroid, or to somehow alter its course, it would already have happened, months or even years ago. It couldn't possibly work now. He'd never thought it would.

As he lies awake the next morning, tucked between the high-thread-count sheets and soft down comforter on the strange, guest-room bed, he can't help but think about Ramona and Carly. Where had they been when the announcement was made? What are they doing now? He's been gone two nights. Has Ramona even noticed? Carly is definitely freaking out. They'd probably both assumed that he left on purpose. It's not like he never thought about it. Why not spend whatever time was left bumming around on the beach? The nights were warm enough, and there would always be people around. It would sure beat tiptoeing around Ramona and one of her epic hangovers.

But Carly would go out looking. And when he wasn't at the docks, or at any of the bars downtown, trying to sneak in with the rest of the underage hopefuls, she'd know that something was up.

Caden turns off the TV. CNN and the other news, science, and weather stations just rehash the same endless, exhausting speculation. The religious stations are just as obsessed. The rest of the channels play a constant loop of upbeat movies, syndicated sitcoms, classic sports broadcasts, nonthreatening cooking shows, and zany children's cartoons. Caden wonders if there is a backlog of programs like these, kept together for this exact purpose. Filed under: BROADCAST WHEN ALL HOPE IS LOST.

He looks down at the grimy stains on his two-day-old clothes and rummages through the drawers of the armoire. His father had said it was stocked with clean clothes when he'd knocked on the door before bed. Caden pretended to be asleep. His father could lock him up for as long as he wanted. It didn't mean they had to be friends.

In one drawer is a stack of plain white crewneck T-shirts, and an unopened six-pack of boxers. In another, a few pairs of stiff, dark jeans. Caden gets dressed, though he's not really sure why. He leaves his old clothes in a heap on the floor, except for his gray, hooded sweatshirt, which he throws back on at the last minute.

The door, which Arthur had locked, is now open a crack. The hallway is lit up by the glow of morning sun, and George and his neck are nowhere in sight. From the kitchen, Caden hears the distinct sounds of a dishwasher being emptied, the clatter of plates and glasses returning to their cupboard homes.

He pads softly down the steps, half expecting to be scooped up and carried back to his room at any moment. But he spies George leaning against the stone wall outside, smoking a cigarette and inspecting the soles of his enormous black loafers.

In the kitchen, he runs into Luisa. Literally. "Caden!" She beams at him, fumbling with the tray she has balanced on both hands. "You were a baby the last time I see you. So much of a man now, yes?"

Caden stares at her, and then beyond her, to where the girl—woman?—from the pool is standing over the stove. Today, she wears a boxy button-up shirt, faded yellow and rolled up at the sleeves, and black leggings. Her hair is messy and loosely pulled back. Somehow, she looks even better in grungy clothes, her tanned forehead creased as she squints at the pan, scraping a spatula around its low, square edges.

Luisa inches toward him with the tray. "I was just bringing you breakfast. Sophie make crepes. You like crepes?"

Sophie smiles shyly at Caden. There's an uneven gap between her two front teeth, which Caden hadn't noticed yesterday, probably because he was busy noticing everything else, and a small bump at the top of her nose, as if it had been broken, long ago. Somehow, these slight imperfections make her face even harder to look away from, as if it needs to be studied, close up. Caden feels his face getting hot. He shifts his eyes quickly to the sand-colored tiles on the floor.

"And bacon," Luisa continues. "You used to love the bacon."

Caden looks at her suspiciously. It's true. He did love the bacon. The smell of it still makes him giddy and warm, though he has no idea why. Ever since Carly spent a summer taking care of the cows at Laughton's dairy, she's been a raging vegetarian. And since Carly does the shopping, Caden eats what Carly eats. He hasn't seen bacon in years. "How do you know that?" he asks Luisa. "How—have we met before?"

Luisa lowers the tray to the counter, the crisp fold of her

starched white shirt cut around her waist by the looping black tie of her apron. "You come to visit," she says. "When you are very small, you, your mother, your sister, you come stay here at Hart Haven." She opens the refrigerator and pulls out a pitcher of orange juice. She pours a tall glass and passes it to Caden, bustling her way out of the kitchen. "I check on the laundry. Sit, Caden. Eat."

She moves the tray to the far side of the kitchen island, across from the built-in stove top where Sophie stands, ladling scoopfuls of gooey batter onto the sizzling pan. Caden pulls out one of the high stools, wincing as the wooden legs screech across the tiles.

Sophie passes him two bowls, one full of berries, the other with peaks of frothy whipped cream. He spoons out a little of each and digs in. Despite Luisa's many attempts, he hasn't had a full meal in days.

"You're still here," Sophie says lightly, once Luisa has gone. She rests one hand on her side as she moves the pan with the other, a subtle smile tugging at the corners of her full lips.

Caden swallows a too-big bite and prays he doesn't choke. His temples throb as he remembers being hauled across the kitchen and up to his room, passing Sophie on the stairs. Not exactly the slickest of first impressions.

"Yeah," Caden says, washing down the syrupy bite with a long sip of OJ, in a way that, he hopes, looks casual and collected. "Figured I'd at least stick around for breakfast."

Sophie turns and reaches into the glass-covered cabinets for a plate on a high shelf. Her baggy shirt inches up toward the curve of her hips, a smooth patch of tanned skin exposed along her side. Caden cuts another bite, the side of his fork squawking across the top of his plate.

"And?" Sophie asks, flipping a new batch of crepes out of the pan. "Was it worth it?"

Caden swallows and smiles. "Not bad," he says with a shrug.

Sophie switches off the burner, the blue flame swallowed in a sudden swoosh. She brings her plate to the other side of the island and sits, her elbow angled on the counter just a few inches from his.

After a few long moments of careful chewing and the clipped clatter of utensils, Caden clears his throat. "Can I ask you a question?"

"You just did," Sophie answers. She takes a small swig of juice and wipes her mouth with a napkin. "You mean another one?"

Caden rolls his eyes playfully. "I guess so."

"Go for it," Sophie allows, between bites.

"What are you—"

"What am I doing with a guy like your father?" she interrupts. She tilts her head to one side, her lips pulled tight in a wry little smile.

Caden holds his fork frozen in the air, a laugh trapped in his throat. "Sure," he says. "Let's start there."

"Probably for the same reasons that you're still here." Sophie shrugs, cutting the rest of her crepe into even, manageable bites.

Caden leans back on his stool. He thinks of the locked door, the heavy weight of George's hands still burning beneath his ribs. She can't possibly think that he *wants* to be here, can she? "I haven't run away because there's a fathead bodyguard watching my every move," he says flatly.

Sophie makes her eyes into wide brown saucers. "Really?" she asks, looking dramatically around the kitchen, under the table, behind the sliding glass doors. "Where?"

Caden stabs a final bite with his fork. He feels the tips of his ears burning and hopes his disheveled hair is long enough to hide them.

Sophie leans across the island, her hair falling over one shoulder. "Hey," she says, gently. "I just meant that he's not such a bad guy. I mean, yeah, he thinks he can do whatever he wants and get away with it, but once you look past the—"

"He had me drugged and kidnapped," Caden says sharply. "It's kind of hard to look past all that."

Sophie looks away. "You're right," she says after a pause. "I'm sorry."

Caden shrugs. The air is suddenly charged between them, and he wishes he hadn't done that, hadn't taken it out on her. So her taste in men is questionable, at best. It's not her fault that he's here.

"I guess there are worse places to be locked up," he jokes. "And I lied before, about the crepes. They're better than not-bad. They're good. Really good."

Sophie smiles into her plate. "Thanks," she says. "I used to work at this French place in Boston. It's where I met your dad, actually. He came in for lunch all the time."

"Waitress?" Caden asks. He quietly stacks his fork and knife on his plate and finishes the last of his juice.

Sophie nods. "I was saving up for school," she says. "But then I met Arthur . . ."

Caden pushes back his stool and brings his plate to the sink. He gives it a quick rinse and puts it in the dishwasher. He knows he could have left it for Luisa, but it feels important to do what he can for himself.

"I know it sounds lame," Sophie says. Caden can feel her eyes on the back of his head. "But . . . I don't know. I guess sometimes it's nice to be taken care of. You know?"

Caden stares through the wall of windows. The glare of the sun paints white streaks across the pool and he wishes he could be out there, underwater, not worried about anything but holding his breath. He wishes he had no idea what she was talking about.

"Anyway." Sophie stands and brings her own plate to the sink, just as Caden is starting toward the hall. Her shoulder brushes the side of his arm and he feels a warm shock. "You should probably go get ready. Arthur likes to get an early start."

"An early start for what?" Caden asks.

Sophie turns to look at him, one hand on the gleaming silver faucet. "He didn't tell you?" she asks. "He's taking you on a trip. Some kind of last-minute bonding thing, I guess. Don't ask me where. I never get any details."

Caden glances down the hall at the closed front door. A trip? Who says he wants to go on a trip? Is it even possible to be kidnapped twice?

Sophie leaves her plate in the sink and grabs a towel from a hook near the patio doors. "See you when you get back?"

Caden nods and offers a hand in a sort of half wave, half

salute. As he makes his way back upstairs, he considers his options. Putting up another fight will only result in more humiliating wrestling with George . . . or worse. And he has to get out of here, somehow. He has to talk to Carly. He has to let them know he's all right.

Caden walks to the closet in his room and spots a generic black duffel bag, tucked away on the top shelf. He opens the dresser drawers and stuffs the bag with T-shirts and boxers, another clean pair of stiff jeans. It feels strange to be packing clothes that aren't his, but then, everything feels strange lately.

# ZAN

"SO HOW'D THEY TAKE IT?" NICK ASKS. HE swings into the harbor, his truck rattling around the sharp corner where the paved road turns to dusty dirt. "Your parents."

Zan shrugs. She spent the morning trying to talk herself out of leaving, silently begging her parents to give her a reason to stay. But Daniel had kept himself holed up in his studio and Miranda was still in town, sneaking her vegetables into the ration boxes and lecturing whoever would listen on the enduring relevance of a healthy, varied diet. It was hard to feel needed when there was nobody around.

"I left a note," she says, hugging the bag she'd stuffed full of random skirts and tops and a few clean pairs of underwear in her lap. Packing was a challenge when she had no idea where they were going, or how long they'd be gone. "I doubt they'll even notice."

"I'm sure that's not true," Nick says, his eyes steady and focused on the tapering road ahead. Zan straightens the beginnings of a smile. She remembers the way Leo used to tease Nick for never picking up on his jokes, for earnestly engaging his every sarcastic remark. There was a time when Zan thought that Nick must be a little slow. He clearly didn't have Leo's sharp wit or dry sense of humor. But now, she's not so sure. Who says everything has to be a joke all of the time? Especially now—why say anything unless you really mean it?

And he's right. Of course her parents will notice that she's gone. No matter how deeply they bury themselves in projects and routine, it's clear that they're anxious, clear that they'd like her around. And for a moment, Zan wonders if she should stay. What if this really is their last week together? Does she want to spend it on some crazy mission, searching for clues and an answer she isn't sure she wants to find?

Before she can change her mind, Nick pulls into a spot by the docks. His boat is tied up before them, a twenty-three-foot Sea-Craft named (without the slightest hint of irony) *My Girl*.

"I have to gas her up," Nick says as they climb out of the truck. "Make yourself comfortable."

Zan stands uncertainly at the edge of the dock. For all of the nights she and Leo spent keeping Nick company as he cleaned *My Girl*, or tinkered with some unidentifiable part or project, she's amazed that she's never actually stepped on board.

Unlike Nick's truck, the boat definitely feels lived in. It's not terribly unclean, but it's clear that Nick and his dad spend a lot of time here, and that female visitors are few and far between. Zan steps around a few upturned crates, careful to avoid the murky water puddled in the corners. She finds a dry spot to sit on the bench near the raised, bulky motor. Half a dozen fishing rods are wedged into holders, jutting toward the sky like wiry antennae, and behind the steering wheel is a complicated-looking panel of knobs, buttons, and dials.

Nick attaches a hose from a diesel pump and hops onto the bow, busying himself at the console. Zan watches as he moves purposefully around her, checking hidden compartments and quickly untying gnarled ropes from the solid metal cleats. She's never seen him so at ease. Even his posture is different, less rigid. He is unquestionably at home.

"Ready?" he asks, reaching to loop the hose back around the pump.

Zan nods and the engine sputters to a slow growl as Nick maneuvers through the harbor. The docks and moorings are at full capacity, and the boat glides carefully through the maze of buoys, toward the open water.

Zan lifts her head to the sun, the warm spray of sea air misting the tops of her cheeks. The early afternoon sun is high and bounces off the gleaming white of the hull as the water stretches out in mirrored sheets before them. Every time she goes out on a boat she wonders why she doesn't do it more often. Suddenly, she is overcome with a feeling of relief. If she had stayed home, if she had said no, she would have missed what might be her last chance to be on the ocean this way. She wonders how many other things she's already missed out on, by not saying yes more often.

Nick pushes a lever and the engine groans, a frothy wake bubbling up behind them. He looks over his shoulder and tips his head at the empty stool. "Come on up!" he shouts over the roar of the motor.

"Thanks for doing this," she says, once she's settled in beside him. His hands grip the wheel easily and he hooks his bare feet around the bottom of his chair.

"What?" he shouts into the wind.

"Thanks for the ride!" Zan yells with a smile.

Nick shrugs. "No problem!" He stares into the distance over her shoulder, and she turns to look, too. The island pulls away, its rocky shore dotted with houses, still and pristine as a painting. She can't remember the last time she saw the island—her home for all of her sixteen years—this way. All at once, she understands why Nick would rather be here than anywhere else, floating in ocean and sky.

"What's it saying?" Nick asks. The car, an old brown Saab that sputters and gasps with every shift of its ancient gears, rolls to a stop in the middle of an abandoned city intersection. The stoplight blinks from red to green overhead.

Zan tries refreshing the map on her phone for the billionth time. The cursor spins uselessly at the center of the tiny screen. They've been driving around the eerily quiet Boston streets for the better part of an hour, and she's starting to think Nick's master plan might have some gaps. "Nothing," she says. "I told you, it's not working."

Nick stares hopefully up through the windshield, as if the street signs might tell him something new. "The circuits are probably overloaded," he muses at the sky.

Zan double-checks her service bars, and sure enough, all she sees is a single dot, blinking uselessly in the corner. "It worked this morning," she remembers, "when I called the bar."

"That was on the island," Nick says. "The city's a different story."

Zan looks at the useless phone in her palm, suddenly anxious to feel so disconnected. Maybe it's better that way, she thinks. At least she won't be tempted to call home.

Nick shifts back into first gear and the car bucks forward. "If I can find Tremont, I can get us there. I think."

Zan stares out the window. The South End is a quaint, tree-lined neighborhood with even rows of short, brick town houses. Scattered among the residential blocks are condensed strips of bakeries, restaurants, and boutiques, most now closed if not boarded up and abandoned. Zan feels her grip tightening on the cracked leather of the seat, sticky beneath her sweaty knees. Of course everything is closed. What were they thinking?

"Don't worry," Nick says, glancing at the whitening tops of her knuckles. "It's a bar. It will definitely be open."

Zan tries to smile as Nick steers them through the narrow streets, made narrower by the double-parked rows of cars on either side. With nothing for people to do and nowhere for them to go, the city seems to be inhabited solely by illegally parked vehicles.

"That's it!" Nick slams on the brakes and leans to look out through Zan's window. There's a thick patch of duct tape at the corner, where the side-view mirror has started to fall off, and he has to stretch around it for a clear view to the street. "Right?"

Zan follows his gaze. The bar is in the basement of a redbrick brownstone, with gold block letters spelling "LULU'S" over the door. Nick pulls up onto the curb at the end of the block, the front tires bumping against an overgrown sidewalk planter. He turns off the ignition. "Ready?"

Nick was right. The bar is serving, and it's packed. In fact, it seems to be the only business open on the block, and even this early in the evening, people pour out onto the tiny stone patio. As they get closer, Zan hears the muffled sounds of a live band playing inside.

The room is long and narrow, with exposed brick along one wall and two dark mahogany bars tucked against a mirror on the other. At the far end, a small group of jazz musicians play on a stage the size of a love seat. The first thing Zan thinks as she squeezes behind Nick and into the lively crowd is that it's just the kind of place Leo would have loved. She searches for a sign, some feeling or sense that he'd been there, that he'd stood exactly where she's standing now. But all she feels is hot and claustrophobic.

Zan feels a nudge behind her and stumbles closer to Nick's back. "Hey," a voice calls out over her head. A guy with slick hair and a handlebar mustache pushes a flyer into her palm. "Sleep-In at the Common," the flyer reads in photocopied print. "Epic slumber party tomorrow night." He smiles at her. "Bring a tent."

Zan folds the flyer into the pocket of her hoodie and searches to find Nick, lost in the crowd up ahead. The bartender, a middle-aged man with a low, round belly and thick wooden plugs pierced through each ear, works quickly and alone. To make his job easier, buckets of ice and bottles of domestic beer have been strategically placed along the bar. They seem to be free for the taking.

Nick shoves his way to an open spot and Zan hovers behind him. On either side, people are calling out orders, trying to get the bartender's attention. Nick watches him hustle past four or five times, at first calling out a polite "Excuse me," and working up to a more forceful "Hey!" Finally, and much to Zan's surprise, he hoists the upper half of his body onto the bar and grabs the man's fleshy upper arm.

"Watch it." The bartender shakes Nick off and levels him with a warning glare. Nick hurries to unfold the receipt in his hand, slapping it on the damp edge of the bar.

"Vanessa!" he shouts over the persistent drink orders coming in all around them. "Does she work here?"

The bartender scoops four glasses full of ice and slams them behind the receipt. "Not anymore," he shouts back, disappearing to hunt for a bottle on one of the low, hidden shelves.

Nick runs his hand through his cropped light hair. Before she knows how it happens, Zan is perched beside him, leaning over the bar to scream into the barman's ear. "Please," she says, her voice near breaking. "Can you tell us where to find her? It's important."

The bartender pauses, a bottle in each hand. He sighs and pours out each of the drinks before grabbing a pen from his shirt pocket. He bites off the cap and scribbles something on the receipt. "Last I knew she was living in Somerville," he shouts. "If you find her, tell her she owes me an apron. I don't care if the world is ending, those things are a bitch to replace."

Zan smiles and feels like wrapping the man's thick, sweaty neck in a hug. She flattens the receipt against her palm. A rowdy group of frat boys fill the bar, shoving Nick and Zan back into the crowd. Nick places a hand on the small of her back and leads her out of the fray. He stops to duck quickly between a couple engaged in a tearful, drunken debate, and reappears with four bottles of free beer hugged against his chest. Zan gives him a look and he shrugs—*Why not?*—as she follows him back through the open door.

# CADEN

CADEN STARES OUT THROUGH THE TINTED
windows of a sleek SUV. The industrial parks and water treat-
ment plants lining the deserted highway slowly morph into
clustered residential streets, until finally the familiar city skyline
rises in the distance: the sun reflecting off the mirrored squares
of the John Hancock building, the proud, boxy Prudential, and
the weird spaceship dome beside it.

"Take the next exit," his father quietly commands. A dark
glass window, rolled halfway down, separates them from the
driver. The driver, the same bearded man who was there the night
Caden was taken from the beach, is named Joe. He's not much
of a talker.

Neither, it turns out, is Caden's father. If Sophie was right,
and the idea behind this trip had been some misplaced attempt
at overdue father/son bonding, his dad sure had a funny way of
showing it.

"You don't have to call me 'Dad,'" he'd said, apropos of
nothing as they bumped over the abandoned construction on
the Bourne Bridge. "Arthur is fine. In case you were . . . feeling
conflicted." Arthur looked out over the channel, his green eyes

following the bubbling wake of a lone tugboat as it slid into the horizon. He pulled a file from his briefcase. "If you don't mind, I have some work to do."

Caden inched closer to his window, the cool artificial air from the vent blowing directly into the sleeve of his borrowed collared shirt. He'd been kidnapped for this? To sit in a temperature-controlled, chauffeured SUV, listening to the intermittent scribble of his father's—*Arthur's*—ballpoint pen, the quiet shuffling of papers as he moved them from one manila folder to another?

Caden closed his eyes.

When he opens them again, they're outside Boston, the only big city he's ever seen. When he and Carly were little and Ramona still had good days, she would take them on the bus for "adventures." She'd drag them through countless discount stores, stocking up on undershirts and school supplies, and reward them with dumplings in Chinatown or steaming slices of pizza in the North End.

The day trips came to an abrupt stop when they got old enough to separate. One spring Saturday, after he'd taken Carly to feed the ducks and watch the street performers at Faneuil Hall, they'd waited for Ramona at their spot, the food court McDonald's in Terminal C. She'd shown up late, slurring and disheveled, and Carly had propped her up with one shoulder, guiding her down the crowded aisle, as a busful of sympathetic passengers whispered and clucked their tongues. That was the end of adventures.

"Where are we going?" Caden asks now. He adjusts the seams of his new jeans, pulling the rough fabric away from his knees.

The folders are closed on Arthur's lap and he taps the pen gently against their fat, worn spines.

"It's a surprise," Arthur says, without the slightest hint of fun or fanfare.

As they pull off the highway, Caden presses his nose against the window. He's disappointed to see that, aside from the eerie quiet that has fallen over the usually bustling streets, not much has changed. The homeless vets who stand between lanes of traffic at the light are still there, maybe a little less aggressive, a little more distractedly drunk. The buses and trains are all parked in the station, lined up along the tracks and snaking down the concrete ramps. The stoplights move more quickly through their cycles, pausing briefly on red before clicking back to green.

Caden isn't sure what he had been expecting. Chaos, maybe. People sobbing in the streets, or looting, like the stuff he's seen in places around the world on TV. Broken glass, babies crying, people sprinting through busted-down doors with stolen electronics.

There's not a busted door or stolen good in sight. Only the sad shuffle of a few lost-looking men in suits; men who probably, like Arthur, had been unable to accept a sudden, mandatory day off.

They've been driving through the still city streets only a few minutes when Joe pulls the car down a side street, sidles up to the curb, and cuts the engine.

"Ready?" Arthur asks, hunching his tall frame to climb out of the car.

"Ready for what?" Caden asks. His father's door slams in his face. Caden sits frozen in his seat.

Joe pops the trunk and goes around to the back, rooting around for a brown paper bag. He hands the bag to Arthur and snaps the trunk door shut before sliding back into the driver's seat. Still, Caden doesn't move. Arthur stands beside the SUV, looking up and down the empty street like he's waiting for a friend to show up.

"He'll win this game," Joe says lightly. "He always does. Quicker you go in, the quicker we can all get something to eat."

Caden sighs again and pushes heavily into the door, slamming it behind him.

Arthur walks a few feet ahead and Caden follows him around a corner. They turn down a narrow alley lined with souvenir shops and makeshift stalls, all shuttered and dark inside. Two hot dog carts appear to have rolled unattended into the middle of the street, and piles of foam fingers and blow-up baseball bats litter one section of the sidewalk. Caden looks beyond his father to where the towering green walls have stretched into view.

Fenway Park.

Caden went to a Red Sox game on a field trip in the eighth grade. That was the year he'd started hanging out with the Roadies, and a group of them were caught smoking butts in one of the outdoor stairwells. They'd spent the last three innings on the bus. Caden didn't care. Once he'd grown out of Little League, he hadn't been much into baseball, anyway. Even after the Red Sox stopped losing every game.

But there was a time when the legendary image of the Green Monster loomed like a sporty Shangri-La in his dreams. Maybe it had something to do with the framed color panorama occupying prime real estate on the wall directly above his bed. It had been a gift from his father on his fourth birthday, the last birthday they celebrated together as a family.

Arthur stops in front of the steps at Gate D. There's a cop sitting on a stool, and Arthur is saying something about "special permission" when Caden shuffles up between them. The cop has a neck like a tree trunk and black, beady eyes; he studies Caden as if he might be wearing a bomb.

"Hang on," the cop says, unlatching a walkie-talkie from his belt and stepping away to mumble into one end.

"The season's canceled," Caden says. A light breeze picks up a paper soda cup and tosses it against the bottom of the concrete steps. Aside from a few scattered guards and a man in a green jumpsuit sweeping the bottom of a handicapped ramp, the stadium is completely deserted.

"That's true." Arthur nods. "Doesn't mean we can't look around."

Caden stuffs his hands in his pockets. "Looking around" Fenway Park hadn't exactly been on his bucket list. Not that he ever had a bucket list. But if he did, it would probably have involved a lot more getting high on the beach with his friends, and a lot less being kidnapped by his long-lost father.

The cop returns and reluctantly ushers them through the metal turnstiles. Arthur pauses at the bottom of the staircase and heads straight for the lower level. The floor is sticky and the thick evening air smells of stale popcorn and old spilled beer. "A friend of mine is part owner of one of the feeder teams," Arthur explains as they pass through a dark hallway and step out into the open field. The sun is just starting to set; a strange, cool twilight illuminates the bleachers. "I asked him to arrange a private tour, but he did me one better: the whole place, all to ourselves."

Arthur takes long, lumbering steps down the cement stairs that lead to the field, the paper bag still tucked beneath his arm. The diamond has been newly brushed and cleaned. The bases sparkle white against the bright green turf.

At the first row of bleachers, Arthur sets the bag on the wall and gently hoists himself over. "What do you think?" he asks, unbuttoning the cuffs of his sleeves and rolling them up in careful, even sections to his elbows. From the bag, he removes a clean baseball and two new gloves.

Caden stops short inside the low wall. He turns to look back at the rows and rows of empty seats, stretching out into the distance. With a loud, buzzing pop, a light tower over the outfield flashes on. On the far side of the high green walls, the sky looks suddenly darker.

Arthur is tossing the ball into one glove, molding the hard leather around it. Caden sighs and throws his legs over the wall. As much as he hates to admit it, he feels a jolt as he lands on the other side. He remembers the dreams he used to have of standing on this field, wearing a uniform and being the best at something, something big. He hops to the turf and grabs the second glove from a bench.

The leather is stiff in his palm. He punches his fist inside, like he's seen people do in the movies.

"Ready?" Arthur asks.

Caden drops his arm to his side and stands with his feet spread apart. The soft, persistent drone of mosquitoes hums threateningly in his ears.

"You don't look ready." Arthur rests the ball against his hip.

"What?"

"Look ready," Arthur encourages, holding his glove in front of his face. "Look alive!"

Caden squeezes the glove in his hand, the unforgiving leather seams digging into the flesh of his fingers. He holds the glove to his chest, imitating his father's stance. Then, he laughs. It starts like a hiccup, an unplanned burst of air. But soon, he's bent in half, the glove buried deep against his stomach.

*"Look alive?"* he finally manages to spit back. He feels his lungs emptying as the laughter fades away. The next few breaths he takes fill him with wild electricity. All of the muscles in his body tense and prepare, like he's standing on the edge of a cliff, facing a rough and powerful wind.

"You've had twelve years to think about this," Caden yells. "Twelve years. We're doing this *now*? Our first game of catch is *today*, in the middle of *Fenway Park*? Did you think I was going to, like, cry, or something? What's next, you teach me how to catch a fly ball? We go out for ice cream? We talk about life, and hug?"

Arthur wipes the back of his free hand against his forehead. He shifts his weight from foot to foot.

Caden rips the glove from his palm and throws it to the ground. "I fucking hate sports," he says. "Which you would know, if you knew anything about me. How's that?"

They stare at each other, the pitcher's mound an anchor between them. Arthur clears his throat. "Caden," he says. His voice is tired, but stern. He looks at the lights. "Pick up the glove."

Caden doesn't move. His feet are like cinder blocks, his fists clenched and pulsing like beating, angry hearts at his side.

"I know you hate sports," Arthur sighs. "I fucking hated sports, too. I hated playing catch. It never made any sense to me. You throw the ball, then I throw the ball? I don't get it. But I've spent my whole life not getting a lot of things, and not doing them because they didn't make sense. And I thought now might be a good time to try something new."

Arthur shields his eyes from the stadium lights high above Caden's head. "Pick up the glove, Caden," he says again. "Please."

Caden eyes the open glove by his feet. He remembers Joe in the car. *He'll win this game. He always does.* He closes the mitt over his fingers and holds it out, like a statue, by his hip.

His father glances up at the darkening sky, and when he looks back at Caden, he's smiling. Something about his face has changed completely, and before Caden can help it, he remembers. He's three years old, and his dad is chasing him through the woods behind their house. He's a prince, and his dad is a dragon, breathing fake fire at the trees. Caden hides beneath a bush and watches his father pretend not to see him, knees bent, his arms outstretched. Caden coughs, then giggles. He wants to be caught.

Beyond the pitcher's mound, Arthur draws back the point of his elbow and sends the ball between them. It lands in Caden's glove with a solid, satisfying thud.

# SIENNA

OPERATION ONE-BIG-HAPPY-FAMILY WAS IN full swing, and Sienna was already exhausted.

First, there was the trip to the beach. Sienna was sure they'd be the only people there. Who could possibly care about getting a tan at a time like this? But the rocky shoreline was sardine-packed with clusters of families, all of whom seemed to share Dad's idea of forced togetherness. When the going gets tough, the tough go swimming.

But Dad was the only one who went in. Ryan brought his three favorite books about caterpillars, and pulled his faded Red Sox hat down low as he read. Denise spent the afternoon flipping through wedding magazines, occasionally asking for Sienna's opinion on everything from flower arrangements to canapés. Sienna managed to grumble a few lukewarm responses ("wow," "pretty," "yum" . . . ) before pulling a towel over her face and pretending to take a nap.

Then came dinner on the patio, a drawn-out presentation of all of Denise's favorites. Luckily, she turned out to be a much better cook than Dad. Sienna did her best to pretend not to enjoy the homemade pasta and fresh tomato and basil salad, but she snuck back to the kitchen for seconds when she thought nobody was looking.

After three rounds of charades, Sienna excused herself to her room. She had hoped that might be the end of it. Maybe one day was all Dad had in mind. They'd done what he wanted. They were nice to Denise. Sienna had even started calling her "Denny" to her face.

But after she'd brushed her teeth, Dad was waiting for her in the hall. A hand on her shoulder, his eyes hopeful and sad. "Denny is hoping to put together some bouquets for the wedding," he'd said. "Could you take her to one of your secret spots tomorrow morning?"

Sienna clenched her teeth and agreed, a quick, silent nod. They'd said good night and she closed her bedroom door.

The secret spots weren't hers. They were Mom's. Sienna hadn't been back since the summer before she died. Fields of wildflowers, hidden deep in the woods, down the overgrown deer paths you had to squint to see.

She sits at the edge of her bed and reaches for her pillbox. She takes half of her anxiety meds at night. A full dose in the morning would make her groggy and weird all day. She'd overheard a few of the staffers at the House, worried that the "kids" would start to boycott. What was the point in medicating themselves, when there was a chance they were all going to die, anyway? Sienna had considered taking a break. The meds did help her to feel more settled, less repetitive in her thinking, but they also made her feel like a zombie. Is that really how she wants to spend the next few days?

There's a sharp *ping* and Sienna turns to the window. She

stands frozen, wondering if she'd imagined the sound, when it happens again. This time, a pebble sails in through the open crack, rolling across the floor to her bare feet.

"Sienna!"

She hears her name whispered in the dark, and carefully tugs at the window. The light from the garage seeps onto the yard and glows on a pair of striped flip-flops. Owen steps slowly out from the shadows.

"Hey," he calls again. Sienna leans forward, fidgeting with the neckline of the flimsy camisole she wears to sleep.

"What are you doing?" She laughs. He's wearing a faded blue T-shirt with thin white stripes, and dark jeans. His hair is fluffier than usual, like it's just been washed.

"What does it look like?" he calls out, his voice soft and hoarse. He picks up another piece of gravel from the driveway and tosses it in the air. "Come on. You owe me a date."

"I do?" Sienna jokes. She looks over her shoulder at the door to her room, open a crack. Denny and Dad have already gone to bed, but she can still hear the murmur of their voices. She holds up a finger and shuts her bedroom door slowly, careful not to catch the creak as it shuts. She gives her bed a quick look—Dad never checks on her at night anymore, but just in case, she stuffs the pillows under the sheets and pulls the blanket up tight. It doesn't look remotely like an actual person sleeping, but it will have to do.

Sienna throws on a pair of jeans and sandals, and grabs a light cardigan from her bag. As she passes her bed, she eyes the pillbox, open on the table. She snaps the box shut and tucks it behind the lamp.

She steps onto the deck, pulling the door shut noiselessly behind her. She leans over the high wooden railing to survey her options. It's only a short hop to the roof of the sunroom below. From there, if she really stretches, she can reach a low branch of the Japanese maple in their yard.

She lands, almost gracefully, on the soft, damp grass, just a few feet from where Owen is standing. She can't believe how easy it was to get out, or that she'd never tried it before.

Owen puts a hand on the top of her head in a sort of improvised half hug. It could be awkward, but for some reason, it's not. Sienna, forever the tallest girl in her class, feels small and protected.

"Sorry," he says, stuffing his hands in his pockets. "I've never thrown a rock at a girl's window before. How'd I do?"

Sienna smiles. He smells like soap and pine needles. "Looks like it worked," she says.

They cut through the high grass and out onto the road, the sound track of chatty crickets and rustling leaves muffling the quiet rhythm of their feet. "Where are we going?" Sienna asks as they round a corner at the bottom of the hill.

Just as they approach the intersection, a pair of headlights cut through the darkness, and an old blue pickup squeals to a stop beside them. "Our ride," Owen announces. He waves to the driver, the dreadlocked girl-drummer from his band, and walks around to the back. Five or six people are already crammed inside, perched against the tailgate or wedged between a rusty silver toolbox and the truck's crowded cab. Owen plants a foot on the bumper and climbs over, leaning out to give Sienna his hand.

She jumps into the flatbed beside him, and feels his arms

close around the tops of her shoulders as the truck picks up speed. She's never ridden in the back like this before, free and untethered. She turns her face to the wind, closes her eyes, and smiles at the darkness.

As soon as they've parked by the docks, Owen grabs Sienna's hand and guides her away from the truck. "See you up there!" Maggie, the dreadlocked driver, calls after them.

Sienna looks back over her shoulder as the group unpacks coolers and bundled-up sleeping bags. "Are they moving in?" she asks.

Owen laughs. "It's kind of a rotating party," he says. "Every night they set up in a new place."

Sienna looks ahead at the crowded, narrow avenues leading to the center of town. People, mostly kids their age and a little bit older, are everywhere—camped out on the curb or dancing in the middle of the street to music playing from speakers, set up every few blocks.

But the stores and restaurants lining the streets, the gift shops and ice cream parlors, the video arcade, the run-down movie theater—every building is shuttered and dark. The deserted backdrop makes the street-side bustle feel wild and lawless. Sienna tightens her grip around Owen's hand and follows him across an empty parking lot.

"How long has it been like this?" she asks. She remembers the nights she used to come into town with her family, for Thai food and frozen yogurt, or a lazy stroll along the harbor. It's hard to believe it's the same place.

"Not long," Owen says. "A few days. The cops tried to shut it down a few times, but I think eventually they gave up and joined the party."

The music changes as they pass from one section of the street to another, first Brazilian pop, then pulsing techno, now classic rock. Kids in colorful and abstract clothing—some wearing little more than bathing suits or wrapped, toga-style, in tapestries and sheets—weave in and out, bumping between them as Owen pulls her along the sidewalk.

"Where are we going?" she asks. Her breathing is ragged and she's starting to feel claustrophobic.

"You'll see." Owen nudges her.

Finally, the crowds thin out, and up ahead, Sienna sees a circle of flickering neon lights. A chorus of polka-themed circus music floats around them, and Owen looks to her with a smile. The Flying Horses, the old-fashioned carousel at the center of town, is the one establishment still up and running. Sienna hears the familiar screeches of joyful riders as the painted horses glide around the track.

She hasn't been to the carousel since forever. It used to be the family's favorite rainy day outing. Even climbing the steps to the open double doors makes her heart heavy with longing, longing for a time when Sienna, too small to ride alone, sat snuggled in her dad's lap, reaching out with their arms entwined, hoping to catch the brass ring.

But as she follows Owen up the steps and past the main entrance, it's clear that things have changed. The ticket windows are boarded up and the friendly, middle-aged attendants who normally preside over the zigzagging line to the front are nowhere to be seen. Instead, chaos reigns, and the horses seem to be zipping by at an unnaturally fast clip.

"As soon as word got out that the carousel was shutting down, a bunch of older kids decided to get it running again," Owen explains as they join the horde of people waiting to climb on board.

"How?" Sienna asks. Ahead of them, a group of girls with glow sticks wrapped around their heads are singing a song Sienna doesn't recognize. She wonders if they all snuck out, as she did, or if their parents know that they're here.

Owen shrugs. "One of them used to work the ring arm," he says, nodding to the hulking metal claw that stretches out from the wall. Sienna used to wonder about the people—usually bronzed, blue-eyed teenage boys—that stood on a pedestal behind the arm, feeding handfuls of rings inside, always struggling to keep up with the riders swiping them out on the other end. At some point, a mysterious voice over the loudspeaker would announce that the brass ring had been dispensed, signaling that the end of the ride was near. The arm attendant would step quietly down from his platform and disappear behind a thick red curtain. It always seemed like such an important job, Sienna remembers thinking, to determine when the last ring would be captured, when the fun would come to an end.

"Hey," Owen says, wrapping his elbow around her neck and pulling her close. "You okay?"

Sienna manages a smile. "Yeah," she says softly. Seeing town this way has made her feel adrift, and uneasy. It's the first time since leaving the House that things have felt so dramatically different. Whatever it is that's happening, whatever comes of the next few days, it's real. And it's big. For the first time that she can remember, Sienna feels afraid.

"We don't have to stay," he says. "I thought it would be fun to go for a ride, but . . ."

"No," Sienna says, leaning the top of her head near his chest, feeling the warmth of his shirt, the flutter of his pulse beneath her cheek. "Let's go for a ride."

Owen rests his palm on the top of her head again, his hand warm and strong on her hair. This time, she turns her face to his and he leans down, holding her chin in his palm. He brings his lips to hers and she feels herself melting, as if every cell in her body is slowing down. Everything inside of her feels suddenly released. Her busy brain is quiet and calm.

They're still tangled together when a shoulder bumps them forward. The line is moving. Owen pulls back and smiles. He takes her hand as they shuffle forward, inching closer to the blurry spin.

# ZAN

"WHERE DID THEY ALL COME FROM?"

Nick taps the steering wheel anxiously with his thumbs, waiting as a large crowd passes in front of the car. Their car is still one of just a few on the road, but the sidewalks are now teeming with couples holding hands, families clustered together, and large groups of students strolling en masse. The sun has slipped behind the boxy city skyline, and Zan wonders if there's something about the darkness that makes people afraid to be alone.

Zan stares at the address, scrawled on the receipt in her lap. First, it was just a name and number. Now, there's a place, a street in a part of the city she knows nothing about. It seems impossible that so much information, so many clues to something she never even suspected, could fit on such a small square of paper.

"My cousins used to live in Somerville," Nick says as the car lurches around a corner. They are slowly making their way out of downtown, the shops and restaurants becoming more spread out as the roads expand. "I think I can get us in the neighborhood, at least."

Zan nods. It seems, suddenly, strange that she and Nick are each other's only company at a time like this, and even stranger that they are driving around the city, in search of a mysterious girl named Vanessa. Strange, but not altogether awful. More like an unlikely coincidence, and one that Zan suspects Leo must have been behind, somehow.

She sneaks a glance at Nick's profile, his square jaw set as he navigates the foreign city streets. She wonders what he'd be doing today, tonight, if she hadn't told him about what she'd found.

"What did your parents say about you leaving?" she asks abruptly. She realizes she knows next to nothing about Nick's family, except for his dad and the boat. What about his mom? Wouldn't she want her only son at home at a time like this?

Nick shrugs. "Not much." He smiles, almost sadly. "My mom's just happy to have my dad around, for once. And my sisters are too busy being little drama queens to notice."

Zan remembers Nick's younger sisters, a pair of golden-haired twins his mother dressed alike until middle school. "What about Clara?" Zan asks. Clara Morrison was one of Zan's best friends, back before Leo, when Zan still had friends. The fact that Clara was dating Nick meant they all saw each other often, though "dating Nick" was something of a contradiction in terms. The only relationship that Nick ever seemed to have much time for was the one he had with his boat. "I mean, doesn't she care that you're gone?"

Nick needlessly checks over his shoulder before pulling into the passing lane. The car whines and rattles as he accelerates. "I didn't tell her I was leaving," he says. "We're not really together anymore."

Zan tries to look surprised. She remembers being at parties

with Leo, who was constantly nearby, his arm slung easily over her shoulder, and watching Clara brood in a corner. Nick was always getting tied up at the harbor, out fishing or working on his boat. He'd show up at the end of the night and kiss Clara hello, before being talked into a late-night swim or game of Ping-Pong with the guys. He just didn't seem to "get" the idea of a girlfriend.

Zan looks through the window at the abandoned streets. They've left the crowds behind them, and are now in a desolate, industrial part of town, the two-lane highway lined with warehouses and boarded-up pawnshops. She wonders what waits for them at the address in her hand, if they ever find it.

The car bucks and hisses in a new and not entirely reassuring way. Nick's bushy blond eyebrows are locked together in obvious concern.

"What was that?" Zan asks.

Nick leans to look through the windshield, where a thin trail of smoke leaks from beneath the bruised and battered hood. "I'm not sure," he says. He checks the rearview mirror and turns the wheel, guiding the sputtering car to the side of the road. They slide to the curb just as the hiss explodes into a whistling screech and the car burps a black cloud of grimy exhaust.

Zan fumbles with her door, coughing and shielding her face with the collar of her shirt. Nick is already standing over the smoking hood, waving his hands to clear the air. Once she's standing a healthy distance from the smell of burning, and mostly convinced the car isn't going to blow up, Zan can't help but laugh.

"I thought you said we'd be okay!" she calls out to Nick, now gingerly attempting to pry open the hood.

"I said we'd make it to the city." He spits and squeezes his eyes shut as the rest of the smoke escapes in a thick puff. "I didn't say anything about a scavenger hunt."

"What happened?" Zan asks, tilting the top half of her body forward just slightly, as if seeing better would somehow make her able to help. She knows exactly nothing about cars. She even splurges on full-service gas when it's an option.

Nick, it doesn't surprise her to discover, knows a lot. He hovers over the mess of wires and rusted springs, careful not to touch anything directly. "I think the cooling system is messed up," he finally says.

Zan folds her arms and wrinkles her nose. "Is that bad?"

"Could be worse." Nick shrugs, slamming the hood. "I could fix it if I had some tools." He leans against the car and glances at the sky. "And parts."

"Where does a person get parts?" Zan asks. She looks up and down the side of the highway, as if there might be a CAR PARTS "R" US on the corner.

Nick rubs his hand over his face and checks the screen of his phone. "Any service station," he says. "But I doubt anything will be open." He looks off into the distance before pushing himself away from the bumper. "Wait here," he says. "I'll check."

Nick jogs a few paces down the road and holds up a hand to let her know he'll be back. Zan lowers herself to the curb, listening as the car's insides seem to rearrange themselves, clinking and settling back into place. She hears Nick's voice in her head. *Scavenger hunt.*

Leo loved scavenger hunts. Actual games, like the one he put together for Amelia's birthday party a few years back, but also adventures that seemed to find him, somehow, wherever he went. Zan remembers the time he walked the entire perimeter of the island, by himself, just because he felt like it. It was when they had first started dating, and he'd asked her along. She'd said no; the thought of camping on the beach, on the island's farthest, rockiest point, scared her more than she wanted to admit. There's a part of her that feels like this trip—solving this mystery, from clues he left behind—is her way of proving that she's changed. That her time with Leo has changed her, for good. She's not afraid anymore.

Now more than ever, she feels like he's watching over her, sending her on one last adventure, setting obstacles and traps along the way, just to see how much she can take.

"Bring it on," she whispers to herself with a smirk.

"Bring what on?"

Zan turns to find Nick panting over her shoulder. "Nothing," she covers. "What'd you find?"

Nick wipes a layer of sweat from his neck with the bottom of his T-shirt, exposing a hard, toned stomach. Zan looks quickly in the direction of the warehouses. "There's a gas station not far," he says. "It's closed. But . . ."

His voice trails off and he stares at her intensely, as if asking for permission to continue.

"But what?" Zan prompts. She looks into Nick's blue eyes and sees a new glimmer, the twinkling kernel of a plan.

"Come with me," he says, walking quickly, the car still rattling and gasping on the side of the road behind him. Zan hurries to keep up.

The gas station is tucked back a bit from the road, attached to a big garage with a sign advertising "Boston's Best Oil Change—Cheap & Fast!" out front. The highway splits off into a quiet residential neighborhood with few signs of life. Zan wonders if everyone has gone deeper into the city, where at least there are more distractions.

First, they try calling for help. They bang on the doors and peer into the darkened convenience shop, scanning the aisles of junk food and batteries for somebody, anybody, to let them in. Next, Nick tries the doors, shaking the pair at the front on their hinges and putting all of his weight into tugging up the heavy door to the garage. The garage is held shut with a flimsy lock, and Nick searches the edges of the pavement for a rock big enough to smash it open.

Zan walks around the corner, behind the tire pump and vacuum machine. There's a sad-looking patch of grass that seems to serve as the outdoor break room, littered with cigarette butts and bottle caps. Above a big blue Dumpster, Zan spots a high window with an angled pane, swung open just a crack.

"Nick!" she calls. "Back here!"

By the time he finds her she's already perched on the Dumpster lid, trying not to inhale the rancid odor of forgotten trash and spilled engine oil. She pushes at the bottom of the window, prying it open as much as she can. "It's stuck," she grunts.

"Let me try," Nick offers. He wedges his elbow into the space between the glass and the garage siding, popping it open a few inches more. He peers inside. "This place is stocked."

Zan eyes the opening before peeling off her sweatshirt. She drops it to the ground and puts a hand on Nick's shoulder. "Give me a boost," she orders him.

Nick looks at her, his eyes wide with alarm. She puts his hands on her waist. "Come on!" she insists.

Nick lifts her easily, and she grabs the dirty sill with both hands. There's a thumping energy inside of her, as if a motor has been switched on. She feels the way she does when she's running, strong and in control. Just as she'd thought, Nick has cleared enough space for her to wrangle her upper body inside. Once her head is through and her eyes adjust to the dusty dark, she looks for an easy way down.

The floor is hard and concrete, so falling headfirst isn't much of an option. But there's a wall of metal shelving a few feet beside her, and she grabs the corner rail with the tips of her outstretched fingers.

"Okay," she shouts. "One more big shove." She feels Nick's hands tighten around her narrow hips, and in one swift motion she's clawing at the shelves and swinging her legs down to the empty railing below.

"I'm in!" she calls ecstatically, starting to scale the ladderlike rungs of shelving to the ground. A pile of hubcaps shudders on the top shelf, and one rolls slowly to the edge. It falls with a piercing clatter, and Zan drops to her feet behind it. She's rubbing the metal marks free from her hands when the whole unit sways ominously to one side. The rest of the hubcaps, followed by half-opened cardboard boxes of bolts and screws, dented cans of paint and oil—it all comes raining down around her. Zan ducks and scrambles to the door, her hands covering her face as the room explodes in a tinny racket.

"Are you okay?" Nick calls out from the window. "Zan?"

Zan slowly lowers her hands from her ears, the din of metal on concrete still echoing in her head. "Yeah," she shouts back. "I'm here. Come around to the side door, I'll let you in."

Zan unlocks the bolted door and starts to pull it open, when she hears a rustling behind her.

"Not so fast."

Zan turns to find herself staring at the shiny, bulbous head of a golf club. Gripping tight to the other end is the smallest old woman Zan has ever seen in her life. Her coarse, white-gray hair is partially covered in a scarf, tribal-looking with swirls of orange and red, and her skin is deep brown and wrinkled.

"What you trying to do here, girl?" she asks, her voice syrupy and thick with an accent that makes Zan think of palm trees.

Zan swallows and backs up toward the sliding garage door. She hears the shuffle of Nick's feet on the other side.

"And who you got there with you?" the old woman asks, nodding at the door.

"I'm, I'm sorry," Zan stutters. "We were just . . ."

The woman struggles to hold the club up to Zan's waist, while unlocking the door and slowly pushing it open. Nick stands on the other side, and she swings the club clumsily toward his face.

"Whoa." Nick dodges the golf club as the woman swipes blindly at the air between them.

"You trying to rob me, boy? The whole world going crazy and

you trying to rob me?" Her voice is high and screechy. Zan stands uncertainly behind her. Up close she can see that the woman is shaking, her petite frame trembling beneath the billowing tent of her housecoat. She's not just angry, Zan realizes. She's terrified.

"Ma'am," Zan tries. "We're so sorry. We, our car broke down, and we didn't think anybody was in here. We just needed some tools. We can pay you."

"Pay me?" The woman turns to look at Zan. She loosens her grip on the club but there's still a wild fury in her small, dark eyes, now glassy and brimming with tears. "What I'm gonna do with your money now? All by myself in this garage, nobody here with me. What I want your money for?"

Zan looks over the woman's head to Nick, who is slowly walking back toward them. "You're all alone here?" he asks.

The woman jumps again at his voice. "My son, this his garage. He tell me 'Come stay with me, Mama, I take care of you.' And then this morning, he gone! Leave me here, with people climbing in, and stealing things, the whole world going crazy . . ."

The woman shakes her head and drops the golf club to the ground. The trembling intensifies, and suddenly she is rocked by loud, violent sobs. Zan knows she should do something, but her arms feel stuck to her sides.

"Where's your son now?" Nick asks, his voice soft and low. He slowly reaches a hand to the woman's shoulder, and Zan winces, expecting her to furiously bat him away. Instead, the old woman crumples like a broken marionette, falling to the floor in a heap.

"He say he be back tonight," the woman says between sniffles. "His girl Lucy, she live out of town, he say he go pick her up and bring her back, and we all be safe here together. Now it's nearly dark and they nowhere." The woman takes a breath and clenches her arthritic hands into trembling fists. "I told him, didn't I tell him, I always say that girl be trouble."

Zan looks to Nick, crouched over the old woman, one hand still resting on her shoulder. It's late, and they should get going. But there's a funny, screwed-up feeling in her stomach that she knows will just get worse if they leave.

"Ma'am?" Zan asks quietly. "Would it be okay if we waited here with you for a while?"

The woman wipes at her eyes with the puffy sleeve of her dress. "What for?"

"Just until your son gets back," Nick interrupts. "In case, in case we need help. With the car."

The woman considers this for a moment. "All right," she says with a sigh. She leans into Nick's arm and he lifts her up to her feet. He guides her back to the door connecting the garage to the shop beside it. She pauses with her hand on the metal knob. "We only have the microwave, but I can find you something to eat. Are you hungry?"

Zan looks to Nick, who shrugs helplessly from behind the woman's hunched back. He holds the door open and ushers them both inside.

"Starving," Nick insists, winking at Zan as she ducks beneath his arm.

Zan smiles and follows the woman into the shop. "Me too."

# SIENNA

"WE'RE ALMOST THERE, I PROMISE."

Sienna clutches Owen's hand in both of hers, her eyes blinking in the moonlight, the uneven ground crackling beneath her sandals. The trees hang close in the darkness, the whispering shadows of outstretched branches clinging to their shoulders as they step carefully along the pine-scented path.

The trail began at Owen's house. After they'd hitched a ride back from town, Owen had grabbed Sienna by the hand and led her up his darkened driveway, turning into the woods just before they reached his front door. Sienna knew she should be getting home; the sun would be up in a few hours. But as she felt Owen's fingers wrap around hers, she knew she wasn't ready for the night to end.

Ahead, the trail opens to a small patch of wild grass that connects to a long, rickety dock. Owen helps Sienna over a knot of burly roots, and in an instant, she sees it. The pond, big and clear as a painting, cut perfectly into the towering pines and maple trees on either side.

"The neighborhood's best-kept secret," Owen says proudly, taking her hand and leading her out to the end of the dock. The moon, nearly full, dances in shimmery white ribbons on the still, dark surface. She sits beside him and peels off her sandals, letting the tips of her toes skim the cool water.

"What do you think?" Owen asks. He rolls up the bottoms of his pants, his feet disappearing beneath the dark surface.

"I think it's maybe the most beautiful place I've ever seen." Sienna laughs. It's hard to believe that it's real, any of it. The pond. The moon.

Being here with Owen.

Owen smiles. He reaches back for her hand. "I had a feeling you wouldn't hate it."

Sienna stares at him, the serious pitch of his dark, full eyebrows, the long, narrow line of his nose.

"What?" he asks, touching his face as if something might be missing.

Sienna shakes her head. "Nothing," she insists. "Just looking."

There's an easy quiet between them. Sienna's ears are still buzzing from being in town. After the carousel, they'd met up with Owen's friends. He'd introduced her to the group of kids that were building the boat, led by a big guy with a beard named Jeremy. Ted, another band member, had played his guitar on the beach, fighting to be heard over the wash of music and voices still thrumming from the streets.

"It's weird, right?" Owen asks. He's playing with her fingers, unbending them one at a time in his palm.

"What is?" Sienna asks.

"Just . . . seeing you again, I guess." He shrugs. "I mean, I really was thinking about you. Wondering where you were. You know how it is when you're a kid, and you have these friends, and then you don't see them for a while? You always remember the way they were, like they're all still out there somewhere, running around with a smaller version of you."

Sienna laughs. She pictures the two of them, little on the beach, Owen chasing her through the waves. "You think you're still running after me somewhere, with seaweed in your hair?"

Owen nods. "Definitely," he says with a smile. "I had the right idea, I guess."

Sienna leans into his shoulder.

"Maybe not the seaweed part." He laughs. "But I'm glad you finally stopped running."

Sienna feels something stick in her throat. "Me too," she says, and realizes it's the truth. It's never felt so good to sit still.

"Thanks for putting up with all of those guys," Owen says, leaning back on his elbows. He smiles. "They can be a little overwhelming."

Sienna remembers the group on the beach, the familiar way they talked and teased, the nicknames they had for each other. "Have you known them all long?" she asks.

"Since preschool. A lot of them live around here. Waited for the bus together, that kind of thing," he explains. "Maggie always calls us the Tribe. Kind of lame, but I guess it's true. We do everything together."

Owen looks out across the pond and Sienna senses a shift in his posture. He hasn't said much about his parents, except that they had finally given up on family game nights. It didn't seem like Owen wanted to spend much time at home anymore, either.

Sienna closes her eyes and she sees them again, two little blond kids playing in the sand. Owen is right. They are still here. Right here. There's nowhere else Sienna would rather be.

"Let's go in," she says quickly. She's already standing, peeling off her sweater and stepping out of her jeans, the crisp night air prickling her arms and legs.

Owen stares at her, his eyes wide with surprise. "You want to?"

Sienna stands facing him. "Turn around," she says. She can't believe what she's about to do. She's never gone skinny-dipping. She's never even been swimming at night. In a quick burst, she pulls off her clothes and jumps in.

The cold of the water greets her with a shock, and she sputters up to the surface. Owen dives in over her head. He wriggles out of his shorts underwater and tosses them in a heavy heap onto the dock. He paddles to her and pulls her into a hug. Her legs wrap easily around his waist, his hands are in her hair. And when they kiss, he tastes cool and bright, like the glow of the moon on his shoulders.

# DAY FOUR

# CADEN

THE STONE STEPS IN FRONT OF THE COTTAGE door are damp and cool from the morning shade. Caden moves to a sunnier spot on the grass. He unpeels the outer layers of a still-warm cream cheese Danish, licking the sticky filling from the sides of his fingers. The peak of Mount Greylock looms over the house like a burly, watchful guard.

It was dark by the time they arrived last night. The drive from Boston to North Adams took over two hours, but Caden had fallen asleep somewhere near Worcester, and the rugged, uneven terrain as they pulled off the access road shook him awake. The "cottage," which was roughly seven times bigger than any cottage Caden had ever seen, clung to the lip of the mountain, and the path from the circular driveway was lit by a trail of hanging metal lanterns, like something out of Edgar Allan Poe.

Only a few lights were on inside, and Arthur had quickly shown him to a guest bedroom at the top of the stairs. Caden fell into the four-poster bed without changing or brushing his teeth.

"Punctual." Arthur's voice startles him now from the doorway. "I like that."

Caden takes another bite of Danish. There had been a note under his bedroom door when he woke up: "Meet by the stables at 8 —A." Caden immediately wondered three things: 1. Where were the stables? 2. What happens there? And 3. Just how sprawling an estate was he dealing with, if his father couldn't just yell to him from down the hall somewhere?

He showered—an annoying ordeal that involved crouching inside a claw-foot tub with a handheld nozzle that looked more like a telephone than a shower—and quickly got dressed, arriving downstairs a little after seven-thirty.

"I see you've met Russell." Arthur pulls the enormous wooden door shut behind him and starts down the steps toward the lawn. He tips his wool hat in the direction of an attached wooden barn—Caden had guessed these were the stables but didn't want to take any chances—and motions for Caden to follow.

"Kind of," Caden mutters, stuffing his face with the last of his pastry. At the bottom of the main staircase, Caden had smelled something sweet, and followed his nose into a formal sitting room. The hardwood floor was covered in pelts—Caden wasn't exactly sure what a pelt was but he was pretty sure these rugs had heads, if not now then very, very recently—and the frozen eyes of an eight-point buck stared down at him from above the giant stone hearth.

No sooner had Caden settled into one of the room's two cracked-leather armchairs than an older man in dirty overalls appeared from a low doorway at the other side of the room. Without speaking, the man carried in a tray of pastries—croissants,

Danish, muffins—a mug of hot coffee, and a single glass of juice, and set it down clumsily on a small fireside table.

"Russell is a man of few words," Arthur continues as they cross the open lawn. The mountain is everywhere above them, brushed at the peak with broken strands of gauzy clouds. "He's been the caretaker here since before I was born."

Caden stops short at the red barn doors. He had eaten his Danish because he was starving. He drank the coffee because it smelled strong and rich. But what, exactly, was happening here? How did he end up at the top of a mountain he'd never seen, with his kidnapper/father, on a private and potentially haunted estate?

"What are we doing here?" he asks, folding his hands over his chest. "What is this place?"

Arthur opens the latch on the door and peers down at Caden from under the brim of his hat. "It's the family lodge," he says. "It's been passed down through generations since the mid–eighteen hundreds. It was in terrible condition for a while, but it's been restored. I come up here as often as I can."

"Why?" Caden asks, looking around. Sure, the view's not bad, but they're stuck at the top of a mountain. Everything in the house looks like it was salvaged from the set of a black-and-white movie, the kind that Ramona was always passing out in front of late at night on PBS. Aside from the baking, all of the rooms smelled like dust and mothballs. It wasn't exactly Caden's idea of the perfect weekend getaway.

"I like the quiet," Arthur says, disappearing into the barn.

"You like that it's yours," Caden says under his breath as he follows Arthur into the dark, dank room.

"Yes." Arthur sighs heavily. "I like that it's mine. One day, I hope you'll like that it's yours, too."

Caden chuckles. "Whatever."

He's done trying to convince his father that none of this matters. The view, the houses, the business, the toys—if this last-ditch rocket launch doesn't work, which he can't imagine it will, all of this could be rubble in just a few short days. Nothing would ever belong to anyone again, and especially not to Caden. Not that he ever thought that it would.

Caden looks around the inside of the barn, the hard dirt floor and the rows of empty stalls. Some are large enough for full-size horses, and some are shorter, wider pens, more suitable for goats or sheep. "What happened to the animals?"

"We haven't kept any since my father died," Arthur explains, walking past the stalls and standing in front of a tall closet door.

"That's dumb," Caden huffs. If it were up to him, if this really was his house, his barn, he'd sure as shit keep animals in it. Horses, for riding up and down the mountain trails. Sheep, for shearing. And maybe some miniature goats and donkeys, just for fun.

Not that it would ever be his house, or his barn.

"So what are we doing here?" Caden asks again, as Arthur opens the closet. He pulls a cord and a dim yellow bulb lights up, hanging from the thick boards at the ceiling. Suddenly, they are face-to-face with three high walls of guns. "Whoa," Caden says, before he can catch himself.

"There used to be an armory in the cellar," Arthur says, reaching for a shotgun by his hip. "But my father preferred to keep the guns out here. I think he thought it kept the livestock in line."

Caden stares at the rows of hanging racks. Shotguns, rifles, even a few ancient-looking muskets, like something straight out of the Revolutionary War.

"What's your pick?" Arthur asks, replacing the shotgun on the wall.

"My pick?" Caden asks. "For what?"

"The hunt," Arthur says. "The season doesn't technically open for a few months, but I can't imagine anyone would be turning us in. We'll be lucky if we see anything. Probably just a few cottontails, if we're lucky."

Arthur holds out a long, narrow rifle, examining it from end to end. "You take the .22," he says, passing it off to Caden. He's never held a real gun before. He'd gone through a short-lived BB phase, but mostly he just hung back while the older kids shot at unsuspecting squirrels and then ran away, whooping and howling like they'd taken out a tribe of enemies on the front.

The rifle is heavier than it looks. The stock is tan with flecks of black and gold, and the barrel looks shiny and new. Arthur selects a shotgun for himself, a bigger weapon with a fat double barrel and a hanging wooden pump, and finds a box of shells at the back of an open shelf. He rests his gun against a stall and locks the closet door.

Caden watches as Arthur takes the rifle from him, quickly loading the chamber with a handful of golden, missile-shaped bullets. Each one pops into place with a satisfying click. Arthur moves fast; it's clear he's done this many times before. Caden feels an overwhelming sense of envy as he watches his father repeat the process with the shotgun shells. Plenty of kids are into hunting on the island, and Caden has never had any desire to be one of them. But now he wishes he at least knew how to load his own gun. Maybe he would have learned, if Arthur had stuck around. Maybe they would have spent weekends building deer stands, high in the trees, staking out their spots before the sun came up.

Arthur holds the rifle by a thick, leather strap and loops it around Caden's shoulder. They walk through the barn and back into the sharp morning light.

"There's a trail through here." Arthur nods at an opening in the woods. Caden falls into step behind him. The woods feel different on a mountain, the ground is soft and the air crisp and dry. The trees are the same white-barked birches, tall pines, and maples he's used to at home, but here they're overgrown and clustered in dizzying rows on either side of the trail. Caden focuses instead on the backs of Arthur's high hiking boots, the green, square tab on the heel. He imagines how they would look from space, two antlike figures shuffling sideways, lost in a blanket of green.

Arthur holds out a branch dotted with red berries, carefully passing it back so it doesn't slap Caden in the face. The butt of the gun jumps against Caden's thighs, the barrel tickles his shoulder blades. He has to admit, it feels singularly badass to be traipsing through the woods with a gun on his back, even if it is a puny rifle, and even if they are just out to shoot a couple of poor, defenseless bunnies.

"You can call your mother when we get back to the lodge," Arthur says suddenly, following the trail down a gentle dip.

Caden jogs to keep up, the momentum carrying him nearly onto his father's heels. "There's a phone that works in the kitchen."

Caden wishes he had pockets. He doesn't know what to do with his hands. He grips the leather strap that cuts diagonally across his chest. "Okay," he says. He almost says, "Thanks."

He swallows hard. He's been gone three nights. He imagines Carly hanging up posters, or organizing some kind of search party through her friends at the Community Center. One thing about living on an island is there's only so much you can do, only so many places to look. Like last winter, when one of Carly's band mates, Ted, lost his dog, a chubby black Lab only a few years old. They'd made signs and announcements on the local radio station, started Facebook groups, even hired a dog psychic. Weeks, then months passed, and people started to guess that the dog had "gone wild." He was living deep in the woods; he thought he was a deer. He wouldn't recognize his owner if he saw him.

The story kept spirits up, but Caden knew it was unlikely. There were woods on the island, but it was still an island. Eventually, the dog would run back to the road, or the ocean. If he didn't show up, it probably meant he'd been hit by a car, or, as it turned out, fallen through the cracks of a half-frozen pond. His body was found in the spring.

Everything turns up on an island. Would Carly keep looking until the end?

"There." Arthur stops suddenly, pointing across an open field. "See that? Just beyond the blueberries." Caden follows his father's arm to a low patch of wild berry plants. Half-hidden by a snarl of low branches, a pudgy brown cottontail stares off into the distance.

"He knows we're here," Arthur whispers. "Be very still."

Caden nods, and they stand in silence for a long moment, watching the rabbit watching them. It's turned in slight profile and one of its dark, round eyes glistens, unblinking, almost calm. Arthur nudges Caden's elbow and Caden realizes he's supposed to take the first shot.

He fumbles awkwardly with the gun on his back, holding the stock away from his body to keep it steady and quiet. His hands are trembling and he hopes Arthur doesn't notice. He holds the gun up with two hands, like he's seen it done on TV. Arthur reaches around his shoulders and steadies the butt above his collarbone. "There," he whispers. "You'll need the leverage."

Caden levels the barrel and peers with one eye through the sight at the very tip. There's a subtle movement in the rabbit's ears, a perking back, and Caden pulls the trigger.

The shot sounds like it was born inside him, and at the same time far away, like an echo. His palms are wet and his pulse drones in his ears.

"Not bad." Arthur claps him on the back. Caden trips forward, steadying himself against a tree as Arthur stalks into the field. He holds the fallen rabbit by the tail and waves it for Caden's approval.

Caden wants to look away, but he forces himself to keep his eyes on the bunny as Arthur shoves it gracelessly into a brown burlap sack. Once it's out of sight, a shapeless lump in the bottom of the bag, Caden takes a breath.

\* \* \*

"Isn't there anything you'd like to ask me?"

It's after noon and the sun is high. The morning's catch has been handed off to Russell, who was charged with cleaning and butchering the rabbit meat for dinner. Caden's first shot had been his only kill. *Beginner's luck,* Arthur had said, but there was pride in his voice. Arthur easily knocked off three or four on their way back to the barn, just enough, he'd said, for a stew.

"Like what?" Caden asks. The back porch is covered and the air is still cool. Dry goose bumps pop up around his elbows.

Arthur pushes himself out of his chair—he insisted they take the two rockers by the railing, where the view of the mountain is clearest—and walks toward the outdoor bar. As far as Caden can tell the porch is the most modern part of the house, with a built-in electric grill on one wall and a stainless steel mini-fridge below. Attached to the fridge is a temperature-controlled wine cooler, which Arthur now opens and kneels beside. "Do you prefer white or red?"

"Neither," Caden replies. What he prefers is not drinking at all. He'll smoke a little weed when it's offered, but he's never gotten into the beer-guzzling or shot-racing that has all but dominated most weekends of his high school career. Maybe it was because he grew up with Ramona, who made drinking look more like a medical condition, and less like something you'd do for a good time.

Arthur reappears at his elbow with a deep, full globe of red wine. "Try it," he says. "It's from a vineyard in the south of France. I think you'll like it."

Caden plants his feet firmly on the porch and takes the glass in his hand. For a moment, he thinks of Sophie. He wonders if she's ever been here, sitting in the chair that he sits in now, sipping fancy French wine and enjoying the view. "Thanks," he says, and takes a small sip. The wine is much thicker than he'd expected, and less bitter, too. It tastes like nothing he's ever had before. He wouldn't even call it a taste. More of a texture, like liquid felt on his tongue. He swallows and feels it warming his insides, all the way down to the hollow of his stomach.

"What do you think?" Arthur asks, swirling the wine to the edges of his glass. He holds it at an angle and watches the liquid pool on one side, as deep crimson veins trail slowly down the other.

"I don't know." Caden shrugs. He can't bring himself to admit that he likes it, that he likes anything about what is happening here. The "cottage," the hunting, the father he's seen only in his dreams for over a decade, now sitting in a rocking chair beside him. "Tastes like wine, I guess."

Caden takes another sip, this one smoother and silkier than the first, and leans back in the rocker. The glass is thin and delicate and feels like a challenge in his hands, like it's daring him to crush it. He sets it down carefully on the low wooden table between them.

Arthur clears his throat. "I guess I figured there would be things you'd want to talk about," he says, staring out at the tops of the red spruce pines that blanket the mountain far into the distance. "I'd hoped you would see this as an opportunity to get to know me."

Caden laughs. "Seriously?"

Arthur looks at him sideways. "Yes, seriously."

Caden shakes his head. "You really are, like, pretty oblivious, aren't you?"

Arthur clears his throat again.

"Do you honestly think I don't know you?" Caden asks. His voice is quiet, but it feels stronger than it has in a while, like it's coming from a part of him that's been underwater, or high on a shelf, impossible to reach.

"I don't know," Arthur stutters. "I just thought—"

"I know you," Caden interrupts. "I know you used to think you were somebody you weren't. You thought you'd come live on the island and marry my mom and just be a regular guy. But you couldn't. The money, the cars, the 'cottages' . . . how could you give it all up? Right?"

Arthur takes another sip and rocks gently, the uneven floorboards creaking beneath his shifting weight.

"I'd say that's pretty much all I need to know." Caden takes another hearty sip of the wine. He's starting to like the way it's making him feel, the richness on his tongue.

"What about you?" Arthur asks. "Is there anything I should know about you?"

Caden leans forward on his knees and twists his fingers together at the knuckles. His pulse is racing suddenly, like he's being chased, and he can't tell if it's from the wine or the conversation. "Anything you should know?" he repeats. There's a tickle in his throat and he coughs.

He wants to say: *Everything.* He wants to say: *You should know everything, because I'm your son. You should know everything about Carly, your daughter, and my mother, Ramona, your wife. You should know what every day has been like since you left.*

*Every time Mom passed out on the porch because she couldn't figure out the latch on the screen door, you should know about that. Every time I cleaned her puke from the floorboards in the bathroom, even after she thought she'd gotten it all. Every night I stayed late at the library, not just because she forgot to pick me up but because I didn't want to go home. The library was quiet and clean and people could take care of themselves. Home was like preschool, except without kids, or games, or snacks. Home sucked. And so do you, for leaving.*

Instead, he says: "Nothing comes to mind."

Arthur doesn't move. Caden pulls lightly at the roots of his hair. He suddenly feels like screaming.

"What about friends?" Arthur asks. His voice is detached, like the questions have been preprogrammed. It reminds Caden of the therapist he had to see in eighth grade. One of his teachers decided that the reason Caden never spoke in class and rarely did his homework was because of "unresolved issues at home." Instead of recess once a week, he was forced to sit in the Resource Room with Dr. Frankel. Dr. Frankel asked questions that were supposed to be deep and powerful, questions like *"Do you ever feel like you're totally alone?"* But she would ask them quickly, automatically, as if she were a disgruntled waitress at some crappy diner, taking her hundredth order for french fries that day. Caden always felt like he was being tricked. He tried not to say anything at all.

"Yeah, I have some friends," Caden says. He has a feeling his friends aren't exactly the caliber of people that Arthur expects. Not that he cares what Arthur expects. He takes another sip of wine.

"And girls?" Arthur asks. He stares at the pointed tops of the pine trees, and Caden realizes that this is new for him, too. He's not detaching on purpose, he just doesn't know any better. For all of the years that Caden hasn't had a father, Arthur hasn't been one. He's making it up as he goes.

Caden swallows hard. There's a burning inside him, a fire that he's feeding with every hot, wine-soaked breath. "Nobody special." He tries to sound light, inconsequential. But he knows the truth when he hears it, and he has a feeling that Arthur does, too. For some reason, it feels almost like a relief, talking this way. Even if he doesn't say much, it feels good to be asked, by someone who almost, maybe, cares.

Arthur rocks slowly back and forth, the round leather toes of loafers lifting up from the floorboards and settling back down.

"I know you think I left because I gave up," he says quietly. "That I wanted a different life."

"Pretty much," Caden quips.

"And part of that's true. I did give up."

Caden sits back in his chair and crosses his arms over his chest, preparing himself for the speech. The speech about why the island isn't for everyone, how his father was young, it wasn't the life that he wanted. The speech he's imagined and played in his head over and over for the past twelve years.

"And I did want a different life," Arthur says. "But that's not why I left."

"Okay." Caden sighs heavily. He's trapped, and he knows it. Let him say what he needs to say. "Whatever."

"I left for one reason. I tried to ignore it as long as I could. I tried to make it work with your mother, despite knowing it never would. I tried for years, because I loved my life. I loved the island. I tried because of you."

"What are you talking about?"

Arthur rests his glass on the table and sits up straight in his chair. "There's a reason why Carly isn't here with you. Why I took you, but left her behind."

"Didn't think she'd be much of a hunter?" Caden jokes.

Arthur slowly shakes his head. "I didn't take her, because she's not mine to take."

"What's that supposed to mean?" Caden furrows his brow. "She's not yours, but I am? Is there some twisted, rich-person law about kidnapping rights to firstborn sons?"

"No," Arthur says. "You're mine, as in I am your father. Your biological father."

Caden turns to look at Arthur. "What do you mean?"

"After you were born, we knew things weren't right. Between your mother and me, I mean. We'd always known it, always known we were playing at something that wasn't real, but all of a sudden we were a family. And we just fell apart." Arthur's voice is quiet and Caden leans closer to listen. "Your mother . . . strayed."

"She what?" Caden almost laughs. She *strayed*? Was she a cat?

"She slept with somebody else. Carly is not my daughter. Do you understand what I'm saying?"

Caden looks out at the peak, the long ridge beyond it. He sees Carly's face in the sky. His sister. The only one who cares anything about keeping the family together, whatever family they have left, isn't really his family at all. Not fully. Not for real.

"Did you know right away?" he asks. For some reason it's the only question he can find. *How did it work? Was there a test?*

"Yes," Arthur answers. "I knew the whole time Ramona was pregnant."

"So why didn't you leave earlier?" Caden asks. He thinks back to the dragon in the woods, the birthday presents, the robots. He is fourteen months older than Carly. His father left when he was four. "Why did you stick around so long?"

"I wanted to believe that we could fix it," he says. "I thought that I could just pretend things were working, pretend we were a real family. But we weren't. I think your mother couldn't forgive herself."

Arthur's voice falls off and they sit together in the quiet. A hawk cuts across the horizon.

"It doesn't excuse what I did," Arthur says abruptly. "I'm not asking you to forgive me for not being a part of your life. I've just always wondered if you knew the truth. And I thought you might like to. For whatever it's worth."

There's a rustling in the trees, a quick, rolling breeze, and Caden feels like he could float away on it, like he's not really there. His body feels like a lie, a hologram, patched together from memories that aren't really his. After a few moments he pushes himself out of the chair. His fingers feel light and tingly, and there's a dull buzzing at his temples. The wine. "I'm gonna lie down," he says. He feels Arthur turn to watch him leave. The screen door slams abruptly behind him.

The kitchen is quiet except for the gentle gurgle of a pot on the big antique stove. It smells like fresh herbs and tomatoes. Hanging on the wall is a rotary phone, the old-fashioned kind that takes forever to dial. Caden walks past it without a second look.

# ZAN

"I HAVE BAD NEWS, AND I HAVE MORE BAD news."

Nick and Zan are huddled around the hood of Nick's car. Zan rubs the tops of her shoulders, bruised and sore from sleeping on the hard tile floor in the cramped room behind the convenience shop. The old woman—her name is Octavia, but she insisted they call her Miss Tavi—set them up with scratchy blankets and some cushions from the tattered couch, turning down the volume on a small black-and-white TV, propped high on a stack of cardboard boxes.

Miss Tavi had tried to convince them she needed to tidy up, and picked up a broom from the corner. But Nick tucked the broom away, warming her a cup of Lipton's tea and insisting she lie down and rest. Sometime in the middle of the night, Zan woke to the sound of running water, and saw, through the windowed door, Miss Tavi mopping the linoleum floor. She wondered if she should keep the old woman company, but Miss Tavi looked strangely at peace as she worked.

As Zan dozed back to sleep, Nick tossed and settled in, one arm resting softly against her back. She thought about moving, but she didn't want to wake him. And it felt nice to sleep so close to somebody again.

When they woke it was nearly dawn, and Miss Tavi's son had returned.

Over a quick breakfast of weak coffee and Peanut M&Ms, the man introduced himself as Dwayne Robert. Zan wasn't sure if *Robert* was his last name, or if he always went by two first names, and so she did her best to avoid addressing him directly. Which wasn't difficult. Aside from asking a few questions about the trouble with Nick's car, Dwayne Robert had very little to say, and soon excused himself to get to work in the garage.

Now he looks at them, his forehead glistening with perspiration, a pained grimace twisting his face. He wipes his hands on the dirty rag hanging from his back pocket and slams the hood shut. "Your water pump is shot," he says, leaning against the driver's side door.

"I know that," Nick says. "What's the other bad news?"

"The other bad news," Dwayne Robert says slowly, with what Zan suspects is the tiniest bit of satisfaction twinkling in his black, almond-shaped eyes, "is that everything else is shot, too."

Nick crosses his arms over his chest. He seems to be trying to stand taller. Zan could tell when she'd suggested they wait for somebody to look at the car, somebody other than Nick, that he hadn't quite warmed to the idea of a second opinion. "What do you mean, everything else?"

Dwayne Robert chuckles. "I mean everything, man," he drawls, taking a long sip of his coffee. His accent is less pronounced than his mother's, but it's clear he was born somewhere else. "It's a miracle this car got you anywhere. Where you say you come from again?"

"Martha's Vineyard," Zan offers. Dwayne Robert whistles through his teeth, and Nick gives her a sideways look. Zan wishes she'd kept her mouth shut.

"Well, you have somebody looking out for you, to get you so far," he says, shaking his head. "I can take it apart if you want, but, you know." Dwayne Robert trails off, glancing wistfully out through the open garage door. "Maybe we don't have that kind of time."

Nick tugs at the ends of his short blond hair. There's something about seeing him—usually unflappably calm and reserved—now so visibly concerned, that hits Zan, the weight of worry quickly settling into her bones. For all she knows, they could be stuck on the mainland for good. Forget about Vanessa. How will they ever get home?

Zan takes a few steps toward the door, grateful for a cool breeze that has picked up, turning the intense midmorning heat almost bearable. She closes her eyes and tries to remember the way she felt yesterday, when it had all been an adventure, a game, and Leo had seemed close by. Now, she can't find the fun—or Leo—anywhere. She thinks about what Dwayne Robert said. If it was true, and Leo had been looking out for them, what does it mean that they've ended up here?

Maybe this is what she deserves. Maybe Leo hadn't been watching them, guiding them, at all. Maybe, instead, she's being punished for wasting her time, Nick's time, hot on the trail of something that has nothing to do with her. Who said Leo wasn't entitled to secrets? Does she really have the right to know absolutely everything about him?

As if through a fog, she hears low voices, Nick and Dwayne Robert talking in the shop. Suddenly, she's crying. She hasn't cried once since the predictions started coming in. It seemed too abstract, and far away. And then, with the announcement, when it started to get closer and feel more real, she was already too lost in Leo's mystery to fully appreciate what it all might mean.

Is this really how it works? The end of everything, and they're stuck, miles away from home, without a car or a plan? She hasn't even called her parents. And Joni, her sister. What about Joni? It's been almost seven years since they've spoken, and even longer since Joni has been home. Could the world really end without her ever seeing her sister again? All of a sudden, finding Vanessa, unraveling Leo's truth, whatever it was, doesn't seem so important.

Nick sits down on the hard concrete beside her. Zan hurries to wipe the fresh tears from the corners of her eyes. She can feel Nick averting his eyes, giving her space and time to clean herself up. "Are you okay?" he asks softly.

Zan nods and sniffles. "Yeah." She smiles. "Just, you know, taking it all in, I guess."

She feels Nick's arm hovering somewhere in the neighborhood of her shoulder, before his hand settles onto the top of her back. She feels his hesitation, but also his warmth, his relentless need, like an involuntary twitch, to make everything all right. She can't believe how long it's been since she's sat this way with somebody, not talking but together, understanding. It makes sense, she thinks. Leo chose both of them to be in his life for a reason. They are connected, and Zan suddenly remembers what it's like to have a friend.

She lets her head fall on Nick's shoulder, feels him tense and then soften.

"He says he'll give us a ride," Nick says eventually. "Wherever we want. He thinks there might still be buses running, out of Chinatown. We could go check."

Zan stares at the lonely gas pumps, the deserted highway stretching endlessly before them. "What do you think we should do?" she asks. She knows what he'll say. She can't blame him. It was crazy, what they did, leaving home at a time like this. Who wouldn't want to go back? Still, she's relieved not to have to make the decision herself.

"Honestly?" Nick sighs. "I think we should keep looking."

Zan sits up. "Really?"

Nick nods. "We've come this far," he says. "And, I don't know . . . I know it sounds crazy, but isn't this exactly the kind of thing that Leo would have loved? Running around on some wild adventure, not turning back, not giving up, no matter what happens?"

Zan smiles. She feels the tears prickling behind her eyes again, but they are new tears, tears of relief. Relief, not just that they can keep going, that there's still a chance they might find what they're looking for, but also relief that she was right:

Nick isn't just her friend. He's the one person in the world who knew Leo almost as well as she did.

* * *

Dwayne Robert pulls his car around front, a restored old station wagon that could comfortably fit a family of ten and smells vaguely of ripe fruit and incense.

Nick stands near the curb, a pile of blankets and a cooler at his feet.

"What's all this?" Zan asks as he pulls open the creaky back door.

"Just some stuff my dad keeps around, for camping and stuff, or when we miss the last boat and have to sleep in the car." Nick shrugs. "Thought it might come in handy."

Zan peers at him, holding back a smile. Of course he'd be prepared. She imagines Nick and his dad roasting marshmallows at a campsite in one of the state parks on the Cape, or curling up with scratchy blankets in different parts of the clunker car. She knew Nick spent every hour that he wasn't in school (and many hours when he should have been) on his dad's boat, but she'd never really understood how much time they must have spent together. She can't imagine being that way with Daniel or Miranda, who prize independence above all else. She knows it's why Miranda never really warmed to Leo. She hated that her daughter was so wrapped up in another person, especially when that person was a boy.

At the thought of her parents, Zan's heart sinks. It's been over twenty-four hours. She knows she should get to a real phone and call. But the only thing worse than leaving for so long, without letting them know where she is, would be the horrifically strained and awkward conversation they'd have to have when they finally spoke. There wouldn't be screaming, or crying, Zan knows. There would be shame, and disappointment, and quiet.

Lots of quiet.

After loading them up with bags of pretzels and bottled water, Miss Tavi waves goodbye from outside the garage. Zan feels a surprising lump in her throat as she waves back. The asteroid, the rocket, the entire Northern Hemisphere, it had all been too much to make her feel much of anything. But Miss Tavi is different. She isn't a continent. She isn't even an island. She's just a frightened old lady who cleans to stay calm. Zan watches her shrink beneath the high neon sign and hopes with everything she has that somehow, Miss Tavi will be all right.

The receipt with Vanessa's address flutters on the long bench seat between Zan and Dwayne Robert. Zan pins it down with the palm of her hand. Dwayne promised he knew the way, but Zan is suddenly aware that they are, technically, being held hostage in a weird-smelling car with a strange man, driving empty streets on a day when the whole world has better things to do than come to their rescue.

Things like pray, apparently. As soon as they turn off the commercial strip of highway and into the clustered streets of two-family homes, they are forced to stop behind what appears to be a parading church sermon. The muffled voice of a pastor is shouting through a bullhorn, and Zan can barely make out the shape of a van far ahead, rolling through the streets, a Sunday service-on-wheels.

Dwayne throws the car into reverse and ducks down a side street as the crowd continues to file in behind them. They are people of all ages and races, some holding their hands to the sky, their eyes closed as they shuffle slowly forward. Others seem to be there just for the spectacle; a few younger kids are laughing and joking around. Zan thinks of the handful of times she's been inside a temple—her mother's family was Jewish and there were a few times when Miranda had dragged Joni and Zan to the Hebrew Center on the island—how the congregation always seemed to be divided between those who truly *believed*, and those who, like her, were there for the free doughnuts. She's surprised to find that it doesn't seem to be any different now. As the pastor's voice fades out behind them, she realizes she hasn't heard a single thing that he's said.

Dwayne Robert shakes his head thoughtfully. "I just can't believe it," he says. "You know? First, they say this thing is coming, and now there's a rocket, going to blow it up. What are we supposed to believe? How are we supposed to know the truth?"

Nick clears his throat in the backseat. The questions are clearly rhetorical and Zan feels a sense of panic that Nick is going to try to answer them anyway. "What about your friend?" she asks, quickly changing the subject. "Your mother said you were picking somebody up, last night."

Dwayne Robert purses his lips and Zan fears she may have stumbled onto a sensitive subject. "I try everything with that girl, man," he says. "I told her come back with me, the kids, too, you know? I love those boys like my own. But she says they need to be with their daddy now. They going to be a family now, because who knows what could happen."

His voice gets soft and sad and he's still shaking his head, as if it's all too much to make sense of at once. "He never do nothing for them, but now, he's family." Dwayne Robert blows air through his teeth.

"I'm sorry," Zan says, because she can't imagine saying anything else.

Dwayne Robert shrugs. "You learn about people, you know?" He smiles, halfheartedly. "What about you two? Your families know where you are?"

Zan catches Nick's eyes in the wide rearview mirror. "Sort of," he says.

Dwayne lifts an eyebrow, not convinced. "This some kind of Romeo and Juliet thing?" he asks. "You running away or something?"

Zan shifts uncomfortably in her seat. "No," she says quickly. It feels urgently important to clarify that she and Nick are not a couple. "No, we're just, we're not . . ."

"We're looking for someone." Nick saves her. "She lives here, at this address."

Dwayne Robert turns onto a smaller side street, lined with nearly identical two-family houses. He takes the receipt from Zan and holds it up to a brown, vinyl-sided house with a small, neglected garden out front. "Well," he says. "I hope you find her. Before it's too late."

Zan closes the heavy station wagon door as Nick unpacks the back. Dwayne Robert waves as he pulls slowly away, and Nick crosses the street first, pulling open a low, iron gate. They start up the shallow stoop to a small, covered porch. Between the two doors is an intercom, and Nick scans the faded yellow tabs. "V. Kent. You think that's her?"

Zan swallows hard. She hears the last thing Dwayne Robert said to them: *Before it's too late,* and she feels a new sense of purpose. It's simple, really. They might not have much time. And no matter what they're going to find out, no matter what it means, or doesn't mean, they have to do it now or they may never get the chance.

She closes her eyes and waits. This time, he's there. Leo, on the trail to the beach, his towel dragging behind him. She searches his face, his eyes, bright blue and convincing. Whatever it is, he wants her to know. He's brought them here for a reason.

Zan pushes the button with her thumb. The bell, sharp and clear, cuts into the quiet.

# CADEN

ARTHUR LOOKS RIDICULOUS IN AN APRON.

Caden stands in the doorway to the lodge kitchen, looking out through the open porch doors. The sky is lit up over the mountain, orange and spooky gray. He's groggy from his nap and it takes him a minute to decide if the sun should be coming or going.

"What are you doing?" he mutters sleepily, stretching his neck. He's still not used to so many pillows.

Arthur hovers near the stove, moving quickly back and forth between a bubbling pot on a burner and the yellowing pages of a cookbook, propped open on top of a wooden butcher's block. "What does it look like I'm doing?" he asks, distracted by a frenzied search for some type of utensil.

"It looks like you're wearing an apron," Caden replies. The apron is dirty white and tied with a delicate lace string around Arthur's waist.

"It was all I could find." Arthur stirs the pot with a chipped wooden spoon. "It probably belonged to one of my great-aunts. Must be ancient."

From the other side of the counter a timer beeps and Arthur's eyes go wide. He rushes to the oven and pulls the door open, as a cloud of bitter smoke engulfs his upper half. "God damn it!" Arthur panics, scanning the nearby surfaces for a potholder or cloth. He settles for the sleeve of his button-down shirt. "Shit. Ouch. Shit!" He slides out a steaming tray of singed dinner rolls and all but throws it on the table. A few of the blackened rolls tumble off the edge and skid like hockey pucks across the floor to Caden's feet.

"Yum," Caden says, a short laugh escaping before he can help it.

Arthur runs the faucet and sticks his hand beneath it. After a brief interlude of incoherent mumbling, he turns back to the pot on the stove. "Russell left."

"Russell?" Caden asks, before remembering the disgruntled butler-type who served him breakfast in the den. "Where did he go?"

Arthur shrugs. "He says he met a lady at the Info Center near the peak. They're going camping."

Caden smirks. "Go, Russell."

Arthur shakes his head in exasperated silence. A wet steam rises from the pot and the thick smell of stock and sautéed vegetables fills the air. Caden's stomach grumbles. He's hungrier than he thought.

"What? You expected him to keep sulking around here, baking you muffins and wiping your ass, when the world is about to explode?" The words are out of him, sharp and fast, but he can hear a shift in his voice. It's teasing, and light, like he's back on the docks, messing with one of his friends.

"I wipe my own ass, thank you," Arthur says with a sly grin.

He clinks the spoon against the side of the pot and flips off the burner. "Hand me a few of those bowls?"

Caden spies a few stacks of ceramic dishware on a high open shelf. He moves carefully around his father, suddenly aware of how close they are standing. Arthur serves up two hearty portions of stew and sets them on the counter. "I thought we'd eat in the dining room."

The dining room table is an imposing slab of mahogany, comically enormous. Caden finds it already set for two, with a white tablecloth and red gingham napkins, goblets for wine and water, antique silverware, and a—now unnecessary—woven basket for bread. He pulls out a chair and feels a twinge between his lower ribs. He can't remember the last time he ate dinner at an actual table, let alone one that was so carefully set.

Arthur appears without his apron and places the bowls on the table. Caden peers into the brownish slosh. It looks like the result of some kind of industrial sewage overflow, but he has to admit, it doesn't smell half bad.

Outside, the wind has picked up and wheezes through the nearby pines, knocking the wooden shutters against the side of the house. Caden's spoon clinks heavily in his bowl. The stew is surprisingly delicious, rich and savory with tender chunks of braised rabbit meat.

"What do you think?" Arthur asks between bites.

Caden feels a trickle of broth running down his chin, and is ready to wipe it away with his sleeve when he remembers the napkin. "It's okay," he says. "I've never had rabbit before."

Arthur smiles. They continue eating in silence. There's something almost peaceful about eating this way, Caden thinks, especially when what you're eating was once, and so very recently, witlessly bounding across an open field. He remembers, in a quick flash, the way the rabbit froze beneath the blueberry bush, almost as if he knew what was coming, and accepted it. There was no panic or frenzied scamper. Death was a certainty, and there was no use trying to pretend otherwise.

In an unguarded moment, he lets his mind wander. How long can he keep this up? Pretending not to care that his life, the lives of everyone he knows and doesn't know, hang on the fate of a single event. Something he is powerless to control. What will he be like, in those final minutes, should it come to that? Calm, like the rabbit, or a total, inconsolable mess?

Arthur clears his throat, resting his spoon against the side of his bowl. "I feel uncomfortable about what I said," he says. "What I told you, about your sister."

Caden swallows and reaches for his wine. There was a brief, confused moment when he woke up from his nap. Had it all been a dream? But, no. Carly is his half sister. Half of her came from somebody else. Half of her has nothing to do with him.

"Does she know?" Caden asks, though he's already sure of the answer. Every Christmas, over a special breakfast of banana pancakes and vegan sausage, Carly abruptly announced what she'd bought that year, before Caden or Ramona had even considered unwrapping their gifts. When she got her first period, she'd complained to Caden about cramps and tampons as they waited on the road for the bus. Carly doesn't believe in secrets.

"I hope not," Arthur says.

Caden looks up from his stew. "Why's that?"

Arthur tilts his bowl and scrapes around the corners with his spoon. "I'm an easy target." He shrugs. "Why add another villain to the mix?"

Caden considers this. Carly will always be his sister, no matter what. But Ramona. It was hardly the first time she'd lied, and he'd spent most of his life wishing she were somebody else, somebody capable and strong. But this felt like a different breed of betrayal. Who knows how Caden would have felt about Arthur all these years, if he'd known the truth? Maybe not much would have changed. But she hadn't allowed him to decide for himself. She'd wanted him to be by her side, an ally in the invisible war against the bad guy who'd left them alone.

It shouldn't have been up to her.

Caden takes a long sip of wine. He feels Arthur's eyes on him. He wishes he could ask what Arthur thinks about how his son turned out. Is he proud? Surprised? Had he been hoping for somebody more like him? Does he regret all the time that he's missed?

A cascade of ringing bells echoes throughout the lodge. Arthur looks up with an almost mischievous gleam in his green eyes. "There she is," he says, wiping at the corners of his mouth with his napkin and folding it carefully on the table.

Caden watches as his father stands. "Who?"

Arthur lays a hand on Caden's shoulder as he passes. "Wait here," he says.

Arthur leaves him through the wide double doors. Caden feels a tingling in the spot on his shoulder where his father's hand had been. It was a small gesture, but to Caden, it felt full of meaning. Full of all of the hundreds of thousands of times a hand might have rested there before, in a different life, where they'd been a real family, or he'd at least known the truth about what family he had left.

# SIENNA

"IT LOOKS EXACTLY THE SAME."

Sienna and Owen stand at the bottom of her driveway, hidden behind the thick trunk of an oak tree. Their shadows fall long on the grass beside them. They'd packed a picnic at Owen's house and spent the day on a quiet section of the beach, talking until the sun started to set. Sienna couldn't believe how late it had gotten, so fast.

Now, she looks up at her house and sees it, for a moment, as it was when she was little. Mom's blue hydrangea bushes crowding the deck, the ones she lovingly tended to like extra, flowering children.

"Almost," Sienna says sadly. There's only one bush left out front, the blossoms now fading gray.

"So." Owen puts a hand on her head. "Jeremy said he'll pick us up around nine. Want to meet at the bus stop?"

Sienna swallows. This morning, when they'd woken up on the docks, cozy and cuddled in the blankets Owen had brought, everything had seemed so simple. He wanted to work on the boat with his friends, and he wanted her to be there, too. She felt her heart swelling inside her. She didn't care what they did, as long as they did it together.

But now, standing in front of her house, she doesn't know how it's possible. Dad will never allow it, and even if he did, is it really what she wants? There's a part of her that feels like she should stay home, even if it means pretending. A part of her that thinks Dad deserves his Happy Family, for once.

"Sienna," Owen says, looking deep into her eyes. "I know it's asking a lot. But think about it. This is so much bigger than anything that's ever happened before. It's being a part of something huge. Something that might save us."

She feels the weight of his hands on her shoulders, the intensity in his brown eyes. She can't possibly let him down.

"See you at the bus stop," she says, and stretches to give him a kiss.

She avoids the gravel driveway and instead pads softly over the grass, hoping to make it back to her room unseen. But something catches her eye in the living room—the quick shifting of horizontal blinds. Her stomach twists into a knot.

Dad is standing just inside the door when she opens it. "Where were you?" he asks. His eyes are red-rimmed and his hair is choppy and disheveled.

Sienna takes a shaky breath. "Dad," she starts.

"I asked you a question, Sienna," he says, his voice clipped and strange. There's a stiffness in his posture, like it's taking a lot of extra effort to stand upright.

"I . . . I lost track of time. I went into town last night with some friends," she says. "You were already asleep. I didn't want to wake you up."

Dad stares at her as if he's having trouble remembering who she is. "I was asleep because it was late," he says flatly. "You've been gone all day. You didn't think I would worry?"

Sienna crosses her arms over her waist. "I'm sorry," she says. "I figured you'd be busy."

"Who was that?" he asks, glancing out the window.

Sienna feels a quick swarm of butterflies in her stomach. It feels, for a moment, like she's watching herself from somewhere else. Or watching a movie about a girl and her dad, arguing in the foyer. Before she'd gone into the House, Sienna had been so lost in herself, so tangled up in her own anxieties, that she hadn't had time to do anything normal, like sneak out, or get caught. However much of her wishes they could just put this all past them, there's a part of her that's almost enjoying it.

"His name is Owen," she says. "We used to play together on the beach. He lives a few streets over. Remember?"

Dad looks up at the ceiling, and Sienna thinks for a moment that he's really trying, trying to see Owen's face. But then he runs a hand through his hair. He walks to the steps and sits with his back against the white paneled wall. "Goose, I know this place feels safe," he says. "That's what I love about it. It's part of the reason I brought us here."

"Then what does it matter if I go out or not?" Sienna asks. There's anger in her belly, like fire, but she swallows it down. Her voice is tight and unfamiliar. "Do you really still have to treat me like some messed-up little kid?" She watches as the words land and Dad's face softens. "I'm better, Dad," she says gently. "I promise."

Dad looks blankly at her before reaching into his pocket. He pulls out her pillbox and holds it between them.

Sienna stares at it, hoping for a minute it might turn into something else.

"You missed two doses," he says. "Last night, and this morning. You didn't think I would check for that, either?"

Sienna swallows. She pulls her sweater tighter around her waist, as if she's been suddenly exposed. She wishes she could close her eyes and be somewhere else. "It's not a big deal," she insists. "They make me fall asleep. And I was planning on taking them as soon as I got home . . ."

"Goose, this isn't like you," Dad says. "I'm worried. You had plans with Denny. She spent the day waiting for you to come home, to pick flowers . . ."

Sienna's hands fly up to her forehead. She squeezes her temples like she's trying to keep her head in one place. *"Pick flowers?"* She laughs, harsh and low. "Are you even listening to yourself? How can you possibly think that's something I would actually want to do?"

"You're grounded, Sienna," Dad interrupts. He says it fast and sudden, like he's ripping off a bandage. The air between them buzzes, tender and raw.

Sienna stands frozen, her hands tangled in her still-damp hair. The scene she's been watching from outside of herself has suddenly taken an implausible turn. She's never been grounded in her life.

"Grounded?" she asks. "I've just spent six months locked up with doctors, getting tested and retested and talking about my feelings, and now, now that there's an *asteroid*, I'm grounded?"

"I'm sorry," Dad says. "I wish I didn't have to do it this way. I wish you'd *want* to be here, but—"

"Why would I want to be here?" she asks. "All you care about is Denny, and the wedding."

Dad sighs. "These next few days . . ." His voice breaks, and he clears his throat. "I think we should spend them together. As a family."

Dad locks his fingers together, twisting against his knuckles. Sienna feels a sharp tug around her heart. He's not asking for a lot. Part of her *wants to want* to be there, too. But she doesn't. She wants to be with Owen, where she can be herself, and not worry about her every move being measured, being held up to some imaginary standard of *Fine. Sane. Not Crazy.*

She swipes the pillbox from his hand and makes a show of emptying the morning's dosage into her palm. She gulps the pills down without water.

"Goose." Dad stands as she brushes past him on the steps.

"I'm going to my room," she calls back over her shoulder. "Isn't that the way this whole grounding-thing works?"

Sienna stomps up the stairs. She doesn't remember having many tantrums when she was little—she was usually too busy consoling everybody else. Now, as she reaches the step that creaks louder than the rest, she lays into it with extra oomph. It feels good, she thinks, to make noise.

# ZAN

Zan and Nick stand just inside the first set of doors, at the bottom of a crooked staircase. They squeeze through the hallway, between an overflowing pile of newspapers and magazines and a pair of rusted bicycles, pushed up against the scuffed white walls.

Nick catches Zan by the elbow. "Hey," he says. "You sure you want to do this?"

Zan wriggles her arm free and forces a smile. She's afraid if she stops moving, she'll change her mind. "Of course," she says. "It's why we came."

Harsh footsteps clatter across the landing above and a shadow hangs over the stairwell. Zan keeps climbing, steadying her nerves with long, deliberate breaths. Whatever she finds, she reminds herself, she'll know. And Leo wants her to know. The truth will set her free.

"Hey!" A girl stands at the top of the stairs, waiting to greet them. Her hair is dyed white-blond and fried into small, wiry curls. Her thin, boyish frame is swaddled in a dramatic red dress, the collar a scandalously low-cut V, exposing a flat section of bony rib cage between two nearly nonexistent breasts. On her feet, she wears shiny gold platform heels, which appear to be three sizes too big. "Come in! Sorry, the place is a total mess."

The girl stumbles a bit as she leads them back into the apartment. Zan and Nick share a look as she closes the door behind them. The apartment isn't so much a mess as it is a total and complete disaster, and probably in violation of a number of health and safety codes. They are standing in what seems to have been once used as a kitchen, but is now a glorified storage space, with clothes, shoes, hats and jackets, jewelry, books and DVDs—basically anything but food or cookware—strewn over every available surface.

"That's okay," Nick finally manages. "Are you . . . are you Vanessa?"

The girl totters unsteadily in her heels to the refrigerator. The shelves are completely bare, except for a large pitcher of something red with chunks of fruit floating inside. "I made sangria. Do you guys want some?" she asks, tossing a pile of sweaters from the counter to the floor. "I thought we had some cups here, somewhere . . ."

"No thanks," Zan interrupts. She's feeling impatient, and more than a little weirded out. Up close, she sees that the girl's eyebrows have been heavily drawn in liquid liner, over a layer of dark stubble. Her bright red lipstick is faded around the corners of her mouth, a blood-colored stain that looks permanent.

"We're looking for Vanessa," Nick says again, this time a little bit louder, as if maybe she hadn't heard him.

The girl shrugs and takes a giant gulp of sangria, straight from the pitcher. Pink drool oozes down her chin. "She's not here," she says through a mouthful of soggy fruit.

Zan feels a tingling in her hands and feet, a weight lifting. The idea of Leo having anything to do with this person was starting to make her feel sick. "So . . . you're not Vanessa?" she asks. It seems important to confirm.

"Nope." The girl shakes her head. "I'm Gretchen. We're roommates. Or, I guess, we were roommates. I'll probably never see her again. She took off last week. Are you sure you guys aren't hungry? There used to be trail mix in one of these cabinets . . ."

Gretchen begins frantically opening and closing cabinet doors. Zan takes a few steps closer to the door. She has a feeling if they don't make much noise they could leave without Gretchen even noticing, or remembering they were there.

"Did she say anything about where she was going?" Nick asks. Zan feels torn. She knows he's doing his job, doing his best to help her learn as much as she can while they're there. But all she wants to do is go home. There's no Vanessa. They tried. They tried, but it was too late.

Gretchen finally gives up the trail-mix hunt and collapses onto a pile of winter coats on the floor. "No," she huffs. "She didn't really talk to me very much. Nobody did. I think it's because I was always studying, you know?"

She looks to Nick as if she's waiting for an answer. He nods slowly. "Sure," he says. "Okay, well, thanks for . . ."

"I mean, I know that's what it is," Gretchen continues, waving her hand around in front of her face like she's swatting a pesky bug. "Even my mom used to tell me to get out more. She'd say, 'Gretchen, take a break. Live a little.'" Gretchen hiccups and gropes for the pitcher, bringing it back to her lips. "So that's what I'm doing. Better late than never, right?"

Zan fidgets behind her back for the doorknob, willing Nick to look her way, willing him to follow her outside. But she can see by the way that he's holding his head, the serious look in his eyes, that he's not going anywhere yet.

"That's right," Nick says, ever the gentleman. "What were you studying?"

"Molecular biology." Gretchen laughs spitefully. "I was getting my doctorate. Doctor of Philosophy. How ridiculous is that? I mean, who even cares? What's the point? What's the point of anything, you know?"

Zan's eyes wander to a framed photo, hung at a disheveled angle on the wall. It's a girl in a royal blue cap and gown, flanked by a sweet-looking, gray-haired couple. The girl has lifeless, mousy brown hair and wears big, unflattering glasses. Bright white tennis sneakers poke out from the bottom of the too-big gown.

"Is this you?" Zan asks, leaning in for a better look.

"Where?" Gretchen crawls on her hands and knees. "Oh. Yeah. A real bombshell, right?" She laughs drily. "I mean, the saddest part is I bought those shoes, special. My parents came all the way from Wisconsin, so I bought new sneakers. I wanted them to be clean."

Zan looks down at Gretchen on the floor. There's a tug around her heart and all of a sudden she feels like crying again. Where are Gretchen's parents now? Why didn't she just go home?

"Vanessa had the best shoes," Gretchen continues, speaking to nobody in particular. "These are hers!" She stretches out one leg and flops her ankle up and down, the sparkly heel knocking against the floor. "Most of this stuff is hers, actually. I figured she wouldn't mind if I tried some things on. She was always telling me to borrow whatever I wanted."

Zan looks to Nick. His eyebrows are lifted, and she almost expects to see his ears and nose twitch, like a dog after a scent. She glances behind him down a long hallway, a pile of skirts and dresses leading toward an open door.

"She was so *nice*," Gretchen continues. "And I was such a bitch! So she never did the dishes. So what? She always invited me places and I never went. Not once. And now she's gone."

"Is that her room?" Zan asks, stepping over a tower of textbooks on the kitchen floor.

Gretchen nods, and Nick follows Zan down the hall. "Take whatever you want," Gretchen shouts. "She won't be coming back. Why would she? She had tons of friends. I'm sure she's with them all, now. Someplace awesome."

Zan steps carefully between piles of long scarves and vintage handbags. The room has two giant windows and dusty sunlight cuts thick beams across the floor. A string of prayer flags hangs over one window, and the walls are covered in quirky drawings, hung in frames of different colors and sizes. An acoustic guitar pokes out of the closet, and the back of the closet door has been transformed into an artful display of chunky necklaces and long, dangling earrings, hung like constellations from shiny nails and hooks.

"Even her mess is cool." Gretchen sighs, her breath hot and wine-soaked on the back of Zan's neck. Zan steps deeper into the room, wishing Gretchen would disappear. Her stomach feels suddenly empty; a dull throbbing starts at the base of her skull.

She hears Nick's heavy footsteps behind her. She doesn't know why, but she wishes he'd disappear, too.

Dresses and skirts are tossed on the bedspread, a colorful patchwork quilt. They are all flowy and long, the kind that Zan always wishes she had the body to pull off. Beside the bed is a pile of books, the spines frayed and tattered. She looks closer to find that they are mostly books of poetry.

The Beats. Bukowski. Brautigan.

All of Leo's favorites.

Zan perches gently on the edge of the bed. The room seems to spin and pull away from her, whipping around as she sits, silent and still, the eye of the storm. Everything about this room has Leo written all over it. Vanessa was just the kind of girl he would have loved.

"What's—" Nick starts to speak from the far corner of the room. Zan looks up to find him crouched over a scattered pile of photographs. Her heart thuds louder in her chest as she lifts herself up from the mattress.

Nick rises quickly to his feet. He has something in his hands. "What is it?" Zan asks.

He looks like he's seen a ghost. His lips are pale as he glares at the floor.

"Let me see," Zan says quietly, holding out her hand.

Nick doesn't move.

"Nick."

Slowly, he unfolds his clenched fingers and hands her a photo, torn in half.

Even before her eyes have fully focused, she knows. She

recognizes the patch of pale sky over Leo's shoulder. The white creases around his eyes, from smiling and squinting at the sun.

It's the same photo she has framed beside her bed.

Only, she's been cut out. Most of her, anyway. All that remains is the tangle of her dark, wet hair, blown by a sudden gust across his forehead.

Before she knows how or why, Zan dashes across the hall to a tiny bathroom. The empty churning in her stomach burns through her esophagus, boiling up inside of her until she's spitting bile into the dirty sink.

Whoever Vanessa was, Leo wanted her to have his picture.

A picture of him, as he'd always wanted to be.

Happy. Carefree.

And alone.

# CADEN

TIME PASSES IN FRAGMENTS, SLOWED TO AN almost imperceptible pace. A few hours, in the world of Caden, used to mean next to nothing. The difference between one video game and the next. Or a party at one beach and a party at another.

Tonight, a few hours hold the universe. A cosmic shift. A forever change in whatever he thought he was starting to know. A mirror of disbelief.

Also: a prostitute.

Her name is Camille, and she stands at the foot of the bed, unwrapping one of what appear to be many silk scarves from around her bare shoulders. Beneath them she wears a cream-colored camisole, lacy and detailed around her neck and cleavage, and flowing black pants that swish around her bare feet when she moves. A collection of silver and turquoise bangles snakes up around her wrist and forearm, and as she turns, Caden notices markings on the back of her toned triceps. It's a tattoo of a tree branch, dark and spindly with pink and red blossoms that crawl up around her back.

Caden shifts on the bed, pressing the points of his shoulder blades against the shiny brass headboard. Camille catches his eye as she wraps the scarves around a bedpost. If it were physically possible to wink without winking, this is what she does.


*"Camille is a healer," Arthur said in the kitchen, after showing Camille to the den. "I've known her for years."*

*Caden felt something inside of him drop. Camille is a healer?*

*"What kind of healer?" he asked, piling the dirty dishes into the sink with a clatter.*

*Arthur stared at him, his gaze blank and unfaltering. "Sit down," he said quietly, nodding at a chair beside the small kitchen table.*

*"No thanks."*

*Caden turned off the faucet and shook his hands dry. He stared through the window at the inky night sky, the blue-black silhouette of the mountains framed like a photograph. His stomach turned and he wondered if it was the rabbit.*


"Do you like music?" Camille asks. She stands with her hands on her hips, her head held at an angle, and her long auburn hair falling loose over one shoulder.

Caden isn't sure if it's a general conversation piece, or if she is about to pull a Mary Poppins and find a musical instrument at the bottom of her floppy leather purse: a tiny flute, maybe, or a ukulele. It's crazy, he knows, but with the way this night is going, not much would surprise him.

"Yeah. I guess." Caden realizes too late that he's squeezing the stiff fabric of the floral bedspread between his fingers, clenched in stubborn fists at his sides. Arthur had told him which room to use, the one at the end of the hall. Caden tries not to imagine what else has gone on in this bed. "I like music." He feels like a foreign exchange student, off balance in a second language, helpless in a world of new customs.

Like the one where you give your son a prostitute.

Camille smiles and moves quickly around the room, with an easy familiarity. She opens a tall wooden hutch and presses a button on a concealed stereo system, adjusting the volume until soft, smooth jazz plays from somewhere in the area of Caden's left elbow. Small speakers, he discovers, have been installed behind the matching end tables. As far as secret love dens go, Arthur has spared no details, though he might have sprung for more comfortable bedding. Caden remembers the luxurious sheets in his room at Hart Haven. He wonders who was in charge of the decorating there.

*"What about Sophie?" Caden asked.*

*She was all Caden could think about. He'd seen her face more than a few times since they'd been gone, usually when he closed his eyes at night, but quickly found it was better to pretend they'd never met. In what world was it fair that his father would end up with someone like Sophie?*

*It wasn't the rabbit. Caden felt like he was going to be sick.*

*Arthur looked at him, long and hard, as if waiting for something to happen.* "Caden," *he said finally, his voice careful and measured.* "She's here for you."


"I'm here for you," Camille says now, perched on the other side of the mattress. Like Sophie, she is of indeterminate age, although in an entirely different way. Her body is slender and flawless, her porcelain skin glows, but there is something older, harsher, hidden in her eyes. She's probably near forty, Caden decides, though she could easily pass for much younger.

Caden clears his throat. "Okay."

Camille reaches her hand toward him on the bed. Caden watches as her fingers crawl nearer to his kneecap, his legs squeezed together with his feet planted solidly on the floor. He is still wearing his shoes.

Her hand is on his knee, light and fluttery, like a hummingbird. A woman's hand. A woman's fingers. He tries to feel aroused, or at least not totally somewhere else. She's not unattractive. She smells sweet and feminine. When she looks at him and smiles, her eyes get warmer.


*"I wanted to do this for you," Arthur said. He took a step forward and Caden wondered just how many times, in the history of fathers and sons, a version of this conversation had taken place. Maybe it was more common than he thought. Maybe it's what dads do. He wouldn't know, he realized with a sudden chill. He never had one.*

*"Camille is an old friend, and a wonderful person," Arthur continued. "She knows a lot about . . . many things. Yoga, Eastern*

*philosophy, religion, the healing arts. I think you'll find her very interesting to talk to."*

*Caden felt his eyes burning, his hands going cold. "Interesting to talk to?"*

"Don't be nervous," Camille says lightly, running her hand slowly up his leg.

"I'm not." Caden tries to smile but his lips are dry and he feels a sharp tingle where they've cracked. He wipes his mouth, hoping not to find it chapped or bleeding. She's a professional, he knows, but he imagines that even hookers have standards.

"Good," Camille says. "We could just talk for a while, if you like."

She moves her hand up to the zipper of his hooded sweatshirt. It's the one piece of his own clothing he brought with him to the lodge, gray and faded and still smelling faintly of the organic laundry detergent Carly uses at home. He tries to focus on the brush of Camille's fingers on his neck as she pulls the zipper down, but now he's thinking about his sister. There's a woman prepared to seduce him, prepared to do anything he wants her to do, and he's thinking about his sister.

"No," he says, too loud. "I mean, that's okay. We don't have to talk."

Camille tugs the zipper free and pushes the sweatshirt down from his shoulders. He feels her hands on his chest and wishes there was more to him. He feels small, like a child, like he's a little boy and she's . . .

Ramona. He sees Ramona as she was when he left for the

beach that night, passed out on the couch. It's Ramona's fault. If she hadn't cheated, none of this would have happened. Arthur would have stuck around. Everything would have been different. Caden would be different. Better. Somebody who knew what to do when a woman put her hand on his knee, his chest.

*Arthur glanced behind him at the kitchen door, swung open. He stood over Caden, the broad range of his shoulders dark and looming as the peaks of the mountain outside.*

*"Camille is a friend," he said softly. "If I've made a mistake bringing her here, I apologize. How you choose to spend your evening is entirely up to you. But she is here, and you will not treat her with anything but respect. Do you understand me?"*

*The hairs on the back of Caden's neck prickled and stood up.*

*"Do you understand me, Caden?"*

*Caden shrugged. "Yeah." He swallowed. "Sure. Whatever."*

*"Good." Arthur gripped Caden's shoulder in his palm, his fingers wide and strong, as he'd done in the dining room. Only this time, it didn't feel like something Caden wanted to remember.*

*Arthur pushed open the door, the light from the den shining, soft and yellow, from the far end of the darkened hall.*

*"Coming?"*

Caden closes his eyes. Not Ramona. It's Arthur. It's a test. His father is testing him. He wants to see what sort of man Caden has become. To know, for certain, if his son is worth saving.

Caden grabs Camille's wrists and holds them tight against

the bed. He feels full of something, he doesn't know what. His fingers are firm and twisting. He feels the faint tremor of her pulse.

"Caden."

His eyes still closed, he feels her struggle, her body tight and tense as she pulls her fingers free.

"Are you all right?" she asks.

Caden opens his eyes. Camille is staring at him, like she was expecting somebody else. There's something small and different in her eyes. A flickering uncertainty. A hint of fear.

"I'm sorry," he says quietly. "I'm really sorry."

Camille shifts beside him, lowering her feet to the floor. Her slender toes barely touch the carpet, hovering near the tops of his sneakers.

Like a toy on a spring, he bolts from the bed. He shuffles through the room and sprints down the hall, stumbling down the stairs. He tugs open the heavy front door, the cool mountain air washing over him.

He runs, like a spooked horse, frantic and wild, not toward, but away.

# SIENNA

"THERE IT IS," OWEN SHOUTS AND POINTS TO an opening between the trees. They have been hiking for so long that Sienna has cramps in the soles of her feet and wishes she'd thought to bring sneakers. In her hurry to sneak out of the house, she hadn't brought much, just a backpack full of T-shirts, a toothbrush (no toothpaste), and, for reasons she still can't explain, the miniature sewing kit Mom kept in the guest bathroom closet.

She had waited until after they'd left. It took a few hours and the promise of ice cream when they got back, but Dad ultimately convinced Ryan to go for a walk after dinner. With most kids, Sienna knew, not even extra dessert would have done the trick, but Dad was starting at somewhat of an advantage. Ryan loved walks, especially when they involved flashlights, the woods, and insects of any kind.

Sienna listened to the complicated negotiation through her bedroom door. She felt a twinge of guilt, thinking that maybe she should go with them. But she was already running late. She waited until she heard the screen door slap shut and Denny turning on the shower, the clanks and groaning of pipes in the wall, before grabbing her bag and hurrying out the front door.

At the end of the driveway, she heard footsteps. Of course, Sienna panicked—Ryan had forgotten something crucial, like his special pencil. But it was only a sad-looking woman walking slow, the orange glow of a cigarette lit up between her fingers. Sienna waited for the woman to pass, thinking she looked familiar. Didn't she have anybody to be with today? She thought of Dad, the look on his face when she'd walked through the door. She imagined what he'd look like when he realized she was gone. Again.

She took a deep breath and kept walking.

Now, after a crowded carpool across the island and a seemingly endless hike up the side of a cliff, a crumbling structure peeks into view, the brick bones of a barn long forgotten. A tall, lopsided chimney breaks through the tops of the trees, and chips of red clay and stone are scattered all around the sandy pit.

"What is this place?" Sienna asks.

"It used to be an actual brickyard," Owen answers. They are, at last, on level ground, and Sienna feels her legs settling back into the familiar, easy rhythm of simply *walking*. "Boats used to sail right up to those docks and load up with materials. The barn was eventually built out of bricks that weren't good enough to sell."

"Is that why it's in such bad shape?" Sienna asks.

"Nah." Owen hops over a waist-high stone wall, a border that seems to enclose the entire area, marking where the woods end and the shoreline begins. "It was a hurricane, I think."

Sienna nods, trying not to think about the irony of trying to avoid one natural disaster in a place that's already been demolished by another.

As they get closer to the barn, Sienna starts to make out a few familiar faces from last night, but mostly, the group—there must be close to fifty of them—is full of people she hasn't met. They seem to be of all ages, some kids like them, a bunch of young families, and a handful of men her dad's age, swarming around the open structure. They are all focused, hard at work, but there's a sense of easy comfort and routine, as if it's not so different from what they do every day.

Owen takes Sienna's hand and squeezes it. "Ready?"

Sienna nods and follows him into the barn. She's not sure exactly what she'd been expecting, but it's clear right away that whatever it was, she was wrong. This is a highly organized operation, basking in the harsh glow of industrial lights. There are hulking pieces of machinery, enormous planks of treated wood, rubber tires the size of full-grown men, and pulley systems that, at first, make Sienna want to run and duck for cover.

The "boat" itself takes up the majority of the indoor space, accessed from platforms on the ground and scaffolding that juts out from the barn loft above. The wheels have been attached and the whole structure sits perched on a wooden ramp, angled down toward the opening that faces the ocean. The whole thing appears to be one pulley-snap away from rolling out to sea, whether or not it's ready.

The buzzing progress doesn't stop for introductions, but Owen carefully leads Sienna around the sprawling space, greeting friends and offering quick explanations of how each fits into the microcosm of his island life. Friends from elementary school. His old soccer coach. The shellfish warden and his wife. Jeremy introduces them to his father, Rex, a ruggedly handsome man who looks too young to have a kid their age. Rex looks up from his nail-gun long enough to greet them, and asks Jeremy to check on the "pit crew."

Sienna raises an eyebrow and the three of them make their way into the belly of the boat, hopping over cables and loose floorboards. "So what do you think?" Jeremy asks as they weave around the upper deck.

Owen laughs. "It's incredible," he raves, running a hand along the reinforced beams that cross the boat's wide center frame.

"Right?" Jeremy starts down a short flight of narrow stairs. "Watch your head," he cautions, pointing to the low ceilings below.

Inside the boat is a maze of small rooms, each stacked with rows of bunk beds built into the curved lower walls. A cheerful group works busily on what looks like a folding table, hanging from one side of the kitchen, a long galley space with one wall full of matching electric stove tops.

"How will you get power?" Sienna asks.

"Good question," Jeremy says, leading them deeper into the cabin. Small LED lights are built into the floor and glow at intervals between their feet. Jeremy pauses in front of a heavy door and pulls it open. Three hulking generators are stacked against the wall, blinking and whirring in the dark. "One beast of a gen-set and two backups," he says proudly. "Dad got them from this hippie commune in the mountains, in exchange for a few reserved spots on the boat."

Owen leans back to peer down the seemingly endless hallway. "How many will it hold?" he asks.

Jeremy closes the closet door. "We're hoping around fifty," he says. "Don't worry, you guys are covered."

Owen puts an arm around Sienna's shoulder and hugs her tight against him. Sienna looks from Owen to Jeremy. She wants to talk, but there's a lump in her throat. She's exhausted, she hasn't slept, and her muscles ache from the hike, but that's not it. She feels more vulnerable, more raw than she's ever felt in her life, and all of a sudden, she knows why.

For the first time since she wound up in the House, for the first time since all the talk about asteroids and "the end" began, she hopes everybody else is wrong. She hopes there's a rocket, and she hopes that it works. She doesn't want this, whatever it is she's feeling, she doesn't want it to end.

She takes Owen's hand and squeezes it.

"Where do we start?"


There is so much work to be done.

Every time Sienna feels like she's finished a particular task—hauling loads of two-by-fours from one side of the barn to the other, folding sheets and towels for the stash of linens down below, assembling kits of medical supplies and storing them in carefully mapped-out locations—somebody is there to assign her a new one.

After a quick and not entirely successful run-in with some power tools, she joins the painting crew, which turns out to be more shellacking than actual painting. Her head is throbbing from the fumes, her body is sore, and she's never been happier in her life.

She hadn't expected to work so hard. In fact, she now realizes, she hadn't really expected anything at all. All she cared about was being with Owen. She could tell how excited he was to show her what was happening, to be a part of the process in some meaningful way, but she'd imagined a more laid-back environment. Maybe with kids drawing pictures of mythical-looking lifeboats, between rounds of a drum circle and hits of the bong.

In other words: These people didn't actually think they could build something that would save them, did they?

They did. And now that Sienna sees the "amphibious boat-type thing" with her own eyes, how absolutely real and solid it seems, all of the people hard at work, so completely dedicated to bringing it into existence, she almost believes that they might just succeed. It's not so much the boat, or the equipment, though it's certainly all very impressive. It's the look in their eyes. At first she thinks it's hope, until she realizes it's something more specific. Faith. They each have faith, and are, as a group, convinced that they can make a difference.

"Careful," a voice says from over her shoulder. "You're dripping."

Sienna quickly flattens her brush on the wooden ledge, soaking up the gooey excess before it oozes onto her lap. A girl with muscular arms and a fuzzy, shaved head steps between Sienna's legs and plops down beside her, choosing a brush and quickly getting to work.

"Glad you guys made it," the girl says. Sienna looks up and

realizes with a start that it's Maggie, the driver from their night in town.

"Your hair," Sienna says, remembering Maggie's knotted dreadlocks.

Maggie beams. She is striking, with enormous blue eyes and big pouty lips, all of which had been completely masked by the wild overgrowth of her tangled mane. "Yeah." She shrugs. "Felt like a good time to lighten the load, you know?"

Sienna smiles. "It looks really nice," she says. "I mean, your head. It's a good shape. I mean . . ."

"I know what you mean," Maggie rescues her. "I was really freaked out after I started cutting. Like, what if I had this massive egg-dome or something? Or, like, all these crazy bumps everywhere. It was a total crapshoot."

Sienna laughs. "Right." She drags her brush along the shiny wooden beams. They are adding a topcoat to the upper deck, a job that Sienna got the feeling was given to people who lacked any kind of real building skills. Maggie doesn't seem to be one of those people, and Sienna wonders why she decided to join in.

"Sienna, right?" Maggie confirms. "What's your story? How did you and Owen get together?"

Sienna feels her face flushing pink and glances across the barn to where Owen and Jeremy are standing, hunched and conspiring over a table saw. "We're . . . we used to be neighbors," Sienna stutters. "I mean, we still are, but we used to hang out. When we were little. My family used to come every summer."

As soon as the words are out of her mouth she wishes she'd found better ones. Now she'll be just another "summer girl." One of probably dozens that Owen has picked up along the years, introducing to his core crew and replacing as soon as the season changes, like a pair of worn-out flip-flops. She waits for Maggie to try to hide a knowing smirk, or maybe not try to hide it at all. Why should she? She's part of the Tribe. She knows how it goes. She's always there when the summer ends.

But Maggie just nods, her smile still glowing and genuine. "That's amazing," she says. "I mean, really cool that you guys found each other again, with all this craziness. And, I probably shouldn't get all sentimental on you, Owen would kill me, but . . ."

Sienna looks up, her heart leaping into her throat. "What?"

Maggie flashes a coy smile. "I don't know," she says. "I'm sure he's told you how he feels. But all I can say is, you know, our band, we're kind of like this little family. And you must be pretty special. You're the first girl Owen has ever brought home."

Sienna swallows, and feels a strange, sudden urge to wrap her arms around Maggie, this near-total stranger. She's never been much of a hugger, not even when she was little. She knows it's probably because Mom wasn't, either. There was something about being so physically close that made her uncomfortable, too open and exposed. But now, Sienna thinks that maybe she's been missing out. Sometimes it's nice to put it all out there, whatever you're feeling. And right now, she feels grateful, and connected.

"Speak of the handsome devil." Maggie winks and looks over Sienna's shoulder. Owen swings out of nowhere over a rickety piece of scaffolding and plops down beside her.

"There you are," he says, tugging gently at the end of her messy ponytail. "You guys ready to call it a night?"

Maggie huffs dramatically, feigning disgust. "Call it a night?" She laughs. "I'm just getting started."

Owen laughs and reaches for Sienna's hand. "What do you say?" he asks. "Should we leave her to concentrate? She's easily distracted . . ."

Maggie pretends to shellac Owen's foot as Sienna drops her sticky paintbrush into the open can. "Definitely."

Owen stands and helps her down from the scaffolding to the solid dirt floor. They snake through the crowded space, stopping to admire the work of a group of kids patching a tear in an old canvas sail. Outside the barn, the night air is warm and heavy.

"Looks like these guys had the same idea," Owen says, gesturing to a group of older guys, building a fire on the beach.

Sienna thinks of Ryan and Dad, out in the woods with their flashlights. They'd have to be home by now. She reaches into her pocket and pulls out her phone. "Give me a second, okay?" she asks.

Owen nods. "Checking in at home?"

Sienna shrugs. "Just want them to know I'm okay," she says. "He was so freaked out earlier. I won't be long."

She walks away from the water. She finds a quiet spot where the sand starts to turn to grass, a low overhang of pine branches marking the edge of the woods.

She dials fast. Dad answers on the second ring.

"Sienna?" he barks. She imagines him pacing the kitchen with the phone in his hand, waiting for her call. Her stomach drops.

"Hi, Dad."

Dad breathes into the phone, a loud, muffled gust that sounds heavy with alarm. "Where are you?"

Sienna crouches into the cool sand and leans back against a knotted tree trunk, wishing any part of her felt as strong and substantial as the ancient, solid wood. "I'm with Owen," she says. "I'm sorry. I'm really sorry I left, but I . . ."

"Come home," Dad says. His voice cracks and Sienna feels her jaw tightening. She never should have called. "Just come home, Goose," he says again. "Please."

"Dad," Sienna sighs, steadying the tremble in her throat. "Something happened. I wanted to tell you earlier, but . . . Owen . . . he has these friends. You have to see what they're doing up here. It's amazing. They're, they're building this . . . it's a boat, but it's . . . huge. And it has wheels that fold up and down. There's room. There's room for all of us, and I want you to come."

"Goose . . ."

"I'm serious, Dad. I know it sounds crazy, but . . . think about it. Everything that's happening is crazy. We're sitting around, living our lives, going to the beach, eating sandwiches, and there's an asteroid out there, an actual *asteroid*. And we're just waiting for it. Like idiots."

"Idiots?"

"Yes, idiots. I didn't realize it until tonight, but what we're doing, what you're doing, it's just dumb. Why wouldn't we at least try to make a difference, while we still have the chance?"

Dad breathes heavily into the phone. "Sienna," he sighs. "I have no idea what to say to you, here. You're right. This is crazy. All of this, every morning I wake up and I can't believe it's real."

"I know!" Sienna agrees. "And . . ."

"And I can see why you'd want to feel like you were doing

something," he interrupts. "But that's the thing. There's nothing to be done."

"How do you know that?"

There's a long, heavy pause. "I don't," he says. "But I know that I'd rather spend time with you guys here than run around in a panic, trying to stop something that can't be stopped."

"It's not running around, it's—"

"You have no idea how lucky we are, Goose. We're so lucky to have this house, this island, a place that's still calm. Where we can be together, and relax. Doesn't that sound better?"

"No," Sienna insists. "It sounds like an excuse."

There's a rustling on the other end and Sienna hears Denny in the background, whispering.

"What if I said I'm staying?" Sienna asks.

"Without us?" Dad replies. "Without Ryan?"

"I don't want to, but . . ." Sienna takes a breath. "I think I love him, Dad. I mean, I know I do. Owen. I love him, and I'm not coming home."

Dad's breathing gets quick and sharp. "You don't love him, Sienna," he hisses. "You hardly even know him."

Sienna feels a fury in her chest. The phone is hot on her ear and she feels her whole body tingling.

"Sienna—"

"I'm staying, Dad," she says. "But it's not too late. Just get in the car, and come. There are lots of kids for Ryan, and other parents, too. You'll see. I promise, when you get here, you'll understand."

"We're not going anywhere, Goose," Dad says quietly, clearing his throat. "But you're old enough to make your own decisions. I love you. Ryan loves you. That's all I can say."

Sienna feels a hand on her shoulder and looks to see that Owen has been standing over her. Sienna wipes her eyes and swallows. "Tell Ryan . . ." she says. Her voice cracks and she takes a deep breath. "I love you guys. I'm sorry. I have to go."

With trembling fingers she ends the call. She feels the rhythm of a sob rolling deep inside her and wraps one hand around her waist, as if she could hold it down.

Owen circles his long arms around her neck. "It's okay," he says into the top of her hair. "It's going to be okay."

"How do you know?" Sienna pulls back suddenly. Tears fall onto the front of Owen's shirt, leaving quick, woven splotches below his collar. "You have no idea what's going to happen. Nobody does. And I just, I just left them. I left Ryan. I didn't even say goodbye."

"I know." Owen holds her face in his hands, drawing his thumbs beneath her eyes to scoop away fresh tears. "It was hard for me to leave my parents, too. They didn't get it at all. But, it isn't really a choice, you know? My mom hasn't gotten out of bed in three days. My dad, he won't stop reading things, hoping for new information. But that's just them. Everybody's different."

Sienna nods, thinking of Dad and the wedding. She had assumed that he was doing it for Denny, that he knew she needed a distraction, that he wanted to keep her happy and calm. But maybe she was wrong. Maybe he needed it, too. And maybe, just maybe, a part of him was relieved that Sienna was gone.

One less thing to worry about, now that worrying was a way of life.

"Everyone's got their own ways of dealing with all this," Owen says. "And we need to be here. We need to help." She feels the taut, stringy muscles in her arms go soft as she slumps against his shoulder. "And we need to be together, right?" Owen hugs her tighter to his side. "That's us."

She breathes the smell of him, his soap, the new dusting of wood shavings stuck in the warm curve of his neck. There's something about being so close to him, so close that it's hard to tell where she ends and he begins, that makes her feel quiet and safe.

# ZAN

ZAN WASN'T SURE HOW LONG SHE'D BEEN standing in the bathroom, staring in shaken disbelief at the grimy mirror over the sink, her reflection bleary and broken through tears.

This is what it looks like, she thought. The undoing of everything she'd held on to since Leo had been gone. His perfect memory. Their perfect relationship. All of it, a lie.

Nick had given up knocking and Gretchen was packing a bag. She had seen the flyer stuck to a lamppost, the same flyer Zan had been given at the bar. *Sleep-In at the Common*. Even in her weepy haze, Zan could hear it in Gretchen's voice. She didn't want to go alone.

"I don't know," Nick hedged. It sounded like he was still in Vanessa's room. The idea made Zan's stomach turn again. How was she supposed to pretend that none of this had ever happened if Nick was still sitting on Vanessa's bed? "We should probably be getting back. We don't have a car, and I have no idea how long it will take . . ."

"People will be there from all over," Gretchen reasoned.

"Tomorrow morning, after the announcement, you'll be able to find a ride. There are no buses running, anyway. You might as well wait."

The announcement. Tomorrow morning they would know for sure if the rocket had hit, and what damage, if any, had been done. Would Persephone break into a million harmless pieces? Or would she charge ahead on her path, untouched?

Zan felt, suddenly, solid, as if something was holding her up. It seemed only right that on the day her world was changed forever, the universe was changing, too. One way or the other, things would never be the same.

She ran the tap, took a cool, long drink from the faucet, and slowly opened the bathroom door.

"She's right," Zan said, walking briskly down the hall, not daring to look at anyone, or anything, until she'd reached the front door. "Let's go."


It's Zan's first time at the Boston Common. Miranda, born and raised in Manhattan, hated Boston, and any time they left the island for "the real world," they headed to her family's apartment on the Upper West Side. Boston was too provincial, Miranda liked to say, and Daniel tended to agree. The art scene was too sleepy, nothing like the galleries in Chelsea, and all of Miranda's old dance pals were in Brooklyn. They called New York "the City," as if it were the only one.

Zan liked visiting Manhattan, but on the few occasions she'd been to Boston, on school trips or outings with Leo, she had to admit that she preferred the slower pace. It felt more like a real place where actual people lived, and less like the set of a hundred movies, all mashed up against each other and competing for attention.

The Common, a big public green in the heart of the city, has been completely transformed. At least that's the way Gretchen tells it. "Usually this place is pretty quiet," she marvels as they cross Boylston Street. She is swaying ahead of them, a giant bottle of champagne clutched in her birdlike fingers. She'd been in charge of collecting the booze, and had stuffed an old purple backpack with whatever she could find in the apartment. Zan had a feeling it was taken from Vanessa's stash, but couldn't bring herself to ask.

Nick hasn't said much since they started walking. Every so often she feels him stealing glances in her direction, probably to make sure she hasn't started crying again. Zan is surprised at how well she's been keeping it together. Something about walking, about the steady pace of Nick's confident steps, is making it easier to breathe.

Nick is much more comfortable in the city than she ever would have imagined. Even Leo, she finds herself thinking, became somebody else when they ventured off-island. Sure, he was full of ideas and adventures, but he was always looking over his shoulder, or getting them lost and pretending it was part of the fun. She always got the feeling that, no matter how hard he tried, he couldn't quite hit his stride anywhere but home. She used to find it endearing. Now, as Nick holds out an arm, shielding her from a group of rowdy bicyclists as they zip around a corner, she realizes it was actually kind of lame.

"I can't believe this!" Gretchen squawks, tilting the bottle back to her lips and passing it over to Zan. "I used to come here on my study breaks. It was totally peaceful and quiet."

Gretchen gestures to a square of open space that is now anything but quiet. The entire green is covered in tarps and tents, and a massive stage has been set up at one end of the biggest field. Amplified music wafts in distorted clouds around them. On the outskirts of the park, there are clusters of performers: A man wearing only a layer of bright body-paint and a thong, throwing devil sticks into the air and catching them easily behind his back. A pair of contortionists, twisted into pretzels on the grass. It's like Cirque du Soleil meets Woodstock, meets Boston, Zan thinks.

Gretchen hurries ahead, quickly losing herself in the crowd. Zan stares at the bottle in her hand, wondering if she should call after Gretchen to return it. Nick stretches to keep an eye on the uneven bob of her purple backpack. "Think we should go after her?" he asks.

"I have a feeling she'll find us if she wants to." Zan shrugs. She brings the bottle to her lips and takes a long, thirsty sip, sharp bubbles stinging the back of her throat.

"Easy there," Nick says with a gentle smile. He reaches for the bottle but Zan tucks it under her arm protectively.

"Come on," Zan says, grabbing on to the soft, worn fabric of Nick's T-shirt and guiding him through the crowd.

They move deeper into the action, stepping over outstretched legs and blankets and half-ravaged baskets of food. "What's happening there?" Zan leans forward to shout in Nick's ear. She points to a big white tent with hundreds of people stuffed inside, clapping and swaying in unison. As they get closer, it becomes clear that it's some sort of religious sermon, with a man in a long white robe leading a choir, and gospel music booming from a pair of tall speakers up front. Hippies, acrobats . . . and God.

They make their way down one of the narrow paved paths to the stage, where hordes of people are pumping their fists to the pulsing rhythm of a local indie band. Zan takes another sip from the heavy green bottle and offers it to Nick. "Are you sure you're okay?" he shouts over the music.

Zan feels herself being jostled by bodies packing in around her. She closes her eyes and takes a deep breath, the tingling bubbles reaching her head. *Okay.* Is she okay? She feels light, like something inside her, something heavy and dark, has been cut free. She feels unattached. Brand-new.

She opens her eyes and takes another deep breath, as if she could harness the energy around them. She looks out at the sea of heads, the hundreds of people who are here, now, together. She thinks of who each of them may have been, before this moment. People with problems, fears, disappointments, broken hearts. Where else should they be, today? Should they be locked in their rooms, alone, crying, afraid? What's the point?

The only thing that matters, she thinks, is that she's alive. Right now, she's alive, and she wants to be here. She wants to be with all of these people she doesn't know. She wants to be with Nick. Even if it doesn't make any sense. If ever there was a time to push boundaries, to be someone she's never been able to be, to stop making sense, this would have to be it.

"Yeah." She smiles. "I'm okay." A stranger knocks her sideways and she steps on the tops of Nick's feet. He puts out a hand to steady her, catching her on the side of her ribs and setting her straight beside him. "Thanks," she yells. He smiles. She hopes he knows that she means it.

# CADEN

ARTHUR IS STILL ASLEEP WHEN THEY PASS back over the bridge.

The highway is all but deserted and the moon flashes in and out, low and orange between a quick series of green exit signs. Joe has the radio on soft, and every so often Caden can make out the hushed intonations of a sermon. Religious leaders of all denominations have taken over the airwaves, reading from sacred texts or preaching words of hope and consolation.

He regrets it already.

Not Camille. Not running away. He regrets letting Arthur find him. He regrets getting into the car.

He'd seen the headlights from his hiding place, which, if he was being honest, wasn't all that hidden. He'd camped out around the far side of the barn, just inside the beginning of the trail they'd taken to go hunting. There was a big cluster of rocks and he'd perched on top of the tallest one. He didn't have a plan, other than never to go back.

He'd heard voices in the driveway, heard the car rumbling down the dirt road. The lights cut across a section of brush and he saw the silhouettes of little creatures ducking for cover. His stomach was twisted in knots. He thought of the little boy he used to be, the prince, hiding from the dragon in the woods. Back then, he'd wanted to be found. Now, he would have given anything to truly disappear.

The car stopped at the barn and he heard a door slam, then Arthur's voice as he tramped across the field. "Caden!" He called for him for a good long while, over and over and into the darkness. "Caden!" After a while, Caden began to think how bizarre his own name sounded out loud.

Eventually, Arthur began to get angry. He kicked a pile of dirt. He squeezed the sides of his misshapen head with his hands. "Caden," he said. "If you can hear me, I need you to know that I'm leaving. I'm leaving, right now, and I need you to come with me. I can't come back for you. This is it. I'm getting in the car, I'm waiting three minutes, and I'm driving away. All right?"

He stood, frozen in the glare of the high beams, before climbing back into the SUV and shutting the heavy door.

Caden weighed his options. There was something uniquely no-nonsense about his father's voice, as if none of what had happened even registered as worthwhile anymore. He knew he could find his own way off the mountain—how hard would it be to find *down*—but what would he do once he got there?

Reluctantly, he slid down the slippery side of the rock. He walked along the trail, the crunch of leaves and twigs a chorus of defeat underfoot. He avoided looking at Joe, who sat with his hands on the wheel, patiently awaiting Arthur's next instruction. He pulled open the door and sat inside, preparing himself for a deluge of questions, a barrage of mortifying curiosity.

But there were no questions. And if Arthur was curious about anything, he did a bang-up job of not letting on. He acknowledged Caden with a slight, courteous nod, tapped Joe on the shoulder, and they were off, winding down the sharp mountain road and back toward civilization.

Now, as they near the coast, the star-studded sky stretching out before them, Arthur snores gently and his chin lolls deeper toward his chest. Caden looks back out the window. There's a weird pulling in his stomach. He thinks it might be disappointment. Why couldn't he be normal, for once? No, Camille wasn't what, or who, he'd imagined, when he'd imagined his first time. But so what? What is he waiting for, now?

It's not like he didn't want to. And it's not like he was totally clueless, either. There had been a few girls at home. One actual girlfriend, even, the summer after freshman year. Ashley Hall. She had been in his advanced English class, before he got bumped off the honors track. They'd done a couple group projects together, and he could tell she thought he was smarter than he was. He tried to play along.

She taught horseback riding to disabled kids that summer, and he would meet her at the stables to help clean up. They fooled around a lot, but she always stopped him when things got too close. She knew it was ridiculous, she said, but her older sister was a sophomore when she first had sex. She always thought she would be, too. She asked if he could wait a few months. Of course, he said. No problem. And it wasn't.

Until she cheated on him with a summer kid, one of the lifeguards at their favorite beach. He didn't have proof, but word travels fast on an island. And the word was that Ashley and the lifeguard had done pretty much everything. Apparently, waiting just wasn't her game.

Everyone assumed that they'd slept together, Caden and Ashley, and, maybe because she felt like she owed him something, she let them believe it was true. Once it was out of the way, at least in theory, he could go back to holing up in his room, playing video games, or loitering on the docks with the stoner crew. He knew, or at least he hoped, that he would get back on track someday. He just wasn't sure how, or when.

And now he's blown it. Twice. First, there was Eliza, on the beach. And now, his dad sets him up with a foolproof plan. All he had to do was show up. Show up, and not freak out.

But he couldn't even do that.

The car slows as they pull into the driveway of Arthur's estate, crunching over the seashell gravel. Arthur stirs. Maybe he won't remember right away, Caden thinks. Maybe they can go back to the way things had been, back before Camille showed up, back when Arthur still thought Caden was worth getting to know. Before he discovered what a helpless, hopeless loser he had for a son.

Maybe, just maybe, they could pretend it hadn't happened.

That it was all just another bad dream.


Inside, the house feels different.

The big open rooms are dark and quiet, but there's a lingering energy, like all of the furniture has been moved around and put back.

"Luisa!" Arthur calls into the kitchen, as Joe shuffles their bags upstairs.

Luisa scurries out from the living room, a confused look in her eyes. "Everyone is already outside," she says in a whisper. "I didn't know they were coming. Should I cook something?"

Arthur shakes his head and unbuttons the sleeves of his shirt. "No, that's all right. It's late," he allows. "Caden, come with me."

Caden follows his father through the foyer and into the kitchen. The pool is lit up, neon blue, and hanging lanterns cast a pale yellow glow around the yard. The sculpted hedges lurk in the shadows like frozen demons, waiting to pounce.

As soon as Arthur swings open the patio doors, Caden hears the voices. Children's voices, first. High-pitched squeals and splashes. Then other voices, boisterous chatter, the clinking of glasses in the dark.

Arthur and Caden stand at the edge of the pool. All around them, men and women are drinking, laughing. A few are swimming, the pale glow of arms and legs squirming in the artificial light. "What is this?" Caden asks.

Arthur puts an arm loosely around Caden's shoulder. "This is your family," he says.

Caden feels a cool hand on the side of his face and turns to see a woman standing beside them. "Is that who I think it is?" she asks. She has dark, tanned skin like Arthur's, and warm green eyes. Two little girls, wrapped in towels, run up alongside her, swinging her hands back and forth like she's a machine. "Girls, he's here!"

Arthur bends down and picks the girls up, balancing one on each hip. "Would you ladies like to say hello to your cousin?"

Suddenly, the splashing stops. There are no more squeals. The men stand frozen, drinks in hand.

Everyone has turned to look at Caden. He feels like he should say something, but he can't imagine what.

"Hello!" the girls yell abruptly, in happy unison. The silence is broken and the crowd laughs, descending on him from all directions.

The woman, their mother, is first. "Hi, Caden," she says, holding out her hand. "I'm sure you don't remember me. Aunt Sarah. Arthur's sister?"

Caden manages a smile and shakes her hand. "Hi," he says. "I'm Caden."

He's swallowed in another burst of laughter and his cheeks start to burn. Of course they know who he is. He was part of the family, once, smaller than the little girls, wriggling in his father's tickling grasp just as they are now.

Arthur passes through the crowd and continues the introductions. He guides Caden around by his elbow, his grasp warm and protective. One after another, new family members are paraded before him. Arthur's brother, Louis, a dentist in Pittsburgh. Louis's wife, Irene, and their heavily orthodontured preteen sons, Max and Liam. A couple of second cousins whose names Caden forgets before they've finished shaking hands. The little girls are twins, it turns out, Ella and Mae. Sarah's husband is a bear of a man named Tobias. He sits ceremoniously at the head of the long patio table, like the Godfather.

Seated beside Tobias is an older woman with thick black hair heavily streaked with silver. A shiny gold crucifix dangles around her neck, twinkling in the moonlight. "Hi, Mom," Arthur greets her, bending to kiss her cheek. "Look who I found."

Arthur nudges Caden forward. The old lady grabs his wrists and shakes them gently. Her eyes are blue and watery and Caden worries for a second that she's crying. "Caden," she says. "Look at you."

Caden smiles, because that's what you do when an old person is holding your hands. At least, he imagines it's what you do. He doesn't have much experience with the elderly. Ramona's father died when Caden was six and her mother lives in Key West. She sends Christmas presents and calls on their birthdays, but he usually pretends not to be home.

"The kids call me Nana," she whispers to him, as if it's top-secret information. "But you call me whatever you want."

Caden nods. "Okay," he says. There's something dreamlike about her, about all of them, he realizes. Like he's seeing a glimpse of the life he could have had, the people who would have surrounded him on holidays, special occasions. The people who would have seen him grow up. Now, he's just an older version of the little boy they barely remember. He finds himself holding on to the old woman's hands longer than he'd planned, as if she might disappear. As if they all might disappear, this family he never knew he had, like a fading hallucination, a mirage.

"Mom says we can go in, if you swim with us." One of the girls is tugging on Caden's wrist. He looks down and the other twin appears from behind his leg.

"Will you swim with us?" she begs.

Caden looks to Arthur, who lifts an eyebrow at the glassy

water, egging him on. He doesn't have a suit, but who cares. This time, Caden thinks, he won't screw it up.

"Why not?"

He takes the girls' hands in his own and leads them to the edge. Together, they jump in.

# SIENNA

SIENNA HELPS OWEN GATHER SPLINTERED pieces of wood, adding them to the growing pile of kindling set back from the brickyard in the sand. All day long, people have been hauling enormous stacks of leftover materials and chucking them into the pit, preparing for the biggest bonfire the island has ever seen.

It starts with a mellow crackle, but by the time Sienna has made her third or fourth trip down from the cluster of tents the fire roars, wild and hungry. The heat comes off in cautionary waves, and Sienna blocks her face from the grayish clouds of floating ash. She passes her offerings over to Owen and hurries back up the sandy cliff, back to where his friends have gathered.

"Something's wrong with your hands," she hears a voice behind her. It's Ted, and he's pointing at her with a sloppy grin. "They're empty!" He leans into one of the many cases of beer piled up beside his tent and tosses her two slippery cans.

She catches them, one in each hand, and smiles. "Thanks."

Ted leans into his tent and grabs his guitar before heading off toward a clearing in the trees. Maggie is already up there, Sienna can see, playing drums on a makeshift set of overturned boxes and empty bottles, and a handful of other musicians—a banjo, it looks like, and a hulking upright bass, which Sienna can't imagine was easy to hike with—are starting to warm up.

Owen tugs at her hair, planting a kiss on her forehead. "Hey," he says, warily eyeing her double-fisted drinks.

"Here you go." She offers him one. She doesn't really feel like drinking. At home, she drank at parties when she was bored, or when there were things she wanted to forget, and she never much enjoyed it. Tonight, there's an electric buzzing inside her, and she can't imagine needing anything else to feel so alive. But she figures she'll hang on to something, if only to avoid more attention from concerned onlookers, like Ted.

Owen takes the beer and rests it back on the top of the crates. "No thanks," he says. "But you go ahead."

Sienna smiles and adds her can to the pile. "No." She shrugs. "I'm good."

Owen grabs her by the hand and they start toward the music, which has grown from quiet plucking to a sudden, raucous performance, like magic. People are up and dancing, and they have no choice but to join in.

Sienna feels an anxious bubble in her chest. She hates dancing. She never knows quite what to do. But Owen makes the decision for her, placing one hand around her waist, and holding the other up to his chest, her fingers clenched tightly inside. They are the only people swaying like an old married couple, but somehow, it feels just right.

"Why aren't you up there?" she asks him, nodding at the impromptu stage.

Owen laughs. "Some people think hiking with eighty pounds

of musical gear on your back is a good time," he says. "I'm not one of those people."

Sienna smiles, her head falling easily into the space beneath his chin.

"And besides," he says, his voice humming against her hair. "It's sort of hard to play and dance at the same time. And I'd rather be dancing, with you."

Sienna tilts her head up to his, leaning in for a quick kiss. Suddenly, she feels a sharp elbow in her back and is thrust forward, nearly knocking Owen into a tree.

"Watch it, Len," Owen calls over Sienna's head. Sienna turns to see a small group of guys, red-faced and wild-eyed, shoving each other on the edge of the cliff. Playful pushing has turned into angry shouting, and before Sienna knows what's happening, Owen is at the center of the fray, holding his arms wide in an attempt to break the fighters up.

The scuffle continues, and Sienna watches as Owen gets knocked down. Her chest feels warm and achy, as if she had been pushed herself. The music comes to an abrupt end, and Maggie is by her side, clutching her by the elbow.

"Stand back here." Maggie guides her, as the brawl intensifies and spreads out along the crater's edge.

"What are they fighting about?" Sienna asks, searching the faces, some now bloodied and covered in sand, for a sign that Owen is all right.

"Who knows." Maggie shakes her head. "They've probably been drinking all day. Everybody's trying so hard not to feel things, you know? But really, we're all scared. And it has to come out, one way or another . . ."

"Knock it off!"

Sienna turns to see a couple of older men, Rex and some of the other dads, sprinting up from the bonfire. They shove their way into the heart of the action and drag a few of the more aggressive fighters away by their elbows.

Sienna feels her pulse racing, her breath short and fast. Where is Owen? There's a hand on her waist and she nearly jumps.

"Only me," Owen says. There's a red lump under one of his eyes and he's holding the outside of his shoulder with his palm.

Sienna wraps her arms around his neck. "Are you okay?"

Owen nods through a wince. "Didn't see that coming," he says. Sienna feels her heart aching for him, not just because he's hurt, but because he looks so disappointed, and even a little bit embarrassed. He'd wanted to show her a good time, she knows. This hadn't been part of the plan.

She hugs him close and follows Maggie back toward the tents, where a smaller, more civilized group has regathered. They've started a campfire and Sienna helps Owen down to a spot on the soft, cool sand, as a couple of girls pass out the fixings for s'mores.

"Our hero," Maggie says, giving his shoulder a light squeeze.

Ted looks up from his guitar. "Let me guess," he says. "O-Man to the rescue again."

The group laughs and Owen blushes. Sienna inches closer to him, careful not to jostle his wounded arm.

"Hey, remember when my brother brought those douche bags over to work on his house?" Maggie grabs a long stick from a pile and pierces it through the top of a marshmallow. "And they tried to take off with all his money, before the job was done?"

Jeremy laughs. "Owen let them get halfway up the ramp to the boat before he tapped the big one on the shoulder," he says. *"Excuse me, sir,"* he mocks.

Owen buries his face in his hands.

"Who did you say you were?" Jeremy asks.

Maggie leaps forward, excitedly. "He said he was the family attorney! I have no idea how it worked, that guy could've wrecked you with one hand behind his back. But they got all spooked, and sure enough, they were back to work that afternoon."

Sienna leans into Owen's side. He looks at her and rolls his eyes, but she can tell he's loving the attention. "You don't mess with the Tribe," he says, and shrugs.

Ted plays a few loud chords on his guitar and everybody toasts, holding up their drinks to the fire. Sienna smiles, but inside her is an uneasy shift. She hasn't heard much about what Owen's life was like before, back when they all were just regular kids, before they were busy building boats and waiting for the asteroid. She knows it's ridiculous, but a part of her is almost disappointed. She had started to let herself think that she and Owen had met when they had, the way that they had, for a reason, and that nothing before that moment would ever matter again. They could both start over, and be nobody to anyone, except each other.

But here was a whole group of people who mattered to Owen, people who had their own stories about who he was. And none of them knew a thing about her. She could have been anyone. So what if she was the first girl he'd brought home, as Maggie had said. *They* were his home. Not her.

Sienna untangles her arm from Owen's elbow and wraps it

around her knees. She thinks about Ryan, alone in his room. She thinks of Dad, of everything she's put him through. There's a dull throbbing in her heart and she has to clench her teeth to keep from crying. Shouldn't she be with the people who truly know her?

Ted strums a few more bars of a song before ending with a dramatic flourish. Everyone claps and cheers, and before she knows it, Owen is reaching across her lap for the guitar.

"Uh-oh," Maggie says, cracking open a new beer. "Is it that time already?"

"Time for what?" Sienna asks.

Owen spends a few moments carefully arranging his injured shoulder while tuning the guitar with one hand. Maggie laughs. "Owen has a secret singer-songwriter fantasy," she says as Owen reaches out a foot and playfully kicks her in the ankle. "He thinks he's got this Bob Dylan thing going on, that nobody knows about. Except when we're all together and he starts to serenade us for no reason . . ."

The group laughs and Owen interrupts them with a sudden strum.

"I am not serenading anybody tonight," he says, his face serious, his eyes unblinking and calm. "It's just something I wrote a few days ago, but if nobody wants to hear it . . ." Owen looks around.

"Oh, just do it already, we don't have all night," Ted says, tossing a marshmallow at Owen's face. "Actually," he reconsiders. "We do."

Owen laughs and slowly starts playing, a simple melody floating up around them. He closes his eyes, in mock serenity, and Sienna forces a smile. She tries to ignore the unsettling feelings, the new uncertainty in the pit of her belly, and focuses instead on Owen's hands, his fingers swift and steady on the strings. When he starts to sing, his voice is clear and unadorned, the kind of voice that makes you lean toward it to hear more.

> *"I met a girl, at the end of the world,*
> *You'd probably think I was lying.*
> *I knew her before, when we were both four.*
> *Four rhymes with 'fore, you should try it."*

There are a few throaty chuckles around them, but Sienna can feel a shift in the group, as everyone turns to her. Her heart is pounding and she feels the tips of her ears start to burn.

> *"I've heard people say, don't get carried away.*
> *No need to take it so fast, boy.*
> *But who cares about time, when the planets align,*
> *Or maybe . . . you, me, and the asteroid."*

At this, the group erupts, holding up their drinks and cheering. Sienna feels her pulse settling down, and a smile springs to her lips.

> *"It's a love story and it ends with a bang*
> *A big one, but that's how they all go.*
> *I met a girl, at the end of the world,*
> *Sienna, can I see you tomorrow?"*

The last chords ring heavily around them, quickly drowning in heartfelt applause. Still seated, Owen takes a quick and modest bow before passing the guitar back to Ted. Maggie gives Owen's good shoulder a gentle shove.

"You big softie," she teases. "That sure sounded serenade-y to me."

Owen turns to Sienna with a smile, goofy and genuine. "Sorry." He shrugs. "I lied."

Sienna blushes. Ted rustles to his feet and says something about restocking the cooler, and soon the rest of the group has taken the hint, scurrying away to different corners of the sandy ledge and leaving Sienna and Owen alone.

"So what do you say?" Owen asks. His hair is wild and he tucks a few dark strands behind his ears, anxiously. "Does tomorrow work for you?"

Sienna smiles and looks into the dark pools of his eyes. Suddenly, she feels a panicked jolt. "Did you . . . how much did you hear, before? When I was on the phone?"

Owen bites his lower lip. "What do you mean?" he asks. Sienna takes a deep breath. Maybe she's being crazy, she thinks. Maybe it's just a coincidence that he's made such a big, grand gesture, on the very night she professed her love for him out loud.

"Oh." Owen nods slowly. "You mean did I hear you gushing about me to your dad, about how madly in love you are with me, you can't stand to be without me, et cetera, et cetera?"

Sienna's stomach drops and she winces, as if bracing for more.

Owen's face cracks into a smile and he leans in closer to her. "Yeah," he says. "I did. But it's okay."

"It is?" Sienna asks, her voice barely a whisper.

"It's more than okay. It's actually really convenient," he says. "Because I'm madly in love with you, too."

Sienna feels all of the blood rushing back to her face, a smile creeping to her lips. Unable to look at him for a second longer, she stares at the tops of her hands, her knuckles pale and raw from gripping the sides of her knees.

Owen sighs. "Good thing that wasn't awkward."

Sienna smiles and stares up at the smooth underside of his jaw, the dimpled chip in his angular chin. Suddenly, he's not a member of somebody else's tribe. She doesn't care who he is when he isn't with her, or who he's been to anybody else. He's still the kid who used to chase her in the waves, with seaweed on his head. And she's the girl who isn't afraid to get caught.

Sienna leans over and reaches with both hands for the sides of his face. His cheeks are flushed and warm as she kisses him, long and solid. Around them, the group is slowly starting to return, and Sienna hears them, cheering and hooting and laughing. But she doesn't pull away. This kiss, this moment, it's theirs. This story belongs to Sienna.

# CADEN

CADEN IS ON HIS WAY UPSTAIRS TO BED AFTER saying his third good night to the twins. His head buzzes, thick and fuzzy from the few warm sips of Scotch that Tobias—Uncle Tobias—had insisted he try. The light is on in the downstairs bathroom, and Caden hears a muffled voice from behind the door.

At first, he catches only broken snippets: "Disrespectful." "Humiliating." "Ungrateful."

It's Arthur, and he's pissed.

Caden steps into the dark hallway beyond the bathroom, glancing over his shoulder to see if anyone else is nearby. Most everyone has gone to bed, but a few of the men are still up with nightcaps, swapping stories in Arthur's study.

Suddenly, another voice. It's Sophie, small and afraid. Caden leans closer, pressing his ear against the crack in the door.

"It doesn't feel right," she's saying. "I shouldn't be here."

"Where should you be? Back in that shithole where I found you? All alone? Not a chance in hell of surviving?"

"What do you care?" Sophie asks, behind a tearful hiccup.

"What do I care?" Arthur shouts. "How do you think it will

look, if I let you go now? After years of defending you, to everyone, to my family . . ."

There's a loud sob and a confused commotion, uneven footsteps approaching the door. Caden ducks back around the corner just as Sophie appears in the hall. She had joined them late, in the pool, and is still wrapped inside one of the big white bathrobes that hang on brass hooks near the hot tub. She wipes her eyes with the sleeve of her robe, leaving a dark trail of mascara on the clean, plush cotton, and walks quickly through the kitchen and back outside. A moment later, Arthur appears, drying his hands on the sides of his pants, as if it was all just a bit of cleaning up.

Caden watches Sophie through the window, her arms hugged around her waist as she gazes longingly up at the sky. He's hardly said a word to her since he's been back. Seeing her in the pool, surrounded by his new family, felt funny. As if, all of a sudden, he belonged there in a way that she did not.

But after hearing the way Arthur spoke to her, his voice so cold and condescending, Caden wants nothing more than to run outside and say something, do something . . . anything to make her smile, the way she'd smiled the morning she made him breakfast. Like they had something in common. A secret understanding.

He stands in the darkened hall, waiting for it to come to him, the perfect line, a good excuse. But it's too late. He hears the muted squeak of the sliding glass door, the gentle padding of her footsteps as she makes her way slowly upstairs.

*  *  *

The house is silent and dark. Caden was surprised to find his door unlocked, and wondered for a moment what it meant. Maybe Arthur forgot. Or maybe he was so disappointed in Caden that he no longer cared if Caden left Hart Haven.

Whatever the reason, Caden can't sleep. He tiptoes into the kitchen, and stops short. Curled on a cushioned bench and gazing out the bay window is Sophie, her profile lit up by the moon.

"Hey," he says softly, before he can change his mind.

Sophie jumps and a hand flutters up to her throat.

"Sorry," Caden says, taking a few steps closer. "I just . . . I couldn't sleep."

Sophie smiles. Her eyes look tired, her skin pale and drawn. "Me neither," she says. "I already tried warm milk. There's still some on the stove, if you want . . ."

Caden glances at a saucepan on the stove, the empty mug beside her on the table. "That's okay," he says. "I was thinking about going for a walk. What do you think?"

Sophie looks up at him, surprised. "With me?"

Caden almost laughs. "Yes, with you," he says, trying to sound convincing. "If you want."

Sophie smiles and follows him slowly, quietly, through the French doors. They walk past the pool and across the open lawn, stepping carefully along the rocky path toward the beach. The sky is dark and dotted with stars, and there's a chill in the air. Caden wonders, on a scale of one to ten, how lame it would be if he offered Sophie his sweatshirt.

"I know you heard us fighting, earlier," Sophie says

suddenly, leaning against a rickety shrub oak to step out of her sandals.

The skin on Caden's forehead wrinkles and pulls. "What—?" he stutters. "What do you mean?"

Sophie points a sandal at his grimy sneakers. "I saw your shoes under the door."

Caden looks down, guiltily, at the tops of his slip-on Vans. They had always been his favorite. Now he wishes he'd never seen them before in his life.

"Sorry," he mutters. "I just, I heard him yelling, and you sounded upset . . ."

"You don't have to apologize," she says, balancing her shoes on a rock and continuing barefoot onto the sandy path. "I just didn't want to go through the whole awkward thing, where you pretend you don't know anything, and I pretend not to *know* that you know . . ."

"Right," Caden agrees, following her through an opening in the beach plum bushes at the top of the dunes. "That would suck."

"Definitely." Sophie heads straight for the calm, dark water and stops at the edge, letting the rush of the tide swirl around her slender ankles. Caden stands to one side, removed. He stuffs his hands in his pockets.

Sophie drags her toes through the sand, a thick line that's quickly erased by the incoming push of the tide. She draws it again, and Caden takes a step closer. There's something powerful in his chest, solid and clenching inside his ribs.

"Can I ask you a question?" he finally manages.

"Sure." Sophie shrugs.

"Why do you want to leave?" he asks. "Or, I mean . . . if you want to get out of here so badly, why don't you?"

Sophie crosses her arms around herself, hugging the outsides of her elbows. "That's two questions." She smiles.

"Sorry."

Sophie catches the flyaway hairs at her forehead and pulls them back behind her ears. "My mom is sick," she says. "And I feel like I should be with her, but . . ."

Caden stops abruptly. "What do you mean, she's sick?" he asks. "He won't let you see her?"

"It's complicated," Sophie says quietly. "My dad died when I was sixteen, and since then it's been just the two of us. When she got sick, I had no idea what to do. I moved back home to take care of her, but it wasn't enough. She doesn't have insurance, and neither of us had any money to pay for the treatments. Arthur is the reason she's still alive."

Sophie gazes out at the water, like she's trying to see something that isn't there. Caden shuffles his feet in the sand.

"But that's, I mean . . ." Caden struggles to find the right words. "That's insane. That he won't let you be with her. If it's what you want . . ."

"It is what I want," she insists. She looks at him the same way she was looking at the horizon, like she wishes he were more. "You don't understand."

Caden doesn't know what to say. He hopes she'll keep talking, but instead, she walks ahead. Caden hurries to catch up, but her steps get quicker and closer together every time he starts to match them.

"Hey," he calls after her. "Hey!" He grabs her lightly at the elbow. When she turns around, her eyes are wet and glossy.

"What's wrong?" he asks. "Whatever it is, you can tell me."

The words sound strange as they float between them. He's never said anything like it, to anyone, before. Usually, it's some well-meaning girl, hanging on his elbow with droopy eyes and a sad, meaningful smile, trying to get him to talk. Insisting that he can tell her *anything*, that she really wants to help. He never asks for help, but he knows there's something about the way he looks, or talks, or breathes, that makes people think he needs it. Ever since Carly grew up and started taking care of herself better than he could, the idea that he could help somebody else has never once seemed a possibility.

"If you want to go," he says. "You should go. Forget him. You should be where you want to be."

"I can't go," Sophie whispers. "He'll find me. He'll find me, and he'll take it all back. The nurses, the medications, all of the equipment—he pays for everything. And he'll take it away. She won't have a chance."

Sophie searches Caden's eyes with her own. She smiles. "I know it's crazy, with everything that's happening. What should it matter if she lives a few more days, right? Would she really want to be around for whatever happens, anyway?" She shakes her head.

Caden swallows. "She doesn't deserve to be uncomfortable," he says firmly.

Sophie nods, looking grateful that he understands her, and more than a little surprised.

Caden kicks at the sand with the sole of his sneaker. "But she doesn't deserve to be alone, either," he says. "And neither do you."

Sophie's eyes fill again with tears and before he can talk himself out of it, Caden wipes the corners dry with the sleeve of his sweatshirt. His blood boils with the familiar frustration of wishing he knew what to do. How to help.

"I'm sorry," he says softly, and through a sniffling sob, Sophie smiles, the smile he's been waiting for. He takes her hand and closes it in his own, holding it just for a moment, as if sealing a promise he hasn't yet made.

# ZAN

"THIS WAY."

Nick grabs for Zan's hand and pulls her across the street. The last act, a soulful jam band that had the crowd dancing until almost three in the morning, has finished its set, and an announcement was made that the music would continue acoustically, per request of the mayor. (Who was, apparently, somewhere among them, and received a mixed greeting of grateful cheers and disappointed boos.)

"Where are we going?" Zan hiccups. Her feet feel funny, like they're loosely attached to her ankles by rusty gears or Lego parts. She and Nick had shared what was left of Gretchen's champagne, which would have been enough to get her tipsy, before moving on to the free beers he'd taken from the bar. Then came the mystery punch, passed around in giant plastic jugs. It tasted summery, like watermelon and berries, and turned their lips and tongues hot pink.

"I have an idea," Nick says, ducking down another, quieter path. They've crossed into a different section of the park, the Public Garden, a sign proclaims. The lawn is still peppered with tents and sleeping bodies, but the vibe is mellower here. Clearly, this is the place where people who actually want to sleep, sleep.

Zan hustles to keep up, suddenly hyperaware that she and Nick are holding hands. She isn't sure when that started. Before crossing the street? During? Why? And more important, why isn't she letting go?

The dark shadows of trees blur around them and the cool breeze feels soft and wet on her face. She feels like she could keep walking forever, and when Nick turns off the path suddenly, she's almost sorry they have to stop.

"Ever slept on a Swan Boat before?" Nick asks. He juts his chin behind her, and she turns. They are at the edge of a misshapen pond. Along one side of the short wooden dock, a series of identical paddleboats are parked, each with a giant wooden swan lurking from the back.

Zan laughs, so abruptly that she covers her mouth. The noise echoes and surprises her. "No," she whispers. "I've never been on one at all."

"You haven't?" Nick asks, surprised. "Really? My mom used to take us on them all the time when we were little. Even my dad loves them. But don't tell him I told you."

"Wouldn't dream of it," Zan swears. The dock sways gently beneath their feet. Or she's the one swaying. It's hard to tell. "You want to sleep with the swans?"

"Sure." Nick laughs. "There are benches. I thought it might be more comfortable than the ground."

Zan looks at him sideways. She wonders how long he's been thinking about this. He has a way of quietly scheming. Just when she thinks that she's figured him out, figured out why he does what he does, or what he's thinking, he surprises her.

And not the way Leo surprised her. Leo was so consistently unpredictable, it was almost impossible for her to be taken off guard. But Nick is different. He seems so stable, so . . . normal, that when he pulls something out of left field—like the trip to Boston, or the Swan Boats—it almost feels more exciting.

Zan stands on the dock and shakes her arms and legs, as if she's physically shaking Leo away. *You're not welcome here,* she hears a strange voice in her head say. *There's no room for you anymore.* She hops the gap beside the dock, her feet landing heavily and rocking the boat back and forth. She keels forward and plants both hands on a bench.

"Careful," Nick says. "I don't think the lifeguards are on duty."

"I'm a very strong swimmer," Zan says, another sudden hiccup jolting her upright.

"I bet," Nick jokes.

"I am," Zan insists. She lies down on the bench, stretching her legs and looking up at the clear night sky. The orange, pointed beak of the oversize swan sneaks into her peripheral vision. It's sort of creepy, being watched by a wooden swan with stiff, feathered wings and dark, painted eyes. "I hate swans," she sighs.

Nick falls heavily onto the bench near her feet. She automatically inches the toes of her sneakers under his leg. She tells herself it's for support. The boat is still sloshing against the dock, and the bench isn't very wide. If she doesn't hold on to something, she could fall.

"Nobody hates swans." Nick shakes his head. He unfolds one of the blankets and lays it around them. The air is cooler on the water and she's glad for the warm weight of thick, musty cotton.

"I do." Zan nods seriously. "I hate them. They're so . . . stuck up."

Nick leans back and laughs. Zan giggles even harder. It's the first time she's seen him laugh, *really* laugh. His head knocks clumsily against the back of the bench.

"Are you okay?" she asks.

"I'll live," he says, rubbing his hair with his hand.

"I'll live," Zan repeats. "Isn't it funny how people say that? Like, it's one or the other? You're either living, or you're not living. Are those really the only two choices?"

Nick looks up at the sky, where the stars are hidden by strings of gauzy clouds. "Um, yeah," he says. "Kind of."

"No." Zan sits up, folding her arms over her bent knees. "There's more. Of course you'll live. Of course it didn't kill you. But just because something doesn't kill you, doesn't make everything else, like, automatically awesome. What's so amazing about not-dying? I mean, shouldn't there be a better goal than just that?"

Nick puts a hand on Zan's knee and looks solemnly into her eyes. "Zan," he says steadily, tapping the top of her knee with one finger. "I think you might be drunk."

Zan puffs some air between her lips and slaps his hand away. "I am not drunk," she says. "I'm thinking."

As soon as the words leave her mouth she starts laughing again. Nick joins in, and soon they are both bent over and giggling uncontrollably. She can't remember the last time she's laughed like this. She loved Leo, truly, with every part of her, but he didn't make her laugh. He made her think, and want to be a better person. At least, she thought that's what he was doing.

Zan catches her breath first and watches Nick as he settles down. The top half of his face is lit up by the glow of lanterns on the dock, and his blue eyes crinkle happily in the corners. She feels, suddenly, weightless, like she could dance all over the clear, dark surface of the pond that surrounds them. It's Nick, she realizes. She would never be here, feeling this way, if it wasn't for him. She's no longer numb. She's grateful.

Nick sighs and holds the edge of the bench with both hands. He studies the panels on the boat's wooden floor. Zan feels her heartbeat in the strangest places, the tops of her ears, the insides of her knees. She reaches for the back of Nick's neck with one hand, cupping her small palm around the soft line of his fine blond hair. His skin is warm, her fingers are cool and dry against it. He turns to look at her, his eyes locking with hers. His stare feels different now, like he's seeing her for the first time. Or maybe, it's the way he's seen her all along, and it's Zan who hasn't been looking.

They lean in together, so slowly it's impossible to tell who reaches who first. The kiss is soft, and controlled. It feels like it could last forever, like they could find a way to do whatever else they needed to do, and stay locked together like this, all the way up until the end.

# DAY FIVE

# CADEN

"NOT HUNGRY?"

Caden eyes Sophie's untouched plate of eggs Benedict as he reaches into the breadbasket for a second blueberry muffin. The patio table bustles with loud conversation and requests for more home fries or another mimosa. Luisa has prepared a brunch unlike anything Caden has ever seen. It's pure gluttony, with every classic dish presented on a flawless serving plate: pancakes, French toast, bacon and sausage. And it's all delicious, which doesn't help to explain why Sophie has hardly eaten two bites.

"I had some cereal," Sophie whispers, disinterestedly picking at the crumbling edge of her English muffin. She's wearing a sleeveless yellow sundress, and Caden finds his eyes wandering to the neat, dark shadow between her small breasts. He steers his eyes quickly back to his own empty plate.

A deep chuckle rolls up from the other end of the table, where Arthur holds court between his mother and Tobias. Seating had been assigned, by printed cards perched over the gold-rimmed charger plates, and it was embarrassingly clear that Caden and Sophie were afterthoughts, stuck at the far end with the kids and a handful of buttoned-up second cousins.

One of the twins—Ella, Caden thinks—slurps her orange juice through a straw, tapping his arm to make him watch every time, as if the outcome might be different. Caden satisfies her with a thumbs-up or a goofy smile, but finds his gaze always pulled back to Sophie. Her light brown hair is pinned up in a scrappy bun, and loose tendrils hang down past her shoulders.

Another honking laugh cuts through the tableside chatter and Caden catches Sophie rolling her eyes. He smiles. "Kind of sounds like a donkey," he whispers to her. "Or a dying goose."

Sophie manages a weak smile. She glances quickly across the table. "You should hear him sing in the shower," she says under her breath. "The first time, I thought *he* was dying."

Caden half laughs, half cringes, trying not to picture Arthur in the shower with Sophie anywhere nearby.

As brunch winds down, Arthur and Tobias are the first to leave the table. The TV in the living room is already on, the low rumble of newscasters filling the house with stalling small talk as everyone waits for the announcement. Every few hours, the Emergency Alert System has been updating them with a series of beeps and a message to stay tuned.

Caden watches Sophie as she walks through the crowd and ducks into the kitchen. He can't believe that Arthur would keep her from her mother, especially on a day like today. Before he can help it, he sees Ramona's face, imagines her and Carly huddled on the couch, staring silently at the boxy TV. It seems impossible that he won't be with them. As if, whatever happens, the news won't actually be real if he's not there to hear it.

As the group trickles inside, Caden finds himself hesitating outside the kitchen. Through the big glass windows he watches

Sophie as she pours herself another cup of coffee. She seems to be looking at things without actually seeing them, as if a part of her is refusing to believe that they're real.

He watches as she wipes away a tear, feeling his own throat tighten, his jaw ache. He has to say something, do something to make her feel better. He puts one hand on the door and is stepping into the kitchen when she turns. She gives him a sad smile before starting for the living room. He has no choice but to follow.


As soon as they reach the landing, Caden knows that something is wrong.

The family is gathered around the television, and there's a new, frantic energy. A terrible quiet. Arthur stands beside the mantel with his eyes closed. The sharp, clipped voice of the president reaches them as they're rounding the corner of the room, and Arthur points a small remote at the cable box, hidden in a wooden console.

Caden hears his heart stop beating, feels the blood stalling in his veins. There's a moment when he thinks they're in trouble, that Arthur saw them last night, walking on the beach. But then he sees Aunt Sarah, her eyes red and raw. The twins, fearfully clutching their father's hands. The older cousins are huddled together, talking in low whispers and gesturing frantically, wiping their brows, crossing and uncrossing their arms.

It's bigger than Sophie. It's worse.

"Shit," Sophie mutters under her breath.

"Everyone, please, stay calm," Arthur says after clearing his throat. "For those of us who may have missed it—" He looks up sharply at Sophie and Caden. "The rocket launch has failed. The bomb was not powerful enough to steer Persephone off course. Instead, we are to brace for an impact, potentially . . . many . . . impacts, as the force of the explosion has broken the asteroid into a number of smaller pieces. This is good news, and bad news. And, to be frank, it was exactly the news I've been expecting."

Arthur straightens and lays an arm on his sister's shoulder. "We are here, together, in this house, on this day, because we are family. And in times of . . . confusion, when things are uncertain, when maybe we're feeling a little bit . . . afraid, that's when family matters most. I've brought you all here because it's the only way I can protect you. And nothing matters more to me than keeping each and every one of you safe."

Caden glances around the room. Arthur's mother holds Sarah's hand, her soft, round chin lightly trembling. The second cousins are now still and silent, with lost, childlike looks in their eyes. Tobias has scooped the twins onto his lap, and moves his hands gently over their fine blond hair.

"The asteroid is expected to make contact tomorrow evening, at sundown," Arthur is saying. "But there is still hope. For the past few months, I have been working with a team of highly skilled engineers to build a private bunker. It is right here, beneath where we are standing, and it is fully equipped with everything we need to survive."

Caden watches his father speak, Arthur's lips moving only slightly, as if he's being controlled by robots. He is confident and strong. He is exactly the kind of person you want to be around in an emergency.

A bunker. Suddenly, it makes sense. Why Arthur insisted on showing him everything that could someday be his. Why Arthur wanted him around. He thought they were going to survive. He had a plan, all along.

"As soon as we're finished here, some friends of mine will take you all down to your rooms," Arthur continues, glancing quickly at George and Joe, who have appeared out of nowhere, flanking the living room doors. "Nobody can say what will happen tomorrow, and it's important for me to know that we're all prepared. Everything you need to make yourselves comfortable is already down there. You will be safe. We will be safe. But only if we're together."

There are murmurings around the room. For a moment, nobody moves, still gripped by stunned silence, frozen in time. Slowly, Aunt Sarah stands and wraps her arms around Arthur in a sideways hug. He looks uncomfortable at first, but gradually softens into the embrace. He reaches an arm out to his mother, and the three of them hold each other. Soon, everyone is reaching out, a hand, a shoulder, a hug, exchanging unspoken words of comfort.

Caden takes a step away, back into the hallway, watching the scene as if he's not there. As if the news is not his own. A flash of yellow catches his eye from the kitchen. He looks up to see Sophie, standing at the open window, one hand over her mouth, her light brown eyes pooling with fresh tears.

Two of these things are not like the others, he thinks.

Two of these things do not belong.

# ZAN

THE GEESE WAKE HER FIRST, LOUD AND BRASSY overhead.

Zan winks her eyes open, one at a time. There's a moment of confusion as she takes in the giant painted swan and thinks it's quacking at her, until she remembers where they are. The concert. The Swan Boat. Nick . . .

"Morning."

Nick sits on one of the shorter benches up front. Zan drags her fingers through her tight, dark curls, attempting to tame the frizzy bedhead that's sure to have found her overnight.

"Hey," she says. There's a pulsing in her brain, a subtle soreness in her joints. Nick hasn't turned completely around, and she studies the back of his neck, seeing flashes of her hand on his jawline, his hand on her bare waist . . .

She closes her eyes and waits. She expects to feel something, maybe a lurch in her stomach, a hot flash of shame or regret stinging the center of her heart. But nothing comes. She feels, simply, quiet, as if the volume has been turned down on the world around her, on the constant nagging of her thoughts. All that's left is the soft swish of the water on the docks, and the easy rhythm of her breath.

Nick takes long strides toward her. His short blond hair is tousled and there is a shallow line indented on the side of his cheek, from where it was pressed against the wooden bench as he slept. He smiles, his blue eyes warm and hopeful, and reaches for the blankets crumpled at her feet. He folds them into neat squares and tucks them under his arm. "Ready?"

Zan tries to smile back, but it feels funny, like her face is struggling to catch up. "Let me just get dressed," she says, making a show of smoothing out her wrinkled jean skirt and adjusting the elastic collar of her hooded sweatshirt. "There we go. All set." The joke falls flat and Zan wishes she'd said something else, something that meant something. Something real.

Nick hops onto the dock and holds out a hand for her to grab. She looks at his palm, strong and calloused from working on the boat. This is it, she thinks. This is where she should say they made a mistake. Before the spell of morning is broken. Before this—whatever it is—before it goes any further.

It was a mistake. Wasn't it? Whatever happened . . . there are foggy gaps in her memory but she doesn't think they slept together. She would have remembered that. Leo was the only person she'd been with, and surely, she'd remember the difference.

No. They didn't. But still. It was a mistake.

Only, she doesn't feel the way she would, the way she usually does, when she's done something she hadn't meant to do. Nick's hand, held out to hers, doesn't make her feel like she's done anything wrong. Instead, it makes her feel like she wants to use it to pull him closer, like she wants to feel what he feels like, again.

She squeezes his wrist with her fingers and stretches her small legs across the gap to the dock. Her hand slips from his wrist to his fingers and he folds them tight in his palm. She thinks for a second that he's going to let go. That he was just being polite. Maybe the mistake was his.

But he doesn't. They begin to walk slowly down the trail, away from the pond and the nosy swans, beneath the tangled canopy of trees. Neither of them says a word, and Zan imagines what they must look like, walking through the park, comfortably quiet, hand in hand. A couple.

Nick glances over her head, an anxious flicker in his eyes. "Something's going on," he says, stretching to see up and down the winding pathways.

Zan squints in the sunlight. "What do you mean?" The park does seem much quieter than it had last night, but that was to be expected, wasn't it? Last night was a celebration, a stop-time party before things got too real. This morning, this morning is when they'll know for certain what to expect. And when to expect it.

"I don't know," Nick says. "It just feels different. And I heard some kind of commotion, earlier."

He's right. There's an eerie quality to the stillness that feels like more than just morning-after calm. In the distance, a siren wails. A breeze picks up, tossing pieces of trash like confetti in the air around them. An empty bottle of wine rolls out onto the sidewalk. It feels like they are the only people awake. For a brief, panicky moment, Zan wonders if it's possible that the asteroid strike has already happened, and she and Nick are the only ones left.

"Did you hear that?" Nick asks, stopping short where the sidewalk meets the trampled grass.

"Hey! Hey, you guys!" Somewhere behind them there's a voice, frantic and high-pitched. "Hey. Wait up!"

Nick shields his eyes from the sun to get a better look. "I don't believe this," he says softly.

As the figure gets closer, Zan recognizes the shock of red, the sparkling gold shoes now clutched in the girl's fingertips. In a park the size of a small town, Gretchen has found them. And she's not alone.

"I thought that was you guys," Gretchen says, leaning over to catch her breath. A layer of dirt and crisp leaves is caked into the back of her dyed blond hair, and grass stains streak the back of her dress. "I wanted you to meet my friend Jeff."

A tiny man in a crooked red bowtie stands beside her. His features are small and delicate and there are dark circles drawn beneath his eyes. "It's Jim, actually," he says quietly, holding out his hand. "Nice to meet you."

"Jim, right, sorry!" Gretchen laughs. "Anyway, I was telling him about you guys, that you were trying to find a ride out of the city."

"You were?" Zan asks, surprised. She is oddly flattered, and then a little bit sad, that on Gretchen's one big night on the town, she managed to find time to talk about her random encounter with Zan and Nick, perfect strangers she'd allowed to ransack her home.

Jim nods. "I have a car," he says. "I was planning on leaving this morning, but since the announcement . . ."

"What announcement?" Nick asks.

Jim and Gretchen share a look, and Zan realizes they are holding hands. "You didn't hear it? The president's speech . . . they played it on the PA at the Common."

"No," Zan says, her heart in her throat. "We must have been asleep."

Jim seems to shrink even smaller. "Oh," he says lightly. "Well, the rocket? It . . . didn't work. Or, it did, but not enough. The asteroid broke apart, but the pieces are still headed this way. Nobody knows what's going to happen, how big the impact will be. But it's definitely happening. Tomorrow night."

Zan feels a tingling in her feet, a dizzying lightness in her head and her knees. She's leaning into Nick before she knows how she got there.

"Are you sure?" she hears Nick asking. He sounds like he's underwater, like they're all underwater, floating, not bound by the borders of their bodies.

Gretchen has her arm around Jim's waist and he's nuzzling into her shoulder. "I'm sorry," she says. "I thought everyone knew. I figured you'd already be gone, but if you still need a car . . ."

"Take mine," Jim says, gazing into Gretchen's bloodshot eyes. "I'm staying here." She kisses him, and they tangle in a groping embrace. Zan looks at the shoes in Gretchen's hands, glinting in the sun. She feels like she's going to be sick.

"That would be great," Nick says, clearing his throat in an attempt to kill the moment.

Jim pulls away and reaches into the pockets of his gray work pants for a key chain. There's a library card attached to one end. "It's the silver Prius," Jim says. "Parked in front of the church on Arlington. Good luck."

In an instant, Gretchen is hanging on to Zan and Nick, circling their necks and breathing into their ears. "Good luck, you guys," she says. "And thanks."

Before Zan can ask for what, Gretchen gives them a meaningful smile and grabs Jim by the hand. They stroll together back toward the park, the identical shapes of their small bodies moving in perfect, silent step, until they've disappeared behind the green wall of trees.

"My sister used to love these."

Zan picks at a chocolate croissant in her lap. Just before they found Jim's car, they'd passed an abandoned catering table, piled to the brim with pastries and fruit. A sign from a nearby bakery read: "Please Take!" and Nick and Zan, who hadn't eaten since leaving the gas station, each stuffed their pockets with sweet, sticky treats.

"I always forget you have a sister," Nick says, staring blankly at the brake lights of the car in front of them. The quiet Boston streets fed them quickly onto the turnpike, which was jammed bumper-to-bumper with people trying to get out of the city. They'd moved roughly thirty feet in the last two hours. Zan's grumbling stomach was grateful for the snacks.

Zan nods. "Half sister, technically. Joni."

"What happened to her? I never see her around anymore."

"She ran away," Zan says, licking chocolate from the sides of her lips. Joni used to peel back the dry outer layers and let Zan have the first bite, right into the center of warm, chocolate core. "When I was nine. I haven't really talked to her since."

It feels strange to be talking about Joni with Nick, but it feels even stranger not to be talking at all. Every so often, she feels her fingers groping for the door handle, jolted by the falling sensation she sometimes gets before sleep. The strange car, the traffic, the city around them, it all feels like a dream. A dream about the days before the end of the world. What other option is there? It can't possibly be real.

And to make matters more confusing, she has no idea what to say to Nick. She feels too much, too many things at once to make sense of anything yet. She's not as angry as she was, at least, and she doesn't know why, but she thinks it's because of Nick. He was exactly what she needed. She looks at the strong line of his chin, his sandy blond sideburns and long, dark lashes. It's strange, that they're together this way. But she can't imagine being with anybody else.

"What?" Nick asks, his eyes darting at her sideways, a tentative smile parting his lips.

Zan laughs. "No," she says. "It's . . . it's nothing."

The smile spreads, his eyes soft and, she thinks, a little bit relieved. "Oh," he says. "Okay."

Zan stares ahead at the sky. There are a few wispy clouds that look like they've been painted onto the canvas of perfect, clear blue. It is impossible to think that something so serene and flawless could ever do anything to hurt them. In the quiet of the car, with Nick beside her, under the never-ending blanket of blue, she feels safe.

There's a buzzing in her pocket and it takes her a moment to remember what it is.

"My phone!" she says. "I have service again."

Nick looks at her suspiciously. "That's weird," he says. He digs into his pocket and pulls out his own phone, turning it on with his thumb. "Me too," he says after a moment. "I guess things have quieted down, now that everyone is pretty much where they want to be."

Zan stares at the screen in her hand—*6 New Voicemails*. Her stomach turns. She thinks of her parents, at home, and Joni, wherever she may be. Everyone else has already checked in with the people they love, the people they know will worry. She imagines all of the hundreds of thousands of phone calls that have been made, friends checking in with friends. Families making plans. Everyone saying the things they need to say before it's too late. Everyone, except Zan.

She holds the phone to her ear and listens to the first message. She doesn't recognize the number right away.

*"Hi, Zan, it's me, Amelia . . ."*

It takes Zan a moment to remember who Amelia is, not because she's forgotten her but because Leo's sister is just about the last person Zan expected to be hearing from, at this second, in a car with Leo's best friend.

*"I hope you're doing okay. I just wanted to tell you something kinda important, and I didn't want to leave it on your machine, but, okay . . . we got a call today, Mom did, from this jewelry store on the Cape. It's called Blue Moon? It's on the little side road next to the boat, you know, near the Indian restaurant Leo was, like, obsessed with, remember?"*

Zan feels Nick's eyes on her profile as he jabs at the radio, searching for a clear station. She inches closer to the window. It's suddenly as if Leo is sitting between them, perched on the console, crowding them out of their seats.

"Everything all right?" Nick asks. Zan holds up a finger and turns to look outside. But Leo is there, too.

*"Anyway, the guy, the owner I guess, he said he was calling people about these leftover items, things that hadn't been picked up, and he says he has something of Leo's. Leo placed an order for something . . . he wouldn't tell us what . . . but he was there, Zan. He was there the day that he died. I thought you'd want to know that. I don't know why. Okay? I hope you're not mad I called. Okay. That's all. Bye."*

There's a quick silence and then the voice mail cuts out, automatically moving on to the next message, an older one from her mother. Zan turns off her phone and tucks it back into her sweatshirt pocket.

"What's up?" Nick asks, switching off the radio, satisfied that there is still nothing but static.

"It was Leo's sister," she says, her voice low and trancelike.

"Amelia?"

Zan nods. "She says they got a call from some jewelry store in Woods Hole. I guess Leo was there the day he died. He ordered something, and never picked it up."

Nick's hands are frozen on the wheel. Zan stares at the torn-up floor mat beneath her feet.

"Okay," Nick says. He sounds different. Disappointed.

"Okay?" Zan repeats.

"Yeah." Nick shrugs. "You want to go check it out, right?"

His voice is cool and raspy, like he's trying to separate it from any part of himself that's real. Zan stares at the side of his face, the pattern of light brown freckles near his chin.

She feels like she might be sick. Not *carsick* sick, but sick like her insides are being wrenched and twisted, like she has no control over anything anymore. She doesn't know what she wants, but something tells her she doesn't have a choice.

She knows she's not going to like what she finds. Everything in her is telling her to forget it. Leo was cheating. Leo had secrets. Why would she put herself through anything else?

But the answer is in her, and she doesn't have a choice. There's a flicker of something, deep in her heart, and whatever it is, she needs to know.

"Yes," she finally says, so quiet she isn't sure that Nick's heard her. "Yeah," she says again louder. "If you don't mind. I . . . I think that we should."

# CADEN

IT'S AFTERNOON WHEN ARTHUR DECIDES TO move them all into the bunker. Tuckered out from a morning of eating and drinking, some of the uncles and older cousins have fallen asleep on the living room couches, their clothes rumpled and dirty among the embroidered pillows and rigid upholstery.

Caden keeps watch from the hall. Joe stands on the other side of the front door, the top of his egg-shaped head looming through the colored glass of a decorative window. Arthur stands with George near an oil painting of the ocean, centered on the far wall. Behind one corner of the gilded frame is a keypad, and as George punches in a quick series of numbers, the wall begins to move, pulling back on either side to reveal a small, steel elevator door.

Arthur looks around the room, quietly dividing the crowd into groups of three or four. The elevator, he explains, only holds so many people at once.

Caden's head is spinning. All that separates him from being trapped in a bunker is that elevator door. He can't do it. Even if it is the only way he'll survive. He can't spend the rest of his life, whatever that turns out to be, knowing that he'd left his family, his *real family*, behind. Yes, his family is broken, but they are his, and he needs to be with them. Now.

He hears a clattering of dishes in the kitchen behind him. He glances around eagerly, still hoping to see Sophie, who has been effectively MIA since brunch. There's a sinking weight in Caden's chest, a fear that she is already down there. That Arthur has locked her away in some dark basement room, and Caden will never see her again.

With Arthur's back turned and Joe safely on the other side of the door, Caden steps silently into the kitchen. Luisa is packing a wine crate full of porcelain dishes, carefully folding each one in bubble wrap and fitting them neatly together.

"Luisa," Caden whispers, keeping watch over his shoulder. "Have you seen Sophie?"

Luisa looks up at him with damp, dark eyes. She's been crying. She wipes her face quickly with a corner of her apron.

Caden looks at her, as if for the first time. Isn't there somewhere else she'd rather be? What has Arthur said, or done, to get *her* to stay? She sniffs. "No," she says. "But if Mr. Arthur has his way, she will be somewhere packing like the rest of us. He didn't say today is the day, you know?"

Caden puts a hand on Luisa's shoulder. "I know," he says. "I'm sorry."

Luisa stops wrapping and grabs Caden's face in her hands. She kisses him on the cheek. "Caden," she says his name sweetly. "You are still a good boy."

Caden's gaze falls, hopeless and sad, to the floor.

"What's wrong?" she asks.

He doesn't know where to start. What's wrong is that he

needs to get out of here, and he needs to do it fast. What's wrong is that he can't leave Sophie behind.

"I understand," she whispers conspiratorially.

"You do?" Caden asks.

Luisa nods, her face solemn, her eyes far away. "It is not right to take a boy from his mother this way," she clucks disapprovingly. "I say to myself, when you first here, it is not right. I know Mr. Arthur has his reasons, and I remember your mother. I know she has problems. But everyone has problems, no? And she doesn't deserve this. Nobody does."

Luisa picks up a fragile plate and studies it, as if she's looking for an inscription or some kind of hidden sign. She glances quickly up at the front door, and then out to the patio. "You go," she leans in to whisper.

"What?" Caden balks.

"Don't worry, I take care of everything." There's an almost happy twinkle in her eyes. Caden looks at her uncertainly and Luisa unwraps one of the plates. "I give him something else to worry about." She smiles. "What is he going to do? Fire me?"

Caden feels a gentle warmth filling his chest. Before he can talk himself out of it, he leans in and hugs Luisa tight, pinning her plump arms to her sides. "Thank you."

The front door opens and closes and there's a shuffling in the hall. "Go!" Luisa orders, her eyes darting to the patio. Caden slips through a crack in the sliding door and pulls it quietly shut behind him.

As soon as he's rounded the corner, he hears the first crash. He crouches between the rosebushes and lifts his head to the lip of the windowsill. Luisa has smashed the first delicate plate on the unforgiving tile floor. She brings her arms high above her head before shattering the next one, wailing in Portuguese, sudden bitter tears drenching her face.

Joe is there first, followed by Arthur and Uncle Tobias. They rush in shouting, but quickly stop short and stare. They are paralyzed by the spectacle, by so much raw emotion. It's a truly convincing performance, and Caden is frozen for a moment himself. More than sad, or afraid, Luisa just looks angry. Every primal wail rings with a sense of injustice, the unfairness of everything that is happening, to all of them, and tearful frustration that there's nowhere else to go and nothing left to be done.

Joe glances over Luisa's head, in the direction of the wall of windows, and Caden quickly ducks. He tiptoes back through the bushes. A moving silhouette catches his eye from an upstairs corner. Sophie. He can make out the shape of her ponytail, the subtle curves of her hips. She walks back and forth from one side of the room to the other, moving slowly like a ghost.

His eyes scan the trellis over the pool, a wrought-iron arbor woven with thick green vines. He ducks below the windows and shuffles to a patio chair. He steadies it against the wall of the house and plants his feet on the wobbly chair arms. In one swift motion he's able to spring up, gripping the trellis bars with two hands and hoisting himself up to the top.

His heart pounds in his ears as he considers the shimmering turquoise of the pool below. He closes his eyes and takes a breath. There's a gap between the trellis and the second-floor balcony outside Sophie's room. He straddles a section of vine and the grated arbor roof, bends his knees, and leaps with arms outstretched.

His hands grasp the wooden banisters of the balcony deck. They rattle in place, warning Caden to act fast. He swings his legs back and forth, once, twice, and on the third time finds enough momentum to kick up onto the deck. He pulls his body over the railing and flops on the porch.

Sophie turns to the window, her eyes wide and startled. Caden waves as she unlatches the balcony doors. "What the hell are you doing?" she asks with a disoriented smile.

Caden holds a hand to his lips. "Quiet," he says, pointing at the kitchen below them. "We don't have much time."

Sophie lets him into her room. Caden assumed she'd be sharing a room with Arthur, but there's no sign of his father anywhere. Along one wall, photographs are hung from clothespins on a line in front of a tall, ornate mirror. The bedding is covered in purple flowers, as are the curtains and a small, star-shaped rug by the door.

"Time for what?" Sophie asks. There's a suitcase on her bed and she continues filling it with clothes from the open dresser drawers.

"We're getting out of here," Caden says. He glances over her shoulder to the balcony, and back at the door to the front hall, quickly wondering which is the safer way to the garage. "You have your keys?"

"My keys?" Sophie pauses with a handful of small tank tops. "What are you talking about?"

"I'm taking you home," he says. "But we have to go now."

Sophie laughs abruptly. "Now? Have you seen the morons he keeps around this place? Their only job is to make sure we stay put."

Sophie looks at him, and he can tell she wants more than anything to believe that he can do it. He reaches for her hand. "I have a plan."

"A plan?" she asks. "What about you? What about the bunker? Don't you want to stay?"

Caden feels a quick drop in his gut. He knows there's a part of him that wishes it were an option. It's the same part that wishes he really did have a dad, a dad who was trying to get to know him, trying to protect him, because he cared. But that's not Arthur. Arthur is exactly the person Caden thought he was, an egomaniacal control freak, determined to get everything he wants, whatever the risk, whatever the cost.

"I'm leaving, and I want you to come with me." Caden shakes his hands impatiently, like he's trying to dry them off. "Okay?" He grabs her hand and pulls her toward the door. Luisa's cries are getting louder, and it sounds like more people have joined them in the kitchen.

Sophie wiggles her small wrist free as he opens the door. "Caden," she whispers forcefully. "I can't. Even if we make it out, he'll know where I'm going. He'll come after us . . ."

"Let him come." Caden shrugs. "There's nothing he'll be able to do once we're out of here. I won't let him."

Sophie searches his face, her big brown eyes simultaneously hopeful and already disappointed, as if she's been here before and she knows how it ends. Caden takes her hand again. "Trust me," he says, in somebody else's voice. Somebody brave and experienced in the art of rescues and quick escapes. Somebody to be trusted. "Can you do that?"

Sophie looks back at her open suitcase. Tiny red splotches have spread across the tops of her cheekbones. She bites the cushiony corner of her pink bottom lip and turns back to Caden. "Okay," she whispers. "Why not."

He squeezes her fingers and leads her out into the hall.

They manage to slip through the front door without anybody noticing. The kitchen still buzzes with activity, and as they leave, Caden hears Luisa's broken voice, calling out a prayer.

Sophie pulls her keys from her purse and unlocks her car, disabling the alarm and emitting a series of jarring beeps. Caden's hand is on the passenger door when he hears a deep voice, behind them.

"Going somewhere?"

Arthur stands with his arms crossed at the open front door. Caden feels a tingling in the bottoms of his feet, like they're begging him to run. He glances quickly to Sophie. "Get in the car," he says.

Sophie eyes Arthur warily before climbing into the car, slamming the door shut behind her.

Caden paces the stone path back to the house. He stands a few feet in front of his father, watching as Arthur's green eyes widen, then narrow into steely slivers. His lips purse until they're invisible. Even his hat looks embarrassed, unevenly tilted at the very back of his lumpy, balding head.

"You weren't even going to say goodbye?" Arthur asks, only he doesn't sound hurt, or even angry. He sounds, Caden realizes, amused.

Caden stands with his hands clenched into fists at his sides. "Sophie wanted to leave," Caden says. "I promised I'd take her home."

Arthur squints at the sun, as if it's an eavesdropping nuisance. "She doesn't need you to take her anywhere, Caden," he says with a tight-lipped smile. "She has a car, see? She's free to do whatever she likes."

"You know that's not true," Caden says. His voice is getting louder and he's suddenly afraid of Sophie hearing them. He plants one foot on the bottom step.

"It is true," Arthur insists. "We had a deal, which I'm sure she's told you all about. She could break it at any time. I wasn't holding her hostage."

"You were going to let her mom die," Caden yells. "Of course she couldn't break your *deal*. What is wrong with you? Can you possibly be this evil?"

Arthur looks at him. There's something in his eyes that Caden at first reads as shame, or alarm. But after a while he realizes it's neither. It's pity.

Sick-tasting bile rises in the back of Caden's throat. He feels his forearms thrumming with his pulse as he folds them tightly over his chest. "We're leaving," Caden says. "Together."

Arthur smiles. "We'll see about that," he says, looking over Caden's head toward Sophie in the car.

He moves to sidestep his son, but Caden turns, blocking him with the broadest part of one shoulder. "No," Caden says. "You won't. We've made up our minds. You have to let us go."

Arthur takes a step back and smiles again. "I don't think you're quite understanding what's happening here, son," he spits.

"I'm not interested in you anymore. I did what I set out to do. I'd hoped we could spend some time together, and we have. I'd hoped we'd get along, that you'd realize I'm not the bad guy you imagined me to be . . ."

"You're right," Caden interrupts him. "You're not what I imagined. You're way, way worse."

Arthur rolls his eyes and tries to push past Caden again. Caden holds his ground in front of the car, this time shoving Arthur back with his chest.

"Caden, don't be ridiculous," Arthur says quietly. "What are you going to do? Take her home, and then what? Seduce her?" He laughs, bitter and dry. "After your little *performance* with Camille, I can assure you that Sophie won't be impressed."

Caden clenches his fists tighter, his heart drumming against the knobby gate of his ribs.

"Oh." Arthur smirks. "You think I didn't know?"

Caden steadies his breath. "I don't care what you know," he seethes.

Arthur shakes his head. "I guess this is what I get for trying to show you a good time," he continues. "Not to mention trying to save your life."

Caden unwraps his arms and lowers them slowly to his sides. He feels his lungs expanding with every cool breath he swallows.

"And here I thought your mother might have raised you to be a bit more grateful," Arthur sneers.

"Grateful?" Caden balks. "You left her. You left me! I don't care what your reasons were. If I really meant anything to you, you could have been around. *I* didn't cheat on you. *I* didn't do anything wrong. And every day you weren't there, every day you didn't call, you let me think that I did. You want me to be grateful for that?"

Arthur's smile fades and his eyes grow smaller and dark. He pauses for a moment, then straightens, standing as tall as he can. "All right," he mutters. "You're a big boy, Caden. If the idea of being around me is too awful for you to stomach, that's your business. But Sophie is my business, and she is staying with me."

Arthur flattens one hand against Caden's chest and presses him against the concrete railing. Caden tumbles backward into the garden, and Arthur takes two giant steps, crossing high over Caden's tangled legs, and walks briskly toward the car. "Sophie!"

Caden looks at Sophie, her eyes wide with fear as she fumbles with the key in the ignition. Caden springs to his feet, grasping after Arthur's legs. Arthur swipes him away, but Caden ducks. Arthur loses his balance and Caden slams into his father's waist, heaving him back against a row of hedges.

Arthur struggles in the shrubs to catch his balance, lunging back at Caden. Again, Caden ducks. This time, Arthur stumbles forward, landing on his knees in the gravel.

All Caden can hear is the whistling of his breath in his nostrils. Arthur looks like he's breathing heavy as he slowly stands. He's facing the door, and for a moment Caden thinks he's going to walk back inside, close the door behind him, and pretend that this—none of it—ever happened.

Then, in a flash, Arthur spins around, barreling toward the car. Caden pulls back his arm, balls up his fist, and swings it against Arthur's jaw. There's an awful clicking sound, all teeth and bones and loosened joints, and Arthur falls back once again. He grabs his face with one hand and crumples from his shoulders to his waist, leaning against the concrete steps.

Sophie has started the car and pulls it up beside him. Caden is breathing so hard that it hurts. He watches as Arthur checks his hand for blood, and snaps his jaw open and shut.

"You know," Arthur says finally, catching his breath. "The funny thing about you, Caden—and I mean this as a compliment: we're a lot more alike than you think."

Arthur adjusts his hat on his head and turns toward the house.

"She's all yours." Arthur waves with one hand on the door. "Good luck."

Caden climbs into the car and Sophie peels out, a cloud of dirt and gravel rising in their wake. Sophie doesn't stop at the light at the end of the driveway, screeching around the sharp corner and speeding away.

# SIENNA

SIENNA AND OWEN HAD CAMPED FAR OFF IN the woods, away from everyone, away from the coming news— good or bad—about the rocket. She had turned her phone off after saying goodbye to her father, and when she powered it on this morning there were no messages. This seemed like good news. But as Sienna and Owen hike back in to the brickyard, where most of the others have slept, she can tell something is up.

People are standing straighter, and some are crying; others have an empty, shocked look about them. By the time Jeremy runs back from the barn, Owen's face is already hard and set, his shoulders pushed back and prepared.

"It didn't work," Owen guesses, before Jeremy has even said a word.

Jeremy nods, his eyes tired and his skin pale beneath the scraggly mess of his beard.

Owen looks frantically around the campsite, as if waiting for somebody to tell him what to do next. Sienna feels suddenly hot, and trapped in her own skin. She looks to Owen, expecting him to hug her, or tell her it will be all right.

There's a commotion nearby, and Sienna grabs automatically

for Owen's hand. She needs him near her and doesn't want to lose him to anybody else.

But this time it's not a drunken disturbance. It's a heated discussion between Rex and a couple of other men Sienna had seen the day before, building a set of stairs with their young sons.

"There's just no way," one man is saying, throwing an arm around his sons' shoulders. "Maybe if we had another week . . ."

"Who knows what we have?" Rex yells, throwing up his hands. "You really think they know anything about when or where this thing will hit? Could be tomorrow, could be next year. Could be never."

"Yeah." The other man nods slowly. "But it's a risk. And I got other kids, you know. My wife, she thinks I'm nuts. I can't just leave them like this."

"Tell you what," the first man says, gripping Rex's arm in his square, builder's palm. "If nothing happens, we'll be back tomorrow night. We'll work until it's finished. But for now, we're going home."

The men lead their sons over the ridge and toward the trail. Jeremy's father spits into the woods behind them, tugging at the roots of his dark, curly hair. He seems so small from far away. Sienna wants to look away, but can't.

She hears Owen's breathing get heavy and rough. "What did people expect?" he says with a half-crazed grin. "That's why we're here, isn't it? I mean, if everyone thought it was all going to just go away, what were they doing busting their asses for the last three weeks?"

Owen forces a harsh-sounding laugh. Sienna can hear the

masked fear in his voice. She knows he's only trying to stay focused, to keep himself, and everyone else, from sinking into a spiral of panic, or worse, despair. But still, she wishes he would take a moment to look at her, at least. She needs to know she's still there.

He works quickly to stow the rest of his belongings in the tent before clapping his hands together and starting out toward the barn.

"Ready?" he calls to Sienna without turning around.

Sienna wants to say yes. She wants to be back up on the rafters, holding his hand, talking about what's left to do before time runs out.

But the truth is that time is up. And it isn't about what she wants anymore. It's about what she needs to do, and where she needs to be. "Owen," she starts.

He must hear it, something, in her voice. He stops and turns to face her slowly.

"Don't say it," he whispers.

Her arms hang loose at her sides and she wishes she could do something useful with them, wrap them around him, or pull him down the mountain and make him come with her, make him understand.

"I have to go home," she says. "This doesn't make any sense."

Owen runs his long fingers through his thick, dark hair. "This is the only thing that makes sense," he says. His body looks tight and condensed, like he carries a charge. "Don't you get it?"

Sienna shakes her head. "I miss my family," she says quietly. "I'm sorry. And I know that you want to believe that this is going to work, but . . ."

"I don't *want* to believe it," he says. "I believe it. That's the difference between you and me."

Sienna crosses her arms. She feels her breath getting choppy and hard. "What?"

"You can't let yourself hope for anything, can you?" he asks. "You think that just because you've had some shitty luck, just because some bad things have happened to you, you can just close your eyes to everything good in the world. It's like you're afraid to imagine a happy ending, even when you have no choice. Even when it might save your life."

Sienna lets his words hang, waiting to see if they'll feel any different the longer they echo between them. "Shitty luck?" she repeats. It sounds almost like a bark.

"Yeah." Owen nods. "Your mom died. And you won't talk about it, but I know you've had a hard time. I'm sorry about that. It's really awful. But really awful things happen all of the time. Another big one might happen tomorrow. And you can either stand up against it, prepare for it, put yourself in the best possible position to meet it head-on . . . or you can give up. Those are your choices."

Sienna crosses her arms and looks farther along the ridge. A new crop of kids is taking down their tents, shouldering their bags, and starting for the trail. If she hurries she can join them, maybe hitch a ride into town.

"Sienna," Owen says. He reaches for her hands, but she pulls them away. "Sienna, I'm sorry. Please. Don't do this. You have to stay. I need you. I love you," he says. "Please don't give up."

The words land like bullets, piercing her skin, burrowing into her heart. "I love you, too," she says. "And I'm not giving up. I'm going home. I know you don't think there's a difference, and yesterday I probably would have agreed with you. But not today." She shakes her head. "I'm sorry."

Sienna waits for a moment, wondering if there's more for them to say. Owen looks at her, his eyes wounded and searching, before throwing up his hands. He walks quickly, each step more determined than the last, down the trail toward the barn. She waits until she can't see him anymore, until he's a speck on the sand inching toward the horizon, before she starts to cry.

# ZAN

HIGHWAYS ARE ALWAYS THE SAME. EVEN WITH
so much traffic, there's a comforting familiarity to a well-traveled
route, the signs always in the same place, marking the same turns
and towns, the landmarks and bridges and tolls. But as Nick
turns off at their exit and they wind along the smaller roads
through parts of Falmouth and into the harbor village of Woods
Hole, it's clear that a great deal has changed.

Everything is closed—the bank, the historical museum, the
bagel places and seafood shacks—but that was to be expected.
What Zan hadn't expected was the dense cloud of panic that
has crept out into the streets, seemingly overnight.

There's something about the word *tomorrow*, she thinks. Tomorrow is the day they've been hearing about, every day, for the
past six months. Even before there was an actual date, when it was
a day that nobody could believe would ever come, it was still a
day. An event. A moment in time that existed somewhere in the
near-but-distant future, looming over their every thought, move,
and prayer.

Today, that day is *tomorrow*. And tomorrow is definitely real.
Too real. As soon as they pass the first gas station, Nick is forced

to slow the car to a crawl. Not because of more traffic, but because of the hordes of people flooding the sidewalks and spilling out onto the road. It's sort of like a parade except that nobody is moving. People stand outside of their houses, hugging each other, sitting on curbs or stoops. It could have had the same free-for-all, festival feeling that they saw in the city last night, but somehow, it doesn't. There are too many tears, too much hand-holding and hard-set eyes. Even the kids look frightened. They're doing their best to "play," set up by well-meaning parents with toys and games, but it's clear by the way they look over their shoulders that they, too, know something isn't right.

"Jesus," Nick whispers as they inch carefully forward. Every so often people glance at them through the windshield, confused, as if motor vehicles are a thing of some long-ago past. They shuffle slowly out of the way, too distracted to notice or care that their toes are inches from being run over. Zan feels the urge to wave, or roll down the window and apologize, as if they are the ones out of line.

Which, in a way, they are. What are they doing, so far from home? What did home even look like, today? Were people they knew doing the same thing that people were doing here? Milling around in the middle of the streets, just to not be alone?

Main Street is too much of a circus to drive down, so they park at the docks and walk. The stores here are closed, too, all except for one: a flag quivers in front of the jewelry store at the end of the block, yellow and white with a big blue moon at the center.

"Ready?" Ever since Zan listened to Amelia's message Nick has spoken only in one-word sentences. At first, she tried to bait him with harmless conversation, but she could feel something charged and tense radiating between them, from the angle of his jaw, the death-grip of his long, freckled fingers on the wheel.

"Hope so," Zan sighs. "You don't have to come in, if you don't want to."

Nick holds the door open and follows her wordlessly inside the darkened shop. A tinkling chime announces their arrival, and the shadow of a small man moves behind a star-spotted curtain, draped from a doorway at the back.

Zan looks quickly around the shop. It's an odd mix of cheap-looking jewelry—rotating stands of plastic earrings like you'd find in a store at the mall—and locked cases of elegant necklaces and rings. She can't imagine what ever would have brought Leo into a place like this.

The shadow flickers and the curtain moves. "Hello," the man greets them. He's middle-aged, with an unfortunate comb-over that flutters like an underwater plant at the top of his head. "Can I help you?"

Zan holds her breath. There's a long moment of quiet before she realizes she's waiting for Nick to do the talking. She turns and finds that he's no longer by her side, having stopped to linger over a rack of souvenir key rings by the door.

"Yes," Zan forces herself to begin. "I mean, I hope so. I got a call, or, a friend of mine got a call from you, I think, about picking up an order?"

"Of course," the man says. He ducks behind one of the glass cases and reappears with what looks like a miniature card catalogue or recipe box. He pops open a latch and begins flicking through the files. "I have so much stuff here. After the announcement, I couldn't bring myself to close up without at least trying to get people what's theirs."

Zan nods, trying to appear grateful and impressed, when really she can't imagine why he would bother. Isn't there anything else he wants to be doing? And does he think people really care about their broken watches or reset rings the day before the end of the world?

"So . . ." The man raps his hands on the counter. "Your name?"

"Oh, right." Zan shakes her head apologetically. "Sorry. It's . . . Leo. Leo Greene."

The man stops rifling through the index cards and lifts a light eyebrow. "You're Leo Greene?"

Zan tries to smile. She feels her face blushing pink. "No," she says carefully. "I'm, I was . . . I was a friend. He died."

The owner's eyes immediately soften and he looks at a spot above her head. "Oh," he says. "I'm very sorry. Though, that explains a lot."

Zan stares at him. "It does?"

The man nods and goes back to hunting through the box of names. "Yes," he says. "He was in here, almost a year ago now, and he ordered a custom necklace. I don't normally do custom jobs anymore, but he had this really unique idea, and you could tell he'd thought about it a lot. I hated to say no. So I told him I'd do it." He pulls out a card and flattens it on the glass countertop. He circles a number in the corner with a pen and disappears again, this time to search through a low, hidden chest of drawers.

"He paid up front. And then he never showed up. I tried him on the number he gave me for months. I was pretty annoyed, you know. I just didn't get it. He was so clear on what he wanted. But I could tell he had some personal stuff going on . . ."

"Personal stuff?" Zan asks. She feels the bizarre beginnings of a laugh in her gut. Of course a stranger, a man who had met Leo only once, would remember so much about a simple exchange that had lasted no more than an hour, over ten months before. It was Leo, after all. If nothing else, he made a serious impression.

The man straightens with a small orange envelope, the kind you'd use to leave a tip in a fancy salon. "He was on some kind of a mission." The man shrugs. "After we worked on his design for a bit, he asked about a girl who used to work for me. I guess that's how he found me in the first place, tracking her down." The man opens a binder and scans through it for a list of names. "Best apprentice I ever had," he muses. "Don't know if he ever found her or not. Never heard from either one of them again."

"Let me guess." There's a sharp voice from behind her and Zan almost jumps. She's forgotten that Nick was even there. "Vanessa?" He spits the name so aggressively that Zan feels like saying it again, but nicer. She tries to give Nick a look but it's as if he can't see her anymore.

"Vanessa," the shop owner repeats. "Yeah, that's right."

Zan doesn't realize she is slumped against the edge of the counter until she feels hard angles digging into the side of her hip. "It is?" she asks quietly. She thought she was prepared for this, but something about hearing it confirmed by a stranger has made her sick all over again.

"At least, that's how I knew her," the man continues. He pushes the small envelope across the counter and turns the binder toward

Zan, marking an "X" where he wants her to sign. "He called her something different, though. What was it?"

He wiggles the pen and Zan holds it in a daze. She moves it over the line, her signature practically illegible from the shaking of her hand.

"Julie? Joanna?" The man crosses his arms and stares at the floor intently. Zan stops with the pen in her hand. "Joni!" the man finally shouts. "He called her Joni. I remember because I wondered why she'd changed it. I used to love Joni Mitchell. And he said that's who she was named after. Guess she had a sister named Suzanne, after a Leonard Cohen song."

There's a loud jangling and Zan turns to see that Nick has nearly knocked over a basket of mood rings on sale. The man looks up quickly, then back at the binder. "Anyway, I told him what I knew. That she'd left the Cape to move to New York, and then she was on the road a while. Last I heard she was working at a bar in Boston. I wrote down the number for him, I think." He stares at the ceiling like he's trying to remember more. "I'll tell you, she wasn't the world's most reliable employee, but she was one hell of an artist." He shakes his head wistfully.

Zan picks up the envelope, the trembling in her hands so extreme that she's sure he's going to notice.

"Well, there you go," the man says. "Hope the necklace finds its rightful owner. Before it's too late . . ."

The jeweler disappears behind the starry curtain. Zan feels suddenly hot, the air close and humid. But the envelope is heavy in her palm, as if it's pinning her to the shop's tiled floor. She can't move. She has to open it, now.

She pulls back the tiny tab and pours the contents into her

palm. The necklace is a silver chain, and at the center, a small square pendant with the image of a vintage typewriter, much like the one she gave Leo for their anniversary last year. On either side of the pendant are two bold-faced letters, glossy and round, like typewriter keys.

An "L" on one side, a "Z" on the other.

Zan lets the necklace fall through her fingers. It trickles to the floor. Zan pushes past Nick—she doesn't know how long he's been standing behind her and she doesn't care—and hurries out into the daylight. She looks for a break in the crowd and ducks into a small passageway between two shops, where she folds in half, clutching her stomach as she waits to be horribly, violently ill.

Joni. Leo was searching for Joni. He wasn't cheating on her. He was trying to give her the one thing she'd always wanted. He wanted to give her her sister back. She'd had it all wrong. He never let her down. Not once.

She had taken care of that, all by herself.

# CADEN

SOPHIE DRIVES FAST, EXPERTLY MANEUVERING the stick shift with one finger hovering in the air. Caden's knees knock against the dashboard and he grips the bottom of his seat with both hands. His pulse is still racing and he tries to take deep, calming breaths, but so far they just seem to be making things worse.

"I can't believe you actually hit him."

Caden stares at his hands curiously, as if they had a plan of their own. "Sorry," he says. "I don't know, I mean, I didn't think that I . . ."

Suddenly Sophie is laughing, her eyes bright and wide as she slaps at the steering wheel with her open palms. "That was incredible!"

Caden swallows. "It was?"

Sophie takes her eyes off the road long enough to look at him, really look at him, like she's seeing him for the very first time. "Nobody has ever stood up for me like that, Caden," she says, before staring back at the road. "Ever."

Caden feels warm all over, but tries to play it cool. He glances out the window, watching the signs as they point back toward

Boston. He hadn't asked where Sophie's mother lived. He'd assumed it was nearby. It feels strange to be free and still moving away from home.

"It isn't far," Sophie assures him, noting as he eyes each passing exit. She fiddles anxiously with the radio dial, finding nothing but coarse, muffled static.

The quiet between them moves from natural to heavy. He wants to say something big. Racing adrenaline still floods his veins. They're free, and it's because of him. He scaled walls and leaped through the air. He changed somebody's life.

Surely he can make a little conversation.

They drive in silence until Sophie switches on her blinker, leading them off an exit ramp and into a small, hard-bitten town. A narrow rural road winds through the dark woods. They pass a deserted gas station, an empty hardware store, an abandoned beauty salon with a neon sign still blinking "Nails" over a padlocked door and barred windows. The town feels sad and lost in a way that's deeper than what's happening, like the desolation isn't new or specific. Caden sees now why Sophie stayed so long with Arthur. He may have been demanding, but at least he wasn't here.

They turn down a crowded cul-de-sac and pull up to a small two-story ranch, a single exposed bulb flickering over the door. Sophie kills the ignition and takes a deep breath. She looks at Caden like she wants to ask him a question, or tell him something he isn't going to like.

"Ready?" Caden asks, stretching his dry lips into a manufactured smile. It feels immediately uncomfortable and wrong. He wishes he'd hung on to the silence.

Sophie stares at the house, as if she's waiting for it to come to her. Finally, she puts a hand on the car door and swings it open. Caden follows her inside.

The house smells like cleaning products and cheap, fruity candles. Across the entryway there's a round red lantern that hangs from the ceiling. It glows eerily over a framed portrait of the Virgin Mary and a string of rosary beads. Caden remembers the haunted house he and Carly and the neighborhood kids used to visit every Halloween. He pretended the masks and cobwebs didn't scare him. It helped that he had to be brave for Carly, but the nightmares had lasted for months.

Sophie quietly drops her keys in a ceramic bowl in the shape of a flower. She steps out of her shoes. Caden does the same.

"She's back here," Sophie whispers. She leads him through a small living room, dimly lit by the reflected red glare from the hall. The low, ratty couch is covered in factory plastic, and a hulking TV with old-fashioned bunny ears lurks in the corner.

Caden isn't sure when he first hears the clicking sounds. They must have been there when he walked in the door, but it's not until he sees the blinking lights of the monitors, the tubes, the frail, sunken woman swaddled in the middle of the reclining hospital bed, that he realizes what's going on.

"Hi, Mom." Sophie crouches on her knees, reaching for a bony white hand under the flimsy hospital sheets. "I'm home, just like I promised. I missed you. Did you miss me?"

Caden stands back, one foot still planted firmly in the living room. The woman on the bed doesn't move; her eyes stay closed, her mouth slack and open just enough for the breathing tube tucked into one corner.

"This is my friend, Caden," Sophie says. "He's the reason I'm here. I was thinking, in the morning, we should make him a big breakfast. Blueberry pancakes and whipped cream, like we used to, okay?"

Sophie looks back at Caden and smiles. He knows it's too late to do anything about his face, the wide eyes or the clenching of his teeth, but Sophie doesn't seem to notice.

"The doctor said she probably can't hear us, but I think she can." Sophie shrugs. "At least enough to know I'm here . . ." She pushes up to her feet and lays her mother's hand carefully back under the sheet. She brushes back a few strands of wispy gray hair and leans over to kiss a spot on the older woman's papery forehead.

"Are you hungry?" Sophie asks. She cuts through another narrow hallway to the kitchen. "The nurse usually leaves snacks."

Caden's socks feel glued to the nubby beige carpet. Sophie's mother is in a coma. She has no idea what is happening. She is completely oblivious to the fact that soon, tomorrow in fact, the world will be forever changed. They will all be gone. And still, Sophie wants to be with her, at the end.

He feels Sophie near him again. She holds out a plastic strainer full of grapes. He shakes his head. "No, thanks."

Sophie considers him for a moment. Caden wonders if she regrets bringing him here. He wonders if he regrets coming.

"Want to see my room?" she asks. She turns on her heels and is halfway up the squeaking staircase before Caden thinks to answer. He watches her feet disappear. He can't believe this is the same girl he met by the pool, so cool and intimidating. Maybe it's being in the house where she grew up, or maybe it's seeing her with her mother. Either way, she seems, suddenly, vulnerable and young.

"Sure," he says to the empty room, to the woman in a coma. "Why not?"

Aside from a small bathroom, Sophie's is the only room upstairs. She leaves the grapes on top of a tall dresser and sinks onto her bed. It's small, a twin, but the comforter is the same as the one she had at Arthur's house: white with big purple flowers. She rests her head on the pile of pillows and folds her hands over her stomach.

She makes a pleasant humming sound. Caden tries to look anywhere but the bed. He starts with the walls. Concert posters, a painting of her name in pastel calligraphy, two small, framed prints of tropical birds. A parade of stuffed animals keeps watch from the windowsill, giraffes and dolphins and a spotted dog with floppy ears. The room feels like it hasn't been touched since Sophie was a little girl.

There's a rustling on the bed as she shifts her legs toward the wall. "Sit," she says. "It's much more comfortable than it looks."

Caden sits on the edge of the bed, his back so straight it feels like his spine is stretching in ways he never thought possible. Sophie laughs. "Relax, Caden," she says. "This isn't the first time you've seen a girl's bedroom, is it?"

Caden laughs. Too loud.

"Oh my God." Sophie holds a hand to her chin. "Is it, really?"

"No," Caden blurts. Technically, it isn't. But close. "Sorry," he says, trying at least to relax his shoulders. "It's been a long couple of days, I guess."

Sophie sits up and folds her legs, holding a pillow in her lap to cover the space where her dress could inch up. "Caden," she says. "Thank you. For doing this with me. I didn't realize how much I wanted to be here, and I never would have done it without you."

Caden shrugs. "Sure," he says. "I wanted to get out of there, too . . ."

"I know," she says. "But you didn't have to take me with you. I mean, you hardly even know me."

Caden's skin feels hot. He feels uncomfortable pricks on the back of his neck and hopes he's not sweating.

"But you knew I needed help," Sophie says. "How did you do that?"

Caden stares at the purple tassels of the shag carpet at his feet. "I don't know," he says. "I guess I just . . ."

He stops talking when he feels her hand on his side. She's playing with the bottom of his shirt, tugging it gently toward her. "What?" she asks.

He looks at her, her ponytail loose and messy and falling down her back. Her eye makeup is smudged in the creases, and her sundress is twisted so that a seam runs crooked down one side. She's never looked more beautiful.

He takes her hand and tangles her long fingers inside his own. The veins in his wrist are throbbing and he hopes she can't feel them, hopes she can't hear his heart pounding in his chest. She scoots closer to him on the bed, and he leans in, kissing her sweetly on the lips. When he tries to pull away, to catch his breath, he feels her hand firm on the back of his neck. She falls easily back on the bed, and brings him on top of her.

He plants his hands on either side of her slim shoulders,

trying not to crush her tiny frame. But her hands have moved to his back, strong and unrelenting, pulling him down, pressing his body against hers until there's no space at all between them. He feels the tension leaving his arms as he falls into the kiss, longer and deeper.

Caden follows Sophie's lead, moving the way her body seems to be asking his body to move, and tries not to think about what's happening, how this, too, isn't anything like what he'd imagined.

It's better.


When he wakes, the sun has set, the full moon a dusky orange, glowing through the window.

He opens one eye and stares at Sophie's sleeping profile, like he's trying to memorize the features of her face. She's tucked between him and the wall, lying on her side. He touches her arm and it's a shock, all of it—the fact that her naked skin is so available for the touching. The fact that she's asleep and he's there. The fact that he is no longer a virgin.

"Mmm," she mumbles into the pillow. She flattens her palm on his face. Her fingers are heavy and warm from the weight of the blankets. She traces his features sloppily. He smiles and she draws his lips with her thumb. "That's better," she says, as if it were a test.

Caden looks around her room, the stuffed animals and picture frames now darkened by shadows. There's something comforting about being surrounded by memories, by who you were when you were small. He thinks of his own room, the secret boxes of toys he has stashed in the closet, unable to throw them away. The computer he's spent countless hours hunched over, the keyboard worn and the letters as faded as the paper-thin camouflage blanket he's slept with since he was a toddler.

"Sophie," Caden says softly. He brushes a few strands of hair away from her eyes. She twitches and blinks.

"What time is it?" she asks, wrapping the blanket around her chest as she sits up against the wall. She stares at the room around her, adjusting to being in her own bed, adjusting to him beside her. She grins, her tongue poking adorably through the small gap in her teeth. "I'm starving."

Sophie rummages around the floor for her clothes, pulling on her dress and scooping her hair into a low ponytail. Caden smiles. He imagines the two of them moving around the tiny kitchen downstairs, making a meal out of whatever they can find. He imagines staying up late, talking, asking each other all kinds of questions. Silly questions, like: *What's your favorite amusement park ride?* But real questions, too, like: *Are you afraid? What comes next? What happens after the end?*

He imagines that they spend the rest of the night, and all day tomorrow, in bed. Just the two of them. He imagines that as it happens, whatever is going to happen, he's holding her, and she's holding him. It's quiet, and peaceful, and all he's ever wanted.

He steps into his jeans and throws on his shirt, following Sophie downstairs. She stands barefoot in the doorway, the pale light from the living room glowing in her hair. She holds up a finger, gesturing for him to wait as she goes to check on her mother.

He hears the faint, staccato beeping of the machines, the

wheezing and clicking that is keeping the woman alive. He watches as Sophie hovers over the adjustable bed, smoothing the sheets, caressing her mother's hair, and worries, for a moment, that he's made a horrible mistake. Without Arthur and his help, how long will Sophie's mother survive?

But as Sophie leans down to kiss her mother's cheek, a sense of calm returns. All that matters is that they are together now. With so few guarantees, they at least deserve that.

Caden thinks of Ramona. She may not be perfect, and she may never change. But she's his family. She and Carly, they're a part of him.

He lets out a long breath and stands in front of Sophie, reaching for one of her hands. "Sophie," he says. "I have to go home."

Sophie's face scrambles. For a second he's afraid she might cry.

"I'm sorry," he rushes. "This has been . . . amazing. Meeting you, and tonight, but . . ."

"You have to go home," Sophie repeats with a quick, binding nod. "I get it."

"You do?"

Sophie leans in toward him and puts a hand on his chest. "You'll probably think this is crazy, but I think I was having a dream, just now. I woke up, and you were gone. I looked for you everywhere, but . . . it was like you were never here. And then I figured it out. Of course. You're an angel."

She looks deep into Caden's eyes and he squirms uncomfortably. He forces a chuckle and rolls his eyes. "I'm no angel," he jokes. "I can promise you that."

"I'm serious," she says. "I think we both ended up in that house for a reason. I needed you. And you needed me."

Caden feels the warm weight of her hand on his ribs. He covers her fingers with his own. Sophie smiles and brings her lips softly to his, a sweet, lingering kiss goodbye.

"Oh, and Caden?" she asks, as he pulls the front door open.

"Yeah?"

"Remember what your dad said? About the two of you being alike?"

Caden looks out at the night sky, at the clusters of stars blinking from behind the trees. He remembers the way he used to see the same stars from his bedroom window, wondering where his father might be as he wished him a silent good night. His jaw tightens, the corners of his eyes start to burn. He wants to go back, back to when his father was just a blurred memory, a benevolent dragon chasing him through the woods.

Sophie touches the inside of Caden's forearm with her thumb. "Trust me," she says, pressing firmly, as if she's trying to leave a mark. "He's wrong."

# ZAN

THE FERRYBOATS SIT, DOCKED IN THE HARBOR, hulking and almost surreal. Zan has never seen all of them in one place before. Lined up in an imposing row, they look regal and a little bit scary. As if, in another life, they could have been battleships instead of gentle ushers, carrying countless people to and from the island every day.

Nick is giving her space, keeping busy with tasks on his boat as he prepares to bring them home. Zan sits at the edge of the dock, looking out at the water, the ocean dark and ominous.

She hears a voice, calling her name, from far away, as if in a memory. For a moment, she wonders if it's him. Leo. What would he say to her now? They'd hardly ever fought. She can't remember a time when he'd been angry with her. They were in it together, whatever *it* was.

Until now. How could she face him? How could she even begin to apologize for betraying him as she had? He wouldn't have expected her to grieve forever, she knows that. But his best friend? No matter how open-minded, how forgiving he was, she knows she was wrong. They were wrong. He'd given them nothing but reasons to trust him, and they hadn't. She and Nick. They'd both let him down.

"Zan!"

This time, Nick hears the voice, too. He turns from the bow of the boat to look back across the parking lot. "Hey, doesn't that kid live on your road?"

Zan turns to see a shadowy figure stepping out from behind the boarded-up ticket office. "Caden?" she calls, pushing herself to her feet.

Caden jogs the length of the dock. By the time he reaches them, he's out of breath, his shirt damp with sweat at the collar. "Hey," he manages. "I can't believe—what are you doing here?"

"What are *you* doing here?" Zan asks. "You look . . ."

"I ran," Caden heaves. "I was . . . I got stuck. My dad . . ."

Caden turns and tosses one arm back behind him, gesturing to the hilly terrain of the mainland. He takes a deep breath and shakes his head. "It's a long story," he says. "I thought I'd make the last boat. They're not running?"

Nick steps onto the dock, leaning down to untie the rope between his feet. "This one is," he says. "You need a lift?"

Caden looks from Nick to Zan. His face looks somehow off balance, like he can't decide if he wants to laugh or cry. The glow from the floodlights catches in his green eyes, and all of a sudden she sees it. The smiling twinkle, the mischievous gleam. The little kid she used to run around the neighborhood with. He's back.

"Thanks," Caden says. Nick shakes his head at the boat and

Caden helps Zan climb carefully on board. The engine sputters to life and the boat slides back from the dock. Zan tucks her knees up to her chest and rests her chin on her hands, watching as the lights of the harbor recede into the darkness, the pull of home drawing them in and away.

# SIENNA

SIENNA IS SURE SHE'LL FIND SOMEBODY TO pick her up, a ride for at least part of the long journey back to her side of the island. And it's not that the streets are quiet. In fact, it is the opposite. Everybody seems to be outside, in large groups or walking in pairs, as if trying to physically soak up as much as they can of the world around them. Who knew what these trees, those beaches, that perfect blue sky will all look like after tomorrow, Sienna thinks. If anyone is around to see it.

But there isn't a car in sight. Nobody is in a rush to get anywhere, or do anything, except be together.

As Sienna walks, she stares at the groups of people gathered in the streets. It reminds her of block parties in her old neighborhood, or the summer street fairs Dad used to take them to on the island. She hated all of them. Mom did, too. At the block parties, they'd often sit on their own front stoop with a bag of chips and a jar of store-bought salsa, intended for sharing but usually polished off by just the two of them, alone. At the fairs, they'd duck into a bookstore, or occasionally wait in the car. Eventually Mom stayed home. She never understood the appeal of large groups, and Sienna realizes now that she's the same way. The last place she wants to be at a time like this, when she's afraid and confused, is with a bunch of people she barely knows, hearing about how afraid and confused they all are, too.

She knows most people find it comforting. But she's not most people. Maybe that's why she's never had a tribe, she thinks, as she walks on, the soles of her sandals wearing thin. A tribe would have been lost on her.

That's probably what Mom thought, too. Sienna feels a familiar fog behind her eyes, a sharp tug in the pit of her stomach. There is no getting around it.

Sienna is just like her mother.

Her shins throb, and there are blisters forming at the backs of her heels. It will take her until morning to get home. If only Owen would find her.

She doesn't know why she's crying. It's nobody's fault but her own. She could have stayed home and been with Dad and Ryan, playing games, being a family. Dad was right. That's all that matters, now.

Or she could have stayed at the brickyard with Owen, the only person who gave her a chance.

But nothing is enough. She has to keep moving. And now, there is nowhere left to run.

She takes a few ragged breaths, wiping the tears from her cheeks. It is suddenly so dark that she can hardly see her feet. She spots a light in the distance, flickering in front of the supermarket, and hobbles to a bench on the porch, rubbing her feet with her hands.

What's the point? What does it matter who she's with

tomorrow? Everyone dies alone. What difference does it make if Sienna stays here, on this bench, all by herself until the very end?

She tucks her sweater tighter around her waist and brings her knees up on the bench, burying her face in her forearms. She is alone, as she's always been. She shouldn't be so surprised. It is her story, it was her mother's story, and the ending is always the same.


She wakes to the soft shush of tires. A cool wash of headlights lands on the crooked row of abandoned shopping carts beside her. Sienna sits upright, squinting into the glare. It's a truck, and the driver, a freckled guy in a T-shirt, leans out the window. "Are you all right?" he asks.

Sienna looks past him to the girl in the front seat. They both look vaguely familiar, but the guy in the back is the only one she really recognizes. Carly's brother. She hasn't seen him since they were practically in diapers, but even in the dark she would know that wild red hair anywhere.

"You live on the circle, right?" The guy in the back leans over a dangling fishing rod. "Hop in."

Sienna hesitates a moment. She knows she was silly to think that Owen might come after her, but she can't help but feel disappointed. She takes a breath. She's doing the right thing. It's time to go home.

"Thanks," Sienna says, climbing over the tailgate. She sits with her back to the wheel well as the guy bangs twice on the side of the truck.

As they roll out of the parking lot and down the main road, Sienna looks at the dark silhouettes of the three people before her, each of them looking off in a different direction, quietly lost inside themselves. Maybe a tribe isn't about fitting in, she thinks. Maybe it's not about the people you've known the longest. Maybe, sometimes, it's just about the right place at the right time, and moving in the same direction, together.

# DAY SIX

# ZAN

IT'S LATE.

The sky is black and starless through the tilted window over her bed. She stares up at it for a while, disoriented by the sensation of falling asleep before the sun has set and waking up later in darkness.

When Nick dropped her off, the house had been empty and still. She'd found Daniel in his studio, working on his Forgiving Wheel, or heard him out there, first. There was a cycle of low grumbles, a sharp crunching sound, finished off with a sputtering cough. Zan couldn't imagine what any of those noises might possibly have to do with forgiveness, and there wasn't any part of her interested in finding out.

She stood for a while outside the studio door, but couldn't go in. She wasn't afraid, exactly. She just didn't feel ready, or whole enough, to explain where she'd been. Daniel would probably understand. He had a way of understanding almost anything, or at least acting like he did. Miranda was the one she should have been nervous about, but Miranda was, as usual, out.

She climbed up the ladder to the loft and lay down on her bed, thinking she'd rest until she heard life in the kitchen. She needed time to work out a story that would make sense. Even now, she knew she couldn't tell the truth. Miranda had always had a hard time talking to Zan about Leo. It was bad enough when he was alive, but even worse after his death. She wouldn't say much, but Zan could feel the way her mother felt, the way she wished her daughter could be more like her. Why couldn't Zan just get a hobby? Or bury herself in schoolwork? Did she have to read his books all the time? So much time on her own, wallowing in her sadness, it couldn't possibly be healthy.

None of this was ever said out loud. It didn't need to be. Zan and Miranda were different creatures, made out of different stuff. Zan had long ago stopped worrying about it or wishing things could be different. As far as she knew, Miranda felt the same way.

Zan sits in bed and a fresh wave of guilt crashes over her, head to toe, as if it had been lurking in some dark corner of the room, waiting for her to wake up. She blinks and sees Nick on the Swan Boat, his mouth on hers, his strong hands pressing into her back. Leo's best friend. Leo, who had spent what turned out to be the final days of his life on a wild goose chase, trying to surprise Zan by doing something nice. No, more than nice. Something extraordinary.

Until the end, he'd been exactly who she'd thought he was. Loyal, dedicated, adventurous, brave. And she'd been weak. She'd doubted him. She deserved an asteroid. She deserved to be wiped out, obliterated, scattered into meaningless dust.

There's a hollow turning in her stomach. She hasn't eaten in hours. She wraps her quilt around her shoulders and starts down the rickety ladder. The kitchen is dark and silent, except for the hum of the fridge and a sad, sporadic drip from the faucet. She fills a glass with water and squeezes the tap tight.

"Don't bother," a voice says from behind her. "It's broken."

Zan jumps and fumbles the glass, spilling water onto her wrist and in a small puddle on the hardwood floor. Miranda is sitting at the kitchen table in her bathrobe, a mug of hot tea clenched between her wiry fingers.

"Mom," Zan sighs. "You scared me."

"Sorry," Miranda says softly. "I was wondering if you would wake up."

Zan leans with her back against the dishwasher. A milky wash of moonlight slips in through the small window over the sink, and Zan can just barely make out the shape of her mother, hunched deeply over her mug, her short black hair frizzing around the long lines of her face. She wonders if she should turn on a light, but something tells her it would be too much.

"I didn't mean to fall asleep," Zan mutters apologetically. "I was waiting for you to get home . . ."

"Where were you?" Miranda asks. Her voice sounds strange. Not furious, as Zan had predicted. But not exactly not-furious, either. She sounds, mostly, tired. And uncertain, which is jarring, and almost worse than flat-out pissed. Miranda is never uncertain about anything. Ever.

Zan pulls out another of the straight-backed kitchen chairs, just enough to squeeze in at the table across from her mother. She takes a sip of her water. It's not cold and tastes vaguely metallic. She should have let it run longer.

"I went to Boston," she says finally. "With Nick."

"Nick who?"

Perhaps as a by-product of all of the time Miranda spent organizing events, or at work at the gallery, or sitting on boards and committees, she's always had a hard time keeping track of Zan's friends. It took her months to acknowledge Leo by name, and longer to consider the two of them an actual couple.

"Leo's friend," Zan reminds her. "He was . . . helping me with something."

Miranda nods. It looks for a moment like she's going to ask more. Zan's mind is racing. The last thing she wants to do is talk to her mother about Leo. But maybe it would be good. Maybe it's only right, the night before they wait for the end, to finally get to the bottom of whatever it is that has always come between them. The strained conversations, the unspoken disappointments. Whatever it was that made Miranda so reluctant to accept that Zan wasn't just like her.

And why had things gotten so much worse, once Leo started coming around? It was as if Miranda refused to believe that her daughter could possibly have fallen in love, or found somebody she wanted to spend all of her time with, somebody more important to her than anything else in the world. Even friends. Even school. Even her *passion*, especially considering that, aside from Leo, she hadn't really found one yet.

And maybe Zan could finally admit that yes, there were times when she did feel like she may have missed out. Maybe she shouldn't have lost touch with all of her friends. Maybe she should have spent more time figuring out who she wanted to be, so that when Leo was so suddenly, so unbelievably, gone, she would have been able to put herself back together again. Or at least she might have known where to start.

Miranda takes a slow sip of her tea, a damp cloud of peppermint wafting from the top of her mug. "Did you find it?"

Zan swallows. "Find what?"

Miranda runs both hands through her dark curls, shaking them at the roots. "Whatever you were looking for."

Zan sets her glass down on the table, above the pale dents where Daniel had accidentally cut through the wood while working on some etchings. The way Miranda reacted you would have thought it was a priceless antique, and not some piece of left-behind furniture that came with the house when they moved in.

That's it? She stares at the tiny cracks, not able to look up at her mother. *Did you find what you're looking for?* This is their big heart-to-heart?

Zan sighs. "Yeah," she says. "Sort of."

She did find something. She found out how little she knew how to trust, even the one person who had never given her anything but reasons to do so. She found out how easily she could forget everything that ever mattered. She found out that she was right to love Leo as hard as she had. As hard as she still does, and always will.

It doesn't much feel like it, but she found Joni, too. Or, she got close. Closer than any of them had been in seven years. She's tempted to tell Miranda. At least it would be something. Something to make Zan feel important, worthwhile.

But she knows it wouldn't do any good. It would be only out of spite, a way to say, *Remember Leo? Who was never good enough? Look what he did. Look what he did for me.* And somewhere, even though there's a part of Zan that wants to make Miranda hurt, wants to make her feel the way she feels, she knows it wouldn't be fair. Ever since Joni left, Miranda has been trying to forget her, forget the daughter who wouldn't be boxed in. The daughter who was strong enough to choose the life that she wanted, instead of the one Miranda had decided would be hers.

Why remind her of all that now? Why remind her that somewhere, not so very far from where they are sitting, Joni is out there. Just a few phone calls away. Leo had found her. And who knows what happened, who knows if they ever really met, but considering that she hasn't turned up, it's safe to assume that still, even now, Joni doesn't want to be found.

Miranda takes one final sip of her tea and stands, carefully tucking her chair back beneath the lip of the table. "I don't know if your father told you, but we've planned a gathering at the beach tomorrow night."

"Tomorrow night?" Zan asks with a bitter chuckle. Tomorrow night. Sunset. The asteroid. Leave it to Miranda to insist on planning even the end of the world.

"Yes." Miranda brings her mug to the sink. "It's important for everyone in the neighborhood to be together. To have a place to go, and not be alone. I realize you might not care about this community, but I do. We do. Your father will bring his new installation. We'll have a picnic. It will be . . ."

Zan holds her breath. If her mother says *nice*, or *lovely*, or anything complimentary and meaningless, she is going to scream. Literally scream, until her body shakes in silent, empty spasms, until there is no sound in her left.

"I hope you'll join us," Miranda says instead. She rests her cup in the sink and passes through the kitchen to her bedroom, where Daniel has been asleep. He sleeps through everything. Miranda, on the other hand, is an insomniac. Zan has spent countless nights lying awake in bed, listening to her mother puttering in the kitchen, making tea, flipping through the pages of the local paper. Sleeplessness was the one thing they'd always had in common, though, naturally, it had never been discussed.

Zan sits in the quiet, listening to the relentless *plink plunk* of the dripping faucet behind her. She's no longer hungry but roots around in the pantry anyway. She takes an open bag of trail mix back to the table and begins picking out the Brazil nuts, to be discarded into the trash. She smiles sadly, thinking of Gretchen, who finally found her soul mate. At least something worked out for someone, she thinks.

She stares at the old grandfather clock in the living room— 11:53. In just a few minutes, *tomorrow* will be here. A sudden, cold fear shocks her inside, all the way down to the smallest bones in her feet. They'd had so many warnings. So much time to prepare. And where had it left them? Was anything better? The world was still ending, and nothing made sense. Nobody had been able to tell her why Leo had to die. Or where Joni was. Or why she and her mother could never have an actual conversation. These were the things she'd always imagined she'd know, some- how, before it was her turn to stop living.

She sits with a handful of sunflower seeds in her palm, a new, anxious tightening at the base of her throat. She hasn't cried much since the news came, the news that nobody knew how to process. How do you think about the end of the world? Where do you file it away? It never seemed to settle anywhere near the place where the tears were hiding. Or maybe it was her. Maybe she'd run out of tears, having spent months and months crying for Leo, and for herself without him.

There's a shuffle outside. At first, she thinks it's an animal. The slow, steady crackle of dirt and gravel. Steps. But bigger than a skunk. Or raccoon. As they near the front door, Zan looks up. The handle, a rusted brass swirl, is turning. Nobody's doors are ever locked on the island, and suddenly, Zan wonders why not.

She hops quickly to her feet and stands behind her chair, as if to use it as a weapon. The door creaks slowly open. In the dark, Zan can only make out the boots, tall black leather with glinting silver buckles.

"Hello?" a voice whispers. "Zan, is that you?"

Zan drops the handful of seeds and nuts in a scattered pile on the table. She runs to the living room and turns on the lamp by the couch. Standing in the door, her long dark hair tangled beneath the thin straps of her flowing dress, is her sister.

Joni, who wouldn't be found, had found her.

# CADEN

He couldn't go home, not yet. It didn't feel right to wake them up in the middle of the night, bombard Ramona and Carly with the news of where he'd been, and what he knew.

He slept on the beach, by the boulder, where he'd slept so many nights before. The steady thumping of the waves on the shore had lulled him quickly to sleep, and he woke as the first rays of misty sunlight glowed from behind the dunes.

Now, he takes a deep breath as he starts up the unpaved driveway. He still doesn't feel ready, but he has no choice. He can't put it off any longer.

The first thing he notices is the trash. Or, more accurately, the lack of trash scattered across the overgrown lawn, usually tumbled from the overturned rubber barrels, listing at one side of the house.

The barrels, now, stand tall, empty, and almost proud—if trash can be proud—at the bottom of the steps, complete with matching lids. Lids that Caden is pretty sure he's never seen before in his life.

As he looks closer, he sees that the lawn, which he hadn't

before considered much of a lawn at all, is no longer overgrown. The grass has been cut back and actually glistens, green and healthy. Even the squat ceramic pots that usually serve as ashtrays have been cleaned out and planted with tiny pink and purple flowers.

Caden looks back at the road, and then up to the house, disoriented. The house is his house, there's no doubt about that. The cracked asphalt on the flat roof is still cracked; the busted heating vent that sags near the basement is still both sagging and busted. But the overall vibe as he approaches the front door is definitely, substantially, better.

Carly must have been on some kind of home-improvement rampage, he figures, fueled by grief and denial. He shakes his head and starts up the back deck. The glare of the sun off the sliding glass doors is bright and blinding, and the piercing shrill of Ramona's scream seems to reach him from everywhere at once.

There's a discombobulated clatter as Caden turns to see his mother, falling from a rusted chaise lounge. She's barefoot, in a red-gold nightgown that matches her hair, and her skin is sun-kissed and shiny. She runs to him across the plywood decking, throwing her arms around him and burying her head under his chin.

"Thank you thank you thank you," she's muttering, more to the air than to him. Caden wants to hug her back, but his arms are pinned to his sides, and he's still trying to make sense of it all—the healthy yard, the flowers, the clean, fruity scent of shampoo in Ramona's soft, wavy hair.

When she finally releases him, she pushes him back to study his face. He looks into her eyes and is shocked by what isn't there: no heavy lids, no sick, glassy sheen, no red at the corners. Just the startling blue of her irises, and the subtle shine of real tears around them.

"Hi, Mom," he says.

She shakes his elbows and the tears spill over onto the tops of her cheeks. She falls into his chest again, but this time he wrestles free and hugs her close, the sharp points of her shoulders tucked under his arms.

"I knew you'd come back," she breathes. "I knew it."

Caden runs his hands through his own hair, greasy and thick. He catches his reflection in the glass. It's been days since he's showered, and his clothes, though still stiff and new, hang on him in a way that looks unnatural.

He takes a deep breath, steadying himself for the wrath that is sure to come. For all Ramona knows, he's been at some non-stop rave, high off of whatever he could get his hands on, with no plans to ever return.

But she doesn't yell. She doesn't accuse. She wipes her eyes carefully with the insides of two fingers and smiles.

"Are you hungry?" she asks. She pulls open the slider and Caden follows her into the house, his eyes splotchy from the sun. Even in the dark he can feel that it's spotless, the kitchen counters glistening, no dirty dishes in the sink. "There are leftovers from dinner last night. The Lowes brought us over some more veggies. I made a stir-fry."

"You cooked?"

Ramona pulls her hair back and ropes it into a bun. She smiles from behind the open fridge. "We've had a big week around here."

"I can tell," Caden says. Is she really not going to ask where he's been? "Where's Carly?"

"She's at the Center, one of her meetings . . ." Ramona pulls out a Tupperware container and spoons the contents into a bowl. "I told her to skip it. Such a gorgeous day. But you know how she is . . ."

She moves quickly, sticking the bowl in the microwave and jabbing at some buttons. The yellow light flickers on as the tray inside vibrates and spins.

"Mom," Caden starts. There must be a tell in his voice, a small signal that he has something serious to say. Before he can take another breath she's rushing across the kitchen to his side.

"Caden, no." She pushes him into one of the mismatched chairs at the dining room table and sits in another, gripping his forearms with both hands. "You don't have to say anything, okay? We don't have to do this. I know why you left."

"You do?"

Ramona nods. She's stopped looking him in the eye, staring instead at the insides of his wrists, the palms of his slender hands. "Of course," she says. "I probably would have done the same. You didn't deserve this. You never did, either of you, but especially not at a time like this. You were scared, and confused, and I wasn't here for you at all. I was the one who ran away first, you know? Without ever getting off that couch, I left you both. And I'll never forgive myself for that. Okay?"

"Mom . . ."

"I know that. And I know you can't forgive me, either. There isn't enough time. There would never be enough time. But the second night you didn't come home, Carly was here with me, and something just snapped inside. I couldn't keep doing it, Caden. I made you leave, and I had no idea if you were coming back, but I knew I had to change. No matter what happened, I knew I couldn't spend whatever time we had left the way I'd been living. I know it sounds stupid, and, maybe not like very much, but . . ." She looks up at him and works on a smile, weak and careful and heartbreaking. "I haven't had a drink in four days."

Caden swallows and peels her fingers from around his wrists, holding them together in his palms. "It doesn't sound stupid," he says gently. "It's really great, Mom."

The smile gets stronger and she squeezes his fingers. She looks happier than he's ever seen her look in his life.

"But you're wrong," he continues softly. "I didn't leave because of you."

Ramona turns her head and the makeshift bun falls out, long tangled strands of her hair falling to her elbows on the table. "You didn't?"

Caden shakes his head. "Actually, I didn't leave at all," he says. "I was taken."

"Taken?" Ramona asks. There's a wild glint in her eyes all of a sudden, like she already knows, like somewhere, deep down, she's always known it would happen someday. "What do you mean you were taken?"

"Dad," Caden says simply. "He had these guys come get me at the beach one night. They knocked me out with something and brought me to his beach house on the Cape. He's got this whole bunker thing, he thinks he's going to survive the asteroid down there, and he wanted me with him, I guess."

Ramona stares at him blankly. Caden hadn't given much thought to what she'd look like when he told her, but now that the moment is here, he's surprised. She doesn't look shocked, or scared, or outraged. She looks, mostly, sad. Sad and sorry. Like she was the one who threw him in the back of a car and locked him up.

"He had all these crazy ideas." Caden almost laughs. "He thought we were gonna, like, bond, or whatever. I think he really, truly, believed it, like he wanted me to be all grateful and, I don't know, happy to be there."

Ramona nods quickly. "Were you?"

Caden scoffs. "No," he says. "I mean, I guess there were a couple times when I was, like, curious, maybe. He took me to his lodge, trying to show off, and we played catch in Fenway Park . . ."

"You did?" Ramona asks. Her eyes are teary again and she's pursing her lips together, so hard that the color in them drains to a clear, pale white. All of a sudden, Caden knows what the sorry face is about. She's sorry he was kidnapped, sure, but she's also sorry he had to wait so long. Sorry it's the first time he's spent with his father, the first time they cooked a meal together, the first time they played catch. Sorry, because she knows it's mostly her fault.

"Mom." Caden holds her hands tighter and looks her hard in the eyes. "He told me what happened. He told me about Carly."

Ramona hangs her head. There's a patch of faded gray spread out along her center part. "Shit," she says quietly, to the speckled linoleum floor.

"Is it true?" he asks. It's not like there's a part of him that believes, or even hopes, that it isn't. He wants, he needs, to hear her say it out loud.

Ramona stares at the floor for a long moment. "Yes," she whispers. "It's true."

"Why didn't you just tell us?" Caden asks. "Did you really think it would make a difference? Carly is my sister."

"I know," Ramona says. "I didn't do it for you. Or Carly. I did it for me. As long as you didn't know the truth, I had an excuse. I could be broken, and useless, because I got left behind. I didn't do anything wrong. It doesn't make sense, but in a way I guess it did to me."

Caden takes a deep breath. He wishes this could be the end of it, but he knows it's not. "It's not fair, Mom," he says. "She deserves to know the truth."

Ramona nods. She untangles her fingers from Caden's and grips the tops of her knees. She still hasn't looked up. "You're right," she sighs. "I'll tell her."

"Tell who what?"

Caden looks over Ramona's head to the deck. Carly stands with her hands cupped over her eyes, her face tight and squinting as she tries to identify the dark shadows on the other side of the screen door.

"Hey, Carly," Caden says, clearing his throat as she steps inside the room.

At the sound of his voice she flings herself toward him. He opens his arms, as if to catch her in a hug. But she's not interested in hugging, and he quickly realizes he'll need his hands to block the fast, sharp blows she's delivering to his shoulders and face.

"You stupid, fucking asshole," she screeches, battering him with slaps and closed-fist jabs. Caden dodges her as best he can, folding her arms together and pinning them across her chest.

Ramona stands off to the side, holding her face in her hands. "Carly," she says. "Carly, stop."

"Stop?" she shouts. "Why should I stop? He has no idea what he put us through. He doesn't care about anybody but himself. He's selfish. You're so fucking selfish, Caden, you know that? You're a selfish little baby who doesn't care about his family. And you know what? We don't care about you. We don't need you. This week has been . . . incredible. Right, Mom? Tell him how much better everything has been since he left."

Ramona shakes her head and covers her face with her hands. Carly struggles to catch her breath, and Caden holds her, feeling her small lungs fill and empty, her shoulders heaving up and down.

"Carly," he says finally. "I'm sorry. It wasn't my fault."

Carly sniffles, something between an angry chuckle and a sob. She wrestles free from his hold and slaps his hands away. "Of course it wasn't," she spits.

"It wasn't," Caden insists. "I was with Dad. He took me and he wouldn't let me leave. I had no choice."

Carly freezes. "What?"

"I know."

"What are you talking about?" she asks, falling into a chair behind her.

Caden shakes his head. "That's what happened, I promise," he says. "I wanted to come back. I wanted to call. But . . ."

Carly waits for more. Caden glances at Ramona, standing

with her back to them, staring up at the cracks in the ceiling above the electric stove.

"Mom?" Caden prompts. What's the use in dragging it out?

Ramona leans against the countertop and takes a deep breath. "Yeah, okay," she says. She steps one bare foot on top of the other and presses down, knees bent, as if she's trying to jump out of her own skin.

"Yeah, okay, what?" Carly asks. She eyes Caden searchingly. "What is this?"

"Mom has something to tell you," Caden says. He tries not to sound like a brat. It's not his secret, not his place. But all of a sudden he feels in control, like his family is something in need of attention and safekeeping and he's the only one able to provide it.

Ramona joins them at the table. She sits across the table from Carly and looks her in the eyes. "Carly," she says. "You know how much I love you, right?"

Carly rolls her eyes. "Jesus, Mom, yes," she sighs. "Please just tell me what the hell is going on."

"Okay, okay." Ramona wipes at imaginary crumbs on the table, scooping them into her open palm. "So. When your father left . . . Arthur, when Arthur left . . . he didn't just, you know, up and leave us. For no reason."

"I know that," Carly says. "He left because he's an asshole and he had more important things to do with his life. Do we have to talk about this again?"

Caden shakes his head and Carly glares at him. "What?" she asks. "Are you guys best friends or something now? You got that kidnapping disease where you fall in love with your captor?"

Caden sits back in his seat. "Can you let her finish, please?" He looks at Ramona and gives her an encouraging nod.

"We do have to talk about it," Ramona starts again, with difficulty. "Because it's not the truth. And Caden thinks, we both think, that the truth is important, now. Just like I don't want to go up against, whatever we have to go up against, tonight, as a pathetic, miserable drunk, I don't want to be there as a liar, either." She bites her lower lip and traces the pale lines of a water stain on the table with her finger. "So, here goes. After Caden was born, things with me and Arthur got really . . . messy. We were both unhappy, all of the time. I loved my son, we both did, but it didn't make us a family. At least, not a real one. And instead of trying to fix anything, I ran away. I ran away, and I started . . . seeing . . . other people. I was a wreck. And then . . ." Ramona forces herself to look up at Carly. "And then I got pregnant."

Carly stares back at Ramona, frozen in her seat. She doesn't say a word.

"I didn't know what to do," Ramona says quietly. "I came back. I came home, and I told him everything. He knew the baby . . . he knew you weren't his daughter, but he stayed anyway. He stayed as long as he could," she says, a thick, phlegmy bubble caught in her throat. "And when he couldn't do it anymore, he left. But it wasn't his fault. Because I left first. And then I lied to you. To both of you. And I'm sorry."

Carly looks at her small hands in her lap. She picks at the frayed bottom of her short jean skirt. Caden watches as the skin around her lips gets splotchy and red, the way it used to when she was little and on the verge of a tantrum. "Why?" she says softly, and coughs. "Why did you lie?"

Ramona sniffs and sits back, resting her head against the wall behind her, beneath the spots of chipped paint where a poster was long ago torn down. It was a copy of a painting, Monet, or Manet, Caden could never remember which, the kind you'd buy in a museum gift shop. Ramona and Arthur had bought it together. It managed to survive years of screaming insults, as if it were somehow to blame for all that had gone wrong.

Then one night, when Caden was eleven or twelve, during one of her infamous, drunken fits, Ramona had ripped the poster from the wall and stormed onto the deck, holding a match to one curled end. Caden watched the growing flames from his bedroom. He remembers thinking he should do something. But there was something about Ramona, waving a flag of fire, her eyes wild and her hair a tangle of moonlit curls as she tossed it into the soggy grass . . . he couldn't move. She was beautiful.

Ramona's eyes are wet and cloudy. "I lied because I couldn't give you another reason to hate me," she says. "I couldn't be the bad guy all of the time. It was wrong. It was disgusting. And I'm sorry," she says, a single tear trailing down her rosy cheek. "I'm so, so sorry."

Caden reaches for his mother's hand across the table. Her fingers twitch and tremble and she hides them in her lap.

He looks sideways at Carly, who is still studying the tops of her knees. Her lower lip quivers slightly but her eyes are dry and steady.

There's a sharp drop in his gut. The silence is too much. What has he done? All of his life, Carly and Ramona have been a team. A dysfunctional team, where one carried the other almost every step of the way, but they were together. They were a family. And in one moment, with one demanded confession, he's screwed it all up.

Carly pushes her hands into her thighs and stands. She trips over the leg of her chair and it makes a sharp squealing sound against the floor. Caden wants to move, wants to stop her from leaving, but he can't. He's done enough already.

But Carly doesn't leave. She walks slowly around the table and stands over Ramona's shoulders. She puts a hand on the top of her mother's head. Ramona looks up, her eyes hopeful saucers. Carly pats her hair in short, gentle strokes, and she smiles.

"You're not a bad guy, Mom."

Ramona wraps her arms around Carly's tiny waist, pulling her onto her lap. Caden coughs and looks away. He feels like he's eavesdropping on a conversation he started and abandoned.

"And you're not so bad either," Carly says to him from across the table. "We're all okay. Okay?"

Caden looks at his sister. He wonders how something so small can be so resilient, so indestructible. "You're not mad?" he asks.

Carly smiles and shrugs. "Mad?" she repeats. "Why would I be mad? Nothing's different. You can't lose something you never had," she says. "And to be honest, I'm kinda psyched about it."

Ramona raises an eyebrow and looks at Carly with suspicion.

"You are?" Caden asks.

"Yeah." Carly nods, twirling a long strand of Ramona's hair in her fingers. "No offense, Cade. But your dad sounds like kind of a dick."

# SIENNA

THE DAY STARTS, HOT AND HUMID.

Sienna sits out back with Denny, the patio table covered in piles of wildflowers, picked on the long beach walks she and Dad had been taking all week long. They've been hard at work for an hour, creating bouquets and arrangements for an arbor, the as-yet-to-be-built structure beneath which the wedding ceremony will be performed, later that night on the beach.

They've been working mostly in quiet. In fact, the whole house has been shockingly calm since Sienna's arrival. When she walked in, late last night, trembling and exhausted from her trek across the island, Dad got up from the couch where he was sleeping and wrapped her in a hug. No words. There was nothing left to say. She was home.

Ryan was in his room. As soon as he'd heard the squeal of the screen door, he bounded down the steps and into the living room. But even their reunion was understated. He hugged her shyly around the waist, told her three important facts about rattlesnakes, and shuffled back upstairs. As if he never doubted she'd make it home in time.

"What about these?" Denny asks, holding up long stalks of

wild lavender and beach grass. Sienna is surprised to find Denny so calm, almost peaceful-looking. She remembers back to that first dinner, when even the mention of the asteroid was enough to send Denny running off in tears. Dad was right: a project of some kind was exactly what they'd needed, all of them, to stay busy, to keep from thinking too much.

Just like Owen. Sienna feels a sharp pain piercing her ribs. She can't even think his name without suffering some bodily ache, a physical reminder of his absence. But every time she feels a pang of missing him, she takes a breath and remembers the truth. It's not Owen, not really. The power of her feelings has less to do with anything real between them and more to do with the strange and terrifying chemistry of her brain.

"Nice." Sienna nods at the flowers, forcing herself to snap out of it. She reaches for some of the long-stemmed Queen Anne's lace. "Maybe with a few of these?" she suggests. The delicate white heads of the flowers poke sturdily through the thin green stalks, adding the perfect matrimonial touch.

"I love it." Denny beams. She sets one bouquet aside and begins work on another. Sienna wipes a fine layer of sweat from the back of her neck. It's not even noon and already her skin feels like it's roasting. A thick, fluttering panic settles in around her heart as she imagines the rest of the day. She closes her eyes and tries another deep breath. There's a hand on her shoulder and she feels the cool of Dad's shadow fall over her face.

"How's it coming out here?" he asks, eyeing the messy floral spread.

"It's coming," Denny sighs. "But I think I need a break. Who wants lunch?"

Denny wraps a slender arm around Dad's waist and leans in for a quick hug. Dad kisses the top of her blond hair tenderly and holds her close beneath his chin. Sienna tries not to look, but somehow the display doesn't bother her. This is what love should look like, she thinks. Quiet, practical, serene.

Dad pulls up one of the heavy patio chairs and sits down, his long legs stretching out into the grass. "Thanks for doing this," he says, folding his hands in his lap and leaning back. Sometimes Sienna wonders what Dad must look like to people who don't know him, his tall frame, long neck, the almost absurdly perfect waves at the front of his sand-colored hair. They probably think he's a politician, or an actor. She's seen people visibly reassess him when he starts to speak. He looks like his voice should be bigger.

"Sure," Sienna says. She watches Denny through the window, starting a salad. "She seems to be doing a lot better."

Dad follows Sienna's eyes and smiles. "Yeah," he agrees. "It was tough for a while there, but she's really been great. Even with Ryan."

Sienna nods and Dad takes a deep breath, sadly shaking his head. "It's hard, you know. We want to be there for you guys, we want to pretend like we're not afraid, like we know what the hell is going on . . ." He sighs with a shaky half smile. "But the truth is we have no idea."

Sienna tears a few long leaves from a flower stalk and wraps them around her fingers. "I know," she says. "I never should have left, Dad. I'm sorry. I don't know what I was thinking."

Dad sits forward and palms the cap of her knee with one wide hand. "You're here now," he says, a grateful smile lighting up the corners of his blue eyes.

Sienna nods. She already feels the lump in her throat, but she pushes it away, determined not to be distracted by tears or emotion. "I want you to know," she says quietly. "I think you were right."

"Right about what?" Dad asks.

"About me," she says. "I wasn't thinking straight. If I had been, I never would have left you and Ryan."

Dad clasps his hands together and leans forward in his chair. "Goose . . ."

"Dad, I'm just like her," Sienna interrupts him, her voice cracking. "I know it. You know it. And, as much as I hope that nothing happens today, that the whole thing was some gigantic mistake and we just get skipped over, or passed by . . . part of me is kind of relieved it might be the end. Because I know what would happen. I know who I'd be."

Dad clears his throat. She can see the beginnings of tears in his eyes, and she knows she should stop, she knows the last thing he wants to think about is Mom, or either of them being sick, but she can't. "It's just scary, you know. I was doing everything I could to get better. The House, and the meds . . . and I thought things were changing, and then all of a sudden, it's like I had no control over anything again. Like I was just taken over by this thing, this thing that was so much bigger than I was, and bigger than anything I could ever think my way through, or talk myself out of. And no matter what I do, that thing always wins."

Sienna sighs unevenly, desperately trying to steady her voice, to keep herself calm and stable. She looks at the patio stones, wishing she hadn't said anything at all. Soon, it will all be over.

What's the use of talking about a future she probably won't ever get to have?

"Goose," Dad says again. Sienna looks up. It takes her a few seconds to make sense of what she sees on his face. He's not crying. He's smiling. And not a sad, helpless smile, or a smile because he doesn't know what else to do. A real smile. He shakes his head and makes a strange noise. Sienna can't be sure, but she thinks it's in the family of laughter.

"Dad?" she asks. "Are you okay?"

Dad nods and covers his mouth with one hand, like he's afraid of getting caught. He takes a long, deep breath and rubs his hands on his knees. "You know the story of how I met your mom, right?" he asks.

Sienna raises an eyebrow. Of course she knows the story. It's her favorite. She used to make Mom tell it at least every other night. "Yeah," she says uncertainly. "You were in law school and she was working in the library. You asked for a book that didn't exist."

"Right," he says. She wonders if he's going to retell it anyway. How he spent weeks inventing an amalgam of various textbook titles and contributor names, something that sounded realistic and would keep Mom busy, keep them busy together, for as long as it took for him to work up the courage to ask her out. "But I don't think you know what happened afterward."

"What do you mean?" Sienna asks. "You asked her out and she said yes. You dated for a while. You got married. You had kids."

Dad squints into the sun and rolls up the thin sleeves of his button-down shirt. "Sort of," he says. "I mean, that's all technically true, but there was a whole other phase there in the beginning that was really, and I mean, *really*, intense."

"Intense?"

Dad nods seriously. "It was awful. The loss of appetite, the endless nights of not sleeping a wink. The last-minute scheming and planning, anything for us to spend more time together. It was the first time I'd seen anything like it, this all-consuming, totally unpredictable, totally irrational obsession. It was . . . well, I didn't know it at the time, but it was a sickness. I had no idea what to do. I was terrified."

Sienna looks back at the ground, her eyes now wet and threatening to overflow. "I know," she says, almost whispering. "That's what I'm saying. I'm just like her."

"Goose," he says again, still smiling. "I'm not talking about your mother. I'm talking about me."

Sienna looks up quickly. "You?"

Dad nods. "I was sick. We were both sick. We were crazy. We were in love," he says. "And sometimes, that's what it looks like. When you're young, or even just out of practice, it can hit you like that. It feels like you're going insane."

Sienna thinks back to their fight in the front hall. She imagines Dad on her bed, counting her pills in his hand. "But . . . you thought I . . ."

"I know I did," he says. "I was wrong. I was worried. I was afraid of losing you again, before I had to. But the more I think about it, the way you've been since you've been back, the way you just described how you feel . . . you're not manic, Sienna. You're not sick. You're in love."

Sienna looks at Dad closely. She tries to imagine him twenty years younger, following Mom in the library like a puppy dog, staying up all night wondering when he'd see her next. It's hard, but if she really tries, she can see it. She remembers the way her parents used to bump into each other in the hallway, or on the stairs, far too often for it to be an accident. They'd always stay locked together, swaying for a moment, like they were dancing to music only they could hear.

"I'm not saying you're not like her," Dad says quietly. "You're a lot like her. She was the most passionate, hard-loving, loyal person I've ever known. You're all of those things."

Sienna crosses her arms. "What about . . . what happened to me? What about what I did?"

Dad's smile fades and he looks at her, strong and steady. "What happened to you is that your mother got sick. You lived with things that nobody should have to live with, saw things that nobody should see, at any age. It nearly killed me, Sienna, watching her go through all that. And I was a grown man, a grown man who knew what I was getting into. You were a little girl. If it hadn't affected you in some horrible way, if it hadn't made you question absolutely everything around you . . ."

Sienna doesn't have time to stop the tears anymore. They're falling fast, her nose wet and runny. Dad reaches across and pulls her head toward his. "You're the strongest person I know. You kept this family a family, all by yourself. And when you needed me, when you needed somebody to take care of you, I wasn't there. That's my fault, Sienna. That's where I went wrong. And it had nothing to do with you," he whispers into her ear. "Okay?"

Sienna buries her face in her father's shoulder, unable to speak. She doesn't know if she believes him, but she almost doesn't care.

Sienna wipes her eyes as Dad gets up to help Denny at the door. She's struggling with a platter of sandwiches and fruit salad. Even Sienna is impressed at how appetizing she's managed to make the rations and few staples they have left in the fridge look on one of Mom's shiny silver trays.

Dad calls for Ryan and Denny sets the platter on the table. As she's pouring the lemonade, Sienna's gaze drifts over her shoulder to the muted blue of the hydrangea bushes that line the stone path.

She hops up with the scissors, crouching in front of the thickest blooms and snipping a handful of full, blue globes.

Ryan races to the table, bug book in hand, and Dad follows closely behind. Sienna joins them with an armful of flowers, adding them to the pile of delicate grasses and herbs on the table.

"These, too," she says to Denny. She takes a tangy sip of lemonade and helps herself to a sandwich.

# ZAN

ZAN CLIMBS BAREFOOT TO THE CLIFFS, SETTLING into her spot against the boulder.

From up here, she can see the long stretch of beach below, and the preparations already under way. At the inlet, Dad and a few former students are digging a pit in the sand where his Forgiving Wheel will soon sit on display. Mom and Joni are walking to Split Rock, already two tiny figures against the shiny backdrop of ocean and cloudless sky.

*Mom and Joni are walking to Split Rock.* She squints harder to make out their shapes, identically tall, dark, and lean, as if maybe the whole thing has been a dream. No part of her had even dared to hope that Joni would actually come home, let alone suggest some time alone with Miranda. An afternoon mother-daughter stroll. Zan laughs. It's nothing short of a miracle.

"Of course you can be dead and still pull off something like this," she says quietly, to Leo's empty rock beside her. She stares at the horizon, remembering how she used to imagine his face on the water, or try to redraw, in her mind, the way his body felt, slouched into the cliff against hers. Now she doesn't see him at all. She feels him somewhere else, somewhere far away, but she knows that he can hear her. That he's been waiting for her to come back.

"I'm sorry," she says. "But you already know that. I know you do. Joni says I shouldn't beat myself up about it. That all this, everything that's going on today, it's making all of us do things we never thought we'd do. I guess for her, that means coming home. Whatever it takes, right?"

Zan smiles. She and Joni had stayed up all night in the loft, catching up and whispering secrets like it was the last night of summer camp, long after lights-out.

"She told me everything," Zan continues, picking up a broken chip of red clay and smudging it into her palm. "How she was in New York, and then working at that jewelry store on the Cape. You found out about her new name, and tracked her down at Lulu's. You told her how much I missed her. You begged her to come home."

Zan hears her voice cracking and she shakes her head. Joni said they'd sat on the stoop on one of her breaks. At first, she'd tried to get Leo to go away. It had been so long, she'd explained, and she'd finally gotten a new start. New name, new job, new apartment. It had taken her years to convince herself that she was doing the right thing, that calling home would be too hard, too much of a reminder of who she was and what she was running away from.

"She said she couldn't do it. But she liked you." Zan smiles. "She said she felt how much you . . . how much we loved each other. You gave her that picture, the one of us on the beach. She cut me out and kept me with her, always. She knew you would look out for me. She knew I'd be okay. That's why she didn't come home."

Joni's face had crumpled when Zan told her what happened to Leo. How he'd been driving back to the boat, just hours after meeting her. She remembered the freak summer storm, the one that came with no warning. The bar had flooded, she said. Cars were stopped in the streets.

Joni had held Zan close. If she'd known, she said, she would have been there.

"I told her it was okay," Zan sighs. "I told her I understood. But I don't. Not really. I don't understand why she did it. I don't understand why, just because she hated it here so much, just because she was so mad at Mom for not letting her be who she wanted to be, she couldn't call me. Not once, in seven years. She couldn't write me a secret letter. Just to say hi, or let me know she was alive. I didn't care where she was or what she was doing. I just wanted my sister back."

Zan tucks her thick curls behind her ears and stretches her legs out across the rock. "You knew that," she says to the gentle breeze, moist and warm off the blazing face of the cliff. "You knew that's what I wanted, more than anything. And you found a way to make it happen."

Something won't let her say more. She wants to apologize again. She wants to get angry, to hate herself out loud for what she did. But instead, she takes a deep breath, inhaling the warm, thick air, the fresh summer smell of sea salt and wildflowers.

She isn't sure how long she's been sitting in silence when she hears footsteps on the path behind her. At first she thinks it's Daniel, coming to nag her about shirking her setup duties.

333

There's a quick, muffled scamper, followed by a flustered whisper. *"Crap."*

Zan feels her breath stick in her throat. Nick. How did he know she'd be here?

He gets a steady foothold on the cliff and hauls himself up into view. "Hey," he says, no doubt embarrassed by his less than graceful entrance. He swings his legs over the ledge and stands behind Zan's shoulder.

She shields her eyes from the glaring midday sun. "Hey."

"My dad and I were helping set up some tables for the potluck, later," he says, nodding his head toward the section of the beach that Miranda has designated for food-related use. "I thought I saw you up here."

Zan nods. She remembers the quiet afternoons they'd spent up here together last summer, missing Leo together. She doesn't think she ever told him it was *their* spot. She wonders if he would have come if he knew about all of the nights she and Leo had spent together here, all of the nights she was "sleeping at a friend's."

"What's it like down there?" she asks.

"Weird." Nick shrugs. He pushes his hands into the pockets of his shorts and kicks at the rugged clay rocks with the edge of one flip-flop. "Everybody's keeping busy, not really saying much. It feels funny setting up picnic tables just a few hours before . . ."

"I know," Zan says. She inches over on her rock to make room. She wishes he hadn't come up, but now that he's here, she can't exactly tell him to leave.

"That's okay," he says, noticing the empty spot beside her. "I'm too jumpy to sit, I think."

Zan studies him. It's true. His elbows shake a little bit at his sides, like he's vibrating with some new, nervous current. He stares at the glassy surface of the ocean. "I just wanted to, you know, I can't stop thinking about what happened, and . . ."

"It's okay, Nick," Zan interrupts. She hasn't had much time to think about the way they left things on the mainland. She'd been too busy feeling guilty, or thinking about Joni, to wonder about Nick. Now, as she tries to help him out of another awkward apology, she realizes she's doing it as much for her as for him. She wants to take Joni's advice, to move on, not spend the whole day reliving something she regrets. But it's easier when she doesn't have to think about it, or see Nick up so close. "You don't have to say anything."

"No." He shakes his head. "It's not okay. I thought it wasn't going to be weird, that we'd wake up yesterday and everything would go back to normal. I figured we'd just keep looking for, whatever we were looking for, and it would be like nothing happened. But it wasn't."

He crosses his sunburned arms over his chest and leans back against the cliff. Tiny pebbles of clay trickle down from the spot where his shoulders meet the rocks, a delicate avalanche that ends in a gritty pile between his feet.

"It was weird. Because I got weird." He clears his throat. "I guess I was mad that you still cared about learning the truth. I thought that whatever happened, with us, you know, I thought it would be enough to make you forget."

Zan hugs her knees into her chest. "Forget what?"

"I don't know," Nick says. He rubs his forehead with one hand, leaving a faint trail of red dirt caked into the skin around his hairline. "Leo, I guess." He shakes his head. "I know. It's the worst. But I guess I . . . I guess I thought you knew . . ."

"Knew what?" Zan asks. The air around them feels suddenly cooler, and she looks up to see a cluster of dark gray clouds moving quickly toward them.

Nick looks down at the tops of his freckled feet. "I've liked you my whole life, Zan," he says. "Since we were little. Since camp. Since before camp, probably. I guess it's more than liking, since it never went away, but it doesn't matter. You were always Leo's. And Leo was always my best friend."

Zan stares at his profile, waiting for him to laugh or tell her that he's kidding. Nick, who never seemed to care one way or the other about any girl, or anything other than fishing or his friends, had felt this way about her, all this time?

But he doesn't laugh. The corners of his mouth turn down and little lines appear around his nostrils. "It gets worse," he says quietly. "The only reason I really wanted to help you do this, help you find the truth about where he was that day, and what he was doing, was because I hoped it was something bad."

A sharp gust of wind picks up the loose clay and sand, swirling it into mini-tornadoes around their legs. "I hoped whatever it was would make you want to forget him, and I wanted to be there when you did."

Zan hugs her goose-pimpled arms around her waist. She remembers that day in his truck, how persistent he was that they start looking. Did he already know what she would find?

She wants him to leave, but can't find the words to say it. She can't look at him, either. She stares instead at the flurry of small, messy waves, kicked up from the sudden, bold wind.

She feels Nick's hand on the side of her arm and she jumps. "Here," he says. His palm is closed tight and slowly he opens his fingers. Threads of silver glint in the sun as he holds out his hand. "You forgot this."

Leo's necklace. Zan takes the chain, the cool pendants pressed inside her palm. Nick must have picked it up when she'd dropped it in the store.

"I'm really sorry, Zan," Nick says. "I wanted you to know that."

Zan stares at the shiny charm letters. She nods. "It's fine, Nick," she says, her voice quiet and small. "Really."

She feels Nick standing behind her for a long moment. He shuffles sideways and plants his hands on the sturdy wall, hanging his legs down over the side. Out of the corner of her eyes she can still see his head, peering up at her from behind the rocky ledge. "I hope so," he says. His voice is lighter and he sounds more like himself, as if that was all he needed. To say it out loud. Zan feels, for a moment, something like jealousy. If only she could talk to Leo, apologize to him the way Nick has apologized to her, and know that she'd been heard, really heard. Maybe that would be enough.

Zan turns and catches Nick's eye. He's looking at her the way he always has, like he wants to know everything that she's thinking, or like maybe he already does. He smiles. "Because I have a feeling wherever we end up, Leo's going to be there, waiting. And I'm sure he can still kick my ass."

Zan feels an almost effortless laugh bubbling up in her throat. Nick holds up a hand, a simple wave goodbye, or the ultimate surrender, Zan isn't quite sure which. He hops down to the path and she listens to his footsteps disappear into the thick woods, winding down the sandy trail to the beach.

Zan unhooks the clasp on the chain. She reaches behind her neck and fumbles blindly until she feels the delicate parts line up with a quiet click. Her fingers flutter over the charms dangling against her collarbone. The "L" for Leo falls slightly beneath the others, tilted at an angle, and nearest to her heart.

# SIENNA

"WHERE'S RYAN?"

Sienna looks up from the armful of long, gnarly branches she's collected from the path behind the beach. Dad stands at the beginning of the trail, wiping a thick gloss of sweat from his forehead with one sleeve. They've been hard at work building an arbor, which has so far entailed gathering wood and carrying it in wobbly bunches to the top of the bluff with the clearest view of the ocean.

Ryan is in charge of making piles of like-proportioned twigs and branches, a job he seems to relish—at least he had, until he disappeared.

"I'll find him," Sienna offers, grateful for the excuse to give her back and arms a break. The branches aren't so much heavy as they are cumbersome to carry, with awkward offshoots and scratchy patches of dead growth that rip into the skin of her forearms. She brushes the dirt and splinters from her palms and starts down the path for the beach. Maybe Ryan has moved his piles somewhere nearer to the bluff, or maybe he's taking a break himself.

The beach is already getting crowded. People from the neighborhood have started to arrive with contributions to the food table, or blankets and chairs to spread out in the sand. To an outsider, it might look like any summer's night at any beach with a worthwhile view of the horizon, where people gather for picnics or to play games before applauding the sun's dramatic descent.

The bluff Dad and Denny have chosen for the wedding is off to one side of the main trail from the parking lot. It's raised just slightly above the shore, so that the view of the beach is long and pristine, but it's still just a short and easy walk to the water. Sienna remembers using the bluff as a landmark when she was little and the walk from the car had seemed never-ending. She knew as soon as she saw the narrow trail at the end, the grassy hill with the cluster of beach plum bushes and a flat, sandy clearing on top, that the ocean was just on the other side.

The piles of wood are here, where they're supposed to be, but Ryan is not.

The ground is cool and damp beneath her bare feet, and she walks quickly, careful to avoid the exposed roots and wedges of driftwood strewn along the path. She's walking toward home, certain she'll find Ryan, scared and overwhelmed, crouched over a book in his bed.

Ahead, near the bus stop, a crowd has gathered. Instinctively, she scans the bodies for Owen's tall frame. She wishes more than anything she could make him appear, just by wanting it badly enough.

What if Dad is right, she wonders. What if she really

was—is?—in love with Owen? Where does that leave her now? What is this steady churning in the pit of her belly? This warm but threatening ache that sits, like a sleeping tiger, on her chest? Is this more love?

Or is this the other side. The loss of love. A broken heart.

Sienna keeps her head down as she walks past the bus stop. Out of the corner of her eye, she can see that the group is all hunched over something, behind the wooden shed. She's almost around the corner when she hears a voice, small and excited.

"Sienna!"

She turns and the crowd parts. At its center is Ryan, on his knees in the dirt, waving at her with both arms. "Quick! You have to see this!"

Sienna jogs over as the crowd pulls back to let her through. "Where have you been?" she asks, trying to sound stern but unable to hide the relief in her voice, relief that he isn't paralyzed by fear, or alone.

The group of kids around him are all staring intently at a spot on the ground. "I was looking for wood for the arbor," Ryan explains, "and all of a sudden, the ground started moving."

Sienna crouches beside him. At first glance, it does look like the dirt is rippling beneath their feet. But as she looks closer, she sees that it's a long, slow-moving procession of caterpillars, inching up the hill and away from the beach.

"They're going somewhere safe," Ryan says. "To be together. It's their animal instinct. They know that something is happening, just like we do."

Sienna puts an arm around Ryan's shoulder and pulls his

head beneath her chin. She breathes in the little-boy scent of his hair.

"Come on, Ry," she says, as the crowd disperses, heading back toward the beach. "Dad's waiting."

She leads Ryan by the hand through the beach parking lot. The trail breaks off in a V, one side winding down to the ocean, the other a smaller path crisscrossed by roots and covered in pine needles. Sienna's stomach flips.

"I'll meet you down there, okay, Bud?" Sienna squeezes Ryan's shoulder as he shrugs and follows the crowd to the water.

Sienna walks briskly, ducking through crooked branches and wiping wisps of cobwebs from her hair. The sun falls in patches on her arms and legs as she picks up into a run, her feet landing firmly between the knotted roots. Her heart races and a silent prayer loops through her mind. *Please let this be the way.*

Ahead, the trail tapers off. She sees the familiar opening, the long wooden dock. She holds her breath as she steps over the fallen tree trunk, the pond stretching out, quiet and still before her.

Her heart sticks. There's nobody there. She walks slowly to the end of the dock. She stands, her arms hugged tight around her waist. Of course he hadn't come back.

There's a rustle in the trees behind her. "Mind if I join you?"

Sienna turns fast to see Owen walking out of the woods, pine needles stuck to his hair. His clothes are wrinkled and his eyes are dark and glassy. It looks like he's been up all night.

"Owen," she gasps. She runs to him on the dock. As soon as she's close enough to touch him, she has no control over anything, not her feet, not her arms, which are reaching out to

Owen's shoulders, not her body, which falls on top of his in a sloppy, gangly heap.

Owen laughs and steadies himself on his heels, holding her around the waist. "Hi," he says into the side of her neck.

"Hi," she laughs back.

"I can't believe you found this place again," he marvels, looking out over the pond.

"Best-kept secret." Sienna shrugs and smiles before nibbling the corner of her lip. "What are you doing here?"

Owen leans against the worn dock footing and looks up at her. "I left right after you did. I wanted to come find you last night, or first thing this morning, but . . ." His brown eyes twitch and he looks suddenly panicked and afraid. "I didn't know what to say."

Sienna puts a hand on the top of his head. His long, dark hair is coarse and dry. He moves away from her gently, shamefully, like he doesn't deserve her affection. "I can't believe I let you go," he says. "I don't know what I was thinking."

"I do." Sienna shrugs.

"You do?" he asks.

Sienna nods. "You were a part of something, up there. It was something you needed to do."

"No." Owen shakes his head. "I thought it was, maybe. But the only thing I need, right now, is you. As soon as you left, I knew it. There was no way I was going to not be with you today. I know we still don't know each other that well, but . . ."

"We do," Sienna stops him. "We know enough."

Owen smiles, the first real smile she's seen. "So you're not mad? Even about all that shitty stuff I said?"

Sienna shakes her head. "No," she says. "A lot of it was true. And some of it was stuff I should have told you. Stuff I probably would have told you, if we had more time."

"You could tell me now," he suggests, leaning easily back into the dock.

Sienna considers this. She could tell him everything. About Mom, what she was like and how she died. About everything that happened afterward. The pills. The hospital. She could tell him, and he'd understand. He'd hold her and tell her that he loved her and maybe they would feel closer, after, because he knew her more.

But she meant what she'd said. They knew each other enough. And she knows enough about herself to know that she really would tell him someday, if it turned out that they had a someday, after all.

Not today, though. Today isn't about reliving, or explaining, or trying to make sense of things in the past. Today is about who she is now, and who she has standing beside her. Owen. Ryan. Dad. Even Denny.

Her tribe.

Sienna smiles at Owen and wedges a hand onto his shoulder. She hops back to the ground and holds both of his hands in her own. "Maybe tomorrow," she says, with a hopeful smile.

Owen drops her hands and holds her face close to his. "To-morrow," he agrees.

# THE BEACH

# CADEN

LEAVING THE HOUSE FEELS HURRIED AND strange.

Carly has everything packed, the salad and plastic cutlery for the potluck dinner, and her backpack of supplies: a blanket, a Multi-Tool, extra batteries, a flashlight.

Caden bit his tongue when he saw her packing that morning. He'd wanted to ask her exactly how much good she thought a plastic flashlight and a screwdriver would do in the event of an actual asteroid strike. But he could see how badly she needed to feel useful.

He wonders now what it is about some people that makes them want to *do* things, to move so fast, in times like this. He's glad these people are out there—even people like his father, who try to do too much, and move too fast—but he's relieved not to be one of them.

Carly calls him from the deck. He knows it's time to go. He looks around his room, the boxes of video games he had hopefully stored in the closet years ago, only to keep dragging them out so often that they'd taken up permanent residence at the foot of his bed. He wonders what his room would have been like in Arthur's bunker. He wonders who will stay there instead.

Carly asked him at lunch, as they ate peanut butter sandwiches on the living room floor, listening to Ramona's old record collection and just hanging out—an entirely normal afternoon made extraordinary by the fact that it had never once happened before—if he'd ever considered staying in the bunker.

"You weren't tempted?" she asked. "You know, to survive?"

Caden shrugged and took a bite of the doughy crust. "It never felt like a real option," he said. "And I guess if I'd thought about it, I would've realized that it wasn't so much a question of *if* we'd survive down there. It was more did I *want* to."

He left out the part about Sophie. It would have been more complicated, he knows, if she'd wanted to stay. Who knows if he would have had the courage, or motivation, to escape on his own?

But maybe she was right. Maybe they had met for a reason. They needed each other to get home, even if going home meant they wouldn't be together.

He can't remember the last time he made his bed, but he makes it now. He closes a dresser drawer, wedged open by a pile of T-shirts. It feels important to leave things in place.

He turns out the light and joins Carly and Ramona on the porch. Ramona has tears in her eyes as she pulls the sliding glass door closed behind them. As they start down the driveway, she grabs Caden's hand, then Carly's, as if they're toddlers, about to cross a busy street.

# SIENNA

THE ARBOR IS FINISHED WHEN SIENNA AND Owen return from the woods.

Ryan had finally been convinced that any and all caterpillars had made their initial escape, along with the other creatures in the forest. Even Sienna noticed an eerie quiet as they made their way back down the path. No birds chirping, no whistling cicadas, no rabbits or squirrels rustling in the underbrush.

Denny is stringing the simple arrangements they'd made that morning to a vine wrapped around the wooden arch. Owen hurries to lend a hand, and Ryan tags along.

Sienna watches a group of people as they lug a wooden cart up the path from the parking lot. On the cart is an oddly shaped box, covered in foil and reflecting the low glare of the sun. Plastic tubes have been fitted together in a sort of figure eight, and a funnel at one end opens into a glass ball that rolls and spins as the cart bumps over the sand.

"What is it?" Dad asks, standing behind her shoulder.

"I don't know," Sienna says. "Some kind of machine."

Dad clears his throat. "I have a favor to ask," he says timidly. "It's kind of a big one, so feel free to say no."

Sienna turns to face him. "A favor?"

Dad nods. "Denny and I have written our vows, and we plan on keeping things very simple, but we need somebody to stand up there with us. You know, make it sort of official."

Sienna looks at the tops of her bare feet. "Official?" she asks. "Don't I have to be, like, ordained on the Internet or something?"

"We're not all that concerned about it being legal," he says, nudging her playfully in the shoulder. "I just thought it would be nice if you'd say a few words. It doesn't have to be specifically about us. It can be anything. Whatever all this—marriage, love— whatever it means to you."

Sienna glances over her father's shoulder to where Owen is cutting into one end of a stringy vine with his teeth. He catches her staring and gives her a shrug and a smile, as if he's still working out the chain of events that landed him here, doing this, tonight.

"Okay," Sienna agrees. "I'll do it."

# ZAN

DESPITE BEING CONSTRUCTED MOSTLY OF cardboard and plastic, the Forgiving Wheel weighs a ton.

They drag it up the path and onto the beach, away from the food, just below a bluff where two of their neighbors will soon be getting married.

"How romantic," Miranda had said when she'd seen the arbor going up. Joni and Zan shared a look. It was the first time either of them had heard their mother use that word in earnest, and it sounded almost like it hurt. But they didn't doubt that she meant it.

Something had happened to Miranda when Joni showed up. Zan had expected more of a climax, more questions, more demands for her sister to explain where she'd been. But by the time Zan had come down for breakfast, earlier that morning, Joni and Miranda were sitting quietly side by side, sipping tea and talking, as if things between them had never been any other way.

Miranda was different with Daniel now, too. Not once, but three times, Zan had seen them kiss. Real kisses, on the lips. With feeling. Zan hadn't seen them so much as touch each other in years. She knows that part of it is the uncertainty that surrounds them, the fear of what's to come, but she can't help but wonder if things would be the same if Joni hadn't come back. There's a real chance that Miranda would have run herself into the ground, ignoring them all and keeping things in order, right up until the very end.

Daniel parks the machine in the hole, still on its rickety wooden cart, and takes a few steps back.

"How does it work?" Zan asks.

Daniel looks at her with a familiar glint in his eyes. Never is he happier than when he gets to explain his projects, the worlds he's been living inside for however long. He loves the solitude, she knows, the time to create on his own, but he loves sharing even more. It's why he's always done installations. The real art, he says, happens when other people get involved.

He pulls open a wooden drawer from the cart, the size of an index card, and removes a stack of colored notepaper. From another, identical drawer, he reaches for a handful of stubby pencils, the kind you'd use to score a round of mini golf.

"First, you write it down," he says.

"Write what down?"

Daniel shrugs. "Whoever, or whatever, you want to forgive," he says. "It doesn't matter what it is, just as long as it's something you want to leave behind. It dies here, is the point. In this machine."

He taps the side of the machine's stocky body, and an electric whirring starts up from inside.

"What's in there?" Zan asks.

"This," he says proudly, as Joni and Miranda join them on

his other side, "is what happens when you stick your paper down the chute."

Daniel lifts a piece of notepaper from the pile and folds it in half before sending it down the first series of tubes. There's some sort of suction from the body of the machine, then a faint flickering sound, until the paper reappears, torn into tiny pieces of colored confetti and whirlpooling around the bottom of the deep glass bowl.

"Look closely," Daniel commands, and the three of them bend down to peer into the globe. The paper has been cut into perfect miniature stars.

"Wow," they coo in unison. It really is beautiful, Zan thinks, but it's nothing compared to the look of pure wonderment that lights up Daniel's face.

"So who goes first?" Daniel asks.

# CADEN

There's definitely enough to go around. Caden imagines all of his neighbors cleaning out their refrigerators, concocting strange combinations of ingredients, like the casserole that appears to have been made out of bread, eggs, and ketchup, or the salad starring droopy lettuce, a full bunch of green grapes, and canned pineapple slices. If, somehow, they're all stranded out here for the rest of their lives, or at least until some form of help arrives, they could make do. But for now, Caden decides, he'll pass.

He's not exactly hungry, and can't imagine anybody else is, either. The beach is crowded and looks strangely festive from far away, but as they get closer and he can see people's faces, he recognizes the familiar looks of frozen panic and quiet, ambiguous alarm.

The biggest crowd is gathered by a pit in the sand, beneath one of the taller bluffs. Carly motions for them to follow her over, and they arrive just as Mr. Lowe, the art teacher, is explaining his latest project.

Caden feels kind of sorry for Mr. Lowe. He was always working on these complex installations that nobody ever seemed to really understand. But as Caden watches him now, gesticulating wildly as he demonstrates his new machine, he sees something new. Maybe it was never really about other people understanding at all.

Carly, obviously, goes first. Caden watches her scribble something on a piece of neon purple paper and fold it meticulously into a small, perfect square. She feeds it through a tube, and an impressive growl kicks up from the body of the machine. At the other end, Daniel waits, pouring little purple shreds into a paper cone and handing it back to Carly.

That's it? Caden wonders, as he shuffles ahead, waiting to take his turn. He can't imagine how transformed he'll feel, watching a piece of paper get torn up and handed back to him in an inverted party hat.

Ramona is next. The crowd of people has fallen completely silent around them, and it feels like even more have arrived from the outskirts of the beach. She steps slowly to the machine and takes a pencil from the box. She looks across the machine at Carly, and then turns around to find Caden. He doesn't know why, or how, but something about seeing her there, the pencil ready in her hand, about to take their lives, her mistakes, everything she wishes she could take back, and put all of it into a few words, a silly sentence . . . he wishes he could rip the paper from her hands.

Maybe it wasn't always the best, what they had growing up. But it was what they had. And look at Carly. She was well on her way to winning every award their school ever offered. And yeah, maybe he had some work to do, but he was all right for the most part. Wasn't he?

Why did they need some machine to tear them apart?

Ramona writes deliberately and carefully onto one side of the paper. Caden looks around and sees that a few people are crying. Ramona tucks the paper into the tube and the machine rumbles to life.

As Daniel hands her the cup of shredded confetti, she does something so unexpected that Caden thinks he's hallucinating. She takes the cup and falls into Daniel's arms, hugging him tight, as if they're the best of friends.

Caden feels an unfamiliar lump swelling in his throat. He doesn't know why, but he feels like crying now, too. Maybe it's because he's never seen Ramona hug another person in his life. Whatever happened in that machine, she needed it.

When his turn comes, Caden debates stepping back. Nobody is keeping track of who has done their forgiving. He could easily duck back to another part of the beach. But he doesn't. He picks up a pencil and a piece of green paper. He thinks for a moment, and then he begins to write:

> *I forgive my parents.*
> *Both of them.*

He stares at the words for a few moments, before adding:

> *(We do the best we can.)*

He folds the paper and sends it down the narrow tube, watching the green square flit and shake as it's sucked into the covered midsection. He hears the metal scraping of a fan, or some other sharp-edged device, and watches as the little green flecks fill the bottom of a clear glass container.

Daniel reaches in and scoops them up with the cone, smiling as he hands it to Caden.

Caden peers into the cup as he walks to join his family by the water. Stars, he realizes, pressing one of the smallest paper cutouts into the tip of his finger.

They're everywhere today.

# SIENNA

THEY DECIDE TO DO THE WEDDING JUST BEFORE sunset, after most people have been given their turn at the machine.

Sienna is surprised that Dad even cares that people are watching. She'd assumed it was Denny's doing, that Denny wanted her wedding to be more than just a quiet exchange of words between two people, that she wanted the whole world, or at least the whole neighborhood, to know what was happening.

But Dad is the one who keeps pushing for an audience. At first, Sienna was hurt. If this is something that Dad is only doing to make Denny happy, what does he care who knows about it?

But as she watches the people spilling onto the beach from the road, greeting each other with warm hugs or pats on the shoulders, she starts to get it. It's not about the wedding. It's about people standing together, being together, and facing whatever happens, together.

Ryan, who has been all over the Forgiving Wheel since they found out what it was, runs back to drag the rest of them over to the growing crowd. Owen holds her hand and squeezes it as they watch from the back. The crowd pushes slowly forward as more and more people take their turn.

"What are you gonna write, Ry?" Sienna leans down to ask her brother.

"It's personal," he answers. His face is set and serious, and Sienna wishes she hadn't pried. She pulls him in for a hug. He struggles at first, his arms stiff and tense at his sides, but she doesn't let go.

"You're an okay brother, you know," she says.

Ryan pushes her away. "That's an understatement."

Owen laughs quietly as they take a few steps closer to the machine.

Ryan goes first. He is, so far, the youngest participant, and Sienna notices a ripple effect in the crowd of people leaning closer to watch him at work. She knows what they're thinking. What can a person so young have to forgive?

Sienna's heart swells with pride as she watches him grip his small fist around the pencil. She has no idea what he's writing. Maybe something about caterpillars, she thinks.

But probably not.

When it's her turn, she works fast. She's thought about it, and though she had a hard time choosing just one, she decided she didn't have to. There were no rules.

*I forgive you, Mom. It wasn't your fault.*

She pauses, and then adds on a separate line:

*I forgive myself.*

# ZAN

ALL ZAN CAN THINK OF ARE APOLOGIES.

She's sorry for what happened with Nick. She's sorry she worried her parents, when they already had enough to worry about. She's sorry she didn't believe in Leo, that she thought he would keep something from her, something that would make her see him any differently than she always had.

But it's not a Sorry Wheel. She can almost hear Daniel explaining the difference, although she's not quite sure she understands what it is. Something about control. Sorry is a feeling, a passive state of heart and mind.

Forgiveness is something you give.

She waits until almost the very end. They all do, Miranda, Daniel, and Joni. It's an unspoken agreement that they will be last, after each one of their neighbors has passed through. Most people were quiet as they wrote. Some smiled. Some cried. A few of the most surprising participants were overcome, hugging Daniel and thanking him as if he'd given them something they'd been waiting for all their lives.

Zan is the first in her family to go. This is also unspoken, but

Joni puts a hand on her shoulder and nods at the cart, and Zan knows what she has to do.

She takes a pencil from the pile, now scattered on the wooden base, and chooses a piece of bright yellow paper. She looks around at her family. Everything she wants to say to them, they already know. Daniel knows how proud he makes her, how much she's loved the quiet times they've spent together, working in his studio, even if she didn't always show it. Miranda knows she always tried. She knows they can love each other without being the same. She knows that Zan remembers what it was like when Joni left, how hard it was to build a normal life again, for all of them. Zan was there. It was hard for her, too.

And Joni knows that, above all else, more than not understanding why she stayed away, Zan is just happy her sister is home. Some things don't need to be said out loud. Or forgiven on a piece of paper.

But some things do.

Zan takes a deep breath and touches the "L" at her neck.

*I forgive me.*
*For doubting you.*

It's what she needs to let go. Before they move on, wherever they're going, she needs to know that it's behind her. It was a part of her, and now, as the machine spits tiny yellow stars into the turning glass globe, it's gone.

# THE WEDDING

# SIENNA

SIENNA STANDS UNDER THE WOODEN ARCH,
the sweet smell of lavender and Denny's hydrangea bouquet floating on the steady breeze.

Everyone on the beach is there. There hadn't been an announcement, but somehow it was understood. After they'd all
taken their turns at the machine, they drifted slowly up the hill,
gathering in a close cluster on the flat part of the bluff.

Denny had changed, at some point, into a simple white sundress. Dad wore his usual uniform of khakis and a button-down,
but he'd taken off his shoes. He looked, for the first time since
Sienna could remember, comfortable and relaxed. He didn't even
seemed bothered by the large group of people, mostly strangers,
who stood, waiting for him to arrive.

There was no music. There was no program. There was just
Dad and Denny, walking together through the crowd, which
parted silently to make a natural aisle.

Now, as they reach the arbor, Sienna glances around the
group. Beside Dad is Ryan, standing tall with his hands clutched
behind his back. Inside his tight little fists are the rings, and he

nods at Sienna with deliberate precision, as if to convince her he has everything under control.

Owen stands a bit farther back, but still very much a part of things, as if he's physically straddling the line between family and friend. She wishes she could pull him closer. He gives her a reassuring smile.

Over Denny's shoulder, she sees the kids from the neighborhood. They're each standing surrounded by other people, people with similar features, the same hair, the same broad shoulders. Families.

Sienna swallows. She can't remember the last time she's had to speak in front of so many people. Maybe a school project, or when it was her turn to share in Group. But this feels different. Not like punishment, or an assignment. It feels like she's playing a part.

"Hi," she begins simply. "I'm Sienna. This is my brother, Ryan, and this is my dad. We're here today because he's getting married, to Denise. We call her Denny. And we're all so glad that you're here."

Dad and Denny squeeze each other's hand and Sienna feels the crowd of onlookers surging closer together, either to hear her better or just because they want less space between them.

"My dad asked me to say something to all of you today. He said it didn't have to be anything in particular, or even anything about them, which I guess makes sense. We don't know any of you all that well. And you don't know us. We're summer people, and we haven't been back here in a while. I used to play on this beach when I was little. I remember some of you did, too. But I have to say, when my dad told me we were coming here now, with everything that's going on . . . I didn't get it. This isn't our home. Not really.

"I don't think he really knew why he wanted us to be here, either. He said it was so we could spend time together, but we could have done that anywhere. I think he thought we were running away, to be honest. And maybe we were, at first. But it didn't work. Nothing magically disappeared because we were on vacation. Or even because of an asteroid. We still disagreed. We wanted different things. I guess there's really no running away from all that."

Sienna shuffles her feet in the sand. Her throat feels dry and the back of her neck is sweaty. She clears her throat.

"I'm sixteen," she says. "It feels funny to be standing up here and talking about things like home and family and love, but I guess those are hard things for anybody to talk about. You just kind of know it when you see it. At least, I do. And it's here."

Sienna smiles at Dad. "Your turn."

# THE END

IT STARTS NOT LONG AFTER THE KISS.

The first kiss, as husband and wife. The stars are falling. It's unclear who goes first, but soon they are reaching into their paper cones, one at a time and all together. They are tossing handfuls, showering the newlyweds and each other in colored confetti, in star-shaped forgiveness, in love.

The wind, a swooning gust that has been building all afternoon, picks up again. First gently, a soft swirling of sand around their feet. Still, they are kissing, the newlyweds, and others, too. They are finding hands to hold, arms to grab on to, shoulders to crouch inside. There are no more empty spaces, no hard lines or angles, only the round, melded shape of people huddled on a cliff, watching as the sun slips lower and lower, the sky behind it shocked with brilliant orange and red.

The wind swallows the scattered confetti, lifts it up and tosses it around, a cloud of color whipping around them, between them, landing in their hair, on their faces, as they strain to look up at the sky.

Like a paintbrush sweeping the horizon, the sunset colors glow deeper and wider, pulling back from the water's edge, higher into the early night sky. Where the darkness had already settled above them, new, dramatic streaks of yellow, crimson, and tangerine ignite, exploding in sharp bursts overhead.

The wind picks up again.

The sky cracks open, now, like lightning, but everywhere at once.

More colors: violet, emerald, and bold, brilliant blue.

The silence falls like a screen, sudden and heavy and real.

The air is still, peculiar and calm.

The people of the island, families, neighbors, strangers, friends, stand together.

And they wait.